Deep

KIMBERLY KINCAID

ISBN: 978-0-9971912-0-2

DEDICATION

This book is dedicated to you, the person holding it.
Without readers, I could not do my dream job.
I am so grateful to have you on this journey with me.

ACKNOWLEDGMENTS

Writing a book is an endeavor. Starting a new series, an undertaking. Branching out to a new series in a new subgenre? There might not be a word big enough for that! I could not have possibly written this book without the following people.

Liliana Hart, thank you for opening the door for the Station Seventeen series by inviting me into your MacKenzie world. Geoff Symon, words cannot express how eternally grateful I am for all your patience and expertise with the forensic aspects of this story. All rule-bending is on me, while the knowledge is entirely (brilliantly!) yours.

To Jaycee Delorenzo of Sweet n' Spicy Designs for a gorgeous cover, and Nicole Bailey of Proof Before You Publish for keeping my commas (and ellipses…and possessive apostrophes…and…) in line. Thank you for holding my hand in Indie waters!

To the usual suspects: Alyssa Alexander, who read all the ugly words and stuck by me until I got it right. Tracy Brogan, whose support is unflagging. Skye Jordan, for kicking my butt through the word sprints that led me to "the end." Laura Kaye and Cristin Harber, who are so gracious with their time and advice. I love you all!

To Robin Covington and Avery Flynn, there aren't enough thanks and love on the planet. There are no finer best friends than you.

Lastly, to my family—Reader Girl, Smarty Pants, and Tiny Dancer, I am ever-proud to be your mom and ever-grateful for your patience during my crazy deadlines. And

Mr. K, to say that I am grateful for your understanding with this transition is pretty much the biggest understatement ever uttered. I could not do what I do without your love and support, just like I would not be who I am without your love and support. You are my heart.

SKIN DEEP

CHAPTER ONE

Kellan Walker stood with an ax in one hand and a sledgehammer in the other, thanking his lucky fucking stars he didn't have an office job. Not that pushing paper was a bad way to go, necessarily—honest work, and all that. But a nine to five fit him about as well as a suit and tie, and since he hadn't sported those particular torture devices since his father's funeral ten years ago, he was all too happy to stick to the helmet and turnout gear he wore every day for the Remington Fire Department.

Better that the fires were literal than figurative. At least those he could put out.

"Is that a sledgehammer in your pocket or are you just happy to see me?"

Kellan looked up from his spot in Station Seventeen's triple-wide engine bay, chuffing out a laugh at the familiar, feminine voice greeting him from the doorway. "I'm always happy to see you when I'm doing inventory, McCullough. Care to help out a brother in need?"

"You want me to pick up your slack again, Walker?" His fellow engine-mate Shae McCullough arched a honey-colored brow at him, and Christ, even in her sleep she probably had enough brass for a band. Cue up the number one reason Kellan liked her.

"I prefer to think of it more as lending your professional expertise. Sharing is caring," he reminded her, putting just enough of a cocky smile to the words to make her cave. Ballbreaker or not, Shae always had his back, just like he'd had hers since the minute he'd crossed the threshold at Seventeen two years ago. Being a firefighter was the closest thing he'd found to the seven years he'd spent in the Army. He and Shae were part of a team, along with everyone else on engine, squad, and even Parker and Quinn on the ambo. They didn't just carry their weight. They carried each other equally.

Still, Kellan knew better than to think McCullough would lower her brass knuckles all the way on his account.

"Caring, my ass. You owe me," she grumbled, although the slight lift of her lips negated any sting the words might otherwise hold.

"I can live with that."

Kellan let go of a laugh along with the words, his work boots scuffing over the smooth concrete of the engine bay floor as he returned both the ax and the sledge to their respective storage compartments in Engine Seventeen. But before he and Shae could pop open the next one down to do a head count on the Halligan bars, the piercing sound of the all-call echoed off the cinder block walls of the engine bay.

"Engine Seventeen, Squad Six, Ambulance Twenty-Two, structure fire, ninety-three hundred block of Glendale Avenue, requesting immediate response."

Just like that, Kellan's pulse tripped into go mode in his veins. "Nothing like a crispy job right out of the chute," he said, double-checking that the storage compartments were all latched tight before quickly hanging the inventory clipboard in his grasp back on the nearby support post. Damn, they'd barely taken a chunk out of their morning shift-change duties. Not that it mattered in the grander scheme of things catching fire.

"You're not complaining, are you?" Shae shot a disbelieving glance over the shoulder of her navy blue uniform shirt as she pulled herself into the operator's seat, throwing on her headset and kicking the engine over into a low growl.

Kellan clambered into the back step behind her, moving all the way down to the spot diagonal from hers, directly behind the officer's seat. "Hell no," he said, because as crazy as it might seem to civilians, he'd rather be busy than bored. He hadn't become a firefighter to sit around the station. Give him the chance to run into a shit storm while all others were running out, and Kellan would take it every day of the week. Twice on Sundays.

He parked himself in the seat where he'd stowed his turnout gear barely fifteen minutes ago, inhaling to counter the physiological responses tempting his body to get jacked up. His heart might want to charge full speed ahead against his sternum and flatten his lungs to boot, but he'd learned how to show his adrenal gland who was boss long before day one at the Remington Fire Academy. Being a sniper for the Rangers tended to teach a guy how to keep his shit in check. After two tours in Afghanistan, the methods for managing his adrenaline were pretty much stitched into Kellan's DNA.

Deep breaths. Quick decisions. Precise movements. No dwelling on what was in front of you or what was already done.

Ever.

Kellan's lieutenant, Ian Gamble, slid his huge frame into the officer's seat in the front of the engine at the same time Station Seventeen's rookie, Luke Slater, scrambled into the back step to sit behind Shae. Gamble turned to pin the rookie with a you-got-lucky-you-weren't-last-in stare, hooking his headset over his ears and jutting his darkly-stubbled chin at Shae in a nonverbal "let's go."

Both Kellan and Slater grabbed the headsets hanging

over their respective seats, because between the hundred and thirty decibel sirens and the rattle and whoosh of cabin noise inside the engine's boxy interior, they didn't have a prayer of hearing their lieutenant otherwise.

"Okay you guys, buckle down because this looks like the real deal," Gamble cut out into his mic, the scraped-up edges of his voice a perfect match for his gruff demeanor. He leaned forward to look at the screen built into the dashboard that connected them with Remington's emergency services system. "Dispatch is reporting flames showing at a residence on the north side of the district. Nearest cross street is Woodmoor," he said, mostly for Shae's benefit.

Of course, she probably didn't need the assist. Shae had operated Engine Seventeen since before Kellan had even set his baby toe in the firehouse for his first shift. She knew Remington's streets as well as she knew her own reflection.

Case in point. "That's up in North Point," she said. "The neighborhood's not pretty." While the fact didn't matter an ounce in terms of how hard they'd fight the blaze, it could have an impact on the scene.

"Mmm," Gamble acknowledged. "Well, if we haul ass"—he paused to slide a glance at Shae, whose resulting grin Kellan could just make out in profile from his spot in the back step—"we'll be first on-scene, so gear up and be ready to look alive. Squad and ambo are on our six, and Captain Bridges is along for the ride."

"Copy that," Kellan said, tugging the headset from his ears. Continuing the smooth circuit of his inhale/exhale, he reached down for his bunker pants, pulling them over his uniform in one methodical move.

"Must be a hell of a fire if all hands are on deck, right?" Slater's dark eyes flashed wide and round from his spot next to Kellan in the step, giving away his jitters despite the guy's obvious attempt at a poker face.

Ah, rookies. Still, while some guys might be tempted to haze a newbie for being a little rattled on his first big fire call, giving the kid shit for turning out to be human after only three weeks on the job seemed a touch indecent.

"Not necessarily," Kellan said, trying to lead by example as he got the rest of his gear into place. "Bridges is a hands-on kind of captain, and squad goes on all the fire calls in the district no matter what." Those guys weren't elite for shits and giggles, that was for damn sure. "But it's not a drill, so keep your head on a swivel and stay on Gamble's hip. And Slater?" He didn't wait for the candidate to acknowledge him, because Christ, the kid looked two seconds away from stroking out. "Breathe in on a three count and out on a five. You're gonna need your legs under you all the way. You copy?"

Slater nodded, his stare turning focused, and what do you know, he actually took Kellan's advice. Good goddamn thing, too, because they were about T-minus two minutes from rolling up on the scene of this fire, and if the thick column of smoke Kellan had spotted through his window was anything to go by, something was burning pretty good.

Time to go to work.

"Bridges is calling the shots on the two-way," Gamble hollered into the step, five seconds before Shae pulled the engine to a stop in front of a two-story detached row home heavily blanketed by smoke. "Listen up for assignments and watch your backs. And each other's."

"Copy that," Kellan said, his response weaving around both Shae's and Slater's as they gave up the same answer at the same time. Doing one last lightning-fast systems check on both his gear and his composure, he shouldered his SCBA tank, his muscles squeezing at the familiar burden of the extra thirty pounds as he hustled his way out of the back step to put his boots on the ground.

Whoa. A sheen of sweat burst between his shoulder blades despite the cool September weather. His pulse knocked hard against his throat at the sight of the thick gray smoke and angry orange flames licking upward from the first and second-story windows on the front of the row home, and even though it was tempting as hell to stare at the fire alone, Kellan was all too well-versed on how danger could spring from the most unexpected places. After cataloguing the immediate no-shit threat posed by the fire itself, he took a swift visual inventory of all of his surroundings.

Fairly well-kept house, although not so much on the neighborhood. Only a handful of onlookers, which would be a plus for securing the scene. No obvious entrapment—no one stumbling from the blaze in a panic about someone still inside and nobody shouting their guts out from a window or the roof. And wasn't that another win, because with the smoke and flames funneling from the Alpha side windows, getting anyone out of the place would be a bitch and a half.

Not that they wouldn't go all just-in-case and get to looking. Speaking of which…

Captain Bridges' voice filled Kellan's ear from the two-way radio clipped just below the shoulder of his turnout gear. "Squad Six, we need a vent on this roof immediately if not sooner. Gates, you and Faurier get a move on. Hawkins and Dempsey, take primary search and rescue, Gamble, you and Slater ready the lines, and Walker and McCullough, back up squad on S&R. I want this fire knocked down before it grows any more teeth, people. Go."

Gamble straightened to the top of his six-foot, five-inch frame, throwing a look from Kellan to Shae. "You heard the captain," he said, but Kellan's boots had already started to thump over the cracked asphalt.

"Yes, sir." Sparing only the seconds necessary to grab his Halligan bar from its spot in Engine Seventeen's storage compartment, he fell into step with Shae, who was right on the squad lieutenant's boot heels on the concrete sidewalk leading up to the house. Under normal circumstances, Hawk probably would've come off with a smart-assed quip in that slow, Southern drawl of his. But pleasantries—hell, anything other than locked and loaded intensity—fell to the wayside the second something went from a smolder to a burn.

This house definitely fit the freaking bill. "All right," Hawk bit out, barely looking over his shoulder as he clanged past the waist-high chain link fence marked with signs warning NO TRESPASSING. "This place is goin' up fast, so don't dawdle. Dempsey, you're my door man. McCullough, once we're in, you and Walker hit the basement and sweep from the bottom up. Dempsey and I will start on the second floor and work our way down. We'll meet you in the middle."

"Copy, Lieutenant," McCullough said, her green stare firm and focused. Their footsteps came to a halt on the timeworn porch boards just shy of the front door. Hawk's tight nod at Dempsey translated to a nonverbal "breach it," and Kellan's gut tightened in a quick jab of anticipation. Dempsey put a punishing kick to the sweet spot in the lower panels, shock flashing both over his face and through Kellan's veins when the damned thing refused to budge in its casing. A breach like that on a house this old should've had the door not just wide open, but halfway off its hinges. No way would the lock hold unless—

"The fuck?" Dempsey grunted, sliding the flat end of his Halligan between the edge of the door and the jamb to visualize the deadbolt. "There's a steel-reinforced protector screwed into the doorframe."

Kellan's brows popped toward the brim of his helmet. Not only was the jamb fortified to the nines, but the deadbolt itself had to be two inches thick. "That's a shit-ton of hardware for a residence."

"It's definitely not your momma's turn-and-go," Dempsey agreed, and Hawk spun another gaze over the covered main-level windows and the thick veil of smoke muddying the morning sunlight around them.

"Put those ridiculous breach skills of yours to work, Dempsey. We need entry like five minutes ago."

"You got it, boss."

Determination shaped Dempsey's features, flattening his lips into a thin line as he turned back toward the door. Blood pulsed over Kellan's eardrums in a white-noise whoosh—thump-thump, Dempsey finessed his Halligan into a space anyone else would've thought microscopic, thump-thump, a chock replaced it for leverage to create a bigger gap, thump-thump, the edge of his Halligan found the hairsbreadth again, rocking once, twice, a third time—

The rip and crack of splintering wood never sounded so fucking beautiful.

Hawk didn't waste so much as a millisecond shouldering his way past the busted-in door and over the threshold after Dempsey, not that Kellan had expected him to. They'd already lost valuable time with the sticky breach, and anyway, everyone's assignments were crystal. Squinting past the haze, he stepped inside the tiny, barely-visible foyer, primed and ready to find the point of entry to the basement so he and Shae could get to work.

A rush of heat slammed into his lungs, chased quickly by the dark, bitter taste of smoke in his mouth, and damn, they had their work laid out for them.

"All right," he barked after he'd yanked his mask into place, the hiss of his regulator punctuating the words. "Let's find a POE to the lower level."

Shae's "copy that" came past the thick shield of her own mask. "Place looks pretty dead," she said, flipping on the high-powered flashlight strapped just to the right of her sternum as she fell in at his six. The beam cut a path through the smoke and the layer of ash starting to pepper in around them, revealing a whole lot of nothing much by way of furniture or belongings. A single couch faced outward from the adjacent living room, its cushions askew. Fast food wrappers and empty beer cans littered the floor around it, but the space appeared empty otherwise. No coffee table, no TV, nothing on the rickety bookshelf propped against the wall.

"Shit." Kellan turned on his own flashlight, although it

didn't do much to help illuminate the place. Heavy curtains blanketed every window from sash to sill, and between that and the smoke, visibility grew more and more difficult with every step farther inside. Still, the ominous glow of flames around them said this fire was eating through the house at an alarming rate. Abandoned or not, they had to make sure no one was trapped inside.

"Even if it's vacant, there could be squatters. Anything goes in this neighborhood," he said, resolve flashing harder in his chest as he scanned the front hallway for a door that might lead down. Forcing his legs into gear, Kellan stabbed his boots into the floorboards with each decisive step, methodically ruling out a hall closet and a tiny bathroom before hitting the jackpot on the third door at the back of the narrow corridor by the kitchen.

"Basement," he called out, pulling the door wide on its hinges and clambering down the unfinished wooden stairs. Visibility went from bad to you've-got-to-be-kidding-me with every downward move, daring his pulse to rattle and his brain to spin back in time.

Thick air, clogging his throat, poker-hot in his lungs. Eyes stinging with sweat and sand and images he'd never forget. Screams. The screams…

This moment. Right now. Nothing else.

Ever.

Kellan's boots hit the concrete landing, slamming his focus back into place. A long, dark hallway stretched out to both his right and his left, and he metered his breath on a three count, using his exhale to bellow, "Fire department! Call out!"

The only response was an eerie silence that sent a chill laddering up his spine.

"Hang on," Shae said from the spot where she'd come to a stop at his nine. She took a handheld thermal imaging camera from one of the deep-welled pockets in her coat, using it to follow the beam of her flashlight from one end of the hallway to the other. "There's a ton of heat building in these walls, Walker. We need to make sure no one's down here and get the hell out of Dodge. I'll take the Delta side." She jerked her head down the left end of the hallway. "You take Bravo. Go."

"Copy that." Kellan pivoted on his heels, angling his body to the right. Visibility amounted to a jack with a side of shit, which meant he was going to have to get creative in order to be thorough and fast. Throwing both arms out from his sides, he exhaled with a hell yes as his glove-covered hands made contact with either wall. Reinforcing his limited vision with feel meant he'd have less of a chance of missing something. Not that there had been a whole lot in the house so far to miss.

Kicking his feet into rapid motion, Kellan moved down the shadow-cloaked passageway. The air down here felt cooler than the main level, which was only to say it wasn't hell-hot and actively engulfed in flames. At least, not yet. But for now, that made the basement a logical place for someone to hide, especially if they thought they'd get into trouble for squatting in an abandoned house, and damn it, there were just enough signs that someone had been here recently to make the unease in Kellan's chest go for a double.

He opened his mouth to broadcast another offer for help, but the words jammed in his windpipe when his right palm skimmed the edge of a doorframe. The knob refused to budge despite the firm twist he tried to put to it, and seriously, what was with the Fort Knox treatment in this place?

Screw it. Not having the time for anything other than brute force, Kellan coiled up his energy on a deep inhale, sending all the power he could muster on a direct path to his leg as he unleashed a relentless kick. The door gave way with a crash, relief filling him in a quick burst as he crossed the threshold into the dank, smoke-tinged room.

"Fire department, call out!" The bellow of his own voice reverberated in his ears. The room was as dark as the hallway behind him, the one small rectangular window in the corner by the ceiling blacked out by a heavy layer of curtains. Kellan aimed his flashlight toward the far side of the space, giving the room a quick yet thorough scan from left to right.

Nothing much. Like the living room above, the furniture in here was sparse, just a large desk in the center of the room with empty pizza boxes and crumpled, grease-stained napkins scattered over its surface. Thankfully, no one was huddled up or trying to hide beneath it, and he turned to complete the sweep of the room. The beam of his flashlight landed on a set of bi-fold doors on the opposite wall, and *finally*, Kellan had found an opening in this place that wasn't bolted shut.

He yanked the closet doors apart on their track, crouching down low to do a quick search of the crawl space beneath a set of crude wooden shelves. But before he could so much as open his mouth for a call-out, a burst of static sounded off from the two-way on his shoulder.

"Hawkins to Command," the lieutenant clipped out. "We're a negative on entrapment on the second floor. The house looks abandoned, but the structure's fully involved. This fire's gonna get worse before it gets better."

"Command to Hawkins," came Captain Bridges' voice in return. "Fall out immediately, before this thing flashes over. Hawkins, Dempsey, McCullough, Walker, I want all four of you in front of me in sixty seconds. Do you copy?"

Kellan's rib cage threatened to constrict, but shit, he had no time for body betrayal. He needed to finish clearing this room and find Shae. Now.

"Walker to Command. Copy. Falling out," he said into the two-way. Steeling his breath, he sent his stare on one last tour of the closet before unfolding himself to standing. The back of his helmet banged against something in a hard thump—ah, fuck, he'd forgotten about the wooden shelves—and Kellan ducked back into the closet out of sheer instinct. His heart slammed in surprise as whatever had been on the now-upended wooden plank tumbled over his shoulder, hitting the concrete subfloor with a metallic crash.

He cursed under his breath, wrangling his pulse back down from its code red. There was no saving the lock box that had burst open at his feet upon impact, so Kellan stepped over the scattered papers and other items spilling over the floor. Racing toward the door, he swung himself back in the direction he'd come, his chest loosening just a fraction at the sight of Shae barreling in from the opposite side.

"I'm clear," she said, and Kellan jerked his head in a nod, leading the way up the steps.

"Me too. Let's get the hell out of here."

They retraced their steps back to the main level, and holy shit, the fire up here had doubled in intensity in the sparse minutes he and Shae had been in the basement. Flames had snaked down the living room walls to grab hold of the curtains in their absence, illuminating the room in a rolling orange glow at the same time heavy billows of smoke clogged their path. But they were a dozen steps from daylight, and Kellan wasn't stopping for love or money.

He charged ahead without pause, sweat stinging his eyes beneath his mask and his chest burning from exertion. Barging back through the front door, his boots punched over the porch boards, the sudden flash of over-bright sunlight leaving him momentarily disoriented. But muscle memory was a powerful thing, and his arms lifted up, his hands tugging off his helmet and mask even though his brain had little to do with the motions.

Breathe. In, two, three. Out, two, three, four, five.

The cool air hit Kellan like a titanium-reinforced wrecking ball. Although he had zero doubt that Captain Bridges had eyes on him, he still reported in over the radio, and by the time he'd heel-toed his way back to Engine Seventeen, he was more than halfway back to all systems go.

"Nice to see you in once piece," Gamble said, one

corner of his mouth lifting in a rare smile. "Heard shit was going a little sideways in there."

"Nothing we couldn't handle," Shae answered from over Kellan's shoulder, still on his six even though they'd more than cleared the hot zone.

Gamble jutted his chin at the water lines he and Slater had prepped per Captain Bridges' orders. "Glad to hear it, because Hawk and Dempsey are clear and squad's got a good vent on the roof. We're about to get this place wet."

The words shifted Kellan back into gear. He replaced his helmet over his sweat-damp head, buckling the straps in seconds. Captain Bridges' command came a breath later, springing Kellan and the rest of his fellow firefighters into action. Move by move, minute by minute, the teams on both engine and squad worked in tandem to control the blaze, first from the outside, then strategically maneuvering their way back over the threshold once the flames had been partially subdued. Kellan tunneled in on each task, methodically completing the necessary steps with his team until finally, the fire had been completely put out.

"Jesus," he breathed once they'd returned to Engine Seventeen, his inhale leaving the acrid taste of smoke on his tongue. "We haven't seen a job this sketchy in a while, huh?"

Hawkins sauntered up from Squad Six's vehicle, fixing him with a slow grin that said there was a whole lot of smartass incoming. "You know the drill, Walker. Just 'cause the fire's out don't mean the fat lady has sung."

"Yeah, yeah," Kellan said, although the words were far from a grumble. Hawk was right—there was a helluva lot more to being a firefighter than the name suggested, and if they didn't want this place to reignite for round two, they still had a lot of boxes to check. "You ready, McCullough?"

"Darlin', please," she said, affecting the heavy Irish accent that went with her heritage as she shoulder-checked him with a wry smile. "I was born ready."

Even though he knew the move would buy him a ration of shit with sprinkles on top, Kellan nudged her right back, just like he would've with any of the guys. "If you say so."

They fell into step next to each other and headed back up the concrete sidewalk. RFD protocol dictated that they monitor the scene of any structure fire with thermal imaging devices post-incident to make sure nothing got hot enough to flare back up. With a blaze this big, chances weren't small that the house still had hot spots in the walls that hadn't been destroyed, and they had to sweep every inch of the place just to be sure nothing lurked where they couldn't see it.

"Okay, boys and girls, let's make this easy," Hawk said, tipping his chin at the front door Dempsey had put a hurt to. "Retrace the ground you covered on your search and rescue circuit. Scan everything you can safely get to, and mark off any rooms too hazardous to reach. We'll use the aerial on Truck Three to get to 'em if we need to. Y'all copy?"

After a chorus of affirmative answers, the four of them crossed the threshold. The bitter tang of waterlogged ash and stale smoke filled Kellan's senses and invited his throat to tighten, but he kept to his smooth cycle of inhale/exhale. He still had plenty of work left to do. No way was he going to take a chance on his system shorting out before this scene was secure.

Or, okay. Ever.

"Damn." Shae whistled under her breath, her footsteps sounding off in soggy splashes as she swung her gaze around the living room. The fire had ravaged the curtains on two of the three side windows, allowing sunlight to spill past the burned-out spaces where the glass used to be. Although the couch and the bookshelf were still recognizable, they were pretty well torched, not to mention waterlogged, and all of the surrounding area in Kellan's line of sight matched.

"Definitely looks like a total loss," he agreed, leading the way back to the basement door and turning on the flashlight still strapped over the front of his turnout gear. "You think this was an accident?"

One shoulder rose and fell beneath the heavy black material of her coat. "I think with a fire this big, the guys at arson investigation always take a glance at the report. But truth? This house is old and vacant. Chances are there hasn't been any upkeep in a while. With how fast the fire moved from floor to floor, it wouldn't shock me if crappy electrical sparked the whole thing."

"Makes sense," Kellan said. The scorch marks spider-webbing over the walls sure backed up the theory.

Shae stopped at the bottom of the basement steps, just long enough to give him one last shrug. "Anyway. Shout out if you find something, yeah?"

"Sure. Back atcha."

Kellan turned his flashlight down the right-hand side of the hallway. The basement had escaped most of the fire and water damage, although there were still signs of both in the musty passageway. He took careful heat readings on the walls regardless, working his way down to the room he'd checked just before getting the order to fall out. Shouldering past the door he'd kicked in, Kellan trailed his flashlight over the space, re-noting the desk, the pizza boxes, the discarded napkins.

His stare snagged on the lock box he'd knocked from the shelf, busted wide on its hinges from the fall, and shit, he hadn't meant to wreck what little was left in the place. Bending down to plant one knee against the concrete, he reached out to gather the papers—no wait, they were photographs—scattered like confetti over the ground. He dusted off their surfaces with his gloved fingers, hoping maybe the move would knock off any ash or dirt marking the photos as a result of their trip over the floor.

But then the images in front of him registered, and all the air left the room.

"Walker to Command," Kellan said into his two-way, trying like hell to steady his voice along with his suddenly slamming heartbeat. "We've got a problem in the basement."

"This is Command," came Captain Bridges' voice over the line. "Do you need backup, Walker?"

"No, sir," he said, dread cranking down on his gut as he looked at the pictures again.

"We need the police. I'm pretty sure they're going to want to see what I just found."

CHAPTER TWO

Isabella Moreno pushed back from her desk, trying with all her might to evil eye the paperwork at her elbow into submission. For every report she'd filed this morning, another three had popped up in its place, and after four hours, she was damn near ready to cry uncle.

Give her thieves, rapists, and gang-banging street thugs any day. But all the requisition-this and document-that required by the Remington Police Department? Now that could really kill a girl.

The sound of her boss's throat clearing kicked her chin to attention and her pulse into third gear. "All right everybody, listen up," Sergeant Sam Sinclair said in a clipped voice that reminded Isabella—and probably every other cop in the Thirty-Third, maybe even all of Remington—that he was as tough as he was dedicated to the job. "We just caught a double. Convenience store robbery over in South Hill and a report of something suspicious found at the scene of a house fire over on Glendale."

"Something suspicious?" Isabella asked, her chest tightening by just a fraction. "Like a body?"

"Aren't you just a ray of sunshine?" Detective Shawn

Maxwell threw her a wry smile from his desk across the squad room, and she worked up an identical twin to the expression in return.

"Yeah, that's me." She snorted, although not unkindly, because truth? Maxwell's sarcasm wasn't poorly placed. "All hugs and rainbows and unicorns."

"And bodies, apparently. Overachiever," he lobbed back. Of the four detectives in the Thirty-Third Precinct's intelligence unit, she and Maxwell had the most seniority at the RPD, and shared a warped sense of cop humor as a result. Kind of funny that he was the oldest detective in the group while she was the youngest, but hey. Experience was experience, and they both had a buttload.

"The suspicious find is not a body," Sinclair said, shooting a glance in her direction. "But first responders are calling it evidence of a possible crime."

Despite the brashness she wore like Kevlar, her sergeant's gruff affirmation allowed Isabella to breathe a little easier. As much as she loved her job and would stop at nothing to get it done, the grim parts were still…well, grim. Victims most of all.

Crimes, she could solve. But saving a victim after the fact was as impossible as hitching a wagon to the moon.

Not that Isabella hadn't spent the last eleven years of her life trying.

Knock it off, she silently chided, pushing back from the stack of paperwork strewn over her blotter and the three half-to-mostly-empty cups of tea surrounding it. "Which call do you want me and Hollister to take?" Isabella asked, reaching for the car keys in the top drawer of her standard-issue metal desk. Grim or not, there were still bad guys out there who needed to be put to justice. It was time to shove up her sleeves and make that happen.

"Actually, neither."

She froze, her eyes darting from her partner Liam Hollister's don't-look-at-me expression to Sinclair's impenetrable blue-gray stare. "Sorry?"

"Hollister's going to back up Maxwell and Hale at the robbery." He jerked his crew cut at the three detectives sitting at their respective desks, all of whom started to move at the action. "You and I are headed to the fire over on Glendale."

Oooookay. Although it was on the tip of her tongue to ask what she'd done to deserve special snowflake status, Isabella refrained. Despite the fact that she and Hollister were technically partners, the four of them worked interchangeably on cases. She worked apart from the group often enough—mostly when she requested extra assignments or volunteered to fly solo, but still. Anyway, the two years Isabella had worked for Sam told her in no uncertain terms that questioning his methods—in front of the team, no less—wouldn't land her anywhere she wanted to be.

"Copy that," she said. Double-checking the Glock and badge combo at her right hip, she grabbed the least cold cup of tea from her desk and followed her sergeant down the hallway of the intelligence office. She steadied her pulse to keep time with her footsteps, smoothing the thump-thump-thump into a steady rhythm until she and Sinclair reached his city-issued unmarked Chevy Tahoe.

"Everything okay?" Isabella lifted her brows just slightly, pulling her seatbelt across the front of her fitted black top. They didn't stand on a whole lot of pretense in intelligence, but that didn't mean she didn't have to play this just right in order to figure out why her boss was acting nine kinds of cagey about this call.

Sinclair's blond brows went up to mirror hers. "You mean other than the suspicious evidence found at this fire?"

Allllrighty. If Sinclair wanted to get right to the case, she certainly had no problem jumping feet-first into work. It was, after all, her MO. "Suspicious evidence is a little vague, huh? We got anything else to go on?"

"Not much, I'm afraid." Sinclair slid a pair of aviator sunglasses over his face and pulled the Tahoe out onto

Franklin Street, headed toward Remington's north side. Having lived in the city her whole life, Isabella knew the place as well as her own last name. Not an entirely small feat considering it was the second largest city in North Carolina.

"Well it's not a body," she prompted, and Sinclair nodded to reaffirm.

"Story I got from the call-in was that RFD responded to a house fire, and after the flames were out, they found something they deemed serious enough to have us take a look at."

The back of Isabella's neck prickled beneath her ponytail. Something about this still wasn't gelling. "And you're doing the walk-and-talk because...?"

"Captain Bridges out at Seventeen called it in."

And there it is. "That's why you're coming out with me instead of sending Hollister or Maxwell or Hale? Because Seventeen is on-scene?"

"I'm coming out with you because I enjoy your sparkling personality, Moreno." God, he put just enough good humor to the words to make the sentiment stick, too. "But to address your concern, yes. Kellan Walker made the find. Since you two have a little history, I thought I'd tag along."

Isabella's stomach pinched beneath the top of her jeans. "Kellan Walker and I don't have any history. And he definitely doesn't concern me," she said. Piss her off? Check. Drive her bat-shit crazy? Check. Hell, he'd even turned her on a little (translation: a lot) with those crystal blue eyes and stupid-broad shoulders and dark, sexy scruff. At least, he had before the whole Chicago debacle three months ago. But nobody—nobody—*concerned* her.

Because Isabella knew far better than to let them.

"Okay," Sinclair said, a pop of surprise moving through her veins as his tone backed up the word. "Then we shouldn't have any issues."

Sure. Just as long as she and Walker didn't have to speak, they'd be peachy. Not that *she* was the one with the problem. She'd busted her ass three months ago on his sister Kylie's case, which had been a doozy and a half, thank you very much. In order to keep Kylie safe after she'd witnessed a brutal murder halfway across the country, Isabella had trusted a former colleague, and Kellan had trusted her.

Funny thing about a house of cards, though. If even one was crooked, the whole lot of them came crashing down. Isabella had unknowingly promised Walker's sister protection she hadn't been able to deliver when a member of her old colleague's team turned out to be dirty, and the case had culminated in a violent shootout. Even though Kylie had ended up unharmed, it hadn't been due to Isabella's slick detective skills. Walker had been furious with her that his sister's safety had been compromised.

But not as furious as Isabella had been with herself that she'd inadvertently put a murder witness in harm's way.

She shoved back the fresh shot of remorse blooming in her chest. "So what exactly did these guys find, anyway?" she asked, focusing her thoughts on this call, where they belonged.

"I don't know, but we're about to find out."

Sinclair pulled up to the uni directing traffic around the sea of emergency response vehicles, flashing his badge to gain entry to the scene. They got as close as they could, which wasn't saying much under the circumstances, but Isabella didn't mind hoofing it a little if it meant she could observe the scene of a crime from the outside in.

She and Sinclair got out of the Tahoe about a half-block from what—as best she could tell—was ground zero for the fire. Every last one of her senses pinged to life as they moved over the seen-better-days sidewalk and past a couple of detached row houses. The neighborhood wasn't great, which meant the intel likely wouldn't be great, either. People in bad neighborhoods tended to have selective memories when it came to recounting suspicious activity. But if the address of the fire had popped anything weird in their database, Sinclair would've mentioned it. So right now, Isabella had to fly on what they had.

Which was a whole lot of French-fried house. Damn, the thing smelled as bad as it looked, the bitter-burnt punch of smoke combining with the scorched siding and smashed out windows to hammer home the suggestion that the structure was a total loss. She scanned the scene, her stomach tightening involuntarily at the sight of the firefighters milling around and storing their gear in various response vehicles.

Stop being an idiot. She and Kellan might not have the best history in the galaxy, or okay, even be on speaking terms right now. But a job was a job. There was no reason for her stomach to get all traitorously jumpy over clapping eyes on him again.

Even if he *did* hate her guts.

"Sergeant. Detective." The familiar voice knocked Isabella back to the present tense. Captain Tanner Bridges, who they'd dealt with from time to time at crime scenes and had always been as helpful as he was fair, greeted them on the sidewalk in front of the burned-out house. "Thanks for coming out so quickly. I wasn't sure who else to call."

"Not a problem," Sinclair said, shaking the man's hand. "Can you tell us what you've got?"

The captain paused, his brown eyes flashing with uncertainty. "Probably best to show you." He jerked his head toward the house's front walk, starting to lead the way. "We responded to a nine-one-one call a few hours ago, and when we got here, the house was pretty heavily involved. Best we can tell, the place looks vacant. Cause of the fire is still unknown, but at first blush, I'd guess some bad wiring kicked things off."

"Okay," Isabella said, all question, and the captain answered with a nod.

"After we put the fire out, firefighter Walker was doing a sweep of the scene to prevent flare-ups when he found something suspicious in a basement closet. Watch your step." Bridges indicated the water and ash-covered porch boards as they crossed the threshold together, and the acrid smell of old smoke hit her like a punch in the nose. "I had some extra lights brought downstairs for better visibility, but no one's been in here except my firefighters."

Isabella took in the scene on the first floor, her heart picking up the pace. There wasn't a whole lot here, and what little was left was pretty torched. What on earth could Kellan have possibly found in a place like this?

She followed Bridges to a staircase at the back of the house, her eyes taking a split second to adjust from the daylight that had spilled in through the main level windows to the shadow-casting glare thrown off by the spotlight lamp at the bottom of the basement steps. He led her and Sinclair down the right-hand side of the hallway and over the threshold to the only room Isabella could see. Her brain smoothly catalogued the scene. Smallish room, maybe twelve by twelve, one desk dead center. Unfinished drywall, cement subfloor.

And one firefighter whose stare had suddenly gone as dark as storm clouds over a raging sea.

Irritation flashed over Kellan's face, along with a hint of surprise as he turned from Isabella to his captain. "You called intelligence?"

Sinclair's brows popped at the same time as her pulse. Her boss knew all about Walker's beef with her, and not only was he fiercely protective of his detectives, but he wasn't exactly known for his stellar composure.

Thankfully, Captain Bridges was. "Of course I called them," he said, just as calm as a lake at sunrise. "This falls under their jurisdiction, and it could be evidence of a potentially serious crime."

The irritation on Walker's soot-smudged face coalesced at the mention, and Sinclair didn't waste time or words getting right to business.

"You want to tell us what you found?" he asked.

After an ever-so-slight pause, Walker nodded. "I covered this section of the basement for search and rescue during the fire. When I got to the closet over here, this lock box fell off the overhead shelf and broke open. Captain Bridges gave the order to fall out before I could see what had been inside—the fire had gotten pretty hairy on the second floor at that point. But when I came back for the prevention sweep after the fire was out, this is what I found."

He gestured to an old, dented metal lock box, the kind someone would store cash in at a yard sale, and a pile of photographs, along with a bundle of thin nylon rope and a plastic baggie containing what looked like a few pairs of women's earrings.

"I gathered the pictures before I saw the images on them," Walker continued, pointing to the tidy pile next to the lock box. "But once I did, I put them down, and I didn't touch any of the other stuff, just in case."

It didn't escape Isabella's notice that he'd kept his eyes lasered in on Sinclair and only Sinclair as he'd recounted the story, even going so far as to turn his shoulder to give her half of his back while he spoke. But screw that. Despite what he thought, she was a damn good cop, and if something had gone down here, she was going to be part of catching whoever was responsible.

"Is this everything you found?" Isabella asked, pulling a pair of nitrile gloves from the pocket of her jeans and snapping them into place.

He looked over the broad ridge of his shoulder, his bright blue gaze covered in frost. "Yes."

The unspoken "duh" riding shotgun with his answer tagged her right in the gut, and she heard the unintended implication in her question just a beat too late. As displeased as they were with each other, Isabella knew Kellan would never withhold potential evidence. He was pissed, not dirty.

She cleared her throat and tried for round two. "What I meant was, are these the only suspicious items your team found from the entire house," she qualified, but still, Walker's expression remained as unmoved as it was chilly.

"Still yes."

Alrighty then. Although she had to bite her tongue to do it, she focused on the evidence in front of her. Kneeling down to the concrete, she picked up the photographs, dropping her stare over the first one in the pile.

And her breath came to a crashing halt in her lungs.

"Jesus." The photograph showed a young woman in profile, her face turned just far enough away from the camera to be useless to any sort of recognition software. Bent halfway over a crushed velvet settee, she wore a lacy black tank top and matching thong underwear, both pulled provocatively low. Her hands were bound behind her with a thin length of nylon rope tied in an intricate knot reaching halfway up her forearms, her back arched at a sharp angle as if her hair was being yanked by someone just outside the camera's range. The corner of her darkly lipsticked mouth was pulled into a tight grimace that further supported the guess, and Isabella's heart took a potshot at her breastbone as the rest of the photo registered. The angry red marks covering the woman's wrists beneath the bindings looked fresh.

The bruises on her throat didn't.

"Yeah," Kellan said, the word going soft at the edges. "That's why we called."

Isabella flipped through the rest of the photos—twenty-two in all, of what appeared to be five different women all in the same setting and same basic pose—before swallowing past the knot in her throat and handing them over to Sinclair. *Don't go back there. Don't think about it. Don't.* "These items were inside the lock box with the pictures?"

Walker nodded. "The rest of the closet is empty and nothing else was on the shelf. These fell out of the box with the pictures." He pointed to the baggie full of jewelry and the bundle of rope, the same thin, white nylon kind used in the photos.

Unfortunately, it was used in a ton of other places, too, and the rope on the floor looked brand new. "Okay." Her brain spun, trying to calculate how long it would take to get a crime scene unit out here. Chances were there was little to no evidence to go on in the rest of the house, especially after the fire, but who knew. They might get lucky. "Thanks for calling this in."

"I take it Seventeen is done with the scene?" Sinclair asked, and Captain Bridges answered with a tight nod.

"The house will still be monitored by the RFD for the next twenty-four hours to make sure nothing flares back up. But yes. We're about to head out."

"Okay, thanks. We'll let you know if we need anything else. Sharp eyes, Walker."

"Just doing my job, Sergeant."

Although he delivered the words without attitude, they bulls-eyed into Isabella's sternum all the same. She flicked a nanosecond's worth of a glance at Kellan, but he'd already aimed his boots toward the door. Which was fine, really, because she had work to do.

I trusted you, and you put my sister's life at risk! That fucking psycho nearly killed her, Moreno. Do you have any idea what I could've lost?

Isabella's heart twisted involuntarily, her mouth going dry as the image of a bright-eyed girl with dark braids and an entire life to live flashed through her mind's eye.

Yeah. Even if Kellan didn't know it, Isabella had every idea of what he could've lost.

And wasn't that all the more reason to focus on nailing whoever was hurting women in the here and now?

"I'll go ahead and do a quick look-see to make sure nothing got missed from the closet down here. Then I'll call the fire marshal's office to let him know we'll need full access for CSU," she said, locking her resolve into place as she turned toward Sinclair. "We can probably get a unit down here by lunchtime. Those guys owe me a favor for—"

"Hold on for just a second, Moreno. Don't you think you're jumping in a little hard?"

She let go of a shocked exhale. "No. I think I'm taking

26

this seriously."

Sinclair measured her with a slow glance that s[...] choosing his words with care. "You take all you[...] seriously. It's what makes you a good cop. All I'm saying[...] maybe we should take a closer look and see if there's something here to pursue before we go all gangbusters."

Isabella's chin hiked, her palms going slick beneath the clingy material of her nitrile gloves. "See if there's something here? Are you kidding me?"

She knew playing Devil's Advocate was a smart way to get all the angles on a case, just like she knew leading with your emotions could give you tunnel vision, or worse yet, get good cops into bad trouble. But the girls in the photos were bound and bruised, for fuck's sake. There was no telling what might've happened to them off camera, if they'd been hurt or made to do things. Or worse. How was she supposed to take her emotions out of *that*?

"This looks like abuse at the very least. At worst, maybe forced prostitution or rape—God, Sam, are you looking at these pictures?" She swiped a photograph from the top of the pile on the desk in front of her, trying like hell to keep her anger in check so her hand wouldn't shake.

"I am," he said, a muscle pulling tight across his jawline. "And I'm trying to see them objectively, like all other potential evidence. Look at the background."

Her stomach churned, but she forced her focus away from the girl in the photograph, taking in the black settee along with the dark red walls behind it. "What about it?"

"It's not here, for one." Sinclair gestured to the dingy, low-rent room around them with a quick lift of his hand. "These pictures look like they were taken someplace way more upscale. Like maybe a sex club."

"Or an Internet porn set," Isabella argued, but Sinclair just nodded.

"Neither of which are illegal all by themselves. As off-putting as these pictures may be to some, others participate in rough sex acts consensually. Including people who star in

...inded her.

...lbeit a thin one. "What about her ...lenged. "This girl looks about as far ... as it gets."

... said, the muscle ticking in his jawline ...no uncertain terms that he wasn't ...oto. "But a large part of BDSM culture, ...rn, is role play. Acting. There are too many ... videos on some of these websites to even count."

Gut clenching, Isabella took a different tack. "Yeah, but the girls in these photos barely look eighteen."

"Barely eighteen and *not* eighteen are two totally different scenarios. I'm not saying I agree with either," he said, cutting off her brewing protest with a surprisingly soft tone. "But you and I both know one of those things won't make a case. Without an ID on any of these women, we have no way of knowing whether what's happening in these pictures is consensual kink or a sex crime."

Okay, so it was going to be an uphill climb. Still... "Age aside, if these girls are being forced to do anything against their will, that's illegal no matter how old they are," Isabella said.

Sinclair paused, his gaze going dark as it landed on the stack of photos, and finally—*finally*—he was ready to play the other side of the coin. "If someone's moving girls, eighteen or not, that'll fall under Peterson's jurisdiction at the FBI."

Isabella's stomach clenched. Derek Peterson was in charge of their local FBI task force unit, and while he was a good agent and a decent enough guy, to say his team was overextended was a gift. "You think he'll open an investigation?"

"Based on just the photos?" A frown bracketed Sinclair's mouth. "Not likely."

Oh, come on. "Sam—"

He stopped her words with a lift of one hand. "Listen,

Moreno. If someone's turning these women out, I want to grab whoever's responsible just as badly as you do."

Isabella knotted her arms over the front of her shirt, and although she was tempted as hell to refresh her argument, she knew Sinclair wasn't the bad guy here.

At her silence, he continued. "RFD's got this place on lockdown, so no one's coming or going. Our best bet is to bag what we have, do our due diligence on making a case, and run all the facts up the chain of command to the FBI field office. If there's something here, we'll do our best to find it."

Dammit, she didn't like this plan. But she didn't hate it yet, either. "I've got a bad feeling about this one," Isabella said, looking down at the stack of photos Sinclair had placed on the desk. The cop in her saw all the variables, heard everything her sergeant had said about the possibility for consensual encounters.

But the part of her beneath her armor saw something very, very different. Something Isabella knew by heart and would never forget.

Something she could not, under any circumstances, let her boss or her fellow detectives or anyone else ever see, so she scraped for a breath and took a step back, focusing on the job in front of her like always.

"Someone's hurting these girls. Or worse. It's our job to help them," Isabella said.

Sinclair scrubbed a hand over the light blond stubble peppering his face. "If that's the case, we'll do all we can to make that happen. But everything Peterson comes at us with will need a solid argument if we want him to open an official investigation."

Isabella straightened, tucking her shoulders in toward her spine. No way would she leave these girls without someone to stand up for them. Without someone to keep them safe.

Without someone to keep them alive.

"Okay," she said. "Then let's give him one."

* * *

Isabella pushed away from her desk, her back creaking as badly as her ancient office chair. The convenience store robbery Hale, Maxwell, and Hollister had caught three days ago had turned out to be a slam dunk thanks to a smart store owner with a lot of security cameras and a stupid thief whose license plate they'd easily lifted from the footage, so she'd thrown the last seventy-two hours' worth of her energy into working alone, making a case *for* her case.

Hell if she hadn't had to throw down for what little she'd been able to scrape up, too. Facial recognition on the girls in the photos had been the bust she'd expected it to be, although of course she'd tried. The rental agency for the house confirmed that the place had been vacant for nearly half a year, and the former tenant was an eighty-year-old woman who'd had no known relatives and a squeaky clean record when she'd passed away five months ago.

Still.

Isabella might be lean on hard evidence from the scene of this fire, but her gut absolutely screamed of things not right. If Peterson sank his hooks into the case, maybe took a harder look at the crime scene, had CSU scour the room in the basement for something they could've missed, she was positive he'd uncover something illegal.

And whoever was responsible for hurting those girls needed to go down.

"Moreno." Sinclair stood in the doorframe of his office, tipping his head to the room behind him. "You got a second?"

Her gaze spun over the open space of the intelligence office, briefly connecting with Hollister's before she planted her boots onto the linoleum and scooped in a deep breath. "Sure."

"Have a seat," he said, closing the door when she'd crossed the threshold, and shit. *Shit.* Getting asked into

Sinclair's office was a fifty-fifty on bad things about to happen, and the odds increased to seventy-thirty when he shut the door. When he told you to sit down on top of it all?

One hundred percent chance you were about to get news you didn't want to hear.

"I just heard back from the FBI on the photos RFD found at that fire call," he said, sliding into the chair across from her. "They've decided not to pursue the photos found at the house fire."

Isabella's heartbeat slammed in her ears. "What?"

"You put together a compelling report, and Peterson gave everything a hard look," Sinclair said, propping his elbows over his desk and steepling his fingers as he gave her a sympathetic look. "But with all this gray area and no clear-cut evidence of an actual crime, he doesn't have a damn thing to go on."

There was no fucking way she was hearing this properly. "That's what an investigation is for," she said, trying—and failing—to keep her words level despite the anger free-flowing through her veins.

Sinclair sat perfectly still, save the barely-there lift of one brow. "An investigation into what, exactly? This case is already cold and it hasn't even been opened. Look"—his voice softened in both volume and tone, and God, she officially hated this as much as possible. "I know this is personal for you, and it's tough to let this one go. But for now, it's what we're stuck with."

Translation: Until one of the girls in those photos becomes a body.

Not on her watch. *Not ever.*

Isabella set her molars together with a firm clack. If more evidence was what the FBI wanted, then she wasn't going to stop until she damn well had some.

CHAPTER THREE

"**B**oss, we got a problem."

Julian DuPree took a deep breath and reminded himself that he was wearing a five thousand dollar suit. If he hadn't been so finely dressed, chances were rather high he'd have murdered the idiot in front of him.

At least his tailor would be pleased. Julian, on the other hand? Remained highly unimpressed.

"Come in, Charles." Julian lifted a manicured hand, ignoring the frown on his employee's normally vacant face as he waved the behemoth into his office. Muscle had its place within Julian's organization, and he knew the value of a good enforcer. Still, he had standards. Calling the man Rampage wasn't going to happen, no matter how deeply he frowned or how long he'd gone by the nickname in other circles.

"So." Julian shuffled through the papers on his antique mahogany desk even though his attention was zeroed in on the no-neck delinquent in front of him. He fucking hated problems. They were so untidy. "What seems to be the issue?"

"There was a fire at the holding facility in North Point,"

Charles said slowly, using all the right vernacular to relay all the wrong things. "The fire marshal says it was caused by bad wiring. Ruled the whole thing accidental. That geeky freak looked up the report online."

Ah, Vaughn. Having a hacker on staff was wonderfully beneficial. Especially one with no conscience.

"We vacated that location several weeks ago, if I recall." Julian kept his expression purposely neutral, calibrating his tone to match even though his senses were on high alert. The only thing he hated more than problems were surprises. "How is an accidental fire in an empty facility we can't be tied to problematic?"

Julian had gone to great lengths to make sure no names were ever used to secure his holding facilities, no rental agreements, no middlemen, no paper trail whatsoever. Using vacant houses in low rent neighborhoods to house his girls meant frequent and strategic movement on his part, but since it also kept him six steps ahead of law enforcement, the effort paid off.

Plus, the girls were filthy anyway. Turning them out in dirty, abandoned flophouses actually seemed quite fitting.

Charles shifted his weight, his cheap work boots becoming suddenly riveting. "The fire is being ruled an accident, but the location wasn't quite empty. There...might have been some photos left behind."

"I see." Julian remained perfectly still even though his anger slithered beneath his skin like a living thing. "Would these be photos of my merchandise?"

He kept his girls carefully catalogued, just as he did with all of his investment property. All hard copy photos, carefully posed for anonymity, and never, ever put on the Internet. Vaughn was good, and so far, loyal. But anyone could be bought. Or sold, as it turned out. No sense in taking chances.

"Uh," Charles said, his beady eyes still focused on the Aubusson beneath his clumsy feet, and the grunt was all the answer Julian needed. "They were just some of the extra pictures, mostly duplicates. But yeah, of the stuff we used to keep there."

Julian's anger flirted with rage, making his pulse pound and pushing his next question between his teeth. "And where are the photos now?"

"I'm not sure. I went back to try and find them after Best Buy over there told me a nine-one-one call had popped on the address." Charles hooked a meaty thumb over his shoulder, gesturing in the direction of the server room down the hall where Vaughn worked, ate, and slept. "But it took a couple of days before I could dodge the cops and the fire department. The place was pretty fucked up. Barely anything left. The pictures might've burned along with most everything else."

"But they weren't there when you went back," Julian said, his rage growing sharper and more focused as the man shook his fat, bald head.

"No, but Vaughn said the fire marshal doesn't have the case listed as pending investigation from the RPD, and—"

Julian silenced him with nothing more than a look. "Even if the police department did open an investigation, they wouldn't get anywhere. Do you know how I know this, Charles?"

"Uh. No, sir."

"Because I don't make errors. And do you know what those photos being left behind at that holding facility is?"

Charles swallowed, but at least he had the decency to answer. "An error."

"Exactly." Julian folded his hands over the long-forgotten paperwork placed neatly on his desk. He had far more important things to deal with than sloppy work. "Tell me, Charles. Why were the photos not moved along with the merchandise in the first place?"

"I thought...the rental company didn't have anyone scheduled to move into the house"—Charles's brick-end chin jerked up at the error, and he took an awkward step back on the ornately patterned rug—"uh, I mean the facility, any time soon, so I thought I had more time to get everything out of there."

Julian knew running an organization like his meant delegating certain tasks. After all, he certainly wasn't going to stay in some hovel on Glendale fucking Avenue to guard a bunch of junkie whores. Bad enough that he had to go to these flophouses on occasion to break their spirits and their bodies in order to show them to whom they belonged. But loose ends and negligent work by his subordinates, in his organization? That simply wouldn't do.

"That's not how we do business," Julian said, forging his words in cool, quiet steel. "The photos should've been the first thing you took care of after the merchandise had been moved."

"I know, boss." Unease flooded Charles's beefy features. "But they were just the extras. I figured keeping them wouldn't hurt. You know. For, uh. Personal use."

One corner of Julian's mouth lifted. Weak bastard. Just like the rest of them.

"Ah, Charles." Pushing back from his desk, he slipped out of his charcoal gray suit jacket, letting the lush fabric slide through his fingers before starting to roll up his shirt sleeves with meticulous care. "That's where you're wrong."

This time, the man didn't frown at the formal address. "I am?"

"Yes." Julian opened his desk drawer, his heart pumping faster at the gleam of razor-sharp stainless steel. Yes. Yes. "Your error is going to hurt. A lot."

Looked like he was going to get his suit dirty after all.

* * *

Kellan hung the last of his gear in the equipment room, finally allowing his muscles to unwind in relief. Considering the flash-bang that had kicked off his tour four days ago, yesterday's twenty-four-hour shift had been relatively quiet in comparison. Two traffic wrecks, both pretty minor, and three medical assists that were more of the same. Still, a shit show could land in his lap at any time, so Kellan knew better than to let his guard down when he was on the clock at Seventeen.

If his emotions didn't stay boxed up, things like those photos he'd found Monday morning would fuck with his head. Being cautious, even to the point of toeing the line of mild paranoia, was better than the alternative. Letting your guard down only made you vulnerable, and people who were vulnerable had a way higher chance of breaking.

And there was one thing Kellan knew for damn sure. With everything he'd seen and done, if he broke, there wouldn't be a chance in hell of putting his ass back together.

"Walker." Gamble's voice caught him by the edge of surprise, and hell, for a guy that big, his lieutenant was freakishly sneaky. "You out of here?"

Kellan blanked the momentary ripple of shock from his veins, re-setting his vitals in less than a breath. "Yup." They'd finished shift change two minutes before he'd come out here to store his gear. Next stop was food, a shower, and bed. In that order. "You?"

"Affirmative," Gamble said, letting his roots as a Marine show.

"See you tonight at the Crooked Angel?" Kellan asked, shouldering the duffel he'd dropped by his feet. The crew on engine, squad, and ambo embodied the whole work-together/play-together thing pretty much down to the letter. Nearly everyone on Seventeen's A-shift, along with a few people who worked in the admin offices at the RFD, killed the clock with one another on a regular basis at the local bar. Given that today was Friday and they didn't have to be back at the fire house until Sunday morning? No way they wouldn't all gather to blow off some steam.

Gamble lifted a dark brow along with one corner of his mouth. "Fifty bucks says I'll see you first."

"Dude." Kellan conveyed his doubt with a look. No need to say out loud that he'd been a sniper in one of the most active Ranger units in the entire Army. Guys who bragged about their experience were either douchebags or posers, and anyway, he and Gamble had worked together for two years. The lieutenant definitely knew whose thread he was pulling.

But he also didn't recant, so Kellan worked up a lazy smile. "Okay by me if you want to give me your money."

"Uh-huh. We'll see."

They walked from the equipment room to the engine bay, parting ways with a pair of easy nods and see-ya-laters. Kellan made his way up Washington Boulevard, where he'd parked yesterday morning before shift. Funny how quiet the city could be before things like rush hour and regular workdays kicked in, all soft sunlight and clean storefronts. He slid in a breath of cool air, scanning the sidewalk and the two-lane thoroughfare where Station Seventeen was situated.

He saw the woman leaning against his '68 Camaro from forty feet away.

Kellan's pulse flared even though his footsteps never faltered. Long, denim-wrapped legs leading to lean muscles and lush, sexy curves. Loose, confident stance that spoke of both awareness and strength. Long, caramel-colored hair that she tossed away from her face as soon as she saw him coming, and God *dammit*, that was the second time this week he'd been blindsided by Isabella Moreno.

"What are you doing here?" he asked, wincing inwardly as the words crossed his lips. Not that he didn't feel every inch of the attitude behind them, because after her fuck-up had put his sister's life in danger three months ago, he so did. But slapping his emotions on his sleeve wasn't on Kellan's agenda, good, bad, or extremely pissed off. Of course, Isabella already knew he was chock full of the emotion behind door number three, anyway.

She pushed herself off the Camaro's cherry red quarter panel, sliding one hand to her unnervingly voluptuous hip while the other remained wrapped around a cup of coffee.

"Waiting for you."

"I got that." His tone left the what-for part of the question hanging between them, and Kellan had to hand it to her. Moreno wasn't the type to mince words.

"I need a favor. I want you to walk me through the scene of Monday's fire."

Jesus, she had a sense of humor. Also, balls the size of Jupiter. "You want me to take you back to the scene of a fire that gutted a three-story house just to give you a play by play?"

She nodded, her brown eyes narrowing against the sunlight just starting to break past the buildings around them. "That about sums it up, yeah."

"It's a little early for you to be punching the clock, isn't it?" he asked. Most people weren't even halfway to the door just shy of oh-seven-hundred on a weekday morning.

Moreno? Not most people, apparently. "What can I say? I'm feeling ambitious."

Kellan resisted the urge to launch a less-than-polite comment about her work ethic, albeit barely. "I already told you and Sinclair everything I know."

"Okay." Her shoulders rose and fell beneath her dark gray leather jacket, easy and smooth. "So humor me and walk me through it again anyway."

His sixth sense took a jab at his gut, prompting him to give the question in his head a voice. "Is this part of the investigation?"

"Why do you ask?" she said, and yeah, that was a no.

"Because you called it a favor, and you just answered my question with a question."

Moreno paused. "I'm a cop. We do that."

Nope. No way was he buying this. Not even on her best day. "And I'm a firefighter who's not interested in putting his ass in a sling just to humor you with an unsanctioned walk-through."

The RFD might offer a little latitude on firefighters revisiting scenes—a fact Kellan would bet his left nut

Moreno damn well knew—but just because he'd worked the job didn't mean he had carte blanche to prance through the place like a fucking show pony now that the fire was out.

Not that a little thing like protocol seemed to bother Isabella in the least. "Your ass will be fine. I'll take full responsibility."

"I'm pretty sure I've heard that one from you before."

The words catapulted out before Kellan could stop them. Moreno flinched, just slightly, but it was enough. "Look, I need to get back onto that scene," she said. "Are you going to help me or not?"

His brain formed the word "no", but all of a sudden, he registered the weary lines bracketing her eyes and the shadows that went with them like a matched set of good and tired, and his mouth tapped into something entirely different. "Did you even sleep last night?"

An image of her in bed, honey-bronze skin against pristine white sheets, barreled through his mind's eye, and Jesus. Maybe he was the one who needed some shuteye if his subconscious was going to go off the deep end like that.

"Not really, no," Isabella said, shifting her weight from one heavily soled boot to the other in order to stand at flawless attention on the sidewalk. "I was a little busy worrying about those girls in the pictures you found."

The answer hit him like the sucker punch it was. Fuck. Fuck. "Your boss doesn't seem to find them quite as concerning," Kellan managed, and at her look of surprise, he continued. "If he did, he'd have opened an official investigation and you wouldn't have needed to haul yourself all the way down here at o'dark-thirty to ask me to get you into that house, right?"

For a long minute, she just studied him with those chocolate-brown eyes. But rather than copping to anything, Moreno said, "And what's your gut on those pictures, hmm?"

Damn. For a detective who had botched the hell out of keeping Kylie safe, she sure was asking all the right questions to get him to cave.

Unease tightened his muscles, speeding his heartbeat by just a notch. "I have a sister. What do you think?"

"I think those photos are evidence of a crime being committed against the women in them, and I think you wouldn't have had your captain call them in unless you do, too."

She's kind of got you there, dude. Kellan exhaled, mashing down on his inner voice. "So how come your sergeant doesn't agree?"

"I never said he didn't," Moreno pointed out. Her expression matched the utterly noncommittal tone of her words, but come on. He hadn't just fallen off the turnip truck, for Chrissake. She wouldn't ask him to bring her back to the scene of this fire unless it was her last resort.

Kellan hit her with a high-level frown. "If you want me to consider helping you out here, the least you can do is not bullshit me before I'm caffeinated."

"Fine." She pressed her lips together, a swath of light brown hair serving as cover for her eyes as she lasered her gaze toward the sidewalk beneath her feet. "*Hypothetically*, on occasion we catch cases that don't have quite enough evidence to pursue in an official capacity."

Seriously? "You have pictures," he said. What better evidence was there?

"Yeah, and that's all I have. Pictures of women I can't identify, who might be of legal age and participating in consensual acts."

Kellan's stomach knotted. He was hardly vanilla when it came to sex, but the girls in those photos had looked terrified, not to mention dangerously young. Role play was in a whole different universe than rape. "You don't really think what's going on in those photos is consensual, do you?"

"You don't really think I'd ask you to take me back to the spot where you found them to look for more evidence if I did, do you?" Moreno asked archly, and *damn*, she was tough.

Too bad for her, so was he. "Let me get this straight. You want me to take you back to a house the fire marshal has almost certainly condemned, without the permission or knowledge of your sergeant or my captain, just because you have a gut feeling that can't be substantiated by any evidence found at the scene?"

"Give the firefighter a gold star. That's exactly what I want."

Kellan took it back. Jupiter wasn't big enough for the stones on this woman. "Give me one good reason why I should put my ass on the line for you."

Before he could move or blink or even breathe, Isabella had stepped toward him, so up close and personal that he could feel the warmth of her breath on his face as she said, "Because I don't want you to put your ass on the line for me at all. I want you to do it for those women. You and I seem to be the only people who think this case is worth pursuing right now, and I can't change that without more evidence, which I can't get if you don't help me. So are you in or not?"

Fuck. Rock. Hard place. Rock. Hard place. Rock...

"Fine," Kellan said, hearing his acquiescence only after his mouth had let it loose. "One quick look, and that's it. But I'm stopping on the way for coffee."

"Already done. No cream, two sugars." Moreno passed over the cardboard cup in her hand, and he realized just a beat too late that she hadn't taken a sip from the thing the entire time they'd been standing there.

Kellan stared at her. Tried to keep his surprise in check. Failed spectacularly. "You remember how I take my coffee?"

She pointed to the front of the navy blue sweater peeking out from behind her jacket. "Detective, remember?"

A bitter taste filled his mouth. Yeah, he remembered. "Right. I'll drive."

"Sounds great."

Flipping his keys in his free hand, he unlocked the passenger door, popping the thing open so Moreno could get in. A few more minutes had him buckled into the driver's seat beside her, Station Seventeen firmly in the Camaro's rearview as he angled the car toward North Point.

"So freelancing on a case like this is a little ballsy, isn't it?" Kellan asked. As a firefighter, bucking the chain of command was a surefire ticket to censure. Not to mention stupidly dangerous.

Isabella's expression said she disagreed. "I'd hardly call this freelancing," she said, twirling her index finger to connect the two of them in an imaginary circle. "We're just going for a ride."

"A ride your sergeant and your partner know nothing about." He couldn't even imagine trying to pull something like that off with Bridges, Gamble, Shae, or even Slater, and the kid had been a firefighter for all of five minutes. But they were still a team, a unit. They trusted each other for backup, even on the small stuff.

"I just want to give the place another look to see if I can find enough evidence to make an official case. That's all," Moreno said, and God, he should've known she'd be fine with breaking the rules.

"If you say so. But this little tour is a one-time deal, so whatever you need, you'd better get it while you can."

"Believe me, I don't like this any more than you do. After today, I'll be out of your hair."

After a minute of silence that lasted for roughly a decade, Moreno took out her cell phone, bringing the screen to life with a flick of her thumb. "So was there anything unusual about the nine-one-one call for this house fire?"

"No," Kellan said, focusing his gaze through the windshield. If something had been sideways about the call-in, he'd have mentioned it to her sergeant days ago.

Her lips pressed into a flat line. "Okay. Did you notice anything out of the ordinary when you arrived at the scene?"

"No."

"Any onlookers acting suspicious or anyone who might not have belonged?"

"No and no." Little wonder she didn't have much of a case. He'd already answered every last one of these questions, for fuck's sake.

Isabella let out a sharp exhale, and whoa, how come she was mad at him? "Look, you hate me for what happened with your sister, and I get that, okay? I trusted Collins without vetting his team, and one of his guys was dirty. But you found the pictures of those girls, and you're the only link I have to this scene, so how about you set your dick aside for just a couple minutes so I can do my job and get somewhere with this case, huh?"

For a split second, Kellan sat completely stunned in the driver's seat, but his irritation didn't leave him speechless for long. "I might be a little more willing to help if you'd do your job without wasting both of our time. I already told you this stuff the other day."

"Right. And I'm sure you think I'm incompetent enough to have no idea that these questions are repeats, and that there's absolutely no good reason to ask them twice."

Her brows arched at the whaaaa? that had to be plastered all over his kisser, and wait… "You didn't just forget?"

"Walker, please." She laughed, although the sound wasn't completely sarcastic. "I remember how you take your coffee, for God's sake. I'm not going to blank on the details of a case I'm trying to break."

Her words sank in good and hard, and hell if she didn't have a point. Kellan turned off of Washington Boulevard, his curiosity doubling with every stoplight and side street, and screw it. "So why ask the same questions again if you already know the answers?"

"Because you'd be surprised how many details get swallowed by the adrenaline of a moment," Moreno said, her shoulders softening ever so slightly against the black leather seatback behind her. "Sometimes witnesses

43

remember particulars from an event after they've had a little time to process, so repeating interview questions after a few days can yield new information from time to time."

Something hot and without a name tempted Kellan to tell her he knew exactly what a person could remember if given enough time to dwell on certain events, and damn it, he needed to lock up his emotions and get this little cloak and dagger mission over with.

"Sorry." He forced his focus out the window to the dingy streets and crowded, weed-choked yards marking the outskirts of Remington's North Point. "I really didn't see anything out of the ordinary, and there were barely any onlookers when we got to the scene. I remember thinking it was a good thing. Less people who might get hurt."

"That is a good thing," she said, dipping her chin in a small nod. "Your captain said he suspected the fire was electrical. Can you tell me why?"

Okay, yeah. Facts. This he could do. "The fire spread pretty fast, and there was a lot of heat in the walls. That's pretty consistent with an electrical fire in an older structure, where the building materials might be out of date. Polystyrene insulation, stuff like that."

Moreno let out a soft *huh*. "So chances are slim that this fire was set intentionally."

"Arson's actually a lot less common than most people think," Kellan said. He'd only heard of a handful of arson cases in his two years with the RFD, all of which had been either wickedly obvious or notoriously difficult to nail down with proof.

"Is that a yes?" Although the question carried all of her trademark sass, her tone didn't, and his answer popped out, matter-of-fact.

"That's a yes. For calls like this, the fire marshal looks at the reports from the responding fire companies, then does a walk-through to determine whether or not a building is salvageable, but actual investigations are pretty uncommon. Anyway, there are only three reasons a person would torch a place on purpose, and none of them really makes sense for this scenario."

"You've got my attention," Isabella said, the spark in her eyes backing up her words and sending a bolt of unexpected heat right through Kellan's bloodstream. "Hit me."

He cleared his throat, collecting the energy to send a sternly worded back-the-hell-up message to his cock. *Focus on what's in front of you, jackass.*

Right. Arson. "So, ah, the first is insurance fraud, which doesn't seem to play in here unless I'm missing a pretty big puzzle piece."

She nodded in agreement. "The house is owned by a rental company, but it's been vacant for about six months. The last tenant was an eighty-year-old retired librarian with no known family, and the rental company had barely enough coverage to rebuild the place. They won't gain much more than heartache from the place burning down. What's the next reason?"

"To set the fire simply to watch it burn," Kellan said, pausing to make a full stop on red before turning onto Glendale Avenue. "But true fire bugs are pretty rare, unless you're binge watching action movies."

"It doesn't seem to fit the circumstances," Moreno agreed. "So what's the last reason?"

He exhaled, long and low. "To cover up a crime. Although if that were the case here, your guy would've attracted a whole lot less attention by burning the photos rather than the whole house. Since the pictures are pretty much the only thing to survive the fire…"

"It looks like this house burning down was not only accidental, but a lucky break."

"You have a very weird definition of lucky," Kellan said, pulling up in front of the house in question. But rather than get snippy or serious the way he expected, Moreno hit him with the full force of her grin.

"You have no idea, Walker. Now let's go catch a bad guy."

SKIN DEEP

CHAPTER FOUR

The optimism in Isabella's chest flamed out about six seconds after she got her boots on the pavement. Okay, so maybe she shouldn't have gotten ahead of herself, thinking that between the evidence she might find at the scene and the fact that she'd convinced Kellan to walk her through this off-the-books recon mission in the first place, she might actually catch the break she needed to take this back to the FBI.

But karma was clearly not waving its pom poms in her corner after all, because the scene in front of her was nothing shy of a total nightmare.

While the street and the surroundings were much like Isabella had remembered, the house itself had sustained an absolute landslide of damage. Sheets of plywood had been slapped over more than half the first-floor windows, all of which bore thick black scorch marks around the casings and the brick beyond. Most of the second floor—and the roof along with it—had burned down to the building's frame, the charred, warped boards completely discordant with the deep blue sky and the glittering, golden sunlight coloring the backdrop above them.

Her stomach clenched before dropping to her shins. How was she supposed to find enough evidence to help these women in a house that was barely standing?

Isabella let go of a heavy breath. "God. This place looks like a war zone."

A flicker of something odd hardened the angles of Walker's jawline, gone before she could tag the expression with a name. "Yeah," he said, flipping the latch on the chain link fence's swinging door. "I guess."

A thought stuck into her, as cold and sharp as a three-inch pin. "The house isn't going to collapse on us or anything, is it?"

Walker paused, his ocean-blue eyes taking a tour of the structure from the top down, but his hesitation didn't last long. "Nah. The foundation and the first floor are still structurally intact, and at this point, everything that was gonna fall in from upstairs already did. We're lucky the house is brick on three sides. It should keep everything from caving in on us."

"Who's got a weird definition of lucky now?" she asked, and hey, how about that? Walker remembered how to smile.

"Yeah, yeah. So how do you want to do this?"

Isabella ran a hand through her hair, sweeping her gaze from one end of the street to the other. Funny, Walker had just given their surroundings the same sort of spot check. "From the outside in. I know you said there wasn't anything out of the ordinary when you got here, but walk me through it anyway. Step by step."

Kellan dialed back his smile, although one corner of his mouth still kicked up against the dark stubble of his goatee. Crossing his arms over the front of his navy blue RFD T-shirt, he pegged her with a cool, impenetrable stare. "You're the boss, Detective."

The words held just enough attitude to make her cheeks prickle. God, between his pushback and the condition of the scene, she'd had her work cut out for her by a blind man wielding a hacksaw. Then again, she probably should've known he was going to sling shit in her direction every millimeter of the way.

"Okay," was all she said, tamping back the *you moody, broody jackass* part for the sake of the greater good. "Let's take it from the top."

Walker studied her for a minute before loosening his arms and turning toward the front walkway. "When we arrived on-scene, there were already flames showing in the first and second-story windows. My captain sent me and three other firefighters to do search and rescue inside the house."

The door to the waist-high fence clanged shut behind them, rattling the NO TRESPASSING sign attached to the chain links. "Is that standard protocol, or did you think someone was in the house?"

A witness—or better yet, a suspect—was a complete Hail Mary, Isabella knew, the same way she was also ninety-nine-point-four percent sure both the captain and Kellan would've mentioned any suspicions that the house had been inhabited when they'd responded to the fire. But in her line of work, assumptions weren't just dangerous. They could be deadly. Better to ask and be sure.

"Standard protocol," Walker confirmed, moving over the concrete walkway that led to the house. "We do S&R on all residences showing flames unless the scene isn't secure enough for us to enter."

"And the four of you went in through the front door?" Isabella gestured toward the porch facing the street, now decorated by wide bands of bright yellow caution tape strung between the two posts on either side of the bottom step.

"Yes. Hawk and Dempsey were in front of me, and McCullough was at my right on the lieutenant's six. There was a lot of smoke. I remember being able to taste it from right here."

Walker dropped his gaze to the midway point of the crumbling concrete path, but his steps didn't slow. His long, jeans-clad legs ate up the distance, and even at five-foot-nine, Isabella had to work to match his strides. Although she kept her head on a swivel to take in their immediate surroundings as they moved toward the house, the neighborhood remained eerily quiet, and damn it, canvassing was going to yield a gigantic goose egg.

This search with Walker had to give her something to help find the women in those photos. *It had to.*

They reached the porch, Kellan's eyes calculating with every step. "Lieutenant Hawkins gave me and McCullough the command to check the basement when we got right about here." He ducked beneath the caution tape, reaching back to hold it up so Isabella could follow. "He also told Dempsey to breach the door, but that took some doing."

Her boots thudded softly on the worn, soot-stained porch boards as she followed him to the entryway in question. Other than wearing a blazing red notice warning KEEP OUT BY ORDER OF THE REMINGTON FIRE MARSHAL, the door didn't look like anything special, and certainly not anything a trained firefighter should have trouble kicking in. "Was the problem with your guy or the situation?"

Walker laughed, the low rumble rippling up Isabella's spine. "Dempsey could break into a bank vault with a hairpin and a smile. You want to know why he had trouble with the breach, see for yourself."

Reaching down, he turned the knob and guided the door in on its hinges. Surprise popped through her that the door was unlocked, quickly chased by the realization that the damage caused by the breach had rendered the hardware useless.

And sweet Jesus, there was a bucketload of hardware. The reinforcement plate triple-screwed into the doorjamb gleamed up at Isabella from its grossly tilted mooring in the splintered wood, and holy *shit*.

"Is that…"

"Steel reinforced," Kellan confirmed. "The deadbolt

isn't exactly standard issue, either."

She eyed the two-inch deadbolt hole in the ruined doorframe, her pulse knocking harder in her veins. She was all for personal safety, but locks like this were damn near professional grade. "Pretty unusual for a residence."

Walker shrugged, but didn't disagree. "The neighborhood's not great. Didn't you say the previous renter was a little old lady? Maybe she wanted the protection."

"Maybe," Isabella allowed, although even she could hear the doubt bleeding through her tone. "But there's a fence all the way around this house, even the front yard, and this hardware is new. Whoever installed it didn't want anyone coming in here unless they knew about it, that's for sure."

Or anyone getting out, whispered a voice from deep in her chest.

Time to move. Right now. "So you and McCullough headed to the basement to do search and rescue while Hawkins and Dempsey checked upstairs?" Isabella asked, forcing her eyes from the lock to the space in front of her as she crossed the threshold into the house.

"Yeah." Walker slid the door shut behind them, his eyes following Isabella's gaze toward the stairs leading upward. "I can't take you up there, though. With the damage, it's way too dangerous."

The hard set of his stubble-covered jaw suggested he was braced for an argument, and part of her was actually disappointed not to offer one up. But it didn't take a rocket scientist to figure out that any evidence that might've been up there was long gone now, and anyway... "I'm determined, Walker, not stupid. Just give me a second to look through the main level here and then we can head downstairs."

His silence held as much surprise as irritation. "Suit yourself. But I'm coming with you."

Great. Isabella moved from the foyer to the living room, taking in what little was left in the fire-damaged space. The flames had eaten away at what looked to have once been a couch, although the jury was still out on what color the thing might've been in its former life, and the patches of wallpaper that had managed to survive curled away from the water-stained drywall in floral-patterned chunks. Every ounce of her gut told her she had a snowball's chance of finding anything salvageable up here, much less anything salvageable that might also be a lead. But Isabella had never let a little thing like shitty odds stop her before. She wasn't about to start today. The silence pressed against her ears, making her hyper-aware of Kellan's eyes on her as she checked out the room, watching in that quiet, cautious way that told her he saw nine times as much as he said.

"So how's your sister doing?" she heard herself ask. God, it was the last thing she'd meant to bring up, which must be a true testament to her pure idiocy right now. But if the mention had thrown Walker for a loop, he didn't show it. In fact, his expression was pretty much carved out of granite, strong and cold and completely unmoving.

"Fine." His arms re-knotted over his chest, the inky edge of a tattoo peeking out from beneath the dark blue sleeve of his T-shirt.

Isabella bit her tongue hard enough to feel the sting. She should just shut up and do the job she'd come here to do. But she'd lifted the lid on the topic. Trying to tap dance around it now seemed stupid. Or worse yet, cowardly. "Kylie moved to Remington, right? From Montana?"

"Yes."

Jeez, he was the high lord of the monosyllable. She moved across the living room, the sunlight filtering in from the few unbroken windows showing her a whole lot of ash and empty space. "It must be nice that she's close by now."

"You think that just because everything turned out okay in Chicago by the grace of God and my buddy Devon's quick thinking, you get to talk about my sister like she's the weather?"

The musty scent of ashes and old smoke filled Isabella's

nose as she sucked in a breath of pure shock. "What?"

Walker pinned her with an icy stare from halfway across the burned and broken room. "You compromised Kylie's safety by trusting Collins. She was nearly killed, and you're treating her like casual conversation."

"I'm not. I'm—" Isabella stopped short, the slam of her heartbeat warning that he wasn't going to believe her no matter how genuine her remorse really was. But she hadn't knowingly put Kylie's life in danger. He had to know that. "We were racing against the clock to keep Kylie safe, Walker. Collins had worked with his team for three years. None of them had ever had so much as an overdue credit card bill. What was I supposed to do?"

"Better," he said, the word hitting her ears like a shout even though he'd barely breathed it. "You were supposed to do better. You have no idea what I had on the line."

"You have no idea what I know."

For a breath, then another, Isabella stood on the ruined floorboards with her throat in a knot and her chest full of thorns. But she wasn't here to argue with him. She was here to help the women in those pictures. Period.

No matter what Walker thought about her abilities as a cop.

Isabella took in the rest of the first floor in silence. Not that there was much to see, but the few pieces of ruined furniture in the living room coupled with the remnants of trash in the kitchen told her someone had been squatting here after the rental agency had cleaned the place out five months ago.

"Okay," she said, pulling a small Maglite from the pocket of her leather jacket as she turned toward the basement door. "So can you walk me through what happened once you and McCullough headed down to the basement?"

"Yeah, sure." Thankfully, Walker seemed to want to get to business just as much as she did. He swung the door open, waiting until Isabella had taken a few steps down before following her into the basement.

"The fire wasn't as bad down here. It must've started on the second floor and traveled down through the walls. Still, we knew time was tight, so Shae and I split the basement," Kellan said, the words sparking fresh curiosity in Isabella's brain.

"Did she find anything at all?"

Walker waited until they'd both reached the bottom of the steps before shaking his head in answer. "A couple of small rooms that were empty, but that was all."

Isabella took a minute to check out the two rooms in question, both of which were barely bigger than a shoebox and about as well-appointed. Both doors bore locks, though, and while the mechanisms were a lot less heavy-duty than the one upstairs, they were still deadbolts installed from the hallway side, and neither room had a window.

The only way out was if whoever had the key opened up.

"Alright," she said, pivoting on her boot heel to shine her flashlight down the basement hallway. Her only hope of finding something—anything she could take to Sinclair—stood twenty paces away, in a nearly-empty room that had come dangerously close to burning down.

The police have no leads, Isabella. They say there's nothing to go on. No way to know who did this to Mari…

No. Not today. If there was any shred of evidence in this basement, Isabella was going to find it.

She forced her feet into a steady gait, following the beam of the flashlight past the stairs to the opposite end of the corridor. Pushing the door inward, she paused in the entryway to examine the room where Walker had found the photos. The blackout curtain had been pulled back from the tiny rectangular window set high up by the ceiling on the far wall, and while the daylight struggling past the dust-smudged glass wasn't much, Isabella would take it. Everything was just as it had been when she and Sinclair had been here four days ago, from the dinged and scratched up desk to the pizza boxes strewn over it, and her gut squeezed with determination as she exhaled.

"Okay. So the lock box was over here." Isabella's footsteps echoed over the floor, the beam of her flashlight sweeping the interior of the open closet. "Now let's see what the rest of the room will give us."

She'd taken the box and its contents as potential evidence the other day, carefully cataloguing the photographs and the jewelry as she'd struggled to find a lead. But there had to be something here, some small shred left behind that would springboard her out of this room and onto the right path. Moving to the center of the musty space, Isabella pulled a pair of nitrile gloves over her hands before bending down low to open the bottom drawer of the desk.

To her surprise, Walker knelt next to her. "So there weren't any hits on these women online? No facial recognition or image matching that might be geotagged?"

Just like that, her surprise doubled down. "No."

The word came out as more of a question than anything else, and he answered it with a quirk of his lips. "My buddy Devon works private security for that new firm over on Lincoln Avenue. I've got some experience with surveillance equipment, so sometimes he lets me freelance to learn new stuff. Dev's company has got some pretty cutting edge tech."

Ah, right, Devon. The guy who'd been traveling with Kylie when they'd gone to take her into custody in Chicago. Guess he'd relocated to Remington along with Walker's sister. They'd definitely seemed like a couple, so the news wasn't exactly earth-shaking.

"The angle of the photos made recognition software pretty useless, and the images don't match any online databases the RPD can access," Isabella said, closing the empty desk drawer and opening the one above it. Damn. More nada. "Whoever took them knows what the hell he's doing."

"Or she," Walker pointed out, and okay, she'd give him this. He didn't have two left feet when it came to the investigation dance.

Still. "While it's possible our guy might not be a guy, sex crimes are overwhelmingly male on female. Especially when it comes to forced prostitution."

He lifted his chin in a brief nod of concession. "Have you got anything to go on other than the stuff that was in the lock box?"

Isabella hesitated. Sharing case details on unsolved crimes was a strict don't-even-think-about-it for anyone in the intelligence unit. But this wasn't technically a case, and what's more, she was pretty fucking desperate to make it one. She and Walker might not like each other, but he clearly wasn't an idiot. How much damage could a little disclosure do?

She said, "No, and even the evidence I've got is running me into a wall. The rope is the most popular brand sold, available at any hardware store or mega-center. There weren't any useable fingerprints on the lock box, the photos or the jewelry, which were all women's earrings, none of them valuable or uniquely identifiable."

Walker propped his forearms over his denim-covered thighs, his dark brows tucked in obvious thought. "How about the desk, or the closet doors? Could you get prints off that, maybe?"

If only. "I'd need a crime scene unit to process the place in order to find out, which I can't do without an open investigation. Even then, any prints they'd find in the room would be circumstantial. Who knows how many squatters might've been in and out of here in the last five months. Getting from the furniture to the photos is a pretty giant leap."

"So you're stuck with whatever you can get to lead you out of this room."

"Pretty much." Isabella's eyes narrowed on the pizza box splayed open over the top of the desk, a spark of hope kicking at her pulse. "Hold on a second." She pressed to standing, flipping the box closed, and halle-freaking-lujah, finally the ball had bounced in her direction.

"What?" Kellan asked, dropping his gaze as he stood. "Three Brothers Pizza. Isn't that the place down by the pier?"

"There are a couple of locations around Remington, but yeah, the one by the pier is the closest. This might be a little thin, but I know someone who works there." She didn't add that the 'someone' was a mouthy former junkie turned CI. The less Walker knew about Carmen, the better.

If his expression was anything to go by, he didn't need to know more to think Isabella was nuts. "Tying prints from the desk to whoever took those pictures is thin, Moreno. Tying a pizza box to the guy? That's anorexic."

Isabella knew he was right. If she went to Sinclair with a pizza box that might have belonged to a suspect, he'd laugh her right out of the intelligence office, and give her what-for over returning to the scene without permission while he was at it. But flimsy or not, the pizza box was more than she'd had when she'd walked into the room, so she borrowed Kellan's cross-armed stance as she fixed him with her very best stare.

"Maybe. But if you think for a second I'm going to back down just because my only lead is a shot in the dark, then clearly, you don't know me as well as you thought you did."

CHAPTER FIVE

Kellan sat back on his bar stool at the Crooked Angel, a beer in his hand and his brain waging an epic battle with his dick. Which wouldn't necessarily be the worst thing in the world if the topic of said battle wasn't Isabella Moreno and his downstairs head wasn't winning by a landslide.

Unfortunately for his sanity, Kellan was a big, fat oh-for-two.

Twelve hours had passed since Moreno had given up that bulldog-fierce conviction that he didn't know her as well as he thought he did, and they hadn't exchanged more than half a dozen words since they'd left the scene of the fire shortly thereafter. She'd spent most of the ride back to Seventeen reading and responding to a string of text messages—presumably from the person she said she knew from the pizza place—and then offered up a brief but sincere 'thanks for the favor' once they'd reached her car. Kellan had headed toward his apartment with every intention of putting the whole morning in his rearview; Moreno's smart mouth and sleek curves, the photos, the fire scene, the possibility of a lead from that pizza box, all of it. The fact that he hadn't been able to come within a thousand meters of ditching his thoughts of this morning had been pretty frustrating.

That Isabella had been sitting less than thirty paces away from him for the last half hour and flat-out ignoring him for just as long?

Now *that* was driving him bat-shit crazy.

Flicking a glance across the Crooked Angel's wood-paneled main dining room, Kellan took in the Thirty-Third's usual four-top over by the plate glass windows lining the front of the bar. His eyes settled on Moreno, then the detectives she worked with, for just a minute before he let out a heavy breath and placed his beer on the table in front of him.

If you think for a second I'm going to back down...you don't know me as well as you thought you did...

Kellan's gut tightened beneath his T-shirt. Yeah, he'd spent the better part of a nonstop week with Moreno after Kylie had called him from Montana three months ago, saying she'd witnessed a brutal murder committed by a thug who ran with dirty cops. Kylie had managed to get as far away as Chicago with the help of Kellan's Army buddy, Devon. And thank fuck he'd been with her, because even though Moreno's work to track the scumbag chasing Kylie had been solid, the case had ended in an adrenaline-soaked shootout, courtesy of a filthy agent on the FBI field team Moreno had vouched for. Kellan had trusted her in the beginning—up until everything went pear-shaped, actually—but then all of a sudden, he hadn't. He couldn't. Although Kylie had ended up unharmed, she could've easily been killed.

But this morning, Moreno had been nothing short of all-in and no holds barred on this case, which begged the question he'd been unable to answer all freaking day.

How well *did* he know Isabella Moreno?

His mind took the rational route, tilting back to their trip to North Point. As much as he wanted to deny it, Kellan had to admit that when they'd been combing the scene of that fire for evidence, she'd been exactly as she had during the bulk of Kylie's case. Determined. Capable. Smart.

Don't forget sexy, came a voice that sounded suspiciously like his mutinous dick, and okay, he officially needed to get laid. Nothing else explained the insanity of his current preoccupation with Moreno's curves or her tenacity. So she'd grabbed the case in front of her this morning with both hands. So what? She'd still made a horrible mistake not vetting Collins's field team three months ago. It had still been her judgment call that had put Kylie's life in danger.

Kellan still could've lost the only family he had, the sister he'd sworn to look after.

And Kylie was the only person keeping his feet on the ground. Even if she didn't know it.

"Hey, there you are! Why are you hiding all the way over here?" A partly stern, mostly teasing voice popped him back to the Crooked Angel, tugging the edges of his mouth into the world's most ironic smile. Speak of the devil had nothing on his little sister.

"I'm in the middle of the best bar in the city on a Friday night," Kellan said, sliding off his padded leather bar stool. "I'd hardly call that hiding."

He refocused his gaze over the dimly lit space as he reached down to fold Kylie into a quick hug. He'd chosen this out of the way spot on the periphery of the Crooked Angel's main room for the dark and private aspect, so he could put his back to the wood-paneled wall and get lost in thought for just a minute. Apparently he'd gotten a little too lost if he hadn't seen his sister make her way into the bar, and wasn't that all the more reason to forget Isabella Moreno's sassy mouth and sexy body and move the hell on?

"Hmm." Kylie's bright blue stare traveled over him with scrutiny, her frown telling him that his response had her far from convinced. "Then how come you're not hanging out with everyone from Seventeen? Normally you guys are all knee deep in nine-ball and trash talk by now."

She gestured toward the back of the Crooked Angel,

where more than half the men and women on A-shift were drinking beer and shooting pool in the alcove by the emergency exit. Leave it to a bunch of firefighters and paramedics to want to have options out of a place.

"I was," Kellan said, his gaze taking a lightning-fast trip to Moreno's table before he constructed an answer that was at least in the same vicinity as the truth. "I just needed to deal with a work thing for a minute."

Kylie opened her mouth, and if he knew her at all, it was to launch an argument. Thankfully Devon—who was never far from Kylie's side now if he got a say so—leaned in from beside her to put a hand on her shoulder.

"Babe, I'm going to grab a few beers. What do you think, Walker?" He tipped his nearly-shaved head toward the bottle on the table by Kellan's hand. "You ready for another?"

Having spent two extended tours with Kellan in the Middle East, Devon knew all too well how strong the urge to decompress could get, just like he and Kellan both knew Kylie would only worry if *she* knew. Troubling her wasn't on Kellan's To-Do list, especially over something as stupid as his unexplainable hard-on for a cop he didn't even like. Clearly, it wasn't on Devon's either.

"Sure, man. Thanks." He slipped Devon a nod to back up the word. Digging deep for a smile, Kellan made sure the gesture reached his eyes as he pushed it over his face and turned his attention back to his sister. "So how's work? I'm surprised they sprung you from the kitchen on a Friday night."

Kylie hopped up onto the bar stool across the table from Kellan, her ear to ear grin lighting up her face and half the city, and bingo. Mission accomplished on the subject change.

"I've worked six dinner shifts in a row," she said, although her tone was a three to one ratio of happiness to irritation. "I love training to be a sous chef at Loulou's, but even I have hard limits. They can suffer without me for a night."

At her mettle, Kellan's smile grew ten times less forced. "There's the girl I know and love."

"Mmm." She arched a dark brown brow, but the remnants of her grin made full-on toughness a hard sell. "You're not just saying that so I'll come cook for you, are you?"

"I'll have you know I'm perfectly functional on my own," he said, picking up the half-empty beer bottle from the polished wood in front of him for a sip.

Ugh, warm. Kylie made a face that likely matched his, as if she'd tasted something well past its prime, and okay, it was time to find the kill switch on her worry, once and for all.

"Ky, I'm fine. I'm not going to tell you not to come cook for me," Kellan added, because while he might be stubborn, he also wasn't an idiot. Kylie could turn boxed mac and cheese into a four-star dish using little more than pantry items and sheer will. "But only do it if you want the kitchen practice, okay?"

"I just worry about you. I know the guys at Seventeen have your back, and that you're really good at your job, but…" Kylie paused, her silence giving in to the jukebox music on the overhead speakers and the ambient crowd noise around them, and for a second Kellan thought she'd finally let go of the topic.

But then she slid a hand to one denim-covered hip and threw him for a rope-a-dope. "Are you happy?"

His pulse tapped out the Morse code equivalent of *what the fuck*. "What kind of question is that?"

"The serious kind," Kylie said, which meant there would be serious work involved in getting her to let go of the serious subject, and oh hell. He needed a redirect. Fast.

Kellan amped up his smile, taking direct aim at a playful joke. "I think living with Dev has made you soft."

"Living with Devon has made me happy," she corrected, the sparkle in her blue eyes backing up her words a million percent, and something heavy and strange shifted in

Kellan's gut. "Come on," Kylie continued. "I know you don't like to talk about your feelings, and normally I don't push. But don't you want to find someone eventually?"

Okay, so he wouldn't mind not waking up alone every morning, but... "Does eventually have to be right this minute?"

Apparently it did, because Kylie didn't blink, not even when Devon reappeared to slide onto the bar stool between them and handed out the fresh beers in his grasp. "No, but when was the last time you went out on a date, hmm?" Kylie pointed her beer bottle at Kellan, her brows up and her determination on full display. "Took a woman to dinner? Had sex?"

Kellan and Devon simultaneously choked on their beers. Devon recovered first. "I get that you guys are tight, babe, but that's a little, uh. Personal, don't you think?"

"No, I don't," she said, leaning back to cross her arms over her chest. "I'm not asking for details, because ew. All I'm saying is there's more to life than work, especially when your job is intense. You should have someone to share that stuff with, Kellan. It's not healthy to keep it all bottled up."

He blew out a breath. As much as he wasn't a fan of Kylie being worried about him, he got it. Hell, no matter how settled or happy she got, he'd still probably worry about her until he was ninety.

"Look, it might have been"—he did a quick count back, and damn. Time to swerve around that pothole—"a little while since I've gone out with anyone, and my job might require me to compartmentalize more than most people. But just because I'm on my own doesn't mean I'm not happy, or that I'm all Vesuvius over here, waiting for my emotions to explode because I'm not hooking up with someone. I'm perfectly fine. There just isn't anyone who does it for me right now."

His gaze moved across the bar completely without his permission, landing on Moreno for just a fraction of a second before he wrestled it away. Christ, going back to the scene of that fire this morning had officially cooked his motherboard.

"Reeeeeeally." Kylie's eyes tapered as the corners of her mouth curved into a smile, and shit. Nothing good could come from the look on her face. "What about Detective Moreno?"

Every one of Kellan's muscles tightened even though he didn't so much as shift his weight over his bar stool. "What about her?"

"You mean other than the fact that I'd have to be blind to have missed the way you've been looking at her?"

"I haven't been *looking* at her," he said, and even Devon's brows lifted in a nonverbal *uh, yeah you have.*

Scrapping his argument, Kellan went for tactic number two: distraction. "Come on, Kylie. Are you really forgetting that Moreno put your life at risk three months ago?"

"Oh, for pity's sake." Kylie rolled her blue eyes sky high and slapped the tabletop in front of her. "Xavier Fagan put my life at risk by chasing me halfway across the country and holding me at gunpoint. Isabella wanted to help me as much as you did."

A muscle ticked along Devon's clean-shaven jaw, his stare going hard around the edges. "I don't know, Kylie. Your brother's kind of got a point. Moreno might not have been the cop on the take, but your life was definitely on the line because of a dirty agent on Collins's field team. She did vouch for them."

"You're a pair of Neanderthals, I swear to God." At their twin looks of are-you-kidding-me, Kylie lifted a hand. "Look, I'm not saying there wasn't any danger. We all know there was. But I am saying Isabella didn't have any way of knowing that guy on Collins's team was secretly on Fagan's payroll, and she went above and beyond on my case. In fact"—she paused, her smile doubling as she looked first at Kellan, then at Isabella across the room—"I can prove it."

Without another word, Kylie placed her beer on the cafe table between them and turned on her heel to march through the heavily populated bar.

Dread crowded Kellan's chest as he watched her move toward the door. "What the hell is she doing?"

"Dude, I have no clue," Devon said, his hands going up in surrender. "She's your sister."

Kellan opened his mouth to pop off with a sarcastic reply, but his words jammed to a halt the second Kylie stopped in front of Isabella's table.

She wouldn't. *She would not.*

She totally fucking did.

"I need this like I need a publicly televised prostate exam right now," he said, his heartbeat dialing up a notch as Kylie led a concerned-looking Isabella across the bar's packed dining room.

Devon shrugged, not even attempting to hide his smirk. "That's what you get for staring at Moreno like you want to get her naked. Don't even bother trying to bullshit me," he added as Kellan started to launch a protest. "I saw how you were looking at her when we walked in here, too."

"I had to work with her on a case this morning. That's all." Seriously. This was above and beyond, even for Kylie.

"If you say so," came the reply from the side of Devon's mouth, but before Kellan could say another word—or better yet, make any sort of a non-obvious exit—Kylie arrived back at the table with Isabella right behind her.

"Oh." Moreno's chest lifted on a clearly surprised inhale as her eyes locked with his, and spectacular. Now Kellan had to deal with his conscience and his cock. "I thought you said you had a question about your case, Kylie."

"I do," Kylie replied. "Do you remember the update you gave me six weeks ago?"

"Of course."

Confusion combined with curiosity, both of them pushing Kellan's irritation to the wayside. "What update?"

Kylie split a glance between him and Moreno, her eyes remaining on the detective as she said, "I know you told me a lot of the details wouldn't be public because the FBI is pursuing federal charges, but what you told me isn't confidential or anything, right?"

Isabella took another slow breath, and Jesus, the neckline of her shirt was going to destroy him. Or at the very least, keep rendering him mute and mostly stupid. "No," she said slowly. "The FBI is obviously keeping the details as quiet as they can since they're pretty sensitive, but the charges are a matter of public record."

Kylie's smile turned cat-in-cream satisfied. "So you can tell Kellan what you told me."

"I…guess," Moreno hedged, although she didn't elaborate, and finally, his brain overrode the dark, indecent part of him secretly wondering what she had on under that deceptively low-cut top of hers.

"Okay, you two. What the hell is going on?"

"You need to hear what Isabella has to say, that's what." His sister turned toward Devon, who come to think of it had remained suspiciously quiet for the last few minutes, and pulled him from his bar stool to his feet. "Come on, Dev. I love this song."

Kylie nodded at the open space by the jukebox where a few couples had twined their arms and other various body parts around each other while they swayed to the slow ballad that had just started.

"You hate this song," Devon said, his forehead creased in total confusion, but Kylie moved beside him and looped her arm around his.

"No. I don't." The smile she speared him with was one hundred percent lethal. "I love it. In fact, I think you guys should dance, too." She pointed from Kellan to Isabella, her expression turning sugar-sweet. "It'll be the perfect chance for Detective Moreno to fill you in on things."

Kellan's chin jerked to attention, his pulse tagging along for the ride. "Kylie," he warned, but funny, it was Moreno who saved his bacon.

"I'm not sure us dancing is a good idea. I wouldn't want to make your brother uncomfortable."

"I'm not *uncomfortable*," he argued, and Kylie's smile became downright beatific. "Perfect. Then it's settled. We're all dancing."

Fuck.

"Is your sister always like this?" Moreno asked after Kylie had tightened her squeeze on Devon's arm, leading him toward the dance floor and out of earshot.

"You mean like a barracuda? Yeah, pretty much." Kellan looked at the boot-scuffed floorboards, unsure whether to laugh or pull out every last hair on his head. "Sorry if she put you on the spot."

"Oh, don't be. I actually like her a lot." At the look of surprise that had to be pinging over his face, Moreno added, "It looks like she gives you a run for your money."

"I guess that makes you two best friends by default."

Moreno's unexpected peal of laughter tagged Kellan right in the sternum. "And I guess I earned that."

Whether it was the sudden ease amidst all their tension or the provocative pretty-factor of her lingering smile, Kellan couldn't be sure, but all of a sudden, he heard himself ask, "So do you want to dance?"

The words seemed to shock them both equally, and God, he needed some damage control, stat. "Uh, we don't have to, obviously. But Kylie seems to think I need to hear this update, or whatever, right from you, so, you know…"

"Yes," she said, blinking twice before blanking her expression and lifting one shoulder in an approximation of a shrug. "I mean, it's just a little dancing, so sure. Why not?"

And wasn't that question more loaded than a Glock at a gun range. Still, he'd asked (albeit gracelessly) and she'd accepted, so Kellan slid off his bar stool and moved toward the dance floor. Isabella walked right beside him, and even though he thought the transition to actual dancing would be chock full of awkward, she simply slipped her hands over his shoulders as his found her waist, their bodies neatly lined up and starting to move in slow, easy rhythm. Her caramel-colored hair spilled over her shoulders, teasing his senses with the warm, heady scent of coconuts as she adjusted to the sway of them dancing, and he instinctively spread his hands wider in search of something concrete to keep him grounded.

But all that did was increase their contact, and despite knowing damn well that he should, he couldn't make his body obey the command from his brain to change it. Kellan inhaled, taking in the strong, lean muscles under the soft material of her shirt, the slight change in texture that signaled the edge of her bra beneath it, and fuck, he needed to put a pin in his emotions if he was going to have a prayer of making it through the next five minutes.

"So." He cleared his throat. *Focus. The FBI. Charges. Facts.* "There was an update on Kylie's case?"

"Of sorts, yeah." Moreno's voice was as metered as her words, and a thought slammed through Kellan's mind with all the subtlety of a wrecking ball on demolition day.

"Don't try to tell me the Feds aren't calling Fagan's death a clean shoot." The suits in DC must be out of their freaking minds if they thought for one second that there had been an option other than putting a kill shot on that son of a bitch.

But Moreno erased his concern with a quick shake of her head. "Oh God, no. The bastard had Kylie at gunpoint, and he'd clearly been tracking her with the intent to keep her quiet, permanently. Collins and his superiors examined both Kylie and Devon's statements and determined the force was warranted. That part of the case is closed."

The tension in Kellan's shoulders unwound by a fraction, making him all too aware of the press of Isabella's fingers over the thin cotton of his T-shirt. "Okay, so what the hell is Kylie talking about with new details then?"

Half of the song's chorus floated through the warm, dimly lit air in the bar before Moreno answered. "The agent who gave up Kylie to Fagan was identified and arrested. He's being indicted on federal charges."

No less than a trillion questions burst through Kellan's

brain, but for right now, he settled on the big three. "What? Who? How?" Last he'd heard a couple of months ago, the case had been so cold, the Feds could've carved an ice sculpture out of the damned thing.

"The agent's name is Mike Burton. He'd been with Collins for two and a half years, and he was slick as hell about playing both sides. It took a ton of surveillance and some really serious digging by our tech guy and a forensic accountant, but we were finally able to catch him siphoning money to an offshore bank account in Seychelles."

"Jesus," Kellan managed, his mind still loaded with questions.

Thankfully, Moreno continued, answering at least some of them as she said, "We grabbed him three days before he was set to fly out of the country on a one-way ride. Of course he's denying everything, but the evidence is pretty damning. We made a good bust, and the FBI indicted him. Burton's currently in solitary at the federal prison in Chicago, awaiting trial."

"Wait." Kellan's pulse sped through his veins, and no way. She couldn't possibly have said—"We? Did intelligence work this case somehow?"

A pause opened up to fill the slight space between them, but Moreno didn't allow it to last for more than a song beat. "Oh. Yeah. No. Not exactly."

"Then who's 'we', *exactly*?"

"I guess 'we' is, um. Me. Collins was too close to the investigation since someone on his team was clearly involved, so I went out to Chicago to lead the task force team that took Burton down."

And here Kellan had thought he'd reached his you've-got-to-be-kidding-me limit for the day. "A case like that couldn't have been a nine to five. How long did the investigation last?"

"I don't know. A few days." At his arched brow, she released a sigh, her breath coasting over his shoulder in a soft puff. "Fine. It might have been eight."

His jaw unhinged. "The FBI just let you waltz on out and lead an extended investigation on one of their own?"

"The investigation was a team effort within the FBI task force," Moreno said, although hell if that wasn't a non-answer to the question. "I'd been in on the original case, so I knew the players, and I've been a cop for over ten years. Burton was a dirty agent who needed to go down. I was happy to work the investigation."

"And Sinclair was cool with that?" Kellan asked, and her body went just rigid enough beneath his hands for him to take notice.

"Sinclair didn't really get a say."

Right. Anyone who'd met the man even for a minute knew there was zero chance she was being straight about that one. "Try again."

"Fine. No one else from the Thirty-Third was involved in the task force. I used personal leave to go," Isabella said, her lashes fanning upward to frame her chocolate-brown stare as she looked him directly in the eyes. "I told Sinclair about the investigation as a professional courtesy. He's my boss and I respect the hell out of him. But as far as whether or not I went, no. Sam didn't get a say."

The same fierceness Kellan had seen outside the row house this morning resurfaced on her face, sending a hard tug through the center of his chest. What kind of cop would burn her vacation time to haul halfway across the country so she could work a case cold enough to warrant its own slab at the morgue?

Here's a hint: not the kind who's as incompetent as you thought.

The realization brought him sharply back to the moment. "Why would you go so far above and beyond for a case outside of your jurisdiction?"

"Because I promised I'd keep Kylie safe. I had no reason not to trust Collins, and he had no reason not to trust Burton, but shit still went sideways. Nailing Burton was the only way to make that right." Isabella lifted her shoulders, and the honesty in her words didn't lessen their punch to

Kellan's gut. "So that's what I did."

"How come you never told me?" he asked. He'd seen her here at the Crooked Angel no less than a dozen times since they'd returned from Chicago, and she clearly knew how to find him at Seventeen easily enough.

Her laughter was self-deprecating enough to put another dent in his armor. "First of all, I didn't go back to Chicago for the recognition. I'd have worked the investigation that led to Burton's indictment regardless of whether or not you or Kylie ever found out. Secondly"—the edges of her mouth tipped up just enough to take her smile into smirk territory—"you made your dislike for me pretty clear. To be honest, I didn't think you'd listen to anything I had to say about your sister's case, even if the news was good."

"I don't dislike you," Kellan hedged, only to be thwarted again by her soft, throaty laugh.

"Walker, please. You went up one side of me and down the other in the motel parking lot as soon as Kylie got the all-clear, and every time you've seen me since, you've evil-eyed me into next week. I think it's safe to say you're not my biggest fan."

For a second, then two, nothing but the song and the ambient noise from the bar passed between them. The familiar crossroads was right in front of him, the one with the fork that led to all the boxes where he locked shit away and the fork with the road he couldn't think about if he wanted to retain his sanity. He had reasons for never taking that path, never digging at anything that would trigger his emotions, and they weren't shitty. Still, Moreno had been straight with him about Burton when she could've just as easily clammed up.

The least he could do was return the favor.

"I was upset that Kylie was in danger three months ago, and yeah, I was pretty pissed at you and Collins over how things shook out. But my sister's all the family I've got. We spent almost seven years apart when I was in the Army, and even though I know she's tough enough to stand on her own two feet, I still want to look out for her."

A flicker moved through Moreno's gaze, coloring it a deep mahogany brown in the low light of the Crooked Angel. "I get that, Walker. I really do, and I'm sorry. I can't tell you enough how much I hate that Fagan got his hands on her, even for a second."

He thought of the vow she'd made to find whoever was hurting those girls, and damn, she really was a good cop. "I know. I'm sorry I flew off the handle in Chicago, and that I was rough on you after that. You didn't have any way of knowing someone on Collins's team would put Kylie in danger. I see that now."

Moreno's lips parted. "You do?"

"Yeah," he said, and as much as he thought the admission might sting, his words came out with ease. "I do."

Of course, he should've known better than to think Isabella would take them without dishing back. "You sure you're feeling okay?" she asked, sliding one hand over his forehead. "You don't have a fever, do you? Should I call a doctor?"

"Funny," Kellan said. He meant to add on to his sarcasm, after all, Moreno was clearly tough enough to take it. But all at once he realized how close they were, their bodies suddenly flush, her fingers cradling his face with her smart, sinful mouth right there in front of his, and every thought in his brain shorted out to head south.

Her smile slipped, awareness edging over her pretty features as if she'd landed in the same place Kellan had. But rather than pulling away, Isabella stood firm, replacing her arm around his shoulder while they swayed to something far more primal than some pop ballad. She pressed against him, her body moving with slow, hot suggestion, and even though he knew it made him a bastard of the highest order, Kellan didn't budge. He tested his grasp on her waist, increasing the pressure of his fingers in slow increments. Moreno's chest melted against his even harder with the weight of her exhale, and a dark thread of satisfaction uncurled in Kellan's belly, taunting his fingers to dig even harder over her T-shirt.

So he let them. And when Isabella cut out another heady breath that warmed his neck and stirred his cock, curling her fingertips into his shoulders with just as much provocative intention, he realized that if they kept upping the ante, neither one of them would back down.

Which meant that if they weren't careful, he and Isabella were going to dare each other right past racy flirting and into a quick, hot fuck in the bathroom.

You helped this woman on a case just over twelve hours ago, you ass. You need to lock it up. Right goddamn now.

Kellan froze as if he'd been hit point-blank with a bucket full of frigid water. As sexy as her body felt against his in the dark of the bar—and fucking hell, it really, *really* did—he knew far better than to let himself get so brazenly carried away on impulse.

Losing control was dangerous. He couldn't let it happen. Not even for a night.

"Ah." He shifted to put some breathing room between them, snapping the moment in half. "So how's that case from this morning going? Did you get any leads from your friend?"

After a handful of rapid-fire blinks, Moreno matched his backward shift, putting clear distance between them as the song on the jukebox shifted into a new one, equally slow. "Oh. Uh, maybe. She's working at the pizza place until eleven tonight. I'm actually going to head over there tonight to see if I can catch her and maybe dig up some more information."

"Is your partner going with you?" Kellan lifted his chin in a slight gesture toward the table by the door, where her fellow detectives had been eyeballing them at regular intervals.

"What, Hollister?" Moreno shook her head, filling the air with the tropical smell of coconuts again even though there was enough space between their bodies to be all-business. "No. I haven't told anyone about this morning yet."

His heart kicked at his rib cage, part concern and part residual want. Damned coconuts. "You're going down to the pier just shy of midnight, by yourself, to grab some intel on what might be a serial rape case or a prostitution ring?"

"Yeah," Moreno said, her tone directly translating to *and why the hell wouldn't I?*

Christ, she was a piece of work. "Don't you think that's a little dangerous?"

"Don't *you* think that's a little sexist?" she volleyed. "I've been a cop for over a decade, Walker. I'm pretty sure I can handle myself."

Nope. He wasn't backing down. Not even in the face of her obvious irritation. "It doesn't have anything to do with you being a woman. It has to do with the fact that your ass isn't bulletproof, and you have a table full of partners right here in this bar, any of whom would almost certainly go with you. Working a case without backup is stupid, Moreno."

Judging by her expression, she'd taken that 'stupid' comment to heart. "I'm not asking for your blessing," she said.

"Good, because you're not going to get it. I want to go with you."

"No." Isabella's spine went rigid. "A CI's identity is strictly confidential. Hence the 'C'."

"Your friend at the pizza place is a CI?" he asked, and wasn't that all the more reason for her not to fly without a wingman. "Look"—Kellan squeezed her waist, just enough to snare her attention so he could say his piece—"I don't want anyone's resume, and I'm not trying to mess with your case. But come on. You're completely off the books, here. You saw those pictures. Digging into this without backup is asking for trouble."

Moreno paused. "And you're going to back me up?"

"You're not willing to trust your partner or your boss. You got a better idea?"

74

"I trust Hollister and Sinclair just fine. I wouldn't work with them if I didn't," Moreno said. "This is just a chat with one of my CIs. Detectives do them solo all the time."

"Not this time," Kellan said, and Moreno pursed her lips, showing off her disdain.

"My CI's not going to like it. She might not even talk to me with you around."

Oh, look. Still no. "Don't worry. I'll charm her."

"Seriously?"

Kellan met Moreno's look of severe doubt with the best smile he could throw together. "What? You don't think I can be charming?"

The song ended, and Isabella slid her hands down his shoulders, pulling back to cross her arms over the front of her T-shirt. "I think you're a pain in the ass."

But Kellan just kept his smile firmly in place as he leaned in toward her, not stopping until their mouths were only a few inches apart.

"Yeah, well like it or not, I'm the pain in the ass who's going with you to that pizza place. Now are you driving, or am I?"

CHAPTER SIX

Isabella stared down the ridiculously sexy firefighter in front of her, and damn it, she was going to regret this. But the glint in Kellan's stormy blue stare told her not only was he not backing down, but he had half a mind to blab her plans to Hollister if she refused to take backup for her meet-and-greet with Carmen, and at this point, she had to pick the lesser of two evils.

Even if this one had just turned her panties inside out in the middle of a crowded bar.

She bit her lower lip, grounding herself in the sting. She'd given him the update on his sister's case, he'd apologized, she'd accepted. So what if somewhere in the midst of that, Isabella had impulsively considered dragging him back to her place to fuck him senseless? She could go home and get herself off later—hell, she could even scream his name when she came all over her hand. But what she *couldn't* do was let a few steamy thoughts of Kellan Walker get in the way of doing her job.

"Fine," Isabella said, snuffing out the heat threatening to bloom back to life between her thighs. "But we can't just go tearing out of here together. If you go with me, we're playing by my rules."

Walker dropped his chin but not his eye contact. "I'm listening."

"Well that works out nicely, because I'm only saying this once." She tilted her head toward the outskirts of the dance floor, continuing when they'd made their way past the people moving to the new, faster song beginning to pulse from the jukebox.

"You're going with me strictly to look out for trouble. No talking to my CI—in fact, no talking to anybody who isn't me—and if I ask you to do something, you need to do it, no questions asked. There are reasons for this that don't involve me being bitchy," she added before he could open his trap to push back. "But they do have everything to do with protocol. I'm already breaking about sixty rules by letting you tag along. I'd like to at least keep you safe."

One nearly black brow arched. "You're going to keep me safe?"

Although she hadn't really pegged Walker as the type to swing his dick around, Isabella was all too happy to set the record straight. "Unless that actually is a gun in your pocket and you're not just happy to see me, then yeah. I'm lead, you're backup, and you need to do what I tell you to. Copy?"

Walker surprised her with a slow nod. "Copy. But if anything goes south, all bets for me being a bystander are off."

"I know how to do my job. Nothing's going to go south." Unless Carmen lost her shit at the whole let's-chat/hot-firefighter-listening double whammy, but Isabella would cross that bridge when she got to it. Speaking of which… "So here's the plan. We're each going to go back to our tables. I've already told Hollister, Maxwell, and Hale that I'm starting to get a headache, so I should be able to jump in about ten minutes. Give me a twenty minute lead, then park your Camaro a couple blocks over and double back to meet me by the diner a half a block up on Delancey."

"That's a lot of cloak and dagger for a meet-up that's supposed to be no big deal, you know."

She had to hand it to him. He wasn't stupid by any stretch. "It's more caution than cloak and dagger. Your car is conspicuous as hell, and your sister's even smarter. If she thinks you left but still sees your car in the parking lot, she's going to grill you into next week about it."

Understanding flickered over his face, followed quickly by a smirk that made her pulse jump without her consent. "I could always tell Kylie I left with you. After all, it'd be true."

"Don't get cocky, Walker, or I'll leave you here." The threat was a bluff, to be sure, but hell if she'd let him rock the composure she'd damn well need to tug any information out of Carmen.

Thankfully, Walker didn't call her bluff. "Fine," he said. "I'll move my car in thirty and meet you on Delancey."

"Excellent." Before Isabella could talk herself out of the move, she pressed up to her toes, brushing her lips right over the line where the scratchy-soft stubble of his goatee met the smooth skin of his cheek.

Kellan froze, his eyes betraying his shock. "What was that for?"

To lower your guard so you don't wreck mine. "The dance. Just don't make me sorry I agreed to the rest of our night."

She sauntered off the dance floor, sights set on the table where her fellow detectives sat by the front door. Although the bold, brash part of her that had pushed to kiss him in the first place wanted nothing more than to turn around to see the look on his face, she refrained. Even with the slam-dunk cases, working a suspect required a dump truck's worth of finesse, from the truths you chose to tell versus the ones you picked to sidestep, or even cover up outright.

Working your partners without them realizing what you were up to? Yeah, quantum physics was a day at the beach in comparison. But as much as Isabella hated the task in front of her, she didn't have a choice.

If she wanted to get off square one with this case, she was going to have to keep her plans to find more intel hidden from her unit.

"Hey. Thanks for watching my beer." She pushed herself back over the bar stool she'd abandoned fifteen minutes earlier, bracing for impact in three, two...

"Don't even think about taking the no-big-deal road, you shameless hussy!" Addison Hale, the newest and only other female member of intelligence, shot a look of total disbelief across the table. "Did you just kiss Kellan freaking Walker?"

"You saw that, huh?" Of course, Moreno had known full well that the woman had. Even the academy's freshest recruit would've caught the glances her partners had leveled at her and Walker on the dance floor.

Hale made a sound dangerously close to a snort. "Um, yeah. Along with everyone else in the bar. Including all of Seventeen's A-shift from all the way in the cheap seats."

"Then I guess I did kiss him," Isabella said, and score the other half of the reason for her lip service. Distraction was a fucking beautiful thing.

Hale's disbelief went another round. "You just kissed the same Kellan Walker who's been trading death glares with you for the last three months over the Fagan case?"

"That would be the one."

"Jesus, Moreno, please." Maxwell laughed and ran a hand over his shaved head, tipping his glass of club soda in Hale's direction. "I know you keep your shit close to the vest, and I'm not really one for gossiping like a tabloid rag. But if you don't throw my partner a bone, she's going to stroke out over here."

Isabella bought herself a no-big-deal pause with a sip of beer. Nice and easy, girl. "Walker's sister wanted me to give him the update on what went down in Chicago last month. Once he heard the Feds have Burton in custody, he came around a little. The whole thing was your basic kiss and make up, no hard feelings type deal. That's all."

"Really?" Clearly, Hale had been looking for way more scandal. God, intelligence rookies were so hungry for the angle with the most bang, it wasn't even funny.

"Sorry to disappoint," Isabella said. "But really."

Hollister leaned his shoulders against the ladder-back on his bar stool, aiming a not-so-subtle frown in the direction of Kellan's table across the bar. "The work you did on the Fagan case was solid. It's about time he got the fuck over it."

Ah, hell. Hollister was one of the most straight-up guys in the RPD. He and Isabella might not live by the share-fest code like most partners, and yeah, no one had ever accused him of being calm, cool, or collected—especially when it came to his loyalty to the intelligence unit. But he was a decent guy and an even better cop.

And she needed to divert his attention from Kellan Walker. Right now.

Guilt pricked at Isabella's chest, but she forced herself to shake her head, literally shrugging off the topic. "It's all good, Liam. The screw up with his sister wasn't a garden variety oops. He was just doing what big brothers do."

The use of Hollister's first name got him, just as she'd known it would, and he turned back toward their table with a lift of one shoulder. "If you say so."

"I do."

The conversation turned toward college football matchups and whether or not Hale's amber lager was better than Hollister's IPA, and Isabella bided her time with a few well-placed nods, staying a half-step outside of the conversation just as she always did. Finally, distractions done, she slid her fingers over her temple, letting them linger just long enough before pushing back from the table.

"I hate to say it, but my head's still killing me. I think I'm going to call it a night," she said, placing the beer she'd been nursing over the soggy and slightly crushed cocktail napkin at her elbow and finding her feet.

"You sure?" Hollister asked, his forehead creasing in

concern. Before Isabella could give up her standard-issue nod and smile and get-the-hell-out-of-here combo, though, a very wry, very familiar male voice interrupted her getaway.

"Come on, you guys. This is Moreno we're talking about. She's always sure. Even when she's snoring."

Isabella turned, arching a brow at the tall, wiry blond behind her. "Damn, Capelli. You really need to stop using that overly large brain of yours to find ways to sneak into this place through the back door. And for the record, I don't snore."

"Of course you don't. That would require you to actually sleep, and we all know you're too busy working to do that," he said, pushing his dark-rimmed glasses over his nose with a grin. "Also for the record, I'm not sneaking. I'm simply testing your awareness along with the security measures of this fine establishment, and logging statistics on the most successful methods of gaining entry to public venues undetected. The findings could be useful the next time you go undercover."

Isabella swallowed the urge to laugh. Leave it to the intelligence unit's tech guru to blame his skulking around on statistical research. James Capelli was the best in the field, although he didn't even have a hairsbreadth of room to talk about going the eat-sleep-breathe route for work. "You say potato, I say see you later. I've got to jump."

Hollister pointed to an empty bar stool at the next table as Capelli commandeered the one she'd just left vacant. "There's still plenty of room if you want to stick around. We can see if they've got any ibuprofen behind the bar, and it's still pretty early. Plus, Capelli's giving me the juice on all of this weekend's football games."

Isabella's nod and smile made their belated appearance as she pulled her leather jacket over her shoulders. *Dodge. Deflect. Make your exit.* "Isn't gambling a bit of a conflict of interest for cops?"

"Online fantasy football is a perfectly legal game of skill," Hollister said, waggling his brows at her you-can't-be-serious expression. "And despite being able to crunch all those stats like soda cans, he never bets on the games himself. Don't you think someone should reap the benefits of this guy's freaky-deaky brain power?"

Maxwell snorted, saving Isabella from having to dig up a comeback. "Hate to break it to you, man, but you reap the benefits every time he hooks you up with high-end surveillance tech or some piece of obscure evidence he uncovers while data mining the entire fucking Internet."

"Now, now, Detective." Capelli grinned, pausing for only a second to flag down a passing waitress and order a beer. "I only data mine most of the Internet."

"Stop being so modest," Hale said, busting Capelli's chops all the way. "You have a photographic memory, for Pete's sake. As far as techies go, I think you're the *king* of the Internet."

Maxwell shook his head. "Laugh now, partner. But when he swaps out your DMV picture with a headshot of Elmer Fudd, you won't think it's so funny."

"Come on, Maxwell. That was three whole years ago, and I changed it back after a day and a half. Plus, Hale here is way more Tweety Bird."

Everyone in the group broke into easy laughter. Isabella's stomach tightened at the camaraderie free-flowing around the table, and she took a step back. Go. Go now. "On that note of brotherly love, I'll see you guys on Monday, yeah?"

Offering up one last round of goodbyes, she cut a quick path out of the Crooked Angel, measuring both her footsteps and her heartbeats until the chatter and pulse of the bar noise gave way to the quiet hum of the streetlights overhead. To calm the unease bubbling in her stomach, she ordered the tasks in front of her into a checklist—*grab keys from right pocket, double-check ankle holster, find an inconspicuous parking spot on Delancey Street*—mentally crossing off each item upon completion. Sinking just low enough into the driver's seat of her Mustang to find the perfect line of sight on the city block in front of her, Isabella killed the engine and let herself blend into the shadows. The laughter-filled banter between her unit-mates filled her mind, tugging at her senses until the strains of a different happy laughter washed over her from a memory.

"Oh, it's awful, prima!" Marisol's face pinched, her girlish features combining with her adolescent disdain. "Are you sure we're drinking it right?"

Isabella had no idea, but she was three years older than Mari, and her fourteen-year-old pride refused to let her cop to her cluelessness. "I'm positive. My papi says black coffee makes you strong."

"It tastes so bitter," Marisol said, her big, dark eyes hesitating over the cup cradled between her palms. "I want to be grown up, but I don't want to drink the rest."

Isabella reached for the white china cup, the light glinting off the gold-rimmed edges as she smiled at her cousin, squeezing her hand. "It's okay," she said, pouring the contents into her own cup even though she'd hated the taste of the coffee just as much as Marisol had. "I'll drink it. Don't worry. You're still grown up for trying."

"Thank you, Isa. You always watch out for me…"

Isabella curled her fingers into fists, focusing on the bite of her nails on the thin skin of her palms. Letting herself go back, even for a second, was dangerous—stupid, really. She couldn't change what had happened eleven years ago, the day she'd made the decision that had changed everything like a stone in still water, rippling all the things it touched. Still, in the dark of her car where no one could see her, Isabella allowed herself to remember. The horrible stomach ache she got that night from drinking that coffee—God, it had been strong enough to take the chrome off a car bumper. The clink of the china cups as she'd finally been able to sneak them back to the kitchen in the house on the south side of Remington where she'd grown up. The trust in Marisol's eyes.

The stark, stabbing fear that had come nearly four years later, when the police had knocked on the door of her mami's house, faces serious and badges bright.

A shift in the shadows had Isabella on full alert, her heart beating a fresh batch of adrenaline through her body and her breath adjusting to temper it. The figure moved up the street on strong, stealthy footsteps, and her muscles released—although only slightly—in recognition. A minute later, Kellan reached the passenger side of her Mustang, his movements perfectly fluid as he hooked his fingers beneath the door handle and settled himself into the seat beside her.

"Nice car. I should've known you'd drive a Ford," he said, a thread of heatless sarcasm woven through the words.

In an instant, Isabella's armor was locked back into place. "Do not speak ill of my baby. I'll leave you here before we even start."

"No you won't." His teeth flashed in a smile that Isabella felt in the pit of her stomach even though she really didn't want to. He said, "The Camaro's two blocks over, in the opposite direction of Kylie and Devon's apartment. Everything's good to go."

"Great." She turned the key, the Mustang's engine growling quietly to life. The job in front of her wasn't small. She needed to pave over memory lane and get to business. "So listen. Before we do this, there are a couple things you need to know."

Walker didn't budge in his seat, but everything about his demeanor said he was all ears. "Shoot."

"Carmen's a little, ah. Prickly. Especially in front of people she doesn't know." The woman had good reason to be rough around the edges, what with the former junkie/prostitute part of her past. But for now, Isabella was keeping that nugget tucked safely away. No need to air her CI's dirty laundry. Carmen might give off nine different brands of attitude, but she was getting her life together. "Her abrasiveness is just her way of testing the water, so don't take it personally. She's going to be on edge enough as it is when she sees me."

"Wait. Doesn't she know you're coming?"

Walker's tone was all surprise over judgment, and

Isabella couldn't help it. She laughed, long and loud. "Some CIs are easier to work with than others. Carmen needs a little finesse. Especially if I want to get useable information out of her."

"Ah." His chin lifted in a single nod of understanding, the passing street lights allowing small glimpses of his expression. "So you think she'll be more likely to come out with the truth if you take her by surprise."

"Now you're catching on." Isabella traded one street for another, the asphalt growing dingier and more warped with poorly patched potholes and faded yellow lines as she headed toward the notoriously rough section of the city down by the North Point River pier. "Carmen's had a hard life. She's on the upside now, but she's still pretty wary. Especially of cops."

"Duly noted." After another minute, he added, "Anything else I should know?"

A ribbon of surprise uncurled in her belly, but far be it for her to say no if he wanted to go the whole knowledge-is-power route. "I might have to withhold some things or even bend the truth when I ask her what she knows about the house and who was in it. You're going to need a decent poker face."

He shifted, his black canvas jacket shushing over the passenger seat as he turned to look at her. "You're going to lie to your informant in order to get her to give you information."

"Not if I don't have to, and I'd never lie about what she'll get in return for useable intel," Isabella qualified. After all, CIs were an asset. Jerking hers around wouldn't get her anywhere, not to mention it was a dick maneuver of the highest order. "But yeah. If I have to massage the truth or be tough on her in order to get her talking, you can bet your ass I will."

"So it's more like angling for what you want," Walker said, and she nodded in reply.

"Yes. Rule number one is to tell as much truth as you

possibly can. People have all sorts of tells when they lie, even for the best of liars telling the tiniest untruths. Plus, Carmen's smart. The more truth I tell her, the less there is to get caught in if she calls me on it." Isabella paused to lift a quick brow at him through the shadows of the Mustang's interior. "For example, it would probably be damn near impossible for me to sell you as my boyfriend than as some nosy, pain in my ass firefighter."

Funny, he raised a brow right back at her. "You wouldn't date a guy like me?"

The suggestion sent enough warmth through Isabella to be fully distracting, and okay, maybe that example had been a bad idea.

She took a breath. "I don't date, period, and Carmen knows it. Anyway, you're bound to infuriate me while I'm talking to her, and I'll probably be as likely to cover it up as I am to bench press a baby grand. In this case, it's just better to tell her the truth."

"That makes sense," Kellan said, waiting a couple of well-shadowed city blocks before adding, "What do you mean, you don't date, period?"

Finally, an easy question. "It's pretty straightforward. The job doesn't leave me much free time, and anyway, dating's too much of a hassle. So I just don't."

"Not to get too personal, but don't you get…"

His tone led her on an easy trip of connect-the-dots. "Horny? Sure. But I didn't say I don't have sex. Only that I don't date."

Isabella shivered. As far as she was concerned, 'relationship' was just a four-syllable word for 'please put all my emotions through a wood chipper and expect me to smile while you're at it.' At least sex was easy enough most of the time, although lately she'd been all work, no play. Jesus, her vibrator was working as much overtime as she was. Her no-nonsense, just-sex approach wasn't the norm, she knew, especially for a woman. In fact, it usually either made men shy away from the topic entirely or propelled them to proposition her.

But Walker didn't do either. "That's pretty jaded," he said, and Isabella pulled her gaze from the road for just a second to arch a brow in reply.

"Don't tell me you're looking for happily ever after over there."

He lifted a dark brow right back at her through the shadows. "Looking for it? Maybe not. I'm hardly Prince Charming material. But I don't want to be alone forever, either. Do you?"

Danger, Will Robinson! Back away from the question. "Being alone has its benefits," she pointed out. Namely that not letting anyone in meant not having to worry you'd lose them. Been there. Done that. Not ever doing it again, thanks.

Walker, it seemed, didn't agree. "And that's why all you do is have no-strings-attached sex? Because you like being alone?"

Isabella opened her mouth, fully prepared to argue. But the last thing she needed right now (or, okay. Ever) was yet another version of the don't-you-want-to-find-someone-and-settle-down speech her mother launched in her direction at regular intervals from her retirement condo in Miami.

And the first thing she needed to do—the only thing—was work.

"Yes, actually. That's exactly why I do it. Now did you want to talk about your sex life too, or should we use these last few minutes to finish prepping for this little fishing expedition with Carmen?"

Walker's stare was a palpable thing through the flashing glow of the overhead streetlights, and for a second, she thought he would push. But instead, after a minute he simply shrugged, turning to look out his window at the inky water beyond the pier that had just come into view in the distance.

"I think we're good on both counts, Moreno. Now let's

go see what we can find out about the girls in those pictures."

CHAPTER SEVEN

Julian looked into the mirror in front of him with a hard, assessing stare. He was as meticulous with his grooming as he was with all things, so he moved his gaze slowly from the top of his white-blond head over his cleanly shaved face before coasting lower to the expanse of his bare, smooth chest. His rigid exercise regimen required no less than two hours a day, carefully cultivating the lean muscles covering his frame. No clumsy bulk for him, nothing ostentatious that couldn't be tastefully covered. Everything about Julian was precise, purposeful.

Clean. Filth could not be tolerated. Under any circumstances.

Filth needed to be purged. Punished.

A knock sounded on the door, the hard, boorish echo filtering through the suite to capture Julian's attention all the way in his dressing room. His pulse quickened at his state of nakedness, but he knew no one in the house would dare even touch the knob to his suite without his consent.

After all, he'd made sure to train his staff properly. Mistakes such as the violation of his privacy were disciplined before the entire group to ensure they never happened twice.

Only one person had ever entered his private rooms without permission. And that one example had been enough.

"You'll wait," Julian said with just enough volume to be heard and obeyed. Turning away from his reflection, he began to dress, following his routine to the letter until his body was covered, his skin and his scars perfectly hidden, just as they should be. He settled into the large Italian leather chair in his mahogany-paneled sitting room, the one that faced the door in planned strategy for meetings such as this, arranging his features just so before shifting his gaze to the entryway.

"Come."

Charles stepped in from the hallway, his beefy face appropriately serious. Good that their last meeting had retained the desired effect. "Evening check-in. Sir," the miscreant added, as if the address would win him any favor.

Julian considered it. Still, best to keep Charles in his place, where he belonged. "You seem to be healing rather well, Charles," he said, allowing his eyes to rest on the man's left arm. Truly, the bandage didn't even show beneath his shirt sleeves. Yet Julian knew from the sudden sheen beading over Charles's forehead that he certainly still required one.

Satisfaction mingled with power, forming a potent cocktail in his veins. "And how are things progressing with my new acquisitions?"

"Good, sir." Charles cleared his throat, his hulking body at rigid attention as he delivered the report. "All three girls are at the new facility with Franco. They should be ready by next Friday night."

"If Franco is training them, I should hope so." The man was abhorrent, giving in to every base urge under the sun. Unfortunately, that made him a prime candidate for effectively breaking in Julian's merchandise, and thus he was necessary. Lord knew Julian wasn't going to subject himself to such disgusting depths. The girls were even more unclean than Franco himself. "And the preparations for tonight's gathering?"

Charles jerked his head in a nod, the movement awkward considering his distinct lack of a neck. "The private rooms are set. Everything is in place for your guests, and the girls are ready to serve them."

"Excellent," Julian said. His thoughts turned to his weekly party, of how his guests would shamelessly suck and fuck and shoot up and share until they were sated, of how the girls they used would take all that was given to them like the dirty little whores they were, and how he himself would watch every move, overseeing it all.

And everyone in attendance would get exactly what they deserved.

* * *

Kellan took in the sun-weathered and timeworn pier off the North Point River, keeping his eyes wide open and his body on full alert. At twenty-three hundred hours, the strip surrounding the docks was just starting to buzz to life, an undertone of bad intentions and even worse actions pulsing through the night air. He turned to give Moreno's car one last look over his shoulder, hoping like hell the thing would be there when they were done with this heart to heart, even if it was a Ford. She didn't seem to have any reservations, though, not even hesitating as she aimed herself in the direction of the long stretch of sketchy bars, tattoo parlors, and seedy convenience stores lining the boardwalk adjacent to the pier, proper.

They fell into step together, her shoulder brushing the outside of his biceps just once before she shifted to give him a wider berth. "This part of Remington gets rough at this time of night. Keep your eyes open."

Kellan had to put his best effort into not laughing. Half the time he still slept with his eyes open. The other half of the time, he didn't sleep at all. "I'll do my best."

Her brown eyes narrowed on him as they began to move side by side over the slim ribbon of concrete leading to the worst section of town, but she didn't say anything other than, "Okay. Just follow my lead with Carmen, and for the love of all that's good, please don't piss her off."

"I told you." Kellan's feet kept time with hers around the corner leading to the main drag, and he sent another wide-net gaze around them to take in their surroundings from the ground-level up. *Focus. Assess the facts.* "I'm all charm."

"That's what I'm afraid of."

They walked for a minute without talking, although Kellan had zero doubt that Moreno was far from aimlessly wandering. Her eyes moved keenly over the storefronts to their right, while his took ownership of the real estate to their left, cataloguing the people standing off in the shadows, leaning on the wooden railing overlooking the glassy black water in the distance. The boardwalk was wide and sparsely lit, with nook-like lookout points off the main drag that allowed for all sorts of semi-privacy among groups of people who chose not to ask or tell. Kellan had counted six couples—no, make that seven—who had been participating in various states of exactly that before the red and white sign boasting "Three Brothers Pizza" flashed in the near distance above Isabella's shoulder.

"I don't suppose you've had a change of heart and want to let me do this chat solo?" she asked, firming her shoulders around her spine as she reached for the door handle next to the promise of "we deliver!" stenciled over the glass in bright red letters.

Kellan lost the battle with his snort. "Not a chance, sweetheart." They were smack in the lap of the worst part of the city. No way was he leaving her to her own devices. Not even inside the pizza place. He didn't care how long she'd been a cop.

"Can't blame a girl for trying." The words slid out under

her breath, quickly falling prey to the sharp staccato of a woman's voice filtering into the otherwise empty storefront from somewhere in the half-open kitchen area.

"Jesus H. Christ on a Popsicle stick, Lamar! Are you sleeping back here *again*? I swear on my *mami's* eyes, I'm going to…" A pause in the diatribe said the voice's owner had registered the electronic door chime. "I'm not through with you, you hear me? Now wake up and start breaking down this kitchen, *pendejo*. We're closing in ten minutes. I've got a date tonight, and I'm not staying late for your lazy ass."

Holy shit. This was Isabella's CI? "Are you serious?" Kellan whispered, and Moreno gave up an I-told-you-so smile.

"As a sledgehammer, *sweetheart*."

Even though he'd bought her attitude wholesale when he'd popped off and called her 'sweetheart' first, Kellan opened his mouth to dish back. His response, however, was unceremoniously cut short by the appearance of a petite, dark-haired woman behind the counter who looked none too pleased to catch sight of them standing there.

"Oh, no." The woman, who couldn't be more than five-foot-zip on her best day, jabbed an inch-long lime green fingernail in Isabella's direction. "Turn back around, *pendeja*. We're locking it up for the night, and we don't got what you want in here anyway. Mmm-mmm."

"Come on, Carmen. I just want to order dinner," Moreno said, pointing to the pair of pizzas sitting under the grease-smudged heat lamps over Carmen's shoulder. "I'll take a slice of pepperoni. For here."

The woman's black-coffee eyes flashed beneath a heavy layer of makeup, her lashes so long and thickly fringed that Kellan wondered how she kept them open beneath the weight. "You want pizza," she said, although she didn't move a muscle.

"For starters." Isabella reached into the back pocket of her jeans, peeling a twenty-dollar bill from the other four in her hand.

"With you, it's always for starters," Carmen grumbled. She turned to slide a piece of pizza onto a paper plate, but clearly, she wasn't done trying to push Isabella's buttons. "So, what," Carmen said in Spanish, suggestion curving around every syllable. "You screwing this one? Because I gotta tell you, I wouldn't throw his ass out of bed for eating crackers just as long as he was eating everything else, you know what I'm saying?"

Kellan clamped down on the urge to let his surprise show at the same moment Moreno froze into place next to him at the counter. "Yeah, I know what you're saying, and no. I'm not screwing him," Isabella answered, also in Spanish.

"But you want to." Carmen's eyes glinted, her lips curving into a hard smile as her stare moved from Moreno's face to his and then back again. "Girl, I can practically smell it on you."

By the time the second wave of Kellan's shock registered, Moreno had the twenty tucked safely back in her pocket and a healthy foot added to the dance space between her body and the counter. "Your mouth always gets you into trouble, Carmen."

The tension between the two women was even easier to translate than the words and shit. *Shit.* Moreno had made it clear that he was just along for the ride. She didn't even have a clue he'd understood her conversation. But they'd come for answers, not a pissing contest, and they weren't going to get anywhere this way. Best case scenario if he butted in was calming Carmen down enough to get her talking. Worst was that Moreno would be pissed that he hadn't stayed quiet, and fuck it. He was getting pretty good at fielding her irritation anyway.

Kellan leaned one arm over the scuffed red Formica and worked up a smile just shy of cocky. "Isabella and I are only friends," he said in Spanish. "But thanks for the compliment."

Although both women gaped at him in clear what-the-fuck surprise, Carmen spoke first, switching back to English. "You're welcome. I suppose you want pizza for starters too."

"That would be great. Thank you."

"You a cop?" Carmen watched Isabella, not Kellan, as she murmured the question softly, and damn, the woman knew exactly what she was doing.

"Nope." He tiled his gaze downward to look her right in the eye, answering just as quietly even though the restaurant was dead empty. "Like I said, I'm just a friend of Isabella's."

"Hmm. All my 'friends' should look like you." Carmen's tone hooked verbal air quotes around the word, and she stood back, shifting her gaze between him and Moreno. Finally, she turned for another piece of pizza, nudging both plates across the counter, and Kellan let go of the breath he'd been holding. "I like you better than the other one she normally comes in with. He's hot too, but bossy. Thinks he owns the place."

"I'll be sure to let Hollister know you said hi," Isabella said lifting a brow along with one corner of her mouth. She passed over the twenty to cover the pizza, putting all the change Carmen handed back into the otherwise empty tip jar by the register.

"Be sure to tell him I said kiss my ass. Now what else do you want? Believe me when I tell you I'm not wasting all night with you two."

She didn't have to ask Moreno twice. "I'm looking for some information on a delivery you guys made to a house not far from here on August twenty-second."

"That was almost a month ago, and we make a lot of deliveries." Carmen folded her arms over her chest, but Moreno didn't so much as bat an eyelash.

"You also have a computer system that keeps great records. Ninety-three-ten Glendale, about four miles from here. Can you look it up?"

"It'll cost you."

"I tip well."

"You'd better," Carmen said, blowing out an exaggerated breath before tapping the touch screen register to life. "Ninety-three-ten Glendale, let's see…oh." Her lips pressed into a hard, flat line. "Looks like we delivered there a bunch of times."

"Anything recent?" Moreno asked, and Kellan could practically see the wheels turning in her mind.

Just like he could see Carmen's expression slam shut. "Not in the last three weeks."

Moreno leaned forward, hands flat over the chipped countertop. "Did the customer ever pay with a credit card?"

"No." Carmen frowned and started to fidget. "Always cash."

"But you remember the house," Kellan said, and bingo. Her frown deepened for a split second before she blanked it from her face.

"Whatever, pretty boy. Like I said, we deliver to a lot of places."

"Carmen." Isabella's gaze narrowed, although with more question than accusation. "Have you been to this house?"

Carmen made a noise comprised of mostly irritation, but it didn't hide the unease pulling at the corners of her mouth. "Maybe I did the deliveries one night when our regular runner was out with the flu."

"And you brought a pizza to this address?" Moreno's tone shifted, softening ever so slightly, and Kellan would bet his paycheck she'd seen Carmen's grimace just as clearly as he had. "Do you remember anything about the delivery?" she asked with care. "Who was in the house? What they looked like?"

Pushing back from the business side of the counter, Carmen scoffed, her titanium-tough attitude right back in place as she jammed her hands into the denim slung dangerously low over her hips. "Yeah, I remember. The guy invited me in to be dessert, then stiffed me for a tip when I told him he'd have better luck fucking himself. Asshole."

Okay, so it was a good start, but being an asshole wasn't

against the law. Sadly. A fact which Moreno hadn't seemed to have lost sight of, either. "What else, Carmen?"

Tap-tap-tap-tap went one bright green nail against the countertop. "Nothing. That's all I remember."

"Bullshit."

Carmen's eyes darted toward Kellan at the same time his darted toward Isabella, but Isabella didn't stand down. "I need this guy, Carmen. I think you know why."

"I know nothing," she snapped, and Moreno's voice gentled to balance out her thorny edges.

"You've seen him around, haven't you. From before you started working here."

The prompt was enough to either take Carmen by surprise or make her throw in the towel. A little, anyway. "Maybe. Look"—her dark stare swiveled over the tiny dining area beside them before moving furtively to the plate glass windows facing the pier—"this is big shit, Isa. These people…you don't understand."

Kellan's blood chilled at the sudden, nameless emotion in Carmen's eyes, then turned colder still at Isabella's reply.

"Believe me, I do. That's why I need to know what you know, mija. So I can do something about it."

Carmen's frown expressed her doubt at the possibility in no uncertain terms. Still, she looked out at the water in the distance and said, "There was only the one guy in the house when I delivered the pizza. I've seen him before. Once. Six, maybe eight months ago. I was at a club and he invited me to a private party." She paused, but only long enough to shrug. "Said I was his boss's type, and if I went, I could have whatever I wanted. Booze, pills, heroin. Said it would be just a taste of the future."

Moreno didn't move, just listened, and even though Carmen's story was kicking him in the gut, Kellan did the same.

"But something about the whole thing felt off," Carmen continued. "A little too good not to have a punch line. I said no, and one of the other girls who was there didn't, so he didn't push. But I never saw her again."

"Would you recognize her if you did?" Moreno asked, but Carmen shook her head.

"I don't think so. She was pretty new to the scene, and I was on my way out. I'd only met her once or twice."

Moreno met the apology on Carmen's face with a quick shake of her head. "That's okay. How about the guy? He got a name?"

"Something weird, like one of those MMA fighters. Fury? Or maybe Rage? Something like that. Huge guy. Longish dark hair. He gave me the fucking creeps. But he didn't recognize me when I delivered the pizza, and I got the hell out of there, fast."

Moreno nodded in encouragement. "Do you remember what club you were at when he asked you to the party?" she asked, but Carmen shook her head, reaching out to check the napkin dispenser by the register even though it was already full.

"No. I'm sorry. I ran the circuit that night, so it could've been half the clubs on the north side. A couple of them have even closed since then. It's been a while." She paused, her chin snapping up as if someone had just snuck up on her to yell boo, and concern washed over Isabella's face.

"Carmen? What is it?"

"No. Nothing."

But this time, rather than going all pit-bull on her, Isabella softened her demeanor and her voice to just above a whisper. "I think this guy is hurting people, Carmen, and I really need to find him. Help me out here. Please."

"Danny Marcus. He and I used to…" Carmen dropped her gaze to the floor tiles. "He's a john. Small-time dealer, he used to trade product for services. I just remembered that Danny was there that night, talking to the wrestler guy. I heard he's running with a high-end group now, moving up in the game. Real fancy."

Kellan thought of the background in the photos he'd found, and his heartbeat picked up the pace. It was a stretch—a yoga instructor's wet dream, actually. But at least it was something.

Apparently, Moreno thought so, too. "You know where I can find him?"

Carmen nodded. "Danny might be moving up in the game, but he ain't gonna forget his roots when they mean he can make a fast buck or get an easy lay. He still slums it sometimes, doing business over by the park on Atlantic Boulevard Friday and Saturday nights. Skinny guy, really curly dark hair. Talks about himself in the third person all the time, you know 'Danny Marcus says he's ready to play,' and stupid shit like that."

She paused to laugh, although the sound didn't hold a whole lot of joy. "He has a thing for Hispanic girls. He'll probably love you. 'Til he finds out you're a cop, anyway."

"Thank you, Carmen. You've been really helpful." Isabella took the other four twenties from the back pocket of her jeans, carefully putting them into the tip jar before taking a step back from the counter.

"Aren't you gonna eat your pizza? I thought you said you were hungry." Carmen pointed to the paper plates still splitting the divide between them, but Moreno just smiled.

"The pizza's for you. Take care of yourself, *mija*. I've got an appetite for something far bigger than food."

CHAPTER EIGHT

Isabella coaxed her cell phone to life with a quick tap of her thumb, the time stamp display cutting through the shadows around the pier and filling her chest with a whole lot of oh-hell-yes. She had just about an hour to scope out the park on Atlantic Boulevard and figure out a strategy for her next move. If—no, *when* she spun this Danny Marcus thing just right and got him to give up the wrestler guy, she'd likely have enough of a lead on whoever was hurting the women in those pictures for Peterson to open an investigation. With the mention of high-end "parties" and the way Wrestler Guy had been obviously recruiting prostitutes, there was no chance the connection between all the pieces was merely a coincidence. All she needed was some sort of hard evidence from Danny to link the whole thing together.

Evidence she was a lot less likely to get with Walker going along for the ride. And judging by the way he was walking no more than a foot beside her on the boardwalk and looking way too sexy for his own good—not to mention way, way too expectant about the next move—convincing him to let her fly solo was going to be a ten-foot-tall order.

"I've got some time to kill before I head down to Atlantic Boulevard." Isabella kept her voice as neutral as possible, as if she were remarking on the weather or hockey scores or anything else that didn't have a massive bearing on breaking the case in front of her wide open. "Nothing starts moving in that neighborhood until at least midnight, so that gives me plenty of time to drop you back at your car."

Walker's mouth curled into a smile, and really, was it too much to ask that he have crooked teeth or bad breath or something that would keep her freaking lady bits in check?

"You're not taking me back to my car," he said, and she stopped short on the pavement leading back to the dilapidated side street where they'd left the Mustang, crossing her arms over her chest so tightly that the seams of her jacket dug into her shoulders.

"I agreed to let you come with me to the pizza place, Kellan."

"Yes you did, Isabella," he replied in the exact same tone, and shit. So much for the first name thing working on him. "And now I'm going to come with you to the park on Atlantic Boulevard to try and find Danny Marcus."

Tread carefully, girl. "I don't need a chaperone."

"Well that's a relief, because 'babysitter' isn't on my resume." Walker spun a gaze over the dusky street, tipping his head toward the spot where her car stood a half a block away before they both started walking again. "I'm not trying to mess with you, but my original argument stands. Pursuing this case off the books in a rough neighborhood without backup is dangerous. Not to mention stupid."

"Thank you," she said, although fuck all, he was right. Atlantic Boulevard definitely wasn't brimming with milk and cookies, especially after midnight. Still, putting her own ass on the line was one thing. Putting someone else's, especially when that ass belonged to a civilian? That was risky with a capital R. "I already bent the hell out of the rules by bringing you to the pizza place."

"You're bending the rules by doing all of this, with or without me. The least you can do is let me make sure you won't get yourself shot, stabbed, or worse." Walker paused, his feet coming to a stop beside her Mustang. "Would it make you feel any better to know I have tactical training?"

Curiosity pumped through her veins, riding her quickening pulse, but she stuffed it back in favor of popping the locks on the car and climbing into the driver's seat. "Unless it's with the RPD and you have a super-secret badge I don't know about, no."

Walker slid into the passenger seat, his body radiating both stealth and strength and his jaw hard-wired in determination. "Even if my training came courtesy of the Army Rangers and I could put a kill shot on damn near anything within two hundred yards of here using nothing more than the Glock in your glove box?"

Holy crap. She knew he'd spent some time in the Army, but… "You were a goddamn sniper for the Army Rangers? How come you never said anything?"

"Because." He blew out a barely audible breath. "It's not something I advertise, just like I imagine you don't brag about being a cop."

Okay. So he had her dead to rights there. "Still. You could've told me when we worked on Kylie's case together."

"Then it wouldn't have mattered," he said with a lift of one shoulder against the leather seatback. "But now it does. All I'm saying is you don't have to worry about me when we go find this Danny Marcus guy. I can take care of myself, and I won't interfere unless you need backup."

"Like you didn't interfere with Carmen?" she asked, the words out before she could cage them. Although the hookup with her CI could've gone so much worse, Walker had thrown Isabella for one hell of a loop by interrupting their conversation with flawless—albeit a little bit formal—Spanish. The last thing she needed was to worry about a distraction that could twist this trip to the park into a disaster.

No, rewind. The last thing she needed to worry about was what Walker had heard Carmen say. God, when this case was said and done and safe in Peterson's hands, Isabella's first order of business was going to be to find a warm, willing bedmate with a whole lot of stamina and some time on his hands.

Walker tipped his head to look at her and added a little more wattage to his smile, which did nothing for the state of her composure. "That wasn't interfering. I'm charming, remember?"

"You're something, all right." Using the pretense of fastening her seatbelt as a cover, Isabella snuck a covert glance at him. Damn it. She'd given him the inch. Of course he wasn't going to let go until he'd taken every last bit of the mile. "You're really not going to let me take you back to your car, are you?"

"Not even a little bit," Walker confirmed. "But don't worry. You won't even know I'm there."

Ha! Pretty flipping unlikely, considering the way his cocky little smirk was suddenly turning her panties into a hot zone. His mouth was weirdly beautiful for being on such a rugged face, those full, firmly set lips set against the backdrop of dark stubble. The occasional flash of straight, white teeth. The suggestive lift at the edges of his mouth that made her wonder what he could do with that quick tongue.

And how many times he could do it.

Good *Lord* she needed to get some air in this car. Like yesterday.

"Fine," Isabella said, jamming her keys into the ignition and her finger over the button to lower her window a few inches. Scrambling for something to focus on other than Walker's potential for superior oral skills, she blurted the first thing that popped into her overly addled head. "I had no idea you speak Spanish."

He nodded. "Arabic, too, although I'm not nearly as fluent."

"That's an interesting skill set," she said, her curiosity bubbling enough to finally override her libido.

"I also sing a mean karaoke version of Springsteen's 'Born In the U.S.A.', and on occasion, I cook," he quipped back.

"Hmmm." Isabella spared him a quick glance before turning onto a side street to head deeper into North Point. "Now it's even more interesting. I assume you learned Arabic overseas?"

"Baghdad. Most of the Spanish is from high school, and Kylie taught me the kitchen skills." Although Walker didn't skip a beat with his cadence, he aimed the words out the passenger window, the small action grabbing every last bit of her attention. He clearly meant to slip around the topic of his deployment, and for a second, she nearly caved. But Isabella had never been anything other than brash, with him or anyone else. Changing her stripes now seemed stupid, and anyway, she couldn't deny the truth.

She wanted to know more about the dark, sexy firefighter sitting next to her in the shadows.

"Nice try with the bait and switch," she said. Hell, she knew every evasive maneuver in the book. And even a couple that weren't. "Too bad for you I'm not that easy."

Walker's laughter deepened both her curiosity and her surprise. "You are a lot of things, Moreno. Easy doesn't even make the top twenty."

Isabella laughed too. After all, he wasn't really wrong. "So you were stationed in Baghdad as a Ranger?"

He paused, but then he said, "For part of my first tour. But I actually spent most of my time in Afghanistan. Kabul and Kandahar."

This time, she managed to check her shock before it made the trip to her face. Two tours as a Ranger were definitely no pleasure trip down Main Street. "That does explain the Arabic. You got any other hidden talents I should know about?"

He lifted one dark brow. "Not unless you've got an

MK24 you need me to assemble or field strip."

Isabella knew she shouldn't flirt with him, with that dangerously distracting smile and those deep-ocean eyes, but God, the words slid out as if they'd been well-oiled and waiting to go. "Be careful, Walker, or I might start to blush."

"Somehow I doubt that," he said, the corners of his mouth edging up. "It figures you'd be the type to get all giddy over high-end weaponry, though."

She lifted one hand off the steering wheel to signal guilty as charged. "I did some extra tactical training with the Remington 700 last year, but those MKs are pretty badass."

"They get the job done." Walker watched the grungy neighborhood scenery for a minute before his own curiosity seemed to get the better of him and he added, "The Remington 700 isn't your run of the mill hardware. Where'd you get your hands on one?"

Isabella grinned. She could talk shop for a month and never get tired of it. "Ah, the guys on SWAT let me sneak in sometimes when they have an open spot in their training schedule. You can never practice too much."

"That's pretty ambitious practice," Kellan said. "Most people just empty a couple of clips at the gun range and call it a day, you know."

Isabella straightened against the Mustang's driver's seat, her pulse knocking against her throat. The last thing she needed right now was to field flak from yet another person over how many hours she put into the job. Hearing the all-work-no-play routine from her mami and papi was bad enough, and there were way worse things to have than a jumbo-sized work ethic.

"Yeah, well I'm not most people. I happen to like a lot of ambition," she said, brows up and bravado at the ready, but Walker's decisive nod had her ballsy defenses screeching to a halt.

"I get that," he said, all quiet truth. "I mean, if I'm going to do a job, it doesn't make sense to go halfway."

Holy. Shit. "Exactly," Isabella answered, giving the word

a slow stretch. Her expression must've betrayed the shock running rampant in her veins, though, because the next thing out of his mouth was a laugh.

"Don't look so surprised, Moreno. I'm more than just a pretty face over here. I go all-in at the firehouse just like you do at the Thirty-Third."

Stone cold busted, she had no choice but to start laughing along with him. "Okay, okay. Point taken. There might not be a whole lot of people who really get my level of job dedication, but I shouldn't have assumed you weren't one of them."

"Speaking of which"—Walker's stare glinted through the shadows—"I've been thinking about what you said earlier."

"I said a lot of things earlier," Isabella replied, blinking in an effort to follow the newly forged direction of the conversation. Where the hell was he headed?

"This morning," Kellan said. "When we were at the scene of the house fire, you said if I thought you wouldn't take a slim lead and run with it, then I didn't know you very well."

She pulled the Mustang to a stop about a block from the park, using the time it took to quiet the engine and cut the headlights to replay their earlier conversation in her mind. "I guess I did."

Walker dropped his voice to a low rumble, matching the relative quiet and darkness of their surroundings. "And I guess I don't. So tell me."

He had to be kidding. "Tell you what?"

"Tell me something about you so I know you better."

Oh God, he so wasn't kidding. "Let me see if I've got this right. You want me to fork over a running biography in the front seat of my car? That's kind of personal, isn't it?"

"Relax, Moreno. I'm not asking for a head count on the skeletons in your closet," Walker said with a shrug. "But we are about to go put the full court press on some dirtbag to try and catch a lead in your case, so the way I see it, a little insight is probably better than a lot of assumptions. Plus, we've got time to kill. So go on. Enlighten me."

"You first," her deeply trained defenses made her say, surprise filling her chest as Kellan answered without hesitation.

"Okay. I like my pizza cold."

Isabella bit her lip two seconds too late to trap her incredulous laugh. "You're serious. We're giving up personal information, and that's what you're going to lead with?"

"You didn't really think I was going to give you something juicy on the first go, did you?" He looked at her through the scant ambient light in the car, his gaze still unwavering even as she leaned in closer to pin him with an inquisitive stare.

"Fair enough. Can't say I pegged you as the cold pizza type, though, what with your sister training to be a chef and all."

"Oh, don't get me wrong," he said, taking off his seat belt and easing a little lower against the passenger seat, melting into the shadows. "I'll eat it warm, too. After a couple of walkabouts through the Middle East, I learned not to be terribly choosy. But the funny part is, the cold pizza thing is actually Kylie's fault."

"Does she know that?" Although his sister was far from stuffy or snobby, Isabella had to imagine cold pizza wouldn't appeal to her culinary sensibilities.

But Walker nodded. "She does. It was mostly just the two of us growing up. Our mom wasn't in the picture and our dad worked two jobs, so we had to fend for ourselves in the dinner department a lot of the time. Frozen pizza was my specialty, but one night we lost power during a thunderstorm and I couldn't warm up the leftovers I'd put in the fridge. We ate them cold because we had no choice, but Kylie ended up liking the pizza better that way. After a while, we both started looking forward to the cold leftovers more than the hot meals."

Isabella laughed, picturing the two of them camped out with their pizza straight from the fridge. "How old were you then?"

"I guess I was about fifteen and Kylie was maybe ten that first time," he said after a pause. "But we shared a lot of pizza in those days, just me and her."

"No wonder you two are close," Isabella said, and the pared-down, God's honest smile on his face slid through her like a summer breeze.

"Yeah, we are." Walker tilted his head, gesturing toward her with a lift of his stubbled chin. "Your turn. Tell me something about you."

Whether it was the cover of the near-darkness blanketing the front seat of her car or the ease at which Kellan had told her such a personal thing about himself, Isabella had no clue. But instead of playing dodge ball with the topic like her gut demanded, she said, "I don't drink coffee."

Surprise streaked over his face, illuminated by the glow of a nearby streetlight as he shifted in his seat. "No way that's a legitimate truth. How do you function?"

"On sheer determination, mostly. Well, that and I drink enough tea to fill a bathtub on any given day."

Walker's soft laughter filled the space between them, easing her tension by another notch. "Is there a particular reason you don't drink coffee, or should I question your sanity in general?"

"I promise, I'm not insane," Isabella said, lifting a hand to caveat with, "At least not where my dislike for coffee is concerned."

"I see." Although his tone was clearly prompting her to continue, he didn't push out loud, and hell if that unassuming, deep blue stare didn't knock the story right out of her.

"When I was fourteen, my cousin Marisol and I wanted to act grown up, but we were too chicken shit to do anything high-level, like take whiskey from either of our parents'

108

liquor cabinets."

A smile ghosted over Walker's mouth. "At fourteen, that was probably a good thing."

"Since Marisol was three years younger than me, definitely," Isabella agreed. "Anyway, we ended up sneaking two cups of coffee from my mami's kitchen one night after a family dinner. We thought we were such a big deal, you know? Drinking coffee like the adults. Of course, we didn't add cream or sugar because that wouldn't have been grown up, and my papi's pretty much notorious in our family for brewing coffee strong enough to kick-start the living dead."

"I like him already." Kellan turned toward her, a subtle thing, really, but God, his quiet focus made it all too easy to keep talking.

"Well, he taught me a lesson that night, even if he didn't know it. Marisol admitted right away how much she hated the coffee, but I was scared we'd get caught sneaking back into the kitchen if we tried to dump out our cups. I couldn't admit that, though."

"Because you were older," Walker said, and her smile was two parts wry, one part bittersweet to go with the memory.

"And because I was stubborn as hell. So I brazened it out and drank both cups of coffee to the very last drop. Marisol had to hold my hair all night while I was sick to my stomach and high as a kite on caffeine. I've never touched the stuff since."

Walker laughed, not unkindly. "Sounds like you two are close."

The simplicity of the words, the glaring reality that they hadn't been true for eleven years now, hurtled Isabella back to reality, and she scraped for a breath to temper her suddenly slamming heartbeat. Was she out of her mind? She had a job to do—not a small one—and yet here she was, letting herself get distracted by a sexy firefighter she had no business revealing her feelings to. Focusing on the case in front of her, on the women in those photos, that was the only thing that mattered.

Even if keeping the past inside hurt like hell.

Isabella turned her attention to the city block outside her window, where it should've been this whole damned time. Christ, she was slipping. "Yeah. Well, anyway, we should probably get a plan into place for this chat with Marcus. Something tells me it's not going to be a milk run, and I need to get as much out of him as I can."

The silence coming from Walker's side of the car was loaded with hesitation, and please, please, she'd need far more energy than she had if he decided to push his luck. But rather than calling her out, he simply lifted a shoulder, turning his body away from hers to scan the other side of the street as if their conversation had never even happened.

"That's what we're here for. So what've you got in mind to get this guy talking?"

CHAPTER NINE

Kellan sent one last glance over Atlantic Boulevard before setting his shoulders and diving headfirst into trouble. Judging by the number of people already beginning to populate the mostly residential area around the park in varying degrees of drunk and disorderly, he wouldn't find a shortage of the stuff, either. In fact, all he had to do was look less than a foot and a half to his right and he'd get an eyeful of mad, bad, and dangerous to know standing right there next to him on the sidewalk.

Or maybe he should make that *difficult* to know, because for as wide-open as she was about her passion for work, Moreno sure did play her personal life close to the Kevlar. Not that her fierceness made Kellan any less curious about her. Or any less turned on with each passing minute they spent together.

On second thought, dangerous might be a better fit.

"Okay," Moreno said, the intensity in her voice stamping the heat from his belly before it could take the quick trip due south. "Remember, this will be a lot different than dealing with Carmen. Once we find Marcus, he's almost certainly going to give chase. Just stick to the plan and follow my lead."

Kellan frowned. "About the plan," he said, but she cut him off with a shake of her head.

"I know you don't like staying in the shadows once we put eyes on Marcus, but I'm not changing my mind on how to run this."

Kellan fell into step beside her. Slipping his hands into his jacket pockets, he swept a covert stare over the block before lowering his chin to keep his words close between them. "All I'm saying is that the plan is a little risky. What if it backfires?"

"It's not going to backfire."

"And you're sure because…?"

Her exhale warmed the bare skin of his neck as she turned to look at him. "Because I need it to work."

"Okay," he said slowly, resigning himself to a nod. While hedging their bets on a probability gave him the fucking shakes, Kellan had to admit Isabella was no slouch in the strategy department. The plan might hinge on one "maybe", but it was otherwise solid. Plus, she'd already made it clear in no uncertain terms that if he didn't like the way she wanted to handle the situation, he was welcome to warm the Mustang's seats while she did it without him.

File that under not goddamn happening. This neighborhood was a crime scene just waiting to go down, and despite Isabella's gut feeling that Marcus would be a runner, Kellan had seen enough scrapes to know that once they got the guy backed into a corner, his fight or flight instincts just might err on the side of getting chippy.

Christ, they really did need the plan to work.

Doing one last check of their surroundings, Kellan took a mental snapshot of their exit paths and any potential obstacles that might cause snags. The entrance to the park sat in the center of the block, marked by a six-foot opening in the wrought iron fence surrounding the heavily shadowed space. A dense network of tree branches arched overhead, still thick with leaves that provided ample cover for the handful of acres that made up the park. What served as winding jogging paths during the day made for all sorts of hidden places for illicit acts at night, and he and Moreno were going to have to be at the very top of their game in order to pin Marcus down and get what they needed out of him.

The shadows around him slipped, pulling at his senses. The night air sent a chill down Kellan's spine despite the cover of his black canvas jacket, and the sensation kicked him in the gut before kicking him back in time. God there was so much irony in how cold the desert got after the sun went down. That first night patrol had damn near ended him, and not from any danger the enemy had posed.

That had come later. Roadside bombs. Ambushes at checkpoints. So many things that could happen in less than a blink.

His heart worked faster against his rib cage, the frenzied rhythm becoming a white-noise whoosh that pressed against his eardrums with every step. Adrenaline threatened to picklock all the boxes in his brain, to make his breath stick and his hands shake, but he reached for an inhale, forcing his brain out of the desert and back into the here and now.

Focus. Nine paces from the car to the other side of the street. Six run-down row homes with mostly darkened windows facing the even darker park. No emotions. Facts only. Breathe.

"You ready?" came Moreno's murmur, soft and sure enough to smooth out the jagged edges of his nerves. She inclined her head at the shadow-lined footpath leading away from the crumbling sidewalk, and Kellan anchored himself the rest of the way into the moment before nodding.

"Absolutely. Let's go make the plan work."

For the first few paces, he moved slowly, staying a half-step behind Isabella as she walked over the dimly lit trail. His eyes adjusted fast enough—shit, learning how to rely on senses other than sight was pretty much Ranger 101, not to mention the first damn thing they taught at the fire academy.

Moreno seemed to adapt just as quickly, leading the way down the path on barely-there footsteps. They walked in tandem, her on the trail and him on her hip, passing couples knotted together and small groups of people smoking and drinking from shared bottles wrapped in brown paper bags. Most of them were far enough off the path not to even notice Kellan and Isabella moving past, but the few that did bother noticing them didn't spare more than a brief glance, seemingly too wrapped up in their activities to care.

Of course, he noticed all of them, cataloguing hair color and build and about a dozen other things with each turn on the winding trail. But no one they passed came close to fitting Carmen's description of Danny Marcus, and the path was becoming less and less populated the farther they went.

Kellan sent yet another furtive three-sixty through the shadows. "You think we're going to find what we're looking for?" he asked quietly, leaning in over Moreno's shoulder. "We haven't even seen anyone for about fifty paces."

Her expression was a tough gauge in the low light filtering down from the street lamp ahead of them in the distance, but her body was strung with enough tight determination to broadcast her answer before she even murmured, "Patience is a virtue, Walker."

"Do I strike you as the virtuous type?" There was no helping the implication laced all over the question, but as soon as Kellan caught the smile hooking at the corners of Moreno's mouth, his boldness became worth it.

"Fair enough. But we're less than a third of the way up the trail, and—" Although her words crashed to a halt, her movements didn't seem to have considered hitching for even a second, and she slid her fingers over his forearm, gripping tight. "There," she whispered. "That's got to be him."

Kellan's eyes lasered in on a man standing to the side of the path about twenty paces in front of them. The guy— who seriously couldn't have weighed more than a buck twenty even if he'd showered in his clothes—stood beneath a street lamp, his back to the pole and his cell phone glued to his ear as he yak-yakked away. An overabundance of dark corkscrew curls sprang out from his head in every direction, and yeah, the guy fit Carmen's description right down to the hey-baby murmurs he was throwing into his cell phone in Spanish.

"Copy that." Kellan checked the immediate area for bystanders and covert exit paths, his pulse tapping out a rhythm of *fuck yeah* at the small stroke of luck that gave Marcus neither. Still… "You sure you want to stick to the plan?"

"Walker." The word was all warning, and damn it, he really had no choice.

"I'm falling back. You're a go to move in."

Moreno didn't so much as blink. Ruffling a hand through her hair, she tugged the hem of her T-shirt down low enough to reveal the swell of her cleavage along with—Jesus, she was going to end him right here in the middle of the park—a good two inches of the black lacy bra beneath it. Slipping a provocative smile over her face, she sauntered over to the guy, and even though it screamed against every last instinct in his gut, Kellan hung back on the periphery, sliding into the shadows just outside the reach of the scant overhead light.

"Hi. You're Danny Marcus, right?" Moreno pressed her hands into the pockets of her jeans to give her breasts maximum lift, and bingo. She had the guy's attention, hook, line, and I-think-with-my-dick sinker.

He murmured something quick into his cell phone, stowing it in his jacket pocket a second later. "And who might you be?"

"My name is Isabella." She leaned on her accent just enough to seal the deal of Marcus's full attention, his eyes taking a slow, filthy trip over her body that made Kellan want to kick the ever-loving shit out of the guy. "I'm looking to score a little fun," she said. "Thought you could maybe help me out."

"You came to the right place, honey. Danny Marcus does know how to have a good time. How come I've never seen a pretty girl like you out here before?"

Kellan took a slow breath, holding it tight in his lungs. For as slimy as the guy was, he wasn't entirely stupid. He was fishing for something to trust.

And Moreno gave it to him, along with a smile that would inspire a hard-on for any straight man on the fucking planet. "I just moved here from Charlotte. I used to hang with Antonio Torres and some of his friends. One of his regular girls said I should come looking for you if I wanted a good time."

Recognition took a turn over Marcus's expression, and Kellan had to admit, she was working him like a pro. "Yeah, I know 'Tonio. He's alright." He paused. "What kind of pick-me-up do you need, sweetheart?"

"Mmm. What've you got?" Moreno asked, the question making Kellan's heartbeat work a little faster in his chest. This was the part of the plan they needed, the part they'd been unable to control or predict with certainty.

Leverage.

Marcus bit. "Molly, oxy, or smack. Pick your pleasure, Isabella."

"You've got heroin?" Moreno paused, pulling her bottom lip between her teeth. "How much?"

Marcus pulled a baggie from his jacket pocket, and damn, he and Moreno couldn't have gotten a better set of circumstances if they'd ordered them gift-wrapped. "I think we can work out a trade. Why don't you bring those pretty tits over here so I can get a better look? Danny Marcus will get you all set, baby."

Kellan's pulse jumped in his veins like a living, breathing, very pissed off thing. Although a primal part of him wanted to say screw it and plant his fist in Marcus's face, he forced himself to inhale, albeit barely. Matching Moreno's steps toward Marcus with noiseless forward movement of his own, he positioned himself off the path about six feet from the two of them.

Focus. Two paces to the path. Five paces to Moreno. Breathe.

"Damn, girl," Marcus said, his voice dropping in greedy approval. "You're going to look so good on your knees, earning your high."

"You want me to blow you in order to get my fix?"

Marcus laughed, the sound rubbing Kellan's nerves raw. "Unless you're up for a fuck. Danny Marcus can make it good for you, baby." He reached down to rest his hand over the fly of his overly baggy jeans. "I promise my cock is worth the smack."

Kellan's molars locked together so hard he was sure they'd self-destruct under the pressure. Even though his brain screamed at him to stand down for just a breath or two longer per the plan, he edged closer, his body bowstring tight and far past ready to act.

A fact that Isabella must have sensed somehow, because she lowered the hand closest to Kellan all the way to her side, flexing her fingers upward in a small, subtle signal of *stand down*. "There's only one teeny-tiny problem with that," she said.

Marcus laughed, holding up the bag of heroin in an obvious attempt to sway her. "Come on, honey. You don't have to be shy with Danny."

In a scissor-sharp instant, her demeanor went from coy to calculating even though nothing moved save her eyes. "Oh, I'm not shy at all. But I am a cop. Which means you and I are about to have a very different exchange than I think you had in mind."

Kellan saw Marcus make up his mind two nanoseconds before the guy tossed the baggie into the grass and lunged down the footpath, and score one for Moreno's gut. But Kellan had been ready for Marcus to jump ever since they'd put eyes on him, and he sprang out of the shadows to block Marcus's trajectory in less than two steps. Whether or not Marcus would see him and stop was a fifty-fifty, Kellan knew, and part of him begged for an excuse to tackle the guy to the asphalt. Marcus recognized the roadblock with just enough space to slow his sloppy advance, though, fear channeling his oversized running shoes in the opposite direction even though in its panic, his brain had clearly forgotten that Moreno was standing there in wait.

"Remember me?" she asked, advancing enough to box Marcus in. His fight or flight instinct was still gunning hard for choice B, and he swung one last time to try his luck on Kellan's side.

Not today, douchebag. Kellan grabbed the guy in a rough hold, spinning him to face Isabella and wrenching both of Marcus's arms behind his back as he nudged him toward the bench and the street light.

"Isabella Moreno, Remington PD." Moreno's badge glinted in a quick flash of gold before she replaced it deep in the well of her pocket. "Let's have a chat, Danny."

"I don't have anything. You don't have anything!" he half-whined, half-pleaded.

To her credit, Moreno refrained from rolling her eyes. "Really? Because I'm pretty sure that between this"—she reached into his jacket to reveal three more baggies, then three more full of pills from the other pocket—"and the heroin you tossed into the bushes there, which I will find with less than five minutes of searching and *will* have your fingerprints on it, I've got enough to call tonight Christmas fucking morning."

Marcus jerked against Kellan's grip, radiating the scent of sweat and fear. "Th-this is entrapment!" His voice lifted a register before cracking. "You propositioned me."

Kellan's pulse thrummed, but Moreno didn't budge or back down. "I told you I was looking for some fun. You're the one who offered me heroin in exchange for sex."

"Alright, alright," Marcus said, his demeanor shifting into a nervous smile. "So Danny likes to party a little. It's Friday night, baby. What's the harm?"

"The harm is that this is enough heroin and pharmaceuticals for you to 'party' with ten of your closest friends." She lifted the drugs to punctuate her point. "Between the possession and the solicitation, you're not looking at being bounced after a night in the tank, Danny."

Marcus froze, his pulse going ballistic against Kellan's grasp on his wrists. "Oh come on, beautiful. You and your partner here don't really want to wreck your night bringing me in, do you? Can't we work something out?"

"Hmm." Isabella's shoulder rose and fell. "Like the kind of 'bargain' you were just trying to sell me a minute ago? I don't think so."

"Wait, wait, wait!" Panic bled through the words, Marcus's stare wild as he threw it over their out-of-the-way spot on the footpath. "Whatever you need, I'm sure I can get it for you. Cash, party favors. Danny's good for that."

Moreno paused. "Now that you mention it, I might be open to taking some information off your hands."

"Information?" Marcus asked warily, and Isabella tipped her head toward the bench a few paces away.

"Mmm hmm," she said, waiting until Kellan had not-so-politely guided Marcus over to the bench and zip-tied the guy's wrist to the arm rest per the plan before continuing. "Word is you've been running with a big guy lately. Like a wrestler. He deals in girls and high-end parties. Ring any bells?"

"Nope. No way. Danny Marcus can get you paid or he can get you high, but he doesn't give up information like a little bitch," Marcus auto-responded, and screw this. They needed answers before this scenario went tango uniform.

Kellan stepped in, close enough to make Marcus shrink against the back of the bench. "I think you know exactly what we're talking about, just like I know you aren't going to get another chance to start sharing before Detective Moreno hauls your sorry ass out of this park with your hands zip tied behind you in front of God and everyone else. Then they'll all think you're a little bitch no matter what, and that word's gonna travel fast. You really like your odds here?"

After a second, Marcus bit out a curse, dropping his voice to a whisper even though the path still remained dark and quiet in either direction. "You don't get it, man."

"Explain it to me," Moreno said, reclaiming Marcus's attention as she moved back into the halo of golden light being cast down from overhead.

Miraculously, he did. "Operations like the one you're after are on a whole different food chain than this nickel and dime shit. Guys like Rampage are bad enough. But his boss? That dude is fucking *scary*, yo. You cross a guy like that, you end up in the dirt."

Kellan's heart beat a steady rhythm of bad things against his ribs as Isabella moved within a foot of Marcus's dance space. "All I need is a little chatter, Danny," she said, her stare never leaving his. "You and me, we're just having a conversation. Nobody's crossing anyone else, and nobody's going to know we talked. I swear it."

Whether it was her dead-serious tone or the look in her eyes that matched, Kellan would never know, but something pushed Danny to say, "There are these parties in one of the penthouse apartment suites at the Metropolitan, you know, over on the south side? Real lush, like Lifestyles of the Rich and Famous, only more tricked out. It's exclusive invite only. I had to introduce Rampage to a dozen fucking girls before he'd even think about name dropping me to his boss so I could get in to play, and I still have to pay my way in with merchandise for his guests."

"Whose does the penthouse belong to?" Moreno asked, but Marcus just huffed out a breath, twisting his hand to not-so-subtly test the strength of the zip tie keeping him anchored to the park bench.

"Beats me. I didn't ask to see the deed."

Kellan had closed half the space between his body and the bench before he'd even processed his brain's command to move. "Marcus—"

Danny's shoulders slumped into his two-sizes-too-big T-shirt, and he finally called no joy. "Look, I don't know whose place it is. But the place is full of fancy art shit and there's more security than most border patrols, so if I had to guess, I'd say it's Casa de Boss Man. Goes by Mr. DuPree. And before you ask, no, I don't know his first name."

Moreno slid a glance at Kellan, stepping forward at the exact moment he orbited back to give the area around them a spot check.

"Sounds like Mr. DuPree knows how to throw a hell of a get-together. Bet he offers his guests some nice party favors to keep them entertained." Isabella's words emerged on a thin, soft breath, but they managed to send a pang through Kellan's gut all the same.

The sensation grew teeth at Marcus's nod. "Liquor, pharmaceuticals, women. Public or private, one-on-one or four-on-one, it doesn't matter. There aren't a whole lot of house rules, but you fuck in public, DuPree gets to watch. Bonus points for banging your girl around while you do it. I don't know that from firsthand experience," he added, jerking back against the bench slats again as Kellan's fingers cranked into hot fists on a step forward. "He just makes it real clear for everybody across the board. Watching is his thing. I told you, he's goddamn creepy."

Jesus. "I'm guessing these women aren't there by choice," Kellan said, the thought souring as it crossed his lips.

Marcus shrugged, although the flicker of unease traveling through his stare canceled out the nonchalance. "I'm not dumb enough to ask any questions. They get tricked out five, maybe six times a night, and some of the guests can get kind of rough. But none of the girls ever try running for the door. I'm sure they get paid for their trouble."

"And I'm sure that's what you tell yourself so you can sleep at night," Moreno said, her stare turning subarctic.

Indignation straightened Marcus's spine. "Hey, I don't smack my ladies around unless they like it that way. I'm a lover, not a fighter."

Yup. There went the last thread of Kellan's already flimsy tolerance. "No, you're a jackass who deals heroin and pays for sex with women who are being turned out, most likely against their will."

Before Marcus could work up a protest or a response of any kind, Isabella said, "But you're going to start making up for the error of your ways. Right now."

"How's that?" Marcus asked, echoing the question in Kellan's brain. But then the look on her face registered, mouth set and eyes glittering with a brand of determination Kellan was beginning to know all too well, and his blood turned to liquid ice in his veins.

"Because, Danny. I'm going to be your date to the next party Mr. DuPree hosts."

CHAPTER TEN

"God dammit, Moreno. Are you out of your fucking mind?"

Isabella scanned the street in front of her, trying like hell and failing just as badly to trap her response between her teeth. "Perfectly sane," she said, inhaling for a count of three clack-clack-clacks of her boots over the broken pavement of Atlantic Boulevard before adding, "As I've told you, what? Four? No, five times now."

Kellan's dark and broody scowl marked him as highly doubtful of her self-assessment, not to mention highly pissed off at her new plan. "You can tell me until you're purple. I'm not going to believe you unless you change your mind about going to this party. How do you even know Marcus will hold up his end of the deal?"

She waited until they'd reached the Mustang and both slid into their respective seats before answering, but somehow, the pause did nothing to slow her irritation. "First of all, I know Marcus will show because I told him that if he doesn't, I'm going to make an anonymous nine-one-one call that will lead a veritable platoon of law enforcement officials to that penthouse, and I'll make sure every last one of the people arrested for drug possession knows he was behind the tip-off. A fact you well know because you were standing right next to me when I said it. Secondly"—she paused again, this time to spear him with a don't-mess-with-my-plan stare—"I'd be out of my fucking mind not to go to this party, Walker. It's the only way I'm going to be able to prove there's something illegal going on with these women and get the FBI to open an investigation."

"It's also dangerous as hell," he said, jamming a hand through his hair hard enough to make the dark edges stick up. "Going to this party with Marcus isn't just doing a little rogue investigating. Shit, fishing for the intel to open a formal investigation practically is its own investigation, only there won't be any other cops there to back you up. You have to tell Sinclair. Or at least tell Hollister."

Now they were back at this again. Stellar. "No. There's no way I can tell either of them. Not when I'm this close."

"You really are out of your mind! You're willing to have the cops go in like gangbusters if Marcus doesn't show, but you won't tell your partner or your boss about the potential to break this case?"

Isabella swung against the driver's seat to face him full-on. "I used that threat with Marcus because I know it'll work, not because I want to actually have to follow through." It was a calculated risk, to be sure, but with the way the scumbag had responded to the leverage she'd used to get him to talk in the first place, her gut said he was too scared of the consequences to call her bluff.

"Fine," Kellan said, turning to match her squared shoulders and lifted chin. "Even if Marcus does show, you still need to tell your partner."

A fresh pulse of frustration heated her veins. Damn it, letting Walker come with her had been a mistake from the get. It was time to end this back and forth, once and for all.

"I can't. I might have a foot in the door with this party, but everything Marcus gave up is still hearsay from a drug dealer. Unless I've got a credible witness, forensic evidence of a crime being committed, or a victim willing to make a statement, there isn't enough for an investigation. Hollister and Sinclair both know this. Sinclair already flat-out said no, and I can't risk Hollister going over my head if I confide in him. I can't go to either of them, no matter how much I want to or how badly they hate guys who do this to women too. Not without one of those three things."

Walker's arms knotted over his chest. "And which one are you looking to find at this party, exactly?"

The images from the photographs flashed up from where they'd been burned into her memory, but she kept her voice steady and sure. "A victim."

"You think you can convince one of these girls to come forward and make a statement against this DuPree guy?" he asked, and at least the surprise in his voice was a step up from the attitude he'd been sporting a minute ago.

"In this case, a victim's statement will carry more weight than anything else. If my gut is right, these women are being held against their will and forced into prostitution, and some of them might not even be eighteen. I don't know if I can convince anyone to come forward." Isabella paused, adding a silent *please, please, please* to her words before continuing out loud. "But this party is the only shot I'm going to get at a face to face with these girls, and a statement is the only shot I'm going to get at Peterson starting a formal investigation with the FBI. I have to do my best to try."

Kellan exhaled, long and low. "You do know this is crazy."

"It might be," she agreed, because as determined as she was, she also wasn't stupid. It was risky. "But I'm still going."

"Fine, but I'm not leaving your side all night."

Isabella's chin jerked up, her heart pinballing against her breastbone as she stared across the front seat at him. "That'll be a neat trick since you're going to be across town in your apartment."

"The fuck I will," Walker bit out, his dark and dangerous attitude winging back in all its glory. "If you won't listen to reason and rely on your unit, fine. Then you are stuck with the alternative. I'm going with you to that party on Friday night. If Marcus can get you in, he can get me in too."

In theory, that might not be untrue. But getting Marcus to agree to escort her to the penthouse had taken a boatload of expertly applied pressure as it was. If she altered the parameters to add Walker to the mix, Marcus would surely balk. Even if by some miracle he didn't, the last thing she needed when she was trying to get one of these girls to talk to her was an overly nervous drug dealer on one arm and an overly furious firefighter on the other.

"No, you're not," she said, mind made up. "I'll have enough to worry about without having to keep track of you."

"We've been over this, Moreno. I can keep track of myself just fine. Plus, I can help you get what you need. You've gotta admit, we did okay having each other's backs and giving Marcus the good cop, bad cop treatment."

Oh, it was official. Walker's faculties were on a complete walkabout. "How about good cop, you're not a cop?" Isabella said, anger and heat and dread uncurling like streamers in her belly. "I shouldn't have even taken you with me tonight."

"But you did." He leaned over the console, his mouth only a few inches from hers as his voice dropped to one notch above a whisper. "You did. And whether you like it or not, now you're stuck with me having your back."

Isabella drew a surprised breath at the same moment Kellan exhaled, warming the slight space between them. There was something odd and unexpectedly intimate about breathing him into her body, and for a hot, impulsive second, she wanted nothing more than to close the distance to discover if that ridiculously sexy mouth of his tasted as good as it looked. A tilt of her chin would get her halfway there, a small push forward doing the rest to put her lips on

Walker's to answer the curiosity rising up in her chest like a tide. Isabella knew he'd let her. The way he'd just shuttered his focus from her eyes to her mouth said so, and oh God—oh God—for as crazy as Walker drove her, how the hell could she want him so badly at the same time?

Whether you like it or not, now you're stuck with me having your back…stuck with me…

"No." Isabella jerked back, cursing her idiot impulses with all her might. Was she insane, letting him get so close even for a second? "No," she said again, locking her molars into place over the word. "You're absolutely not going with me."

Walker gave up a slow blink before his expression hardened back to its sharp angles and unyielding lines. "Isabella—"

She didn't think. Just spoke. "I heard you, and I get that you think me going to this party is too dangerous for me to do by myself. I really do. But it's far more dangerous for me to take you with me, so the answer is no. I'm not arguing with you, and I'm not budging," she added, each slam of her heart hammering her certainty farther into place. "And if that means you tell Hollister, or Sinclair, or hell, your favorite reporter at the *Remington Sun Times*, then I guess I'll have to live with the fallout. But I am not, under any circumstances, taking you to that party. Are we clear?"

Thump-thump. *Please stand down.* Thump-thump. *Please let me do my job and help these women.* Thump-thump.

Please don't get close.

Walker reached for his seatbelt, his stare as cold as his tone as he said, "If you're so bound and determined to get in over your head with nobody to back you up, then I guess I can't stop you."

* * *

Isabella looked at the five-inch stack of paperwork at her elbow, and seriously, how had all her police reports become a mini Mount Everest in the span of only half a work week?

Maybe because you're trying to juggle your regular cases with getting prepped for this illegal drugs/forced prostitution/bad-man-doing-very-bad-things party you're not supposed to be going to in T-minus forty-eight hours, and oh by the way, don't forget trying to forget the galactically furious firefighter you haven't heard a single peep from since you dropped him off at his car five nights ago.

Well. At least that explained the size of her backlog.

"Burning the midnight oil, huh Moreno?"

The sound of Sinclair's voice coming from the entryway to his office bumped Isabella back to the reality of the precinct, and she worked up a smile as she tamped down her thoughts. "Nah. It's only"—she paused to throw a glance at the clock on the wall beside her, doing her best to keep her surprise to herself, because damn, when had it gotten so late?—"ten-thirty. Plus, you're still here."

"That's because I live here." He ran a hand over his crew cut with a smile even though Isabella knew he was only thirty percent kidding. Sinclair had been divorced three times over, and his daughter, January, was only five years younger than Isabella herself. He might have an apartment a hop-skip away from the police station, but he was as much of a fixture in the Thirty-Third as the handcuffs and holding cells. Not that she was too far behind.

"Everyone else took off for the Crooked Angel a good three hours ago," Sinclair continued, leaning one shoulder against the doorframe leading to his office. "You didn't feel like taking a breather too?"

"And miss out on all this glamour?" She pointed to Mount McPaperwork. "Not a chance."

"Ah. Well, I got the final report from the fire marshal on that blaze over on Glendale earlier today."

Isabella's pulse tripped, but she managed a nice, steady, "Did you?" in reply. Although she'd given the women in the photos no less than a thousand thoughts over the last five days, she'd been meticulous about avoiding mention of the case that wasn't a case (yet) with Sinclair. The more she kept off the table, the less she had to swerve around.

Not to mention, the less he had to suspect.

"Mmm." Pushing off the industrial gray doorframe, Sinclair crossed the room and pulled out the spare chair next to her desk. The metal feet scraped over the linoleum as he turned the thing around backwards and sat down, his eyes never leaving her face. "The cause of the fire was bad electrical, just like Bridges said. The fire marshal ruled it an accident and condemned the house, so the insurance adjusters and the property owner will take things from here. Thought you'd want to know."

Surprise lifted her brows. "And what makes you think that?"

"Because you've had the evidence box containing the photos, the rope, and the jewelry under your desk for the last week even though the FBI passed on opening an investigation."

Well shit. Of all the clutter on all the desks in the thousand-square-foot office space allotted to intelligence, her boss just had to have eagle eyes for the one thing she'd hoped no one would notice. God, she was going to have to play this just right in order to reroute Sinclair's attention.

Isabella pushed back from her desk, her chair sounding off in a geriatric squeal as she threw a haphazard glance at the box in question. "Oh, yeah. Guess I forgot to bring it back downstairs to the evidence locker after I worked up that report for Peterson last week."

Again, Sinclair's gaze didn't move. "You want to try again, only without the bullshit this time?"

She forced herself not to react despite the all-out rampage of her heartbeat in her chest. If she dodged the topic completely now that he'd thrown it front and center, every last one of Sinclair's red flags would start waving in the wind, and anyway, as much as she didn't want him to know she'd been doing some personally motivated freelancing, she didn't want to dodge the topic at all.

"Fine. I know Peterson passed, but I still think there's a

case here. Something about these photos…" Isabella dropped her stare to the box again, to the plain, ordinary white cardboard that held the suggestion of terrible things, and something twisted deep inside of her. "I get that there's only circumstantial evidence to go on right now. But I'm telling you. Someone is hurting these women."

"We've been over this," Sinclair said, not unkindly. "If there was anything solid to go on, we'd investigate."

"I know." For a second, Isabella itched to tell him what she'd learned last Friday night from Carmen and Danny Marcus. She hadn't been planning on keeping the truth from Sinclair forever anyway—the whole point in trying to turn up a useable lead was so she *could* tell him, and then he could tell Peterson. Sinclair would be pissed that she'd fractured the rules to nail down the intel, she knew. But he'd been pissed at her before, just like she'd worked cases outside of intelligence before. If it got them the proof they needed to help these women, Isabella would take the fallout.

And if she told Sinclair about the party before she got said proof, he just might pull the plug on her recon mission, which meant she had no choice but to ask for forgiveness later than permission in the here and now.

"I get it," she said, biting her tongue so she wouldn't add that while she understood the technicalities, she also thought they sucked. "There are only so many cases we can pursue, and without concrete evidence, this one is a shot in the dark."

"Listen, Moreno." Sinclair paused, the edge that normally filled his blue-gray stare suspiciously absent. "I know calls like these are tough for you."

"They're tough for all of us." She'd never met a cop who didn't get jacked up over a case every now and then, particularly when the details were brutal.

But Sinclair didn't let up. "Yes, but they're particularly tough for you. I just don't want us passing on this investigation to turn into a banana peel for you."

"I'm sorry," Isabella said, her confusion and shock

merging together to form a great, big tangle of what the fuck. "I'm not really sure what that means."

Lifting a hand, Sinclair gestured around the intelligence office, all the desks still and empty and dark except for hers. "It's ten-thirty on a Wednesday night, and here you are working."

"You're not really going to rattle my trap because I'm doing my job, are you?" Isabella let go of a soft laugh in an effort to lighten the tension thickening the air, but Sinclair didn't laugh back, or hell, even slow down.

"Actually, I am. You were here last night at the same time. Night before that, too. You've been triple-timing it for months."

"I have cases, Sam." They'd caught a brutal assault/robbery just this morning that she'd spent four hours doing background on while Maxwell and Hale had taken statements and worked with CSI.

"So do the rest of your team, and they manage not to live here." Sinclair leaned forward over the metal backrest of the chair, and hell, Isabella hated every shred of the honesty she saw in his eyes. "Look, you're dedicated as hell, and you're a great detective. Fierce. Smart. But you take on a lot, and you hold a lot in. I'll be honest. Sometimes I worry."

Her chin hiked along with her pulse. "Are you questioning whether or not I can do my job?"

"No. I'm questioning whether or not you're okay after you do your job. With everything that happened to Marisol, it's understandable—"

She held up a hand to put a quick end to the subject. "What happened to Marisol was a long time ago, Sam."

"What happened to Marisol was a tragedy," he corrected. "Eleven years ago or not, it's understandable that things like those photos might upset you."

Isabella nearly laughed at the irony. She wasn't upset. She couldn't be upset. There were too many cases that needed to be solved, too many victims who needed help for her to let her emotions get in the way of anything other than her job. "I appreciate the concern, but really, I'm fine."

The edges of Sinclair's mouth lowered in a frown that said he was unconvinced. "Your cousin was kidnapped, Isabella. She was sexually assaulted and murdered, and the case was never solved."

"I know exactly what happened to her," Isabella snapped, her breath tightening her throat upon exit. God, she would give anything not to know, to un-hear the details and un-see the photos that were there every single time she closed her eyes, even just to blink.

"And I know you're not fine." Sinclair straightened, sending his gaze over her paper-strewn desk. "You're working seventy, sometimes eighty hours a week."

"So I don't mind the overtime. I like my job."

"No," he argued. "You're in love with your job."

Her patience slipped another notch. "And what's so wrong with that?"

"No matter how good you are or how many cases you solve, this job is never going to love you back. And it's sure as hell not going to *have* your back unless you start trusting the people around you."

The words forced the air from her lungs, stunning her into place behind her desk as Sinclair continued.

"You volunteer for extra cases outside of the unit." Up went one hand, ticking off each point, finger by finger. "You've never turned down overtime. Not even on Christmas. You're at the precinct when your partners are blowing off steam together, and even on the rare occasion you do go to the Crooked Angel with them, you're always a step removed—even with Hollister, and he's your partner. You think I don't see that? That the rest of the unit doesn't see it too? Hell, they don't even know about Marisol. They don't know a damned thing about you."

Isabella's shoulders met the back of her chair with a soft thump. "I'm private with everyone. It's not personal."

"Except this job is personal," Sinclair said. "We do more

than just punch the clock together. We have to trust each other in life and death situations every day. You keep Maxwell, Hale, Hollister, and Capelli at arm's length, and they feel it."

"So, what?" She managed to push the question past the shock bursting through her chest, but only just. "You think they don't trust me?"

"No, Isabella." Sinclair shook his head. "I think you don't trust them."

The words sent a good, sharp kick all the way through her, and oh, it hurt. But her defenses swiftly locked down over the ache, covering it up with the reminder of why she could not, under any circumstances, let her partners, her boss, or anyone else get too close. If they got close, Isabella would care about them, and they would care about her in return.

And the last person who'd been close, who'd cared for her and trusted her, had been tortured and murdered, lost in the blink of an eye even though the pain would last until she took her dying breath.

Going through that again wasn't an option.

Which meant letting anyone in—letting them close enough to really know her, to know them in return—simply couldn't happen.

Folding her hands over the forms on her desk, she tucked her shoulders in tight and opened her mouth to kill this conversation, once and for all. "If I didn't trust the people in this unit, I wouldn't so much as direct traffic with any of them. Just because I don't want to sit around the campfire and share all my feelings and hug it out with my partners doesn't mean I don't trust them, or that I'm not a good cop."

Just like that, the chilly edges of Sinclair's stare came winging back as he pushed himself out of the chair to stand in front of her, his stance just as unyielding as her own.

"It doesn't mean you're okay, either. Now do me a favor and go home. And take that box back to the evidence locker on your way out."

* * *

Isabella took a deep breath of crisp nighttime air, sending a glance over the shadowed city block in front of her. The four-inch heels she'd had to buy specifically for this party pinched at her toes, but she anchored them into place on the sidewalk. Using her throwaway cell phone as a guise, she did a covert scan of her surroundings while she pretended to check her voicemail messages.

No people on either side of the street. No suspicious sounds raising her hackles.

Nothing standing between her and the intel she needed except for two city blocks and the word of a drug-dealing john.

Isabella tucked her cell phone into the miniscule clutch designed to hold it and little else, forcing her feet into a steady stride. She'd quadruple-checked her reflection in the tiny pop-down mirror on the Mustang's visor, the gold-tinged light doing damn little to soften the smoky gray eyeliner and shimmery copper-colored lipstick that had taken her far too much time and energy to apply. Everything was in place, from her micro-mini halter dress to the small but lethal two-inch ceramic blade she'd tucked behind the lining of the belt around her waist. She had to admit, she'd been a little surprised not to have gotten a last-minute "you're not still thinking of doing this, are you?" phone call from Kellan. But since she also hadn't gotten a last-minute "get your ass in my office right now" demand from Sinclair, Isabella had to assume Walker had washed his hands of both her and her recon mission.

Which was really for the best, because between the reluctant drug dealer she was going to have to rely on and the high-level security she was going to have to get past in order to talk to one of these girls, she had one hell of a task in front of her tonight.

Isabella's heels clipped out a smooth rhythm over the concrete as she walked the pair of city blocks to her meet-up spot with Marcus. Although she had come up with an airtight plan before she'd even cut him loose from his park bench last Friday night, there were still variables that couldn't be predicted, the first of which was whether or not he'd make good on his end of the deal. Just because she'd promised Marcus she wouldn't sleep, eat, or stop relentlessly searching for him in addition to making that nine-one-one call if he ditched her didn't mean he'd actually do the smart thing and show up.

The sight of him standing beneath the street light across from the glittering high rise of the Metropolitan was enough to make her pulse pitch with relief.

"Marcus." Isabella kept her voice utterly neutral, her first cover-up of what would probably be hundreds tonight. "Good of you to show."

"Damn, girl." Danny's brows shot up, an appreciative leer mixing in with the unease that lurked in his expression. "You look—"

"Don't finish that sentence," she said, stabbing an index finger at him to hammer the point all the way into place. "Because then I will have to harm you, and as much as the idea has its merits on some level, I need you to get me into this party. Speaking of which"—she softened her words, trying on the coy smile from her bag of distraction tricks— "You need to relax. Nothing sends off warning flares like a jumpy drug dealer."

Marcus jammed his hands into the pockets of his dress pants and sent a withering frown in her direction. "Coulda mentioned that last fucking week before I ended up zip-tied to a park bench."

"And ruin all the fun? Not a chance. You remember the drill?"

"Yeah," he mumbled, but they had zero margin for error.

So she said, "Run it through for me one more time, just

for grins."

"Same story you gave Danny last Friday night," he said, and okay, at least he was relaxing enough to keep with his usual personal quirks. "You moved here from Charlotte and we hooked up in the park a couple of weeks ago. You like to party and you're looking for a girl to spice things up, so I invited you upstairs to find you a good time."

Isabella nodded her approval, a wisp of hair breaking free from the loose up-do she'd pinned to the crown of her head. "Once you get me in the door, we can part ways. It'll be less distracting for both of us, and easier for me to slip out once I get what I'm looking for. But Danny." She leaned in to look at him. "Don't do anything you're going to regret."

"Danny Marcus ain't stupid, baby." He focused his stare on the halo of streetlight at their feet for just a split second before lifting his chin to look Isabella in the eye. "I don't take you upstairs, you haul me to the clink along with everyone in that penthouse. But if I tell anyone I breathed a word of this to a cop, let alone brought one all the way upstairs with me, Mr. DuPree will lose his shit, and...well, there's worse things that could happen to Danny Marcus than prison."

God, he so wasn't wrong, and wasn't that all the more reason to get up to that penthouse, stat. "No one's going to find out I'm a cop, Marcus. This whole thing is going to play out just like we planned. Now let's go."

Isabella smoothed a hand over her skirt and crossed the street, making sure Marcus remained relaxed and right by her side as they made their way to the Metropolitan's front entrance by way of the neatly paved sidewalk. Taking one last deep breath, she smiled at the uniformed doorman as he pulled open the gleaming, brass-handled door leading into the lobby.

And found herself face to stormy blue stare with Kellan Walker.

CHAPTER ELEVEN

Kellan had known that as soon as Isabella saw him standing there on the Italian marble floor tiles of the Metropolitan's lushly appointed two-story lobby, she was going to be mad enough to spit fire. What he hadn't counted on, however, was that she would look so ridiculously hot that he'd lose the element of surprise to the independent thinking of his dick.

Moreno strode over to him, her heels working up a riot of sound that echoed off the frescoed ceilings of the lobby. "What the hell are you doing here?" she hissed, and although she'd dropped the words into the tight sliver of space between their bodies to keep them private, the anger bleeding through her tone hit him like a shout.

Focus. Breathe. "Is that any way to greet your date?" Kellan asked, pairing the question with a smile in an effort to take the edge off her supreme irritation.

If his tactic worked, it was only by the tiniest margin. "Marcus is my date," Isabella said. Kellan knew she wasn't going to like what came next, but truly, she'd given him no choice.

"Not anymore."

Realization had her chocolate-colored eyes springing wide. "Oh my God, you're *serious*."

He nodded, spinning a lightning-fast glance around the lobby to make sure the elegant space was still empty of anyone other than Marcus, who was still a few steps behind them and just out of earshot. "I'm afraid so."

"You aren't going upstairs with me, Walker. This isn't up for debate." She flashed a quick give-me-a-second look at Marcus—who had remained impressively reaction-free at the obvious monkey wrench Kellan had just tossed into the party-of-two plan—linking her arm through Kellan's to lead him farther into the lobby. To anyone passing by, they might look like a couple meeting up for a late-night outing to a bar or an upscale club, her game face was that good. But Kellan could feel the tension in Moreno's body all the way through his suit jacket and shirt sleeve, which meant he had to proceed with extreme caution if he wanted to get anywhere with her.

But he still wasn't backing down on the truth. She wasn't going upstairs without someone on her hip.

And if that someone had to be him, then so be it.

"You're absolutely right," Kellan said, murmuring quietly in her ear as they pretended to admire an ornately framed painting on the lobby wall. "It's not up for debate. I'm here, and I want to help you. You're taking me upstairs as your date."

"You knew," she whispered, understanding parting her lips into a tawny O even though her gaze never left the painting. "You knew this whole time that you were going to show up tonight and give me no choice but to take you to this party, didn't you?"

Kellan nodded. No point in lying, and even if he did, she'd only call him out and get even madder. Not necessarily in that order. "Coming up with your plan right in front of me before you cut Marcus loose last Friday probably wasn't your best move," he admitted. Before she could jump in with a renewed protest, he tacked on, "Yes, this has been my plan all week, and yes, I knew you'd be this pissed off. But I also know there are a lot of things in that penthouse that you can't control, and tonight is your only shot to get what you're looking for. Let me help you, Moreno."

She didn't agree, but she didn't balk out loud either, so he took the momentary win and continued.

"This is no different than the other night in the park. I know how to work recon, and I want to help you help those girls. Just trust me to do that, okay? Just trust me to have your back for tonight."

For a minute, she said nothing. Then the minute slid into another, then another, Kellan's heart beating faster and faster against his sternum until finally, Isabella turned toward him.

"Listen to me very carefully." Her fingers moved softly over his chest, stopping to straighten the black wool of his suit jacket in an oddly intimate gesture. "Nothing about the plan changes, except now you and I are a couple who want a third for a good time. Danny will get us in the door, and you'll follow my lead to the letter. Do you understand?"

The vise-like grip on his lungs released on a completely silent exhale. "I do," he said, but Moreno's hands didn't budge.

"Be sure you can do this. Because once we get into that elevator, there's no going back."

He didn't hesitate. "I'm sure, Isabella."

"Good. And Walker?" Although a smile played on her lips, her words arrived on a dead-serious promise. "Don't think that just because I agreed to this, I'm not furious with you. When we get out of here, you and I are going to have an argument you won't win."

Without so much as a blink, she lowered her hands from his slamming chest, looping her arm through the bend in his elbow and walking back toward the spot where Marcus had been waiting just a few paces away.

"Slight change in plans," Moreno said. She fixed Marcus with a stunner of a smile, likely to water down any panic that might go with the news, and man, she was good. But where her smile was concerned, Kellan had seen the genuine product, and as subtle as the difference was, this one was just the slightest bit off from the unfettered expression she'd given up the other night at the Crooked Angel.

"What do you mean, a change in plans?" Marcus darted a glance from Isabella to Kellan, but she stepped in closer, recovering his attention in one long-legged swoop.

"Relax, Danny. I'm just your friend looking for a good time, remember? Only now, my boyfriend wants to watch."

Kellan sucked in an involuntary breath. But he'd promised to follow her lead to the letter and they had to get over the threshold somehow, so he nodded and said, "I'm sure that's not an unusual request for a party like this, is it, Danny? No big deal for a boyfriend to watch."

The point seemed to hit its mark. Thank fuck. "Oh. Well, there aren't usually a lot of women at these parties other than the ones working for DuPree, but yeah. Most of the clients do like to watch," Marcus agreed, his shoulders loosening from around the collar of his dress shirt. "I guess it won't be any different to sell it with two of you. But I can still, uh, go, though, right? As soon as you two get past the door, Danny Marcus is done?"

"Like I said. Everything else stands." Isabella shifted back on one glossy black high heel, gesturing toward the bank of mirror-paneled elevators behind them. "Now what do you say we get to work?"

Marcus nodded, his black curls springing up and down. "Alright, yeah. Let's get this over with."

Leading the way to the elevators, Marcus pulled an electronic key card from his back pocket and inserted it into the slot above the elevator control buttons. At Isabella's raised brows, he said, "The code to get up to the penthouse level changes every week, and there's a new key for each party. They're couriered to people who have been approved for the guest list to keep things exclusive."

Now it was Kellan's turn to send his brows on a one-way trip up. "Nice security."

"Yeah. Just wait."

A soft ding signaled the elevator's arrival seconds later, and the three of them stepped onto the empty car. The space was lined with black lacquered paneling from the waist down and mirrors the rest of the way up, and didn't that just offer about a thousand opportunities for security cameras. From here on in, they were going to have to assume they were being watched.

A fact that wasn't lost on Isabella, apparently. Tightening her grasp on his arm, she leaned in toward him. The curve of her breast brushed over the outside of his biceps, sending a bolt of want deep between his legs, and hell, this was going to take all the restraint on the goddamn planet.

But Kellan steeled himself against her touch. The whole thing was for show, and there was no denying the anger-fueled tension still thrumming through her body. He'd promised Moreno he could stay on the level and do whatever it took to help her.

There was no turning back now. No room for error or impulse or emotion of any kind.

Focus. Thirty-eighth floor. Thirty-nine. Forty. Breathe.

On another muted chime, the elevator doors slid open to reveal a small alcove leading to a set of intricately carved double doors. The stark white walls were offset by the glow spilling down from regularly spaced sleek gold light fixtures that Kellan recognized as more places for cameras to hide, but being watched seemed the least of their worries since the path to the doors was being blocked by the biggest man he'd ever seen.

And between the three years he'd spent with the fire department and the seven he'd clocked in the Army, that was fucking *saying* something. But as daunting as the roadblock was, this had to be their wrestler guy, which meant they were on the right track. Provided they could get past him, anyway.

Marcus took point, probably in an effort to rip off the

Band-Aid of getting everybody over the threshold as promised to save his skinny ass. "Hey, Rampage! How you been?"

The guy didn't move a millimeter from his post in front of the doors leading into the penthouse as he gave Marcus a slow, flat stare. "Missed you last week, Danny Boy. Mr. DuPree's parties starting to bore you?"

"Oh. Ah, of course not." He stiffened, and Kellan's gut slid south. At least the dirtbag was quick on the upswing. "Sorry I missed out," Marcus said, his smile turning appropriately sleazy as he turned toward Moreno. "I was spending a little time with my girl Isabella, here. She and her boyfriend like to party, and they're looking for a pretty young thing to keep them company. Thought I'd bring them along tonight. Show 'em a good time."

Thankfully, the human boulder didn't seem to notice Marcus's hiccup. "Hmm." Rampage's beady stare slithered over Isabella, making Kellan grind his molars hard enough to test their integrity. "We don't get a lot of chicks looking to join in. Girl on girl is pretty fucking hot." He didn't even bother with subtlety as his gaze lingered on Moreno's breasts. "But she and her boyfriend aren't on the list."

Marcus's eyes flared, although only for a second. "They're cool, man. Looking for Mr. DuPree's kind of fun, you know what I mean? Would Danny Marcus steer you wrong?" he asked with a smile, but Rampage's bulldog status remained unchanged.

"They're still not on the list."

Isabella unwound her arm from Kellan's, her hips swaying provocatively as she stepped around Marcus on her shiny black stilettos. "Okay, Rampage. It is Rampage, right?" She pulled just enough of her bottom lip between her teeth to make Kellan's pulse spike, and Jesus, he didn't know which he wanted more—to kiss her or kill her. "My boyfriend and I really want to play. What do we need to do to get on the list?"

Rampage's stare stayed fixed on her mouth for a full

three seconds before he answered. "Mr. DuPree has a strict no-hands rule, so unfortunately, you can't earn your way in with me. But if you want a taste of what his parties offer, you're still going to have to show me you want it."

The protest burned on Kellan's tongue, but Moreno's catlike smile kept the guy's attention. "What'd you have in mind?"

"You said you came to play, right?" His upper lip lifted in a filthy leer, but Moreno held steady.

Her fingers tightened ever so slightly over Kellan's forearm as if to say easy. "Among other things."

"Then prove it," Rampage said, jerking his brick-end chin at Marcus. "Put your mouth on him. I'll even let you pick your spot, but you'd better make it good."

Kellan's composure slammed to a complete halt. The heavy bassline of some song thumped from behind the doors, lifting the hair on the back of his neck and pulsing along with the white-hot anger in his veins.

"No." The protest was out before he could trap it between his teeth, making Marcus flinch and Rampage take a step forward. But Isabella slipped into the hairsbreadth of testosterone-soaked space between all three of them, flattening one palm over Kellan's chest as she turned to face Rampage.

"My boyfriend's just a little territorial when it comes to other men, but don't worry," Isabella said. "If proof is what you're after, I can show you how bad I want it."

Before Kellan could speak or move or even think, her mouth was on his.

For a split second, he was paralyzed, too thrown by surprise to respond. But then the feel of Isabella's lips, hungry and insistent, registered all at once, and Kellan lost all thought, answering instead with pure, raw instinct.

Cupping her chin with a single hand, he spread his fingers over one side of her face while his thumb found the other, anchoring her mouth under his. He pushed past her lips without pleasantries, coaxing her mouth open with his hand and his tongue. She opened for him readily, letting him delve deep again and again until—*fuck*—a moan drifted up from her chest, vibrating a path from his lips all the way to his cock.

Rather than giving in and letting him keep the lead he'd claimed, though, Isabella began to meet the brash invasion of his tongue with pressure of her own. Hot fists formed over his jacket right where his shoulders met his arms, pulling their bodies into a full-frontal connection that did nothing to slow the blind, reckless need building in Kellan's gut.

Faster. Harder. More.

Now.

Another greedy sweep of Isabella's tongue was all it took to break him. Crushing his chest against hers, he thrust roughly into the cradle of her hips, impulse daring him not to stop until he'd yanked her dress up and her panties down, burying his cock in the warm, wet heat of her pussy. He broke from her mouth just long enough to reach for the hem of her dress, and the sight of her through his shuttered eyes forced a moan past his lips.

Back arched. Nipples tight and hard, pressing provocatively against the thin red fabric covering them. Mouth parted in wordless desire with heat in her stare to match.

Holy shit. Isabella genuinely wanted him. As badly as he wanted her.

And he'd been two seconds away from doing his level best to make her come in public.

The thought brought him smashing back to the alcove, to the reality of what he'd been doing—to the even harsher reality of what he'd almost done—and Jesus Christ, was he out of his goddamn mind?

Kellan froze. He took a swift step back, his body sending up a primal and thoroughly pissed what the fuck? to his brain. But as much as the kiss had shredded every last ounce of his control, he couldn't blow their cover, which meant he damn sure couldn't look at Isabella.

Jam these feelings into a box, Walker. Right. Now.

Shifting forward to remove her from his line of sight, Kellan reached up to swipe his thumb over his bottom lip, lifting his eyes to level Rampage with an emotionless stare.

"Good enough for you?" he asked, the smudge of Isabella's coppery lipstick glittering on his hand in the soft light.

Rampage lifted his chin just once, but it was enough. "Never seen a pair of undercover cops do that." After scanning all three of them with a handheld metal detector and checking the contents of Isabella's purse, he added, "Enjoy the party."

He entered a code on the keypad set discretely on the wall beside the double doors, fitting an electronic card identical to the one Marcus had used for elevator access into the adjacent slot. The locks sounded off in a heavy click that sent relief spiraling through Kellan's veins, and he waited until both Isabella and Marcus had crossed the threshold before moving past Rampage to step into the penthouse.

The music that had only been indistinct sound in the alcove became clearer, albeit not overwhelmingly loud, filling the space of the foyer and two living rooms in front of them with a background of seductive suggestion. Lavish didn't begin to cover the décor—twelve-foot ceilings with inlaid crown molding, marble pillars delineating the rooms while keeping the space wide open, soft lighting focused on the gilt-framed art and the expertly placed sculpture throughout. Well-dressed couples and small groups of guests dotted the shadowed corners and lushly upholstered furniture, and Kellan realized with a start that the man in the leather armchair less than ten paces away was cutting cocaine over a small mirror just as easily as he might channel surf, while the man across from him received an overly enthusiastic blow job from a woman in a gold-sequined dress.

They were definitely not in Kansas anymore, Toto.

"Danny Marcus made good on his end," Marcus said quietly, his eyes nowhere near Kellan or Isabella, and she nodded in reply.

"You did. The two of us can find a friend from here. Just remember not to do anything stupid."

Marcus's laugh carried zero humor. "You either, sweet cheeks. I'm not looking to leave this party in a body bag. Have a nice life."

Turning on his heel, Marcus made a beeline for the farthest spot from where Kellan and Moreno stood by the entryway, and finally, Kellan chanced a full glance in her direction. Her expression was impassive, as if she stood smack in the middle of illegal sex parties all the time, but a provocative flush still rode her cheeks, her kiss-swollen lips betraying her ease by just a fraction. The careful sweep of her eyes told him she was taking in ten times more than her face let on, though, just as he'd done the second they'd stepped into the room. While he didn't want to blow his focus—or hers—he wanted her pissed off even less, so yeah. Time to bite the bullet.

He leaned toward her, dialing his voice to a low murmur that only she could hear. "Are we good?"

Isabella tilted her head. The scent of coconuts hit him with an unexpected punch that damn near answered his side of the question with a big, fat, fucking negative.

But then she said, "Of course. Why wouldn't we be?"

Her answer held no drama, no anger or passion or anything other than straight-up nothing much. But just as he'd seen the authentic version of her smile last week versus the almost-there version she'd been handing out tonight, Kellan had seen the pared-down desire on Isabella's face when he'd kissed her. Her want had been the real deal, just like his.

"Because I kissed you," Kellan said, and Moreno shocked the hell out of him by replying with a soft laugh.

"Actually, if you want to get technical about things, I kissed you and you kissed me back."

Only this woman would argue semantics in order to claim the upper hand at a sex party. "You're splitting hairs, don't you think?"

"Maybe," she said, pressing up to bring her lips level with his ear and getting as close as possible without actually touching him, and even though it made him a top-shelf bastard, Kellan enjoyed every second of the game.

Moreno continued, her teasing smile curving right below his jawline. "But there's no sense in making a big deal where there isn't one. We did what we had to in order to get in the door, and I don't regret that for a second. Do you?"

Kellan blinked back round two of his surprise—Christ, her tenacity knew no bounds—but he answered in truth. "No. I don't."

"Good." Isabella paused, her mouth remaining close enough that he could feel the warmth of her exhale before she shifted back to slide her arm through his and led him farther into the room. "Now do me a favor and tell me what you see."

Damn. Kellan couldn't tell if he should be a little impressed or a lot turned on by her fierce dedication, but since neither feeling would get them what they'd come for, he leaned in toward her while surreptitiously re-scanning the room.

"Well, Marcus wasn't kidding about security," he said, sliding the words quietly under his breath as he poured a glass of scotch from the self-serve bar that he had no intention of drinking. "I have eyes on two video cameras here in the foyer, two more in each living room, which means there are probably twice as many I don't see yet."

Mirror cams and similar garden variety "hidden" surveillance devices were easy enough to spot with a quick glance if you knew what you were looking for. The higher tech stuff…well, that was a whole different ball game. But Kellan had tagged along on enough here-and-there jobs with Devon lately to be able to pick up on the surveillance devices most people couldn't.

Spinning another slow gaze over the lush settees, the crystal tumblers glinting from the corners of the low, sleek tables, and the men dressed in suits that probably cost more than he earned fighting a month's worth of fires, Kellan continued in hushed tones. "Between the music and the size of these rooms, general audio's got to be a no-go, unless this DuPree guy has got access to some high-level tech I haven't heard of yet."

"Mmm. Whoever he is, he definitely likes to watch. You see anybody you like as being him?" Moreno leaned in on the guise of nuzzling Kellan's neck, and he reminded himself—and his dick—that in order to pull this off, they not only had to look like a couple, but they had to be convincing. Especially if someone had the ability to put a visual on them from one of at least six angles.

"Nope. Everyone I've got eyes on looks like a guest or a woman." He channeled his want into a dark smile that would look like a proposition to anyone monitoring the feed from the camera on his left, dropping his mouth just low enough toward Isabella to draw cover on the off chance one of the security staff could read lips. "So how do you want to play this?"

"As quickly as possible without rushing." Moreno's glance lingered on the ten scantily clad women in the room, two of whom were on their knees and another two who appeared so strung out, they were barely standing upright on their five-inch heels. Jesus.

Isabella's breath grew shaky against his skin, but both her expression and her tone betrayed nothing as she continued. "We have to choose the right girl. If we pick someone too skittish, or worse yet, too far gone, she might tell DuPree someone's sniffing around. That'll make him more cautious and a lot harder to catch, not to mention burning the only chance we have to get the proof of what's going on here."

"Copy that." Kellan fought the anger starting to churn in his belly, focusing instead on the feel of Isabella's arm folded closely in the crook of his elbow. "How about the one in the blue dress over there by the piano?"

Moreno led him a handful of steps farther into the main room, perching on the armrest of a richly upholstered wingback chair that gave her a better vantage point to study the blond. "Looks like she's already got company," Isabella said, her expression tightening as a dark-haired man with a nasty scar on his forehead walked over to the woman and passed over a syringe before placing a sharp slap on her ass.

Kellan's fingers curled into fists. Damn it, they couldn't help these women fast enough. "The redhead at four o'clock looks pretty unsteady on her feet, but we might be able to try our luck with her."

All at once, Moreno's body went bowstring tight, her spine unfolding against the gold brocade of the armchair. "That girl," she whispered, her eyes unmoving. "In the white dress, with the feathers tattooed on her shoulder. She's the one."

He waited six painfully long heartbeats before letting his gaze follow hers. The dark-haired woman—Christ, even in her low-cut dress and heavy makeup, she didn't look more than seventeen—stood by herself by a tall potted palm, clearly trying to use the leafy fronds as cover. Turned in profile, Kellan could see the edges of an intricate tattoo scrolling over the back of her thin, bare shoulder, cascading out of view beneath the strap of her dress. Her lower lip seemed to have found a permanent home between her teeth, giving away her hesitation despite the openness of nearly everyone else in the room.

Of all the women at the party, she looked the most out of place, both scared and comparatively sober. Still, if she was too scared, she'd never talk to them. "Are you sure?" he asked.

"Absolutely. That's her. That's our girl."

Isabella looked up at him, her pretty brown eyes brimming with so much certainty that Kellan trusted his gut by trusting hers.

"Okay," he said. "Do what you need to. I'll follow your lead."

CHAPTER TWELVE

Julian had seen the woman in the red dress the second she'd stepped off the elevator outside the main doors of the penthouse. He'd been sitting in his private quarters in the security room, in the exact spot he occupied still, when he'd caught sight of her and her companions on the surveillance monitor for the main entrance. Under normal circumstances, Julian would have punished Charles severely for allowing in two guests who hadn't been vetted. The word of that degenerate drug dealer with the penchant for the cheapest and most strung out whores on Julian's payroll was less than worthless, the man's tendency to lie back like a lazy pig while these women serviced him—usually in seven minutes or less, start to finish—equally so. These women were meant to be used, to be violated until they begged for an end and then fucked even harder for their weakness. Yet Danny Marcus was one of Julian's few clients too soft to show these repulsive females what they deserved.

Julian swallowed hard, straightening his French silk tie over the disgust in his throat. Like everyone else, Marcus served a purpose. He was a somewhat reliable source for bringing in new, albeit low-end, merchandise, and for

151

supplying the girls with the heroin that kept them so dependent, they'd do anything for their next fix. That was the sole reason that Julian allowed the wretched man to attend his exclusive gatherings.

And it was definitely why he didn't have Marcus beaten into a bloody carpet stain for arrogantly bringing not one, but two guests with him tonight.

The woman in the red dress was striking.

She had a fire about her—the defiant lift of that chin, the quiet strength in the way she carried herself. She'd manipulated Charles easily, and hadn't been ashamed to show her base desire for her companion in public, just as the rest of his guests did. She had spirit, this woman.

And that made Julian want to break her.

"The woman in the red dress who accompanied Mr. Marcus," he said, the glow of the sixteen monitors in the main security office illuminating the space as he turned to raise an eyebrow at Vaughn. "Who is she?"

"No idea, Mr. DuPree. I've never seen her at a party before." Vaughn straightened from where he sat hunched over his keyboard, shoving at the sleeves of his oversized hooded sweatshirt. Pulling up the video of the woman in the alcove, he watched her shamelessly kiss her goateed companion for a full minute before adding, "Pretty hot, though. From the look of the feed, she came to play."

Much to Julian's dismay, the ability to obtain clear audio to accompany the live feeds from the dozen or so video cameras strategically placed throughout the main rooms of the penthouse was still a work in progress. The private rooms were easier to accommodate with their smaller space and lack of background noise, and of course, Julian did. Perhaps he'd have a stroke of luck with his lady in red.

"Mmm." Julian smoothed a hand over his suit jacket, admiring the feel of the hand-tailored wool for just a moment before pushing back from the surveillance desk to find his feet. "If she and our other mystery guest take a partner into a private room, be sure to record the feed.

Audio and video."

"It's a little unusual for a woman to sign on for your brand of fun. No offense," Vaughn added, a sheepish smile splitting the untamed stubble trying so valiantly to become a beard. "But hey, she looks eager enough. Maybe the guy with her will share her when he's done."

Julian's heart pumped with the dark thrill of anticipation at the thought. To see such a woman dominated, fucked and then shared with one of his guests, or better yet, two at the same time.

Yes. Now *that* would be a sight. But first, he needed a safeguard.

"Run facial recognition on both her and her companion, if you would," he said, buttoning his suit jacket and straightening the cuffs of his dress shirt until they were just so.

Vaughn lifted his dark head in a nod. "Might take a while to hit some of the bigger databases. Gotta keep our tracks covered, you know."

Ah, but Julian appreciated meticulous work. As well as honesty. The wait was an annoyance, but overall, the spent time was inconsequential in the face of what he wanted. "Understood. Do it as quickly as possible and report back to me as soon as you get the results."

"Roger that. You headed out to the floor, boss?"

Vaughn's brows shot up toward his unkempt hairline. Julian could understand the man's surprise. Much of the time he enjoyed the parties from his private viewing room, where he would no doubt retire soon enough.

But not yet. Not tonight.

Julian smiled, the gesture cold and cunning on his mouth. "We do have new guests this evening, Mr. Vaughn. It would be quite rude of me not to welcome them to the party personally, don't you think?"

With that, he turned toward the door.

* * *

Isabella set her sights on the woman in the white dress, one million percent certain that she was the key to breaking this case wide fucking open. Although girl might be a more accurate description—God, she couldn't be old enough to vote, let alone old enough to legally drink—her eyes told a story Isabella knew all too well.

This girl had seen things. Done things. Knew things. And if Isabella and Kellan played their cards exactly right, she just might be able to get her to talk about them.

She just might be able to keep this girl safe.

"This is going to be a tightrope walk," Isabella whispered, but Kellan surprised her with a nod.

"Understood. I'll keep eyes on the room while you talk to her. Looks like her current location is out of earshot of any other guests."

"Copy that." Setting her shoulders beneath the spaghetti straps of her halter dress, Isabella pressed her stilettos into the ornate and very expensive-looking area rug at the feet of the armchair she'd been perched on. She linked her arm through Walker's, trying like hell to blank out the steel of his muscles beneath his shirt and suit jacket as she took slow, precise steps across the penthouse's main room.

"Hi there." Isabella stopped four paces shy of the woman, wanting to give her enough space to feel comfortable, but not enough to run. "My name is Isabella."

The woman looked up, her black-coffee eyes darting from Isabella to Kellan and then back again before lowering back to the white marble floor tiles. "I'm Angel."

"That's a very pretty name."

"Oh. Thank you," she said, speaking more to her patent leather platform pumps than to anyone else.

Isabella tried again. "I suppose that explains your tattoo."

Now that she was closer, she realized the ink on the woman's shoulder depicted a curved line of feathers shaped into an angel's wing. Not a small victory, since it likely meant

Angel was her real name.

The woman nodded, chancing the slightest glance in Isabella's direction. "Yes."

Background chatter and pleasured moans from other party-goers filled the quiet between them as Angel fiddled with the silver chain at her throat, and damn, getting this girl to come out of her shell was going to take some doing. Not an easy task in front of all these people, one of whom had to be the man forcing her to be here.

Time to get more private.

Isabella smiled. "Well, Angel, my friend and I were wondering if you'd like to spend a little time with us tonight."

Angel's head sprang up. "With both of you? Like, together?"

Shit. "We were just hoping we could get to know you better," Isabella said. As if to underline her no-pressure request, Kellan let go of her arm to take a step back on the marble floor, putting a nice-and-easy smile on his face.

Thankfully, it seemed to do the trick. At least for now. "I've just never done it with a woman before. Not yet, anyway," Angel said.

Isabella's heart pumped faster with hope, but she waited out a few beats of the music before taking the opening. "So you're new to parties like this?"

Please, please, let her not be too far in to try for a way out.

Again, Angel's eyes went wide, and she swung a look at the man over by the piano before stiffly moving toward Isabella and running an awkward hand over her shoulder. "Yes, but you don't have to worry. I like to try new things, and I'll do whatever you want. You wanna get high first? We could shoot a little H before I make you happy. I'm up for anything."

Isabella shook her head, catching Angel's hand with her own. The words were intended to be sexy, she knew. But they fell short of their mark like an overly rehearsed line from a B-grade porno, and Isabella felt Walker's body go tense beside her.

She reached back with her free hand and squeezed his forearm to keep him—and maybe herself—steady. She couldn't reject Angel outright. With all the cameras in this place, someone was bound to notice.

Isabella moved her hand to the girl's shoulder, trying to make her touch as comforting as possible while keeping up pretenses. "You don't look too happy to be here, Angel."

"I could look happy for you, if that's what you want." Panic streaked over Angel's face, and Isabella scrambled to regain what little ground she'd gained.

"That's not what I meant."

"Oh." Angel chewed her lower lip, leaving streaks of dark red lipstick on her teeth. "I could...I could cry instead." Again, her gaze darted toward the piano. "Some people like that. It turns them on when I cry. Or I can do whatever you and your man want me to. You're the guests. I'm here to serve you."

"No, no, no. I didn't mean—" Isabella forced the emotion in her chest to stay the hell away from her face. Just because they were somewhat tucked away over here and Kellan had her back didn't mean she could give her emotions any wiggle room. The job was more important. Always. "I only meant that if you'd like to take a break, we can go into one of the private rooms and just talk."

"He's always watching."

"Excuse me?" Kellan asked from over Isabella's shoulder, his voice soft with concern.

Angel tipped her head just slightly toward the man with the scar on his forehead, who was now roughly encouraging the blond in the blue dress to dance with a man who looked twice her age. "Franco keeps an eye on us girls from out here, but Mr. DuPree watches the private rooms with hidden cameras to make sure we're doing our jobs. We're not..." She paused for a wince. "We're not really supposed to tell the guests that, though."

Isabella's stomach tightened. Damn it, she should've

figured the bedrooms would be under just as much surveillance as the rest of the place. "That's okay. We won't tell anyone you said anything. You won't get into any trouble."

"Angel." Walker kept his tone low, probably as much to keep from spooking her as to avoid being overheard. "Do you know if Mr. DuPree listens to what goes on in the private rooms too? Or does he just watch on the security feeds?"

She edged closer, although cautiously. "I don't know. But he's not watching because he wants to keep me or any of the other girls safe. He likes to see us work. The rougher, the better. You take me to a room and don't fuck me or make me fuck you, he's gonna be mad. And you don't want to know what happens when he gets mad."

"No, you're right," Isabella reassured her. "I don't want that."

Angel leaned in toward Isabella, her expression growing panicked. "So can we please just go fuck now? I promise I'll try my best. I'll do whatever you tell me to. Just don't make him mad. He cut me off from my stash, and I…I need the fix, okay? Please."

Isabella steadied her hands over Angel's shoulders, but just barely. "Easy, Angel. Mr. DuPree won't be mad. You don't have to worry, okay?"

Taking a deep breath, she sent one last look around the space in search of a more private place to talk without being eavesdropped on or easily seen, but damn it, between the chance they'd be caught not screwing on video or overheard by one of DuPree's lurking goons, talking here was too risky.

Isabella was going to have to talk to Angel outside of this penthouse if she wanted to get enough of a statement to go after DuPree. Plus, the longer she and Kellan stood here, the greater the chances someone would notice they were both still dressed and sober.

She closed the softly lit distance between her and Angel,

putting her mouth close to the woman's ear but stopping well shy of contact. "I don't want to get you in trouble, but I do want to talk. If you're not here because you want to be, I can help you."

Angel stiffened, her chin turning in surprise. "How?" she asked, the flash of vulnerable hope in her eyes negating the toughness she'd tried to stick to the word. "You some kind of fairy godmother or something?"

"Or something."

The girl's dark eyes grew round. "You're a—"

Isabella squeezed Angel's shoulder, not hard, but enough to cut her words to the quick. "Friend, Angel. I'm just a friend."

"I don't have friends. Not anymore." She looked across the room at the spot by the piano, where Scarface leered openly at the blond, who seemed far less sure of her balance and her surroundings than she had five minutes ago. "Rampage and Franco and Mr. DuPree made sure of that. Me and the others, we're not even allowed to talk to each other most of the time."

Isabella's heart slapped at her sternum, but God, she had to stay steady. "Well, you can talk to me."

"Yeah, right," Angel said. "Like I got time for conversation. If I don't start blowing your boyfriend in about fifteen seconds, Franco's gonna come over here and backhand me into next week."

"No one's going to lay a finger on you," Walker interjected, the vow quiet but fierce enough to make the back of Isabella's neck prickle.

"We can't talk now, you're right. But you can come talk to me away from here. Would you like that?"

"Mr. DuPree will kill me," Angel whispered, the look on her face backing up the fear.

But Isabella had had enough. "No, he won't. Look at me, Angel." The girl hesitated before lifting her gaze to Isabella's, and holy hell, no one's eyes should look so haunted. "If you come talk to me, I'll keep you safe. We can get you clean, and you won't ever have to go to a party like this again. I swear it."

A minute ticked by, then another before she finally gave up a broken nod that sent relief careening through Isabella's veins. "Rampage and Franco keep us locked up most of the time when we're not here for parties, but they don't watch us as close as they do the girls they're still breaking in. My room has a window. It's not too big, but I think I can get out." She paused, her voice growing small. "I don't want to do this anymore. I want to get out."

Something twisted, hard and deep in Isabella's chest, but she buckled down over the sensation. "Good. This is really good," she said, although it was the world's most gigantic understatement.

She'd just smashed this case wide open. She was going to help these girls and make it so no one could ever hurt them again. Ever.

Isabella lowered her hands from Angel's shoulders but kept the connection of their eyes firmly in place. "I want you to meet me at the diner across from the Thirty-Third precinct, tomorrow morning at nine. Can you do that?"

Angel fiddled with the silver chain at her throat. "So soon?"

God, as far as Isabella was concerned, right now wasn't even soon enough. But giving Angel time to get scared or reconsider wasn't on her agenda. "This will be your last party, Angel. I promise."

"I'd...really like that," she whispered. "Okay. Tomorrow morning."

Not wanting to leave anything up to chance or circumstance, Isabella said, "In a few seconds, I'm going to go into the bathroom down that hallway." She paused for a brief second to flick a glance at the just-visible doorway off the living room where they stood. "I'll leave my card hidden behind the toilet tank for you. If you run into problems—anything at all—I want you to call me, day or night. Okay?"

Angel's nod was answer enough, and they were running

out of time. Turning toward the hallway, Isabella took a forward step so she could get into that bathroom then get the hell out of Dodge, when Kellan's hand slid around her body to pull her in close.

"Keep walking," he said in a quiet demand, and really? He'd trusted her this whole time, for God's sake, even though he'd surprised the hell out of her while he was at it. Was he really going to get bossy about chaperoning her now?

"You can't go to the bathroom with me," Isabella argued under her breath, but his proprietary grip around her shoulders grew even tighter as he dipped his mouth to her ear.

"Yeah, well, the blond guy in the million dollar suit who's been watching us talk to Angel for the last couple minutes is moving in on our six, so I hate to break it to you, but you're not going into the bathroom *without* me."

Ten more seconds had them to the threshold of the bathroom, two more and Kellan had shut and locked the door, and dammit, she needed to breathe, to form an exit plan, to *think*. She moved to say just that, but Walker's fingers pressed hard and quick to the center of her mouth, stopping her words before they could form.

"Wait." He surveyed the bathroom, his eyes ice-blue and meticulous as they moved over the cream-colored hand-embossed wallpaper, the marble and mahogany vanity topped with copper fixtures and a mirror large enough to span half the wall behind it, and the four corners where the crown molding met the ceiling on perfectly drawn seams. After one quick slide of his fingers around the mirror's frame, he lifted his chin in a nod.

But just because this tiny, windowless bathroom didn't seem to be under video surveillance didn't mean there weren't listening devices they'd missed. Or that the man who had been following them wasn't listening in at the door the old fashioned way. She couldn't be careless now. Not when she was so close.

Isabella pulled the burner cell from her purse, flicking the screen to life. DuPree? she typed into an empty text message field, showing the screen to Walker before deleting the single word.

He took the phone from her with a nod. Best guess. Don't think he knows what we came for. But he knows we're here, and that we're not regulars. We're probably going to have to talk our way out the door.

Her gut squeezed, but still, she typed, copy that. Making sure to delete their back and forth, she placed her phone back inside her purse, lifting the edge of the satin lining to pull out the business card she'd tucked beneath it. Reaching around to the back of the toilet tank, she slipped the top corner of the card noiselessly under the spot where the smooth porcelain tower met the tank lid, trapping it into place.

"Okay," Isabella mouthed, squaring her shoulders and standing tall. She took a step toward the door, her intentions set on beating the fastest path to the elevator without being noticed.

But then Walker was close enough for her to breathe in the dark, spicy scent of his skin. With a swift advance, he pressed her back against the vanity, dropping his hands to either side of the edge of the countertop and caging her body with his own.

"Laugh."

He placed the word just behind her earlobe in the barest of whispers. Isabella pulled back in shock, attempting to gain some space between them to figure out what the hell he was up to.

But again, he leaned in to put his mouth to her ear. "Trust me, just laugh. Out loud. Right now."

It might've been her adrenaline, which had been free-flowing long enough to shred even the calmest composure. Maybe it was the absurdity of the situation—of being stuck in one of the most luxurious bathrooms in all of Remington with a ridiculously hot firefighter and a Hail Mary exit plan.

But something prompted Isabella to do what Walker had asked. While her performance wouldn't win her any Academy Awards, she pushed out a laugh that seemed to do the trick. As good as he smelled all pressed up against her (and damn, he smelled good enough to eat with a spoon), Isabella wasn't about to just comply without getting a little information.

She slipped her hands into her clutch to produce her phone, pressing both against the front of his crisp black dress shirt as she keyed in, Why laugh?

Walker eased back, but only a fraction as he took the phone to answer. Because there's no video in this room.

Her brows shot upward in a silent so? and he continued to thumb-type in the tight space between their bodies. So that gives us an advantage.

Isabella paused, rolling through the tactics in her head until…

A bolt of heat arrowed down her spine, landing directly between her hips. You want whoever's on the other side of that door to think we're having a bathroom quickie?

The smile hooking over Walker's mouth was all the confirmation she needed, although he typed in an answer anyway. It's a solid explanation for me following you in here in case DuPree is watching. Plus, when in Rome…

Ah, hell. Isabella had to admit, he had not just one point, but two.

She shifted, her lower back still pressed against the cool marble of the countertop. So how much longer is our quickie going to take? Because no offense, but I'd really like to get out of here.

Wasn't it you who said patience is a virtue? Walker typed, but she had his number, big time.

Yes. And you said you weren't virtuous.

Clearly. Since I'm having sex with you in a bathroom.

Isabella couldn't help it. A laugh that came suspiciously close to a giggle barged out of her mouth. Touché. What do you say we go at it for five more minutes then get gone?

Walker nodded. His step back allowed her the room to replace her phone in her purse and muss her hair just enough to look appropriately sex-tousled. The five-minute wait-time eased her adrenaline and set her determination in bedrock, and as soon as it was up, she pointed to the heavily paneled mahogany door.

"Shall we?" Isabella purred, throwing her persona back into place.

Faking a sexed-up flush wasn't tough as Walker fixed her with a slow stare. "After you, sweetheart."

Unlocking the latch with a flick of his wrist, he pulled the door quietly inward. The hallway beyond was shadowed but empty, and nothing about the party seemed to have changed. Although it took all the effort Isabella could muster, she kept her eyes far from the side of the room where they'd left Angel—God, had it really been less than ten minutes ago? She followed Walker's lead as he aimed himself toward the exit, but they'd barely made it past the piano in the living room before a man with white-blond hair and the world's most calculating smile stepped smoothly into their path.

"Pardon me. I don't mean to interrupt your evening," he said, his platinum cufflinks winking coldly in the overhead light as he extended a well-manicured hand in her direction. "My name is Julian DuPree. I'm hosting tonight's party."

Isabella's stomach pitched like a rowboat on the open sea. "How lovely to finally meet you, Mr. DuPree." She sweetened the bitter-burnt taste of the lie with a splash of truth and a smile she had to work for. The guy's stare alone made her skin crawl. "We've heard all about you and your gatherings. You certainly don't disappoint."

"That's very kind, Miss…?"

"Isabella," she said, biting past the urge to gag—or worse yet, punch him directly in the perfect white teeth—as DuPree lifted her hand to his mouth.

A move Kellan cut short with an unsubtle clearing of his throat. "Walker."

DuPree's clean-shaven jaw tightened just enough to be visible, hardening the edges of his smile. "Yes, well." He lowered Isabella's hand. "My security specialist has told me you're quite the jealous type. It's good to see I haven't been misinformed."

"I like control," Walker grated, and damn it, if this quick exit turned into a testosterone-fueled pissing match, she honestly didn't know which of them she would strangle first.

But much to Isabella's shock, DuPree laughed. "I understand perfectly. And with a companion like Isabella here, how could you not?" He paused, raking her with a gaze that made the feather-fine hairs on her arms stand at full attention. "At any rate, I must apologize. I would've introduced myself sooner, but I saw you were chatting with Angel, and I wanted to give you three a chance to get to know one another. Was she not to your liking?"

Dread exploded in Isabella's chest. "Oh no, quite the opposite," she said, forcing her words to a slow, steady drawl. This guy might be a creeper of the highest order, but he was shrewd. Calling too much attention to Angel would trip his trigger, no doubt. "We found her very eager to please."

"And yet you didn't take her into a private room to play."

Thank God for fake bathroom quickies. "Of course, we considered it, but…" Isabella leaned forward as if confiding a secret even though she'd rather cuddle up with Hannibal Fucking Lecter. "Angel inspired us to get creative. Walker and I decided to play in a private room on our own."

She aimed a pointed gaze at the hallway leading to the bathroom, where she'd bet her next six paychecks DuPree had seen her go with Kellan on her four-inch heels.

"I know the powder room is a little unconventional." Isabella paused just long enough to let a manufactured smile unfold over her face. "We came here looking for a third, but we got so caught up in the moment. We just couldn't help ourselves. Surely that happens at this type of party, doesn't it, Mr. DuPree?"

He straightened, lean shoulders coiling tight beneath his navy blue suit jacket, and for one pulse-rattling second, Isabella thought he'd call her bluff six ways to Sunday. Kellan must've made the same logic leap, because he tensed ever so slightly beside her, and oh God, oh God oh God. She had everything she needed to get the FBI to investigate this bastard. She had not come this far only to get busted twenty yards shy of the goddamn door.

But then DuPree stepped back, gesturing to the wide expanse of the living room around them. "Yes, of course. Impulse can be so difficult to deny."

"I knew a man like you would understand." Isabella pinned her very best sexy smile to the words, sealing them into place to cover her relief.

Thankfully, DuPree bought every word. "Well, I won't keep you from indulging those impulses further. Do enjoy the rest of your evening, and please. Feel free to take that third when you've regained your energy. I wouldn't be a good host if I didn't see you...fully accommodated."

"We'll keep that in mind," Walker said, his smile all teeth.

Isabella lifted her lashes at DuPree to soften the sting. *You got what you came for. Play the part. Get out the door.* "We certainly will. Thank you."

"It's my pleasure, I assure you. I'm sure I'll be seeing you both again quite soon. Isabella." With one last up and down look, DuPree turned on his polished heels and moved his way through the crowd.

Holy hell, she'd done it. She'd found a victim willing to make a statement. She was going to make sure none of these women ever got hurt again.

She was going to take this asshole down.

After a beat, then two, Kellan sent a covert glance over the party-goers, still caught up in every possible level of debauchery. "DuPree just went through the service door at your three. Path to the door is clear," he murmured.

"Copy that. Let's get the hell out of here. I have to be at work bright and early tomorrow."

CHAPTER THIRTEEN

Kellan waited until he and Isabella were a block and a half away from the Metropolitan before he allowed himself the luxury of relief. Between the endorphins from their kiss and the anger-laced adrenaline at their getaway conversation with DuPree (holy *hell* had Kellan wanted to smash the guy's face in. Smarmy bastard), he was so redlined on emotion that getting it all to fit into the boxes in his chest was a mountain-sized chore.

Isabella, however? Looked cool as a cucumber in the middle of the Arctic Circle. At least, she did when she wasn't smiling her face off. But with the meet-up with Angel set up for tomorrow, Isabella would have everything she needed to nail DuPree.

Kellan threw a healthy dose of satisfaction on top of the giant pile of emotions zinging through his bloodstream. They might have done a risky thing—a downright fucking dangerous thing—not going by the book. But they were going to get the bad guy, and Kellan couldn't deny it.

That felt pretty goddamn outstanding.

Isabella moved her fingers to the small of her back, sliding a two-inch ceramic blade from its hiding spot in the fabric of her belt and putting it safely in her purse. Ah, he should've known she wouldn't come to this party unarmed. He had to admit, the weapon was pretty slick—not only would it not trip metal detectors, but the tiny, razor-sharp knife was small enough to be hidden in any one of a dozen places, even as scantily dressed as she was. Hell, she could be damn near naked and still be armed enough to do some serious damage.

The thought of Isabella naked slammed into him in an oh-so-sexy slideshow, and okay, yeah, he needed to focus on something else. Now would be good.

They took a handful more steps over the well-tended sidewalk before she finally set aside her grin. "Tonight might've been a total win on recon, but I'm still mad at you, you know. You completely ambushed me."

"You didn't give me much choice," he argued, albeit with more reason than heat. "I'd never run into a fire without Shae and Gamble and Slater on my six. Not even if the place was burning down at my feet."

She examined him with a sidelong glance. "No offense, but how does that make you a good firefighter? It's your job to run into burning buildings."

"It's my job to fight fires," Kellan corrected. "And I can't do that if I'm dead."

He knew the adrenaline still pumping through his system was making him loose-lipped, just like he knew he was going to crash like a semi on a steep grade as soon as he got home. But as mad as Isabella might be that he'd showed up unexpectedly tonight, she still should've trusted her team, or hell, someone to back her up.

"You want to know the absolute hardest part of my job?" Kellan asked, her silent, surprised expression giving him the leeway to answer his own question. "When I can't go into a building that's burning down at my feet."

Isabella's brow folded. "I'm not sure I follow."

She wrapped her arms around herself, giving up a shiver against the nighttime air around them, and he slid the jacket from his shoulders to place it around hers.

"One of my first big fire calls was at a warehouse down on Edgemoor. Huge, three-story building, and the place was showing flames from every freaking window it had. Of course, we all wanted to run inside like gangbusters." God, he could still see Hawk and all the guys from squad practically jumping out of their boots to vent the roof and bust down the door. "But Captain Bridges took one look at the scene and gave the order to stand down."

"What?" Isabella came to a stop beside her street-parked Mustang, disbelief coloring her shadowy features as she pivoted to face him. "But you just said the fire was huge."

"Yup." Kellan nodded. That damned blaze was still one of the biggest he'd ever seen, even two years later. "I couldn't believe it. In fact, I was so pissed that I tried to go in anyway."

"You did? What happened?"

He let his gaze take an ingrained up-and-down tour of the sidewalk where they stood and the street beyond it before telling her, "Bridges stepped right in my flight path and said, 'Son, you know what happens if I don't stop you from going into that warehouse right now?'"

The sheer curiosity glittering in her pretty brown eyes under the light of the streetlamp prompted him to continue, and so he did. "When I mouthed off with a 'what?' Bridges just looked at me and said, 'Your whole team runs in after you, and then whoever gets here next pulls us all out in body bags.' Three minutes later, the roof collapsed. Warehouse came down like a house of cards."

"Holy shit," Moreno said on a soft exhale. But her lack of mettle didn't last for long. "I know you think that what I did tonight was stupid. But there are lives on the line here, Walker. What if someone had been trapped in that warehouse? Then what would you have done?"

"I don't know," Kellan admitted. "But what I do know is that whatever we'd have done to save them would've been done as a team. Look"—he stepped in, his body only inches from hers, and even though he knew it was impulsive, he really didn't care—"I don't think you trying to help those girls is stupid, Isabella. In fact, I think it's really fucking brave. But you're working without backup, and sooner or later, no matter how brave you are, that's going to blow up in your face if you don't let someone help you."

She didn't acquiesce, but she also didn't argue, simply angling her head to look at him. Her expression, so serious and tough, was completely at odds with the understanding glinting through her wide-eyed stare. The suit jacket Kellan had wrapped around her swallowed the slim line of her shoulders, making her look that much smaller than him despite her larger-than-life moxie, and damn, he couldn't tell what was more enticing. The brass she flashed like armor or the softer side she was surely guarding underneath.

Finally, Isabella released a sigh. "All right. Angel's meeting me tomorrow morning. As soon as I get a statement from her, I'll loop Sinclair and the intelligence team in on everything. I swear," she added.

"Okay. That's all I can ask for."

For a second, they stood there, face to face on the pavement, and the urge to kiss her—not for show or pretense, but really kiss her—stole through him. But Kellan knew all too well that adrenaline was a bitch best left undisturbed.

Damn, Isabella was beautiful.

Even though his body sent nine kinds of what-for and why-not to his brain, Kellan took a step back on the pavement. He'd done what he'd come here to do. Moreno was safe at her car. The scene around them was secure. "I guess I should get out of here. I called in for the first couple hours of my shift tomorrow, but I still have to punch the clock at oh nine-hundred."

"Oh." Isabella swiveled a glance over the quiet street. "Did you park nearby?"

Ah, hell. "No, I…walked."

"You walked?" Her tone painted the question as a direct

descendant of *are you crazy*? and screw it. He nodded, letting one corner of his mouth drift up into a half-smile.

"I was in the Army. I'm used to humping it places. Anyway, the trip's not too far."

At Moreno's lifted brows, he caved the rest of the way. "Okay, okay. My apartment is six miles from here. But the walking clears my head."

It would have to do for an explanation, because if she thought the walking part was nuts, he was pretty certain the whole *I walk to get my emotions in check otherwise there's a decent chance I'd fucking self-destruct* thing would go over like a two-ton boulder.

"If you say so." Isabella laughed, the soft, throaty sound hitting him right in the center of his chest. "Six miles is kind of a lot, though, and you've already done it once tonight. Do you want a ride?"

Kellan realized in that moment that she'd stepped toward him to regain the space he'd given her; that suddenly, her body was very much within touching distance, and that despite the warning coming from the small corner of his brain still allowing rational thought, the darker, baser rest of him wanted nothing more than to make their earlier kiss a prelude to better things. Hotter things.

Naked things.

"I'm not sure that's such a good idea," he said, the roughness in his voice spotlighting the words as a lie. But the hungry look in her eyes, along with the current of want burning in his veins at the sight of it, was the product of circumstance and nothing more. They'd just snuck into a sex party thrown by a highly dangerous criminal and garnered a lead that would blow Isabella's case wide open. Of course they were wired. They probably had more adrenaline winging through their bodies than blood right now. But Kellan of all people knew that actually acting on those keyed-up endorphins was dangerous as hell.

Fuck, he wanted her anyway.

Isabella's catlike smile—this one genuine, sweet and sexy

and shared like a naughty secret—ensured he wouldn't get a blink of sleep tonight, even after the six-mile haul home. "Not a good idea," she repeated. "Because?"

He weighed his options. Saw that he had no good ones. And went with the truth.

"Because if you give me a ride back to my apartment, I'll be tempted to ask you to come upstairs."

"Ah." But rather than retreating or clamming up in awkward silence, Moreno tilted her head to bring her mouth mere inches from his. "Is that what you want? For me to come upstairs with you?"

"Yes." His honesty flew out, hot and unchecked.

Isabella met it with a twist of her lips that made his cock go hard and his pulse rush fast against his throat. "Good," she whispered.

And then she slanted her mouth over his.

Her heels gave her enough of a height advantage to line their bodies up with near perfect precision, and Kellan wasted no time taking full advantage. Pressing his chest flush with hers, he cupped her face between both palms, hooking his fingers into the wild fall of her hair. Of course she gave as good as she got, her tongue darting over the seam of his lips in an eager bid for entry. For a wicked second, Kellan considered denying her just to hear the noise of want she'd make in the back of her throat as she tried again. In the end, his greedy impulses won out, and he deepened the kiss with a sweep of his tongue, then another.

Isabella sighed, and he caught the sound with another greedy kiss. Her lips opened easily, her tongue stroking and seeking, but Kellan held off her advances. He wanted her—Christ, his cock was hard as steel, begging to be pushed deep into the heat between her legs—but that was the point. *He* wanted *her.*

And so instead of letting her have control, he took.

Tightening his fingers in her hair, he angled closer, parting her mouth with his tongue. He sucked and licked, pulling her bottom lip between his teeth and applying just enough pressure to pull that noise from the back of her throat after all.

Ah, the gravelly moan shot straight to his balls, but still, he didn't hold back. Kellan ravaged her mouth, exploring her tongue and teeth and lips until he'd tasted every part of her mouth, priming her for what was to come. Coaxing his way back inside, he pushed deeply with his tongue again and again, fucking her mouth the way he'd fuck her pussy, until he realized the truth with startling clarity.

Kissing Isabella wasn't going to be enough. And if they didn't stop *right now*, they weren't going to stop at all.

Kellan broke from her mouth, his breath heavy against the line of her jaw. "Moreno," he warned, but she captured the rest with a quick slide of her lips.

"Get in the car and ask me upstairs, Walker. My answer's not no."

CHAPTER FOURTEEN

Isabella tried as hard as she knew how not to break every land-speed record in existence on the drive to Kellan's apartment. True to his word about the distance, the six miles took as many minutes, the walk from the building's parking lot to the elevator bay in the lobby only a few more. He stood beside her in the small but nicely decorated space, their shoulders and the outside edges of their pinky fingers just close enough to share warmth but not contact.

They said nothing. Hell, they weren't even looking at one another.

She'd never wanted anyone inside of her so badly in her life.

The elevator doors trundled open with a soft, rolling thump, but before Isabella could make even the slightest move forward, Kellan caught her hand.

"Be sure you still want this."

Lust and adrenaline and a thousand other things answered under her skin, but they were all in agreement about one thing. "I've been sure since the second I kissed you. I want this. Right now."

"Good," he said, his eyes glittering so dark, they were

nearly navy blue.

And then he pulled her into the elevator.

"Kellan," she said, but his name got lost on the moan that followed as he walked her back against the mirrored wall adjacent to the control panel, taking only the briefest of seconds to hit the button for the fourth floor and wait for the elevator doors to shut before refocusing his undivided attention on her body.

"Mmm." Dropping his lips to her neck, Kellan fisted the lapels of the suit jacket he'd loaned her, yanking the fabric apart to reveal her flimsy dress and heated skin. "Do you know how hard it is to concentrate with you in this dress?" he asked, stringing a line of slow, seductive kisses all the way to her shoulder, and oh God, his mouth had to be each and every one of the seven deadly sins.

Isabella arched her back to increase their contact, because she was pretty sure that if he stopped, she'd lose her mind. "All the more reason to take it off."

"Oh no, sweetheart. I'm not letting you off the hook so easy."

Surprise burst through her, followed by a quick shot of confusion. "But you said you wanted this too."

"Make no mistake." Kellan's lips parted in a smile that she felt more than saw as he lifted his mouth to her ear. "I am dying to fuck you. But this isn't going to be a quickie in the bathroom where I shove up your skirt and finish hot and fast. I'm going to take my time with you, Isabella. I'm going to make you come with my fingers and my mouth and my cock, and when I'm done, you're going to remember every inch of where I've been."

Sweet God in heaven, what was taking this elevator so damn long?

As if the car and cables had heard her, the control panel by her side sounded off in a muted ding, the doors sliding open to reveal a blessedly empty well-lit hallway. "Please tell me you don't live at the end of the hall," Isabella said, because truly, her deep, dirty need to lose her clothes and let Kellan make good on his promise was reaching critical mass.

The cocky half-smile tugging at the corners of Kellan's lips? Not helping. "Three doors down on the left. 405."

"Excellent."

They took the half-dozen steps necessary to reach his door, barely making the trip over the threshold before they crashed back together in a tangle of tongues, arms, and really bad intentions. Isabella recognized the bright power of an adrenaline rush all too well—Lord knew it was an occupational hazard for someone who could be shot at or sideswiped on any given day. There were far worse ways to burn that energy than mutually agreed upon, no-strings-attached sex, and anyway, she'd stretched the truth with Kellan a few minutes ago.

Isabella had wanted him for days, months if she counted that initial spark of attraction between them before their trip to Chicago.

Right now, she meant to have him.

"You're wearing too many clothes," she said, placing the murmur against his mouth as she reached for the buttons on his shirt with one hand and the buckle on his belt with the other.

He stilled both of her hands in a move so fast, her pulse clattered. "I meant what I said. I want you, but I'm not rushing this."

"But—"

"No." Walker softened the harshness of his insistence with a brush of his lips. "Look, I'm not trying to make this into something it's not. We're attracted to each other and we're looking to blow off some steam. You don't date and you don't do relationships. I get it. But I'm still not rushing. Now come here."

Under any other circumstances, she'd rather be skinned alive than bossed around, especially in bed. But something about Kellan's tone told her he hadn't asked to be domineering, and his shockingly gentle touch as he twined his fingers through hers backed up the sentiment. "There, see?" he said, guiding her through the darkness of what had to be the foyer and pulling her farther into his apartment. "Not so bad."

"Not so bad," she agreed. "Is this the way to your bedroom?"

"Nope." A few more steps with nothing to lead them but the ambient light filtering in through the two floor-to-ceiling windows on the far side of the room, and damn, how could he see so well in the dark?

Impatient, Isabella tried again. "Funny, I didn't take you for a sex in the kitchen kind of guy."

"As a matter of fact, I have very sturdy countertops. But that's not where we're going."

"Kellan—"

"Relax." He came to a stop in front of the pair of windows. "This is where I wanted to take you."

"We're in your living room." Although the apartment was still as dark as when they'd entered, the twinkling lights from the city below allowed her to make out the silhouette of the basics—a couch, a flat screen TV, and a pair of bookshelves shrouded in the shadows behind them.

"Mmm hmm." Walker tugged her closer, making her heart race. Lowering his mouth over hers, he coaxed her lips open, and she nearly got lost in the magnetic power of his kiss.

Nearly. "Do you really want to do this in front of your windows?" Isabella asked, something odd jangling in the very bottom of her stomach.

"Don't tell me you're secretly harboring a shy streak." His dark brows raised just enough to make her laugh, and she tipped her head toward the thick panes of glass.

"Hardly. But there are no curtains at all. Anyone could see in."

There was a pretty big difference in not being shy and not wanting some pervy passerby to snap cell phone photos of her in a compromising position. She might be on her own time, but she was still a cop.

Still, Kellan seemed undaunted. "Anyone who? We're standing in the dark, four stories up, and there's no building directly across the street. I have extensive tactical training as a sniper. Vantage points are my thing, and I'm here to tell you, no one could see us right now, even if they wanted to. We can do whatever we want in front of the whole damned city, and no one would see a thing."

"Oh." A dark thrill surprised her by rippling the length of her spine. "I guess you're right."

"Mmm," Kellan said, sending her surprise into a double as he swung her body to face the glass, then stepped in to press his chest to her back. "You don't like to let people see you, do you?"

Isabella's heart knocked a warning against her ribs. But the adrenaline still left in her system coupled with the fact that even he couldn't see her face right now, and they both made her admit the truth. "No."

"You have the perfect cover up here. You can do anything—feel everything—and no one will see you. No one will know."

Kellan dropped his mouth to her neck at the same time she melted against him, his hard chest and even harder erection flush against the back of her body. Squeezing her thighs together did nothing to ease her throbbing clit, and she thrust back against the ridge of his cock to try and quell the ache.

His breath hitched at her ear, but only for a second before he circled an arm around her hips to stay her movements. "Nice try, but we're still going slow. You smell tropical, like coconuts. Has anyone ever told you?"

A shock of laughter startled her. "No. It's my body lotion."

"It's all of you," Kellan countered. "And you suck in your breath every time I kiss you right"—he paused, grazing his mouth over the juncture where her neck met her shoulder—"here. It's very sexy."

Isabella exhaled, her skin still tingling with residual pleasure from the soft scrape of his stubble on her overly sensitive skin. "I do that because it feels…" *Yes, yes, yes.* "Really good."

He lingered there for a minute longer before sliding his jacket from her body and focusing his attention on her shoulder blade, then the center of her back. Kissing his way down her spine, he dropped to his knees behind her.

"You remember what I said? About how I'm going to make you come with my fingers and my mouth?"

All she could manage past the slamming of her heart was a broken nod.

"Good. Open up for me, Isabella." He slid both hands up the length of her thighs, lifting her skirt higher and nudging her feet apart. "Let me in."

She complied without thought. Widening her stance, she shifted her weight, planting both feet on the floorboards. The leverage of her stilettos kept her anchored in place, and Kellan made a dark sound of approval from behind her.

"Now put your hands on the glass."

The bare scrap of Isabella's brain left for logical thinking knew this should be awkward. They were fully dressed and barely touching, not even close to being face to face. But the fact that he *couldn't* see her, that she was truly hidden in plain sight, made her hotter than she'd ever been.

She flattened her palms against the window in front of her, her pussy clenching at the heat of Kellan's exhale on her thighs.

"That's it. Lean forward," he said, allowing her space to bend slightly at the waist. The thin material of her thong slid easily over the slick wetness between her legs, and Isabella couldn't hold back her moan at the pleasure the friction sent deep into her core.

Kellan slipped his palms farther up her thighs, not stopping until her skirt was bunched around her hips. "Christ, woman. I could spend all night just looking at your pretty ass."

At her whimper, he chuffed out a laugh, his breath coasting over the small of her back. "Don't worry. I don't want to go that slow. Come here and let me give you what you need."

Without another word, he hooked his thumbs around the thin strings holding her panties in place over her hips, pulling them down in a slow glide. Isabella's clit ached with the need to be touched, her nipples turning to tight points as they hardened in anticipation, and Kellan cupped her ass with both hands, angling his shoulders against the hot, needy space between her legs.

And then his mouth was on her sex from behind her, and she forgot how to breathe.

"Ah." The gasp tore from her throat on a wordless noise, and Isabella arched, desperate for deeper contact.

Although Kellan didn't draw back, he also didn't give her what she was after. "Easy. Let me get to know you." He slid his tongue along the seam of her body, testing her folds with soft flutters and firmer flicks. "Let me find what you want."

Sensations crashed through Isabella's body—dirty, needful, sweet—one right after the other. But Kellan refused to rush, giving her no choice but to slow down and feel each one. He licked and tasted, learning her pussy with his mouth while he spread her wider and explored with his fingers. Heat built in a steady demand between her thighs as he kissed her over and over, until finally, Isabella curled her fingers into the window in front of her.

"Oh God," she moaned, her inner muscles tensing with delicious pressure as Kellan pushed his tongue deeper inside.

"There." He did it again, then one more time, and she was helpless against her sigh in response. "That makes you want to come, doesn't it?"

Another slow thrust of his tongue, and every part of Isabella's body trembled with awareness. "Yes."

"Then I'm not stopping until you do."

Shifting slightly, Kellan wrapped an arm around the

front of her hip, dipping two fingers to circle her clit while he worked her pussy from behind with his mouth. The thrusts of his tongue grew deeper, faster, and her breath pushed out in shorter bursts, fogging the glass. She closed her eyes, concentrating on his fingers and the wicked pleasure of his mouth as he fucked her with his tongue.

And he was right. Isabella felt him everywhere.

"Kellan." Release spiraled, bright and hot between her hips, but he didn't hold back.

"I'm right here, sweetheart. No one can see you. Go ahead and let go."

Her orgasm crashed into her, stealing her breath and making her cry out all at once. Waves of pleasure rolled over her from the inside out, and oh God, they seemed to last forever, making her legs shake and her heart slam and her body feel totally brand new. After every last tremor had been wrung from inside of her, Kellan slowed his movements, righting her dress over her hips as he pushed to his feet behind her.

"Jesus. Isabella, you are—"

"Not even close to done."

She pivoted just in time to see surprise take hold of his features, his eyes widening in the city light filtering up from below. But they'd done things his way, with him in control of her pleasure.

Now she was going to return the favor.

With a bold smile, Isabella pressed up to kiss him, tracing the curve of his bottom lip with her tongue. "What, you thought I'd let you have all the fun?"

"Sorry, did you not just have fun?" The corners of his mouth lifted into a cocky smirk. "Because you sounded like—"

"Yes." She kissed him again, arousal rebuilding in her belly at the primal, earthy taste of sex on his mouth. "I know what I sounded like. But you had me nice and slow. Now I want you."

Kellan pulled her close. "I want you, too."

"No. I want you. I want you fast." Isabella pulled her dress over her head. "I want you hard." One twist of her wrist, and her bra followed. "And I want you inside me, right now."

He took a step back, his up-and-down stare as palpable as a touch raking over her naked skin. "You are the hottest fucking woman I have ever seen. C'mere."

Grabbing her by the hands, Kellan cut a direct path to what turned out to be his sofa. He undressed in just a few economical moves, his shirt and shoes and pants landing who knew where, and finally, he stood in front of her in nothing more than a pair of black boxer briefs.

"Oh." Isabella's throat worked over a swallow. Holy shit, he was beautiful, all chiseled shoulders and flat abs. The dark, scrolling edges of a tattoo spanned one arm from the bottom of his shoulder to his biceps, and her fingers ached with the urge to touch him, to learn him by heart the way he'd uncovered her.

But she was going to have to take the scenic route next time, because right now, what Isabella really wanted was to fuck him.

Wrapping one arm around Kellan's shoulder, she lowered her free hand over the tightly bunched muscles covering his midsection. Although his chest was mostly smooth, her fingers rasped over a crisp trail of dark hair leading down toward his low-slung waistband, and a fresh wave of desire bloomed between her legs.

That desire made Isabella's mouth water as soon as her hand skimmed over his cock.

"Isabella," Kellan grated, thrusting into her touch.

She didn't deny him. "Shhh," she whispered, stroking him with firm intention. "It's okay if you want to let go, too. Go on, Kellan." She slid his boxer briefs lower to palm his cock, hot skin on skin. "Lose control a little."

A spear of wicked satisfaction moved through her chest as he pushed into the circle of her fingers. Isabella pumped her hand from root to tip, each one of Kellan's heavy breaths against her neck daring her to move faster. On an upward glide, she swept her thumb over the head of his cock to capture the bead of moisture there, and he broke from her with a curse.

"Now," came the dark demand from the back of his throat, making her even more wet. But a thought pricked at the back of her mind, and shit. *Shit.* As prepared as Isabella had been for every other situation tonight, fitting a condom in her itty-bitty purse had never even occurred to her. She was on the pill—no such thing as too careful—but as desperate as she was to let Kellan bury himself inside of her until they both screamed, horny didn't trump smart.

Fortunately, he seemed to be on the same thought train. Bending to grab his pants from the floor, he slipped a condom from his wallet, sheathing himself with only a few deft movements. After exhaling her relief, Isabella splayed her fingers over the hard line of his shoulders, sending him to the couch behind them with just one push. She straddled Kellan's lap, balancing the cradle of her hips over the corded muscles of his thighs. His stare glittered over her in the darkness that her eyes had grown accustomed to, and he claimed her waist in a rough hold.

"No." Although she whispered the word, it stilled him completely. Isabella curled her fingers around his wrists. "I want *you*, remember? I want you to feel me. I want you to know where I've been, too. So no moving," she said, guiding his hands to his sides and shifting her body over his. "Let me fuck you, Kellan. Let me find what *you* want."

Isabella reached down to the slight space between them. His cock jutted up from the low center of his hips, thick and gloriously hard, and even though her heart was pounding so fast she was sure the damned thing would try to make a jailbreak, she angled her aching sex against him and pushed.

Oh. Holy. Hell.

Biting back her moan was never going to happen, so she didn't even bother to try. With her thighs spread wide and their bodies joined to the hilt, Kellan stretched her inner muscles and filled her completely. Isabella sucked in a breath at the heat and the pressure and the dirty, wanton feel of his cock inside her pussy, and oh God, he could bury himself like this all night and it still wouldn't be enough.

"*Ah,*" Kellan grated, the noise grounding her in the here and now. Bracketing his shoulders with both arms, she leaned forward and lifted slightly, pressing her palms into the soft leather of the couch behind him. The change in angle sent another round of sensations winging through Isabella's core, but she tamped them down. She rocked back and forth with purpose, listening to Kellan's breath and feeling his body tighten beneath her as she moved faster, then slower, then harder against his cock.

"Show me what you want," Isabella said, pleasure filling her chest at the look of intensity shaping his face.

"Just you, sweetheart. Now don't stop."

The words arrowed deep, daring her to roll her hips and dig her nails into the back of the couch behind his shoulders. For every thrust, she retreated a little farther, riding the entire length of his cock over and over. Kellan's hands formed fists at his sides, his eyes locked on the spot where he disappeared deep inside again and again, and the intensity sent a curl of want licking between Isabella's legs. She lowered her fingers, sweeping them over the sensitive knot of her clit, shock moving through her as his hand covered hers.

"So hot." His fingers joined in, testing the slick folds at the top of her sex while he filled her so thoroughly below, and the provocative sensations twined together to send her unexpectedly over the edge. Her climax pulsed through her, taking control of her voice, and Kellan tensed beneath her at the sound of her cries.

"Isabella. Oh, fuck, I—"

Gripping her hips, he pushed her all the way down on his cock as he thrust up to meet her. The sweet invasion sent another wave of pleasure through her pussy, and she arched to take every inch of his shuddering release.

Minutes passed with nothing but the sound of their ragged breath. Isabella slumped over Kellan's body, her arms around his neck and his hands still locked around her waist, both of them inhaling and exhaling against one another. Her brain knew she should move, commanded her to do it, even. But her body was boneless, refusing to hear a damned thing her neurons said. Finally, Kellan moved her gently aside, slipping down the hallway for only a minute before returning to the spot next to her on the cushions.

"Here." He reached for the blanket draped over the arm of the couch, pulling the edges around his shoulders and pressing his chest against her back.

Isabella's brain snapped back online. She stiffened despite her body's bid to melt into the warmth of Kellan's touch. "Actually, I should probably go."

His answer came quick and matter-of-fact. "No you shouldn't."

"I should," she said again, unease beginning to form in her belly. The sex had been great—other-worldly, even. But she didn't do this. She didn't stay.

At least, she'd never wanted to.

Isabella's heart nudged faster against her breastbone. "I have to be up early," she whispered, but Kellan tightened his grip from behind her, and jeez, how could any man feel so freaking good when he wasn't even touching her naughty bits?

"I have to be up early, too. I'll wake you."

"But—"

"Moreno." He slid a kiss into her hair, putting yet another kill shot on her determination. "It's two o'clock in the morning and I'm not wearing any pants. Don't make me get up and walk you to your car."

Dammit, she laughed. "I carry a Glock instead of a purse and I'm trained to the teeth in self-defense. I can make it to my car just fine, you know."

"I do. But the thing is, I don't want you to go right now. So could you do me a favor please, and just lie down with me and close your eyes? We're talking a couple of hours of shuteye on the couch, here. No big deal. Plus, after the night we've had, you've got to be tired."

Well, shit. Of course he had to go and have a point. "Okay," Isabella finally said, letting him guide her back to the oversized cushions of the couch, which just so happened to be deceptively comfortable. Her breath found a slow, steady rhythm, and her body finally gave in to the full letdown of her adrenaline rush. Her muscles unwound one by one, their tight hold of awareness slipping into relaxation. Walker's chest was warm against her back, which was oddly comforting considering how hard-bodied he was, and didn't that just make it that much easier to let him hold her.

"Mmm." She settled in against his back, trying—and failing—to stifle her yawn. "I'm still really mad at you for ambushing me," she murmured. Whoa, how was keeping her eyes open so difficult all of a sudden?

Kellan tightened the circle of his arms around her, her relaxation growing even deeper as he dropped a kiss to her temple. "I know," he said.

It was the last thing Isabella heard before drifting off to sleep.

CHAPTER FIFTEEN

Between two years in a fire house and as many tours as a Ranger, decent sleep was one of those things that Kellan had pretty much written off. He wasn't a robot—of course he needed (and got) a few hours here and there. But considering he'd spent his night on a rush of endorphins topped off with incendiary sex, managing even the slightest bit of shuteye was a complete fucking no-go.

Especially since his partner for both parts of the evening was curled up in his arms.

Kellan scooped in a breath, watching the very first strains of daylight color the room from the windows behind him. For the thousandth time, he catalogued the events of the past six hours in his head—watching Isabella's uncut determination as she brazened her way past security at the Metropolitan, then again as she fast-talked her way past DuPree to get out the door. The certainty in her eyes as she'd told Kellan to invite her upstairs. The seductive fierceness that gave way to the tremble beneath it before rebuilding into even hotter intensity as she'd screamed his name and made him scream hers.

And for the thousandth time, he was shocked down to

his balls that she'd agreed to stay.

Not that he hadn't put effort in trying to convince her. With Isabella's arm's length, I-don't-date attitude, Kellan had known that even asking her to go down the hall to his way more comfortable queen-sized bed would likely make her balk. But despite her initial bid to race out his door mere minutes after they'd finished having sex, he'd seen the vulnerability in her eyes when he'd asked her to stay, and felt the tension leave her body when he'd pulled her in close to hold her as she fell asleep.

So what was Isabella hiding beneath all that armor?

As if her stalwart defenses had somehow honed in on the question filling his brain, she stirred beside him. "Mmm." Her drowsy murmur lasted for only a fraction before she stilled. "Walker?"

Easy. If sticking around after sex wasn't her thing, chances were, morning-after conversations were pretty far from her repertoire. "Were you expecting someone else?" he asked.

Isabella let go of a laugh, and bingo, mission accomplished. "Of course not. I thought you might be asleep."

"Nope."

"What time is it?"

Kellan eyeballed the degree of muted daylight now beginning to creep over the wall in front of them in earnest. "Just shy of six, I'd guess."

She turned her chin in obvious surprise, her hair rustling over the bare skin of her shoulder. "Did you sleep at all?"

"A little." He'd closed his eyes. For now it would have to serve. "You slept."

After a pause, she said, "Yeah, but I really should get up."

He didn't tighten the arm he'd slung around her over the navy blue fleece blanket keeping them covered, but he also didn't move to let her up. "It's Saturday. You're not meeting Angel until nine, right?"

"Right." The response came out with a heavy flavor of *what does that have to do with anything*, making Kellan's pulse flash faster through his veins. The smart thing to do would be to cram all these weird feelings back into their boxes and let Isabella be on her merry way.

But fuck it. He was never going to get past her armor if he didn't earn his way in. "So give me five more minutes."

She tilted her hips, just enough to brush her ass over his morning hard-on. "If I'm remembering correctly, you take longer than five minutes."

Okay, so his brain wasn't the only part of him that was wide awake and standing at attention. But come on. He might be aiming at decency, but Isabella was still hot, not to mention pressed up against him and oh-so-naked.

Kellan sucked in a breath, channeling all his willpower into a redirect despite his cock's raging protest. "And if I'm remembering correctly, you don't hate when I do. But that's actually not why I wanted the time."

"Oh? What could possibly be better?"

"Tell me something about you."

"What?" Isabella's entire body tensed against his, her shoulder blades on his chest, her back on his belly. Kellan knew he could retract what he'd said. He could take back the words and she'd walk out the door and he'd put everything he'd felt over the last couple of weeks back into their allotted spaces, hidden away. If he took it back, Isabella would pretend she'd never heard him ask.

But he *had* asked. And as crazy and impulsive and as dangerous as it was, Kellan didn't want to take it back.

He wanted more.

"Tell me something about you," he repeated, and she shook her head in a quick back and forth.

"I told you the other night, I'm not good at this."

Nope. He'd come this far. No sense in scaling back now. "Yes you are. Look, I'll even go first again. My favorite color is blue."

"Oh." Isabella's shoulders unwound by the tiniest

margin. "I…um, I like red. Dark, like a nice merlot."

"Hmm. I'm pretty much a beer guy," Kellan said with just enough challenge to make her rise to greet it.

"You don't know what you're missing," she answered, her trademark feistiness on full display. "A good bottle of red isn't just a handful of drinks. It's an experience."

Damn, he'd never be off his toes with her, that was for sure. "You'll have to show me," he said, adding on, "I have a thing for political thrillers."

"There's a stash of romance novels on my bedside table."

Unable to help himself, Kellan let his surprise ride out on a laugh. "Ah. You'll *definitely* have to show me. What's your favorite season?"

"Spring, right when the leaves start growing," Isabella replied. Shifting beneath the blanket, she turned to her back, dipping her chin to look at him expectantly.

"Mine, too. Favorite pizza topping? If you say anchovies, I might have to kick you off my couch."

"Black olives." She laughed, a deep, throaty sound that came up from deep in her chest, and man, she was seriously beautiful.

Kellan propped his elbow against the couch cushion, holding his head up with one hand while nudging her with the other. "See, you are good at this."

"You haven't asked me any hard questions yet."

"Why don't we cross that bridge when we get to it?"

"Walker," she started, but didn't back the protest up, and hell. He was already in for a penny. No way was he going down without fighting for the whole damned pound.

"Look Moreno, I'm not going to lie. I like you, and I'd like to see you again. But for now, none of the questions have to be hard. Okay?"

"Okay," Isabella whispered, blinking as if the answer had surprised her. Another minute passed before the shock on her face turned into a smile. "So, I gave you five minutes. Does that mean I get five back?"

His cock stirred beneath the blanket. "What'd you have in mind?"

Turning to her side to face him, her smile became a grin as she leaned in to kiss him, slow and sexy. "Something that'll wake you up better than coffee."

Hell yes. Impulsive or not, Kellan rolled her beneath him in less than a blink. "Oh, sweetheart. Your wakeup call is going to take more than five minutes. But I wouldn't be a good host if I let you leave without a proper sendoff."

* * *

Julian sat in the leather wingback chair behind his desk, his tie still straight and his suit jacket still buttoned despite the last of his guests having departed about an hour ago. Under normal circumstances, he'd have retired to his bedroom with the choicest video selections of the evening, letting the primal grunts and pained cries on the feeds from the private party rooms lull him to sleep. But this pre-dawn was far from normal, because what he was looking at instead were the photographs of two people he was going to murder.

Julian stared at the pair of printouts Vaughn had placed on the antique mahogany in front of him, forcing his hands to impeccable steadiness despite the utter rage tearing through his veins. "Are you certain this information is accurate?"

If Vaughn took offense at the question, he was wise enough not to let it show. "The RPD database might be a bitch to crack, even for me," he said, shrugging even deeper into the hooded sweatshirt he wore like a sloppy second skin. "But it doesn't lie. Isabella Moreno is a detective in the intelligence unit at the Thirty-Third."

"A detective," Julian repeated, looking again at the printout showing a black and white photo of Isabella in what looked to be her headshot for the department.

Vaughn nodded. "I'm as shocked as you, boss. But I

triple-checked our security measures, and there's no active investigation into you or anyone on your payroll, with the Remington police or the FBI. These parties are still completely under the radar." After a pause, he said, "I pulled all the footage of her for a closer look. She obviously knows Danny Boy, and she seemed pretty into the guy she was with—something tells me he didn't go into that bathroom with her to help powder her nose. There are plenty of cops with dirty secrets. You think she might just want to party?"

Julian considered the idea for a moment, but dismissed it just as quickly. If Isabella had come here to partake in sex or drugs or both, she'd have done so more openly. His reputation for secrecy was flawless, and besides, Julian had a condensed history of her case records right here in front of him. Detective Moreno seemed to have a penchant for pursuing crimes against women. Clearly, her interest in him was professional.

Anger locked his jaw hard enough that his words barely slipped out. "No, Mr. Vaughn. I do not."

"There hasn't been so much as a mouse fart about this operation anywhere online," Vaughn said carefully, which was smart on his part. Drawing attention to the fact that they'd unknowingly hosted a fucking police detective last night wouldn't win him any favors with Julian's foul temper right now. "I can assure you, Mr. DuPree, the cops know nothing."

"While your vernacular is quite charming, your statement seems a bit inaccurate," Julian shot back. "Detective Moreno was here, after all, so she knows something. The questions that remain are how and how much."

A bitter taste filled Julian's mouth. Oh, but he detested the police. A useless lot, far too easily fooled, blackmailed, or bought off with the promise of having their cocks sucked. They were just as weak as the rest of the men who frequented his parties, either ignorant or swayed by overindulgence and depravity.

But not Isabella. No. She, it seemed, was searching for justice, and that simply wouldn't do. He needed to teach her a lesson about what happened to those insolent enough to challenge his power. The question was, how to hurt her best.

A thought turned over in Julian's mind, and he focused his attention on the second sheet of paper Vaughn had brought him. "Mr. Walker is a curious companion for our Detective Moreno, don't you think?"

"Yeah, I'm not really sure how fire boy plays into things," Vaughn agreed, shifting his weight from one beat-up sneaker to the other over the edge of the cream and blue Aubusson. "It's definitely not standard operating procedure for the RPD to let a civilian tag along on any kind of undercover operation, even if the dude was kind of a badass in the Army. His record's cleaner than most surgical instruments, so chances are he's not an informant or here for the party, either."

Julian thought of Walker's brutish flashes of overprotective temper as well as the way he'd taken Isabella's mouth so savagely in the alcove outside the penthouse doors, and no, the man wasn't in this out of forced obligation or for the thrill like Julian's other guests. But why would Detective Moreno bring such unconventional protection when surely, she had a partner in the intelligence unit?

It was just one of the many questions that needed answers, and Julian was not a patient man. "Run everything you can on both of them, and don't sleep, eat, or so much as pause to use the bathroom until I get a full report."

"You're the boss," Vaughn said. "Anything else?"

Julian took a moment to think. The information he'd tasked Vaughn with finding would dictate how best to eliminate Detective Moreno and Mr. Walker, but in the meantime, he could still give that bitch and her guard dog the dressing-down they deserved for daring to think they could expose him, not to mention dole out some well-earned punishments.

A plan unfolded in Julian's brain, dark and twisted and absolutely perfect. Yes. Yes. This would do nicely.

He checked the Patek Philippe on his wrist before sending his gaze across his desk. "Do we still have access to the holding facility on Oakmont?"

"The flophouse by the pier in North Point?" Vaughn straightened at the censure Julian had channeled into his stare. Really, was the terminology so difficult to remember? "Uh, yeah," Vaughn said. "That...facility is still vacant."

"Excellent. Have Franco escort Angel there immediately. Oh, and instruct Charles to find Mr. Marcus and bring him as well. We'll also need some pharmaceutical supplies to use as an accelerant for a fire."

Shame, really. Now he'd have to replace one of his whores and find a new source for his heroin. But there was no sense in dirtying his hands on two separate occasions, and perhaps Angel would be encouraged to speak freely if she saw firsthand what happened to anyone who double-crossed him.

No matter if she wasn't. Julian had a cure for insubordination, and he intended to use it until that dirty, drug-ravaged whore begged for mercy either way.

Vaughn's brows popped in obvious surprise. "You want to set the place on fire? Don't you think the cops will get suspicious when the RFD calls in the bodies?"

"The police are imbeciles who won't see anything more than a drug dealer and a prostitute who were stupid enough to cook methamphetamines without proper ventilation," Julian said. "The deaths will be ruled a sad accident, and will barely be a blip on the news outlets in three days' time."

Vaughn paused, tapping one finger against his lips before shaking his head and smiling. "Damn, Mr. DuPree. I've gotta tell you, that's pretty brilliant. Turning abandoned house into a fake meth lab won't take much. I bet one of Franco's associates would be willing to donate some supplies in exchange for an invite to next week's party."

"Make it happen," Julian said, his heart beating faster and filling him with anticipation that bordered on arousal. What better way to get the message across to both Detective Moreno and Mr. Walker that he wasn't to be trifled with than to show them what he was capable of, and ensure that there was nothing they could do about it?

Speaking of which… "Make certain when the nine-one-one call is placed that Mr. Walker's home station is routed to the scene. I also want Detective Moreno notified, anonymously, of course. But first things first. I'll need that word with Angel. And Vaughn?" Julian waited to be sure they held eye contact before continuing. "Do tell Franco I hope he's saved some energy. He can fuck the truth out of her any way he likes, just so long as she talks."

Julian would find out what Isabella Moreno knew. And then he would silence her in the most painful way possible.

CHAPTER SIXTEEN

Isabella sat back against the corner booth at the Fork in the Road, scanning the busy diner around her even though she'd memorized the description and location of every last occupant fifteen minutes ago. The layout of the place itself was already a gimme. She knew the diner's bright blue high-backed booths, silver-flecked white Formica counter, and fifties-style checkerboard floor tiles as well as she knew her own apartment.

The Fork was as standard a hangout as the Crooked Angel for the cops at the Thirty-Third, although Isabella had known the place by heart far before her first day at the academy. The throwback diner had been Marisol's favorite place to eat—besides Isabella's family's home in south Remington, anyway.

She glanced at the chrome-and-vinyl bar stools lining the front counter, her mind giving up the image of a girl caught firmly in adolescence, with long dark braids and a trusting smile and quarters for the jukebox in the corner. God, Marisol had loved that jukebox, poring over song after song to make sure she'd considered them all before making her selections, then the two of them would sing along with the words, laughing as if they'd had all the time in the world.

Oh, Mari. I miss you.

Isabella straightened, rubbing one hand over the center of her black and gray top to snuff out the bone-deep ache blooming there. Yeah, the thought might be true, just as it had been yesterday, and the day before, and for the last eleven years before that. But she didn't have time to go skipping through her memories. Angel would be here in five minutes, and Isabella was going to need every last ounce of her focus to take the girl's statement and figure out the best plan of attack from there.

She needed to clear her head. To breathe. To relax, just as she had when she'd fallen asleep in Kellan's arms last night, then again when she'd had out-of-body-experience sex with him this morning.

Annnnnd just like that, Isabella's thoughts leaped right from the frying pan to the firefighter.

Oh, come on, she thought, taking a sip of the tea in front of her even though it was lukewarm at best. So she'd had sex with Kellan (really, *really* good sex. Holy hell, the man's stamina and attention to detail were practically awe-inspiring) and taken a four-hour power nap on his couch. So what? She hadn't exactly been virgin material, and anyway, he'd been clear that their night together had been no big deal, just like she'd wanted.

Except now, sitting here with the bright morning-after sunlight pouring into her booth through the window beside her, all Isabella could think of was that what she *really* wanted once this meet-up was said and done was to sleep with Kellan again.

She returned her teacup to its saucer with an ungainly clink. She had a job to do, for God's sake. A woman in peril, who had promised to meet her and give a statement that would have the FBI crawling up every last one of DuPree's orifices by sunset. Isabella needed to channel all her energy into keeping Angel safe.

Provided the woman showed up.

A minute ticked by, then another, before Isabella checked the time stamp on her iPhone. Okay, so Angel was two minutes late. She'd said getting through her window might take some doing, and Isabella would rather Angel be cautious and late than get caught slipping out.

Her chest constricted as if it had been wrapped in steel bands, but she forced herself to inhale. No. Angel hadn't gotten caught, and she hadn't backed out. She was coming. Isabella had sworn to keep her safe.

You worry too much, Marisol. It's twelve blocks, not twelve miles! Just walk over here. If I come pick you up, I won't have enough time to take a shower before we go to this party, and Connor Washington is supposed to be there. Come on, please? I promise you'll be safe...

Isabella slid her clammy palms over her denim-clad thighs, slapping the memory from her brain. But the two minutes turned into four, then became a full ten, and come on, come on. Where the hell—

Isabella's phone buzzed a good three inches across the Formica at her elbow, sending her pulse rocketing through the stratosphere. But intelligence wasn't on call this weekend, and she could count the number of personal calls she'd gotten this month on one hand, minus five fingers.

Unknown caller.

Her throat went dry and tight, the combination doing nothing for her calm. Under any other circumstances, she'd send the call to voicemail with a muttered curse about stupid telemarketers. But Angel was now eleven—she checked her watch—no, twelve minutes late.

Oh God. She'd promised to protect her. She needed Angel safe.

Isabella needed her here. Now.

She flicked the phone to life, making her way to the alcove by the restrooms in the back of the diner for better privacy. "Moreno."

"Detective Moreno." The voice was male and unfamiliar, and the air in the narrow hallway seemed to grow thicker.

Still, she strong-armed her voice into smoothness. "Who is this?"

"You might want to think less about who this is and more about who I have here with me. Or more specifically, who isn't with you at the Fork in the Road right now."

Adrenaline punched through her lungs in a panicked substitute for breath. "Where's Angel?"

The man laughed. "It wouldn't be very fun if I gave you all the pieces to the puzzle, now would it? Can't lead you to any conclusions beyond the shadow of a doubt."

"Okay." Isabella's mind raced. The longer she kept this guy on the phone, the more information he might give up, and even the smallest detail might help her find Angel. "What is it that you want?"

"Aw, your police tactics to keep me talking are so cute. But you're not going to catch me now that I know you're a cop. I know all your little tricks."

Her chin snapped up. "And how's that? Are you a cop, too?"

The man's laughter curled over the line as he thoroughly ignored her question, and damn it, she should've known he wouldn't take such easy bait. "I just called on the boss man's behalf. He wanted me to tell you he'll see you real soon. Oh, and sorry you've got to work this weekend. Dead-end cases are so tough. Bye, now."

The line clicked once and went dead.

No. No, no, no, no, *no.*

Fear cemented Isabella's boots to the black and white floor tiles for only a second before her adrenaline surged, propelling her back to the table she'd abandoned. With her thoughts moving at warp speed, she yanked the paper placemat from beneath her cup and saucer, whipping a pen from the pocket of her leather jacket and writing down the entire conversation in all the exact words she could remember.

All the pieces to the puzzle…beyond the shadow of a doubt…now that I know you're a cop…dead-end cases…dead…

No.

Panic grabbed her chest, sinking its nails in and gripping without mercy, but she crammed a breath into her fear-choked lungs. She couldn't get emotional. She couldn't break down, not now. She'd already gotten this far, and on her own at that. She had to think. To work.

She had to find a way to save Angel before it was too late.

* * *

Kellan worked up his very best poker face before walking through the side door leading to Station Seventeen's engine bay. True, he hadn't taken so much as a nanosecond off in the pair of years he'd been on the RFD's payroll, and true again, he'd only missed the first two hours of his twenty-four-hour tour, plus he'd covered said hours in advance with one of the guys from C-shift so his engine-mates wouldn't have to run light. But if anyone Kellan worked with caught so much as the tiniest glimmer of post-coital satisfaction on his face, he'd have to field a never-ending ration of shit from every last person in the house.

Although considering how hot the sex had been, not once but twice, the ribbing might be worth it.

"Hey, you guys." Blanking the idiot grin threatening the corners of his mouth, Kellan lowered his duffel to the scuffed concrete of the engine bay floor, turning toward the equipment room to grab his gear and get it prepped in case they got a call on the fly.

Shae's laughter stopped him a few steps shy of the door. "Heyyyy! Look what the cat dragged in." She looked up from the inventory clipboard in her grasp, arching one light brown brow. "You all caught up on your beauty sleep, Walker?"

"He does look nice and refreshed, doesn't he?" asked their head paramedic, Parker Drake, from the spot where he was restocking his first-in bag at the back of the ambo. He ran a hand over his short black hair, striking an exaggerated pose like a cover model. "Practically GQ."

Kellan swallowed the urge to dish up the good-natured fuck you the guy deserved. He needed to dodge the topic, not shine a spotlight on his tardiness—or worse, the reason for it. "Thanks, Ace. Unfortunately, I wasn't sleeping in. But clearly McCullough here was kind enough to get enough beauty sleep for the both of us."

The smartass deflection struck a bulls-eye, prompting Shae to give him the finger and Parker to laugh, and Kellan exhaled in silent relief. Ducking into the equipment room, he grabbed his bunker gear from the oversized cubby where he'd stored it just before he'd clocked out after last shift. The sharp scent of smoke and soot invaded his nose despite the fact that both the gear and the equipment room where it was always stored off-shift got very regular, very thorough cleanings. But some things simply couldn't be blotted out or washed away.

Stifling heat, scorching his lungs with every inhale. Rectangular patterns of merciless sunlight burning in through the glassless windows. A shift of unexpected motion, the pinch of dread that arrived in his gut just a second too late.

"If you move, I will kill your friend…"

Kellan's chin snapped up, his heart going Mach 2 against his navy blue RFD T-shirt. Dammit, all the intensity of last night's recon mission was really cooking his composure. Thank fuck Isabella was going to get what she needed from Angel in order to put DuPree's bastard ass in a federal prison.

Isabella, with her iron will and her gorgeous face and her deliciously wicked smile. Isabella, who'd opened up to him this morning, giving him a taste and making him want more. Isabella, whose tight, sweet body had trembled beneath his as the sun rose, and yeah, he needed to get all these emotions locked up right now.

Walking back out to the engine bay, Kellan stored his gear in his regular spot in Engine Seventeen's back step, checking, then double-checking his SCBA tank and mask before securing them in the compartment behind his well-worn seatback. He stuck his head into Bridges' office to officially check in with the captain and start his shift, but he hadn't even made it six steps out of the man's office before the shrill sound of the all-call turned his pulse into a playground.

"Engine Seventeen, Squad Six, Ambulance Twenty-Two, Battalion Seventeen. Structure fire, hazardous materials, forty-two fourteen Oakmont Boulevard. Requesting immediate response."

Kellan moved toward the engine bay out of pure instinct, and he was far from alone.

"Woohoo, looks like they're playing our song, y'all," Hawk drawled, hustling his way into the hall from the fire house's common area with the rest of the rescue squad on his heels.

"Nothing like a hazmat call to make your dick nice and hard in the morning," Faurier said, tacking on an apologetic shrug as he caught Shae's eye roll from the doorway to the engine bay. "No offense, McCullough."

But Shae just smirked in response as she beat feet to Engine Seventeen and grabbed her bunker pants from the operator's seat. "All good, Sammy boy. If you've got to apologize for your dick, you've got bigger problems than offending me."

Faurier laughed and lifted his hands in concession before quickly hoisting himself into Squad Six's vehicle. Although the conversation seemed relaxed, maybe even to the point of being inappropriate considering the potential seriousness of the call they were about to go on, Kellan knew better. Every single one of their adrenal glands was pumping out a fucking truckload of go-go-go right now. Letting the conversation crank that tension even higher wouldn't do them—or the people they were hustling to help—any favors. Keeping cool was an absolute imperative if they wanted to get their jobs done right. One split second of panic could be the difference between life and death.

Focus. Block out everything that isn't right now. Kellan set his shoulders around his spine and rounded the back side of the engine, where Gamble greeted him with a single lift of his chin.

"Nice timing. You fucking slacker," his lieutenant added, toeing out of his plainclothes work boots and yanking his turnout gear over his navy blue RFD T-shirt in a well-practiced move.

"Yeah, yeah." Kellan was tempted to jaw back, but he'd already ducked the radar with McCullough and Drake. Plus, something out there was on fire, and from the all-call, it didn't sound like a family barbecue gone awry. Hazmat was no joke.

Pulling himself into the back step, Kellan sucked in a few rounds of inhale/exhale to meter his pulse as he slung his headset into place and began to gear up. Gamble swiveled a lightning-fast three-sixty through the engine's interior, his eyes landing on Kellan, then their rookie Slater beside him before giving Shae the signal to haul balls out of the engine bay.

"Okay, boys and girls. Let's see what we've got," Gamble clipped through the mic, hitting the words with enough volume to be heard over the wail of the sirens and the rattle and whoosh of the interior vehicle noise. He turned his attention to the display screen on the dashboard, scrolling through the updates from dispatch. "House fire, and from the sound of things, not a small one. Dispatch has a report of flames showing on the entire first floor and some kind of explosion. Huh," he added, his voice hitching in surprise. "That's weird. Only one nine-one-one call."

"Really?" Slater asked, pausing with one arm halfway through his coat. "On a Saturday morning? With an explosion?"

The rookie was right. That wasn't just weird. It was fucking crazy.

Shae's honey-colored ponytail swung from the back of one shoulder to the other as she checked the intersection in front of them and hung a sharp right. "Oakmont Boulevard marks the eastern edge of North Point. That neighborhood is as bad as it gets. People tend to mind their own business and not much else around there."

Kellan pictured the layout of their call area in his mind's eye, and damn, looked like weird was just their jumping-off point today. "Why the hell did we get called all the way out there? Isn't that Station Twelve's territory?"

"Dunno," Gamble said. "Might be the hazmat though. Squad always gets dibs on those calls, and if the fire's big enough, the guys from Twelve will be there, too. Speaking of which, this is a hazmat situation. Dispatch has the nine-one-one caller IDing the house as having a meth lab inside, so we're gonna have to be on our toes. Gear up and get your shit together."

"Copy that," Kellan said into the mic, Shae and Slater's identical response layering in with his over the headset. He put his senses on full alert as he shouldered into the heavy material of his coat and fastened the thing without looking. Following with the rest of his gear, he looked over at Slater to make sure the guy was all systems go with both his equipment and the nerves that had to be filling the kid to the goddamn brim right now.

Not that Kellan didn't get it. On this job, you were either scared or you lacked a pulse. The trick was learning how to throw your fear back like a double shot of Crown Royal and not let the afterburn kick your ass for the effort.

Inhale on a three-count. Exhale to five. Thump-thump. Thump-thump. Focus.

Kellan reached out to slide open the small window at his side. Breathing in, he took in every detail of the surroundings flying by him, from the bright blue sky to the crisp morning air that said autumn had truly arrived. The tightly knit buildings on both sides of the city streets made getting a clear visual on the fire's smoke-line tough, but the sharp, charred-ash scent beginning to filter in through the window made the back of Kellan's neck prickle.

Here we go.

CHAPTER SEVENTEEN

"Looks like we're first on-scene," Gamble said, pointing through the engine's windshield at the empty street in front of them, and Kellan didn't waste any time taking in the details. Small, squat houses lined either side of the narrow strip of pavement, each one in various states of dinginess or disrepair. A thick haze of gray smoke blanketed the block, chugging steadily from a two-story cottage midway up the street, and whoa, fighting this fire was going to be a goddamn chore. Not that he and everyone else from Seventeen wouldn't rise to the challenge of kicking this thing's ass, but they were going to sweat for every penny of today's paycheck.

Kellan shouldered into the harness of his SCBA tank, his heavy-soled boots thudding to the asphalt the second Shae pulled the engine to a stop in front of the house. Bright orange flames illuminated each of the four main-level windows in angry, persistent streaks, their color a direct contrast to the dark smoke funneling up toward the roofline. The second floor looked pretty intact, but with how fast this fire seemed to be moving, he was shit-sure that wouldn't last.

The radio on his shoulder crackled to life. "Alright, people," came Captain Bridges' voice over the line from the spot where he stood twenty paces away in full gear. "Dispatch has a report of a methamphetamine lab on the premises, so mask up and proceed with care. Hawk, Gates, get a vent on that roof. Dempsey, you and Faurier take Walker and McCullough for search and rescue. Gamble, you're on the nozzle with Slater once the house is clear. Go to work."

"Copy that," Kellan said, his pulse flaring faster and his feet already in go-mode toward the storage compartment in the engine that held his Halligan bar. Taking one last mental snapshot of the scene, he fell into step with Shae, following Dempsey and Faurier over the scraggly excuse for a lawn. The front door easily succumbed to Dempsey's well-placed kick, and a blast of heat and smoke rushed out to greet them like the world's rudest hostess.

"Masks," Faurier barked, each of them tugging their equipment into place over their faces. "McCullough, you and Walker take floor two. Dempsey and I will shake and bake down here. Let's make it quick."

"Copy," Shae hollered past the hiss of her regulator. Following Faurier and Dempsey into the hazy space of the foyer, she and Kellan cut a quick path toward the set of stairs to their left. He counted his paces, making a fast mental note of how far the exit was in case visibility got any worse. Sweat formed a hot band of moisture over his forehead, and he did his best to blink it back, taking slow, even breaths to make the most of the oxygen from his SCBA. The house seemed less fire-ravaged the farther they ascended, but only just. Whatever had sparked this blaze had dug in hard and deep.

After a few more steps, he and Shae reached the top of the staircase, a dark, narrow hallway splitting off to either the right or the left. "I'll take Bravo, you take Delta, we'll meet back here in the middle. Good?" she asked, turning toward the left side of the hall.

"Copy that." Kellan's knuckles tightened over his Halligan bar even though his Teflon-reinforced gloves padded much of the contact. Six paces over the floorboards brought him to a door on his left, and he shoved his way over the threshold without pretense.

"Fire department! Call out!"

The only answer was the crackling whoosh of flames trailing up the far wall. Kellan moved farther into the space, and wait—he spun on his boot heels—the room was completely empty. No furniture, no curtains on the single window allowing a few feeble shafts of sunlight past the soot and smoke.

No nothing.

A prickle of unease slid over the back of his neck, but he shoved the feeling aside. This house was on fire, and not a little bit. He didn't have time for weird coincidences.

Another ten seconds turned up a just-as-empty closet, and Kellan strode back toward the hallway, jamming the door behind him shut so the flames had less of a chance to spread. The radio chatter at his shoulder told him Hawk and Gates were more than halfway to getting the roof vented, and once they did, chances were high Bridges would want to hit this place with enough water to fill an Olympic-sized swimming pool.

"Fire department. Is anybody in here?" Kellan tried again, shouldering his way past the only other doorway at his end of the hall. The room on the other side was way smaller and way more darkly shadowed than the bedroom he had just checked, and despite the limited visibility, he instantly recognized the space in front of him as a bathroom.

He caught sight of the woman curled up in the bathtub a half-second later.

"Whoa!" He dropped to his knees, his Halligan bar jangling to the tile and his pulse sending a steady stream of adrenaline to every last cell in his body. "Ma'am? Can you hear me?" Kellan put a firm shake on the woman's shoulder, but her head simply lolled, sending her dark hair over her face. Dammit.

Sucking in a breath, he slapped one gloved hand over his radio. "Walker to Command."

"Command to Walker," Bridges answered, all business. "Report."

"I have an unconscious victim on the second floor, Delta side." He needed to find Shae and get this woman out of here, now.

"McCullough to Command, the rest of floor two is clear." Shae's voice filtered through the two-way, calm and controlled. "Walker, fall out to the primary exit. I've got your back."

Relief spilled through him. "Copy, McCullough," Kellan said, and Bridges' voice followed.

"Command to McCullough, copy that. Walker, you're a go. Drake and Copeland are standing by at the primary exit to assist."

The second the words registered, Kellan's arms shot out. Turning the victim to her back, he took a cursory look at her, just to make sure she had no obvious injuries he'd make worse with a fireman's carry...

And then he saw the woman's face.

"Angel?" His heart ricocheted against his ribs. For a stop-time second, Kellan thought surely his brain was playing some adrenaline-fueled, nasty-bastard trick on his eyes—how the hell could Angel be here, in the bathtub of a burning house, when she was supposed to be with Isabella?

After a single blink, he smashed down on his confusion. This fire was getting meaner by the second. He couldn't afford to do anything right now other than move.

Move.

Shoving away anything that wasn't uncut instinct, Kellan lifted Angel out of the bathtub and propped her over his shoulders. The threshold back to the hallway—two steps— the smoke-clogged stairs—twelve plus the landing to make a baker's dozen—the handful of paces to the front door—

all six. Each set of strides became a blur of shapes and sounds as he counted his way to the door. Sweat poured between his shoulder blades, his lungs constricting beneath the crush of adrenaline filling his chest, but he couldn't stop. Couldn't think.

Couldn't be scared Angel might be dead instead of at the diner with Isabella, where she was supposed to be giving the statement that would put DuPree away forever.

Sunlight blasted Kellan's field of vision, stunning his senses but not his movements as his boots pounded over the threshold and into the front yard. His muscles screamed with every step, but he refused to give in until a familiar female voice penetrated his consciousness.

"Easy, Walker. Let's see what we've got." Quinn Copeland, the second half of Station Seventeen's paramedic crew, rushed up to meet him with a gurney. Kellan lowered Angel to the thin mattress dividing the space between him and Copeland, reaching up to remove his helmet and his mask but not budging an inch as she began her rapid trauma assessment.

"Damn it." Quinn's face went from zero to shit-storm serious in less than a breath. "She's not breathing, and I can't find a pulse."

Kellan's gut took a hard slide toward his knees. "We need to help her. We need—" He yanked his chin in a rough glance from side to side. "Where's Drake?"

"He's on the other victim," she said quietly, her gloved hands moving fast enough over Angel's body to turn them into a purple blur.

"What?" Oh hell, how many women had been inside that house?

Copeland flattened her palms over Angel's chest and began CPR, and shit. Shit! This couldn't be happening.

"Gates found someone else inside just seconds after you radioed in, and from the sound of things, the guy's as bad off as this woman." She completed a round of compressions, pausing for a lightning-fast vitals check before shifting to resume CPR. "The paramedics from Twelve are on their way to help us get both victims to Remington Hospital. Until then, Drake and I have to divide and conquer here on-scene."

"You're not taking her to the hospital?" Kellan asked, dread filling his belly, and Copeland pegged him with a light gray stare that defied her sweet, all-American looks.

"Drake's guy is critical too, Walker, and they won't both fit in the ambo. We have to wait for the guys from Twelve to help us with transport, so right now I'm all this woman's got."

"No you're not," Kellan said. "Let me help." He jerked his chin toward his radio before she could protest. "Walker to Command, requesting to assist Copeland with the victim."

"Command to Walker," came Bridges' voice. "Affirmative. You are a go for medical assist."

Relief left his lungs on a hard burst. "Copy that, Command," Kellan said, quickly shucking the soot-stained leather on his hands in favor of a pair of nitrile medical gloves and squinting through the sunlight to look at Quinn.

"I've got your back, Copeland. Just tell me what to do to help you help her."

She didn't hesitate. "Okay. Take over compressions so I can get her hooked up to the monitor."

Copeland shifted her hands to make room for his to replace them, and Kellan leaned in from the other side of the gurney. Willing his hands not to shake and his focus not to falter, he laced his fingers together, palm over knuckles. He pressed them to the front of Angel's once-white dress, his brain making the startled realization that it was the same one she'd worn last night.

She hadn't even changed clothes from the party.

A fresh shot of adrenaline bloomed in his veins, but he stuffed back the heart-twisting detail. He had to focus on helping Angel, right here and right now. No emotions. Just actions.

Kellan flew into motion, starting CPR. *One and two and three and four…* Christ, she felt so small and frail, his hands spanning more than half of her chest. "Come on, Angel. Breathe. You need to breathe."

Copeland's white-blond brows winged up, her hands hitching over the leads to the portable monitor at the foot of the gurney. "Do you know this woman?"

A thread of warning uncurled in Kellan's chest despite all the go-go-go flooding through his bloodstream. Even a small admission would risk outing Isabella's off-the-books recon. "I…I've seen her before. She's an informant for the RPD. Or she's supposed to be."

"Well, you and I are going to do everything we can to help her."

Blocking everything from his brain that wasn't part of the trauma response, Kellan completed a few rounds of compressions before rotating with Quinn to monitor Angel's vitals. He registered his surroundings in clips of awareness—the radio byplay between Gamble and Slater as they moved through the house with the primary water line, the acrid scent of smoke tightening the back of his throat, the crease that deepened between Copeland's brows with every check of Angel's nonexistent vitals.

Jesus. How had this even happened? Angel was supposed to be with Isabella. She was supposed to be safe.

Instead, she was fighting for her life.

Kellan and Quinn completed a five-minute cycle of compressions, then another. His muscles burned to the point of cramping, and he whipped his coat from the frame of his shoulders to keep himself from overheating. His body processed the cool blast of air even though his brain refused to let him enjoy the relief, and come on—come on—for fuck's sake, why wasn't Angel responding?

"Command to Copeland, Command to Drake." Captain Bridges' voice cut a path into Kellan's awareness from the radio slung over the shoulder of Copeland's uniform. "Ambulance Twelve is on-scene."

"Thank God," Copeland murmured, sliding a gaze toward the flat red line moving over the screen of the portable monitor. A few seconds later, a dark-haired paramedic appeared at her side, and God damn it, Kellan hated every last bit of Quinn's expression as she greeted the guy.

"Unresponsive female pulled from the scene," she said, giving the paramedic the bullet in low, serious tones. "No breath sounds, no pulse. Began compressions fourteen minutes ago. No response."

"Fourteen minutes down is a long time." The paramedic looked from Copeland to Angel, then back again before adding, "You want to take her to Remington Hospital so the docs can call it?"

"No." Kellan heard the protest only after it had catapulted from his mouth. But they had to do something here. He had to do something. "Can't you intubate her? Or shock her with the defibrillator? Maybe she just needs a jolt to get her heart going."

Quinn's hand curled around his forearm. "Walker, we can't. Intubating her won't make her breathe on her own, and we can't shock her if she never had a heart rhythm to begin with. We'll continue CPR on the way to the hospital, but I'm sorry. She's gone."

Anger cranked Kellan's jaw hard enough to make his molars beg for forgiveness. Ripping his gloves from his hands, he grated out a harsh curse as Copeland and the paramedic from Twelve loaded the gurney into the back of the ambulance. Kellan swung his gaze over the scene, taking in the ruined, now-smoldering house and Parker's grim expression from where he knelt over a man about forty feet away.

...Drake's guy is critical too...Drake's guy...

Kellan strode across the pavement, his heart locked in his windpipe. Drake's eyes were on the monitor propped beside the crumbling curb, the other paramedic from Station Twelve doing CPR across from him. Kellan lasered in on the victim's face, shock and fear combining to punch him right in the throat.

The second victim was Danny Marcus.

Parker looked up as Kellan came to a clumsy stop a few feet away. "Hey, man. You okay?"

"I..." Kellan shook off the question, because answering it with a yes would make him an epic fucking liar. "How is he?"

Although the other paramedic didn't slow her compressions, Drake gave up a tight shake of his head. "No vitals. Gates found him in a hall closet. Looks like they were cooking meth in the kitchen, and somehow the chemicals ignited. He must've been trying to hide from the fire until you guys showed up. I did all I could, but that smoke is pretty toxic. Once you breathe enough of it in..."

"Yeah," Kellan said, already in motion. "Thanks, Drake."

No emotions. Just what's in front of you. Go.

Pushing past the adrenaline-fueled shake of his legs, he cut a straight path to Engine Seventeen. The details were far too tidy to be accidental, the victims too connected to him and Isabella and last night's party to be a coincidence. Angel and Danny Marcus were both dead.

Which meant Isabella was in danger of being next.

Although it took all of his waning strength, he crammed the thought down long enough to haul himself into the back of the engine and grab his cell phone from the storage compartment behind the operator's seat. His fingers jerked in broken motions over the screen, but somehow, he managed to pull up Moreno's number and hit "send."

Come on, sweetheart. Kellan's pulse slammed against his eardrums. *Answer the phone. Be okay. Answer the—*

"Moreno."

Relief hit him in a hot wave. "Isabella? It's Kellan."

"Walker?" She sounded odd, her voice laced tight with surprise and a tone he'd never heard her use and didn't recognize. "Oh God, are you safe?"

214

Wait, how could she already know about the fire? "Yeah, are you?"

"Yes, I'm…" Isabella broke off in confusion. "Angel never showed, Kellan. DuPree's got her."

Dread leaked through his limbs, but still he said, "I know."

"What? How?"

As much as Kellan knew he needed to tell her what had happened, he couldn't deliver the news over the phone. "I'm at a fire scene in North Point. How fast can you get here?"

CHAPTER EIGHTEEN

Isabella didn't even wait for her Mustang to make a full stop behind the cluster of lights-flashing emergency vehicles before throwing the car into park and flinging the driver's side door wide on its hinges. Her boots flew over the pavement, temples pounding from all the thoughts trying to wedge their way into her over-crowded brain, but she swiped them out of the way in favor of the only one that mattered.

She needed to find Walker.

"Excuse me." Station Seventeen's rookie—Smith? No, Slater—stepped into her path over the weed-infested sidewalk. "Ma'am? I'm sorry, but you can't—"

Isabella didn't even slow by a fraction. Thrusting her badge over her head, she half-hollered, "RPD," continuing over the concrete and crab grass. She searched wildly for Kellan, the tang of smoke strong enough to leave a bitter taste in her mouth as her breath moved in and out. The small clapboard house in front of her was no longer on fire, but from the look of things, the status change was recent. First responders milled around the front yard, some returning hoses and equipment to the half-dozen emergency vehicles lining the block, some moving into and around the house, probably to make sure the fire stayed out. Isabella looked at every face, her eyes darting over the names emblazoned in reflective letters across the back of every coat, and for the love of all things sacred and holy, where the hell—

"Walker!" Isabella's heart slammed into her sternum as she caught sight of him by the side yard, away from the throng of other first responders. He stared at the scene, his bright red suspenders locked in a tight line over equally tight-looking muscles, and sweet Jesus. He looked awful.

"Isabella." Relief flared over his soot-streaked face, although the emotion lasted less than a second. His dark hair stuck up in a thousand directions as if he'd been tugging on it without mercy, and his T-shirt and turnout gear were covered in heavy layers of sweat and grime. But none of those things froze her to the grass in panic and fear.

It was the look in his eyes that did that, pinning her into place with the sort of bone-deep sadness that felt like it went on forever, and oh. Oh God.

"Tell me," she blurted, closing the rest of the space between them with a handful of brisk strides. Kellan's hands found her shoulders as he swept a gaze over her from head to toe, and she reached up to curl her fingers over his. "I'm fine, Kellan. *Please* just tell me what the hell is going on."

"How do you know DuPree had Angel this morning? Do you have proof?"

"N-no." She shook her head, trying to process the question. "Someone working with DuPree called me this morning after Angel didn't show. Somehow he found out I'm a cop, and he knew she'd agreed to meet me, but…"

Realization clicked like a row of dominoes falling one right into the other, sending a hard shot of fear through her blood like ice water.

DuPree didn't have Angel. She was here. Inside.

Dead.

Isabella felt herself lunge toward the house only after her

legs had started to go, but she barely made it three steps before Kellan moved in to stop her.

His arms hooked around her shoulders, her waist. "Easy, Isabella. Hold on for a second." His grip was tight enough to be unforgiving, but she struggled against it anyway.

This wasn't happening. Not again. Isabella had promised. *She'd promised.*

Panic seized her lungs, turning her breath to sand. "I need...you have to let me..."

"The fire's barely out. You can't go inside," Kellan said, his mouth somewhere by her left ear, but no, no, no, she had to help Angel. She had to get into that goddamned *house.*

With another push, she struggled against the vise-like hold keeping her grounded. Kellan shocked her by letting go of her shoulders, then shocked her even harder by staying in her path and cupping her face between both palms to keep her from running.

"Isabella, *stop.*"

Her chest hitched at an unnatural pace, hot, traitorous tears burning beneath her eyelids. "Angel is in there, isn't she? DuPree killed her."

"Isabella..."

She gripped the sleeves of his T-shirt so hard, her knuckles ached. "Yes or no! Walker, I need to hear you say it."

"I'm so sorry," Kellan said, sadness scraping over the words like sandpaper. "We did everything we possibly could, but yes. Both Angel and Danny Marcus died in this house fire."

Oh. God. "Danny Marcus is dead too?" Isabella's knees buckled.

But Kellan stepped in closer to steady her. "Yes."

For a second, she couldn't speak or think or breathe. Angel had trusted her. She'd promised the woman safety, and instead, Angel was dead.

Just like Marisol.

Isabella closed her eyes and fought the urge to be sick.

She had to focus. She was standing in front of a crime scene, and it needed to be processed. If she could get inside, if she could just find one sliver of evidence linking DuPree to this fire, if she could figure out a way to trace the phone call she'd received, then maybe she could fix this. She had to fix this. She had to shut out the pain and work.

"Isabella."

Although her name was little more than a whisper on Kellan's lips, it cracked her wide open, and she sagged against him. Angel was dead. DuPree had murdered her. Isabella couldn't fix this.

But she knew someone who could.

Pulling back from Kellan's sturdy embrace, she slid her cell phone from the back pocket of her jeans. Her fingers flew over the screen, her heart racing along with them as she pressed the phone to her ear.

"Come on. Come on, come on, come on," Isabella murmured, her heart catching in her throat when the call connected after the second ring.

"Hey, it's me. I need you down in North Point, right now. It's urgent."

The next fifteen minutes were some of the longest of her life. She had questions—Christ, no less than a thousand of them—but despite the spinning in her brain and the pressure crushing her chest, she stood still and waited and remembered how to breathe. Kellan stood beside her, not saying anything but not budging either, until finally, a voice sounded off from behind her, low and serious.

"Would you like to tell me what the hell is going on here?"

Isabella turned to meet the unreadable expression Sinclair had paired with the demand, unsure whether to feel relieved or filled to the brim with dread. "Julian DuPree murdered two people here this morning. I don't know if I can prove it, but I'm absolutely sure he's responsible."

With a deep breath, Isabella told her boss what she'd uncovered, from the intel Carmen had given her last week to the deal she'd struck with Danny Marcus in the park. Things got a little dicey when she got to the party she and Kellan had crashed off the books, but despite the steel-gray glint in his stare, Sinclair listened silently until she finished.

"Is that everything?" he asked, and she nodded.

"Yes. Look, I know you're mad"—the glint in his eyes simmered darker, and she amended her statement— "furious. But Angel is dead. DuPree has to be stopped."

Sinclair stepped in, his eyes moving from Isabella to Kellan, who still stood beside her on the front lawn of the fire-eaten house.

"Talk to me about this scene. Are there any signs of foul play?" he asked, and Isabella's stomach pitched at the full ten seconds Kellan took before responding.

He swept a long gaze over the house before turning to look at Sinclair. "Best we can tell right now is that the fire started in the kitchen, where there's evidence of a pretty big meth lab. It looks like someone got careless with the chemicals and the heat, which sparked an explosion that made the flames spread rapidly. Angel and Marcus appear to have been hiding to stay away from the fire, but the smoke inside the house was highly toxic. We did everything in our power to try and revive them both, but neither one made it."

"Wait." Isabella blinked. Processed. And came up with a big, fat *oh hell no*. "Are you saying these deaths look like an accident?"

"This fire hasn't even been officially out for more than thirty minutes," Kellan said slowly. "I can only tell you what things look like right this second, but the fire marshal will have to put all the pieces together to give you anything concrete. If he can even find anything in that mess."

Deep inside Isabella's chest, something snapped. "I don't give a shit what this *looks like*! This fire, these"—her throat knotted, turning her words high-pitched and wobbly—"deaths, they aren't an accident. DuPree is behind this, Kellan. These are *killings*. Angel and Marcus were *murdered*, and DuPree is responsible."

She sucked in a breath to keep arguing, but Kellan's next words stunned her into silence.

"I know, Isabella."

"Y-you believe me?" she asked.

"Of course I do." His expression went pale and grim as he shifted his stony blue gaze from her to Sinclair. "I'm just not sure you're going to find enough evidence to prove it."

Oh, yes she would. Isabella didn't care if she had to comb every inch of this scene and not eat, sleep, or stop until she had DuPree dead to rights.

Just as long as Sinclair opened an official investigation.

"Sam," she started, but he cut her off with a lift of one hand.

"All I need is a yes or no. Do you believe DuPree is behind this, and that he either killed these two people or was directly involved in their deaths?"

Isabella's heart pounded, but she stabbed her boots into the unkempt grass and stood tall, sparing only the briefest of glances toward the scorched clapboard and the smashed-out windows on the house before saying, "Yes. I'm absolutely certain."

"Okay." Sinclair's face showed no emotion even though his single word had just filled her with too many of them to count. "Let's go talk to your Captain, Walker. I'm going to need a very detailed walk-through of everything your people saw today. As of right now, this is no longer a fire scene. It's a potential crime scene. And I'm in charge of the investigation."

* * *

Isabella sat in the chair across from Sinclair's desk, her temples throbbing and her heart full of holes. Sam had been painfully quiet during the course of the three hours they'd spent at the house on Oakmont. Not that he was an overly chatty guy otherwise—in fact, Isabella would swear he'd emerged from the womb with his poker face fully intact and nailed into place. But he'd been one hundred percent business as they'd worked the scene, then dead silent after they'd reached the Thirty-Third. The fifteen minutes they'd been sitting across from each other as he wordlessly read and re-read the notes she'd kept on everything she'd discovered over the last week and a half had quickly become torture, and she'd had to bite her lip to bleeding to keep herself quiet.

Isabella might have plenty to say, but Sinclair still hadn't made the call to officially open this case. Hell, he hadn't even called in the rest of their team to help with gathering and examining the facts so he could run them up the chain of command. And she could not, under any circumstances, risk even the tiniest chance that he wouldn't do either.

They had to catch DuPree. She had to work. Because if she didn't work, she'd think about Angel. Angel, whose body was at the morgue at Remington Hospital. Angel, who was supposed to have met Isabella for breakfast, but instead she'd been trapped inside a burning building, terrified and alone. Angel, who she'd sworn to protect.

On second thought, screw biting her tongue. Julian DuPree needed to go down for this. Hard and fast and right goddamn now.

"How quickly can we get Peterson to okay an investigation and order search warrants for the penthouse at the Metropolitan?" Isabella asked. The surveillance equipment alone had to hold a gold mine of guilty-as-charged.

Sinclair fixed her with an unreadable blue-gray stare. "We need to rewind a little here, Moreno. I'm not calling anybody just yet."

All the emotion from the morning—fuck, from the whole week and a half since Kellan had found those photographs—surged past the tipping point, and something hot and without a name exploded in her chest.

"You cannot be *serious*," Isabella cut out, her spine going ramrod straight against the office chair behind her. "Julian DuPree is a psychopath who has forced God knows how many women into prostitution by keeping them locked up and stringing them out on heroin. He gets off on watching from behind the scenes as these women are violated five and six times a night, and he murdered two people—that we know of—in cold blood!"

Sinclair matched Isabella's fire with a whole lot of ice. "Actually, I'm *very* serious. And so are the actions you took to pursue this guy off the books when I told you in no uncertain terms to back the hell off."

And there's the rub. "Look, I know I took some liberties with regard to this case—"

"Liberties?" He let go of the word as if it tasted rotten. "You ignored my orders. The chain of command doesn't exist for you to piss on it, Moreno."

A ripple of warning traveled the length of Isabella's spine. Yeah, she'd known Sinclair was going to be shit-slinging mad that she'd taken matters into her own hands. She just hadn't thought he'd be completely unreasonable on top of it.

DuPree was insidious. He had to be stopped. Period.

"There's no way these deaths were an accident," Isabella said, diving right in to round two. "Somehow DuPree found out I'm a cop, and he connected the dots from the video footage from the penthouse to put me with both Marcus and Angel. Then he killed them to keep them quiet."

"Or they were cooking meth and accidentally sparked a fire, then died from smoke inhalation before they could be rescued by the RFD. There's evidence that points in both directions here."

Sinclair's words were quiet and far from an argument, but Isabella's nerves were beyond frayed, her composure completely shattered.

"You're really not going to have Peterson open a case after you just spent three hours walking that scene with me and half the freaking fire department?" Her voice came out unnaturally shrill, but she was so far past caring. "What was the point in even asking me if I was sure these are murders if you weren't going to *act*?"

"Of course I'm going to act," Sinclair said, the stone cold certainty both in his voice and on his face killing the rest of the argument she'd been about to launch. "I'm calling Peterson with a recommendation to start a full investigation, starting immediately. If DuPree is behind these murders, I want him to answer for them, along with every other heinous thing he's ever done or even thought about doing."

Isabella opened her mouth. Tried like hell to verbalize an intelligent thought. Couldn't make it happen for all the world.

"I don't understand," she finally managed. "You just told me you weren't calling him."

"No. I said I wasn't calling him *yet*."

Nothing followed but the far-off ringing of phones from the homicide office down the hall and the muffled white noise of afternoon traffic moving over the street two stories below, but she wasn't about to get shy—about this case or anything else—now. "What are you waiting for?" Isabella asked.

Sinclair scrubbed a hand over the dark blond stubble peppering his jaw and leaned back in his desk chair, although the increased space between them did nothing to dilute the seriousness in his expression. "I'm waiting for you to go home."

"E-excuse me?" Isabella sputtered, her pulse tripping through her veins. "Why would I go home if we're opening an investigation?"

"You're going home because that's where I'm sending you. As of this moment, you're off this case."

"Sam." The single syllable was all she could push past the dread keeping her pinned into place. But he couldn't kick her off this investigation. Not when Angel had been killed for agreeing to meet her. Isabella had to make this right.

Sinclair shook his head. "You're a great cop, Moreno. But even great cops can't freelance in this unit. And they sure as shit don't get to buck the chain of command that starts with me."

"You bend the rules all the time," she said, clamping down on her lip as soon as the words were out. Okay, so pointing out his rules-are-mostly-just-guidelines mentality might've been a teensy bit brash. But Sinclair didn't exactly go by the book all the time, or hell, even *half* the time.

Just when she was certain she'd surpassed her daily quota for total fucking shock, Sinclair said, "You're right. Sometimes I do. But there's a huge difference between massaging the rules to get the job done and going completely rogue. You repeatedly put yourself in danger for evidence the State's Attorney can't touch because you had no search warrant when you obtained it, you showed a blatant disregard for a direct order given to you by your commanding officer, and don't even get me started on the fact that you brought a civilian on not one, but all of these field trips of yours."

"Believe me, that part wasn't by choice," she argued, but Sinclair wasn't having a single word of it.

"Everything you did was by choice. Your decision to pursue DuPree off the books—"

Despair drove her to interrupt. "You wouldn't let me pursue him on the books!"

He interrupted right back. "Your decision to keep me and the rest of this unit at arm's length rather than trusting us to back you up once you'd talked to your CI—"

No. Way. "Is that what this is about? You're booting me from this case just because I don't want to share my feelings while we all have s'mores around the campfire?" Un-be-fucking-lievable!

"No," Sinclair bit out. "I'm booting you from this case because you need to learn that being a cop isn't just about you. It's about solving cases as part of a team. And if you can't work with me and Hollister and Maxwell and Hale and

Capelli—if you can't trust us when you need us, either out there or in here—then you're not working this case."

Isabella blinked through the afternoon sunlight slanting in past the shades. Sinclair knew her. He'd read her personnel file cover to cover a thousand times—shit, he'd put the full court press on her recruitment to the intelligence unit the second she'd been promoted to detective. He knew why she'd become a cop, why she'd made it her mission to become a detective so she could stop men just like Julian DuPree. He couldn't. He *wouldn't* do this to her.

"Sam," she whispered, her throat rasping over her words. "You can't take me off this case. Please."

But Sinclair simply shook his head. "I'm sorry, Moreno, but I just did. You're on restricted desk duty, updating your unrelated paperwork until further notice. And if you so much as look at this case again without my permission, I'll see to it personally that you walk the beat at the shopping mall for the rest of your career. Are we understood?"

CHAPTER NINETEEN

Kellan pulled himself from the driver's seat of his Camaro, every one of his muscles feeling as if it had been strung up and stretched thin. Captain Bridges had given him a lot of latitude during yesterday's shift, sparing him from his duties on engine in order to take Isabella and Sinclair through the scene of the fire, inch by inch. But Seventeen had rolled out on four back-to-back calls after that, and while two of them had been relatively minor, the three-car smash-up on the highway and the utility worker they'd rescued from a drainage pipe had sucked away energy he'd had to manufacture out of sheer will. Add to it the fact that DuPree had somehow managed to ID Isabella as a cop and kill both Angel and Danny Marcus, then cover it up while still flaunting the crime in their faces?

Yeah. Stick a fork in him. He was freaking cooked.

Kellan sent a few extra covert gazes around the parking lot in front of his apartment complex, his awareness on full-alert as he walked the path from the asphalt to the building's double-wide glass front doors. If DuPree knew who Isabella was, chances were high that the bastard had ID'd Kellan, too. He'd called Kylie and Devon as a precaution, his sister kicking into what-the-hell mode and Devon kicking equally hard into oh-hell-no mode. Kellan had assured Kylie he'd be fine (and Devon had assured Kellan *she'd* be fine—thank fuck), passing along the same assurances to Bridges and everyone else at Seventeen when Sinclair had told them all to be extra vigilant for the time being, just in case. Gamble had even gone so far as to get all Special Forces on his ass, making him swear to check in at regular intervals between now and their next shift. And Kellan thought he was paranoid. He didn't even want to know what had happened to make Gamble so sharp around the edges.

Speak of the devil. Kellan liberated his ringing cell phone from the back pocket of his jeans and tapped the icon to take the call. "I left the fire house ten minutes ago, you know."

"Yeah. You home?" Gamble asked without pretense.

Kellan swiped his way into the building with his electronic key card, stepping into the empty lobby and hitting the button for the elevator. "Copy, jackass."

"That's all I needed to hear," Gamble said. Leave it to a Marine to set their code word for the all-clear to jackass. "Later. Jackass," he added, and Kellan could swear he heard an oh-so-rare smile in the guy's voice just before he disconnected the call.

"Nice talking to you, too," Kellan said to the dead air, a small huff of laughter crossing his lips. Sharp around the edges or not, there were far worse people to have his back.

The elevator arrived seconds later and he stepped on, looking down at the cell phone still in his hand. Scrolling through his list of contacts, his finger hovered over the icon labeled *Moreno*, his brain doing the yes-no-yes-no dance the whole way to the fourth floor, and screw it. He might have some ironclad impulse control in all other situations, and Isabella might be more than your average badass. But DuPree was a psychopath who had killed two people in direct connection with her investigation, and she'd taken Angel's death as hard as he'd expected. Kellan needed to know Isabella was okay.

Shit. For all her tight-lipped caution and chin-up bravado, he missed her. And dangerous or not, he wasn't quite ready to lock that feeling away with all the rest.

His finger came down on the icon two seconds before the elevator doors opened, but it wasn't the sound coming through his phone that shocked him into place as soon as he stepped into the corridor.

It was the sound of someone else's phone, ringing from a few doors down, that blew Kellan the fuck away.

"Moreno?" He blinked, certain his weary, bleary eyes weren't cooperating with reality. But Isabella looked up at him from the spot where she'd been sitting outside the door to his apartment, her cell phone in her hand and a look of total shock on her face.

"Hey, I...are you calling me?" she asked as she stood, and Christ, could Kellan be any less suave?

"Sorry, yeah." He hit the *end call* icon with the edge of his thumb, and her phone fell silent. "I wanted to make sure you're okay."

"Oh." Isabella nodded, her hair spilling forward to shield her eyes. "Sorry to just show up like this. I'm sure you're really tired. Or, you know. Maybe busy. This was probably a bad idea."

Kellan lowered his brows in confusion, and what was that look on her face? "No. I'm glad you're here." His smile lasted only briefly before he asked, "So, *are* you okay?"

"Not really. No. I mean, I'm safe," she added, likely in response to the swift step he'd just taken in her direction and the tactical stare he'd just lasered over either side of the narrow, empty hallway. "But yeah. I'm not okay."

"You're not hurt," he said, and looked like his tactical tendencies weren't on the shelf just yet.

"No."

"Are you hungry?" While he might not share the chef-level cooking gene with Kylie, he could still throw together some basics. She needed to eat if she was going to keep up her strength for this case.

But Isabella shook her head. "No."

Remembering the look on her face when she'd arrived at yesterday's fire scene, he quietly asked, "Is it Angel?"

She didn't answer. Unable to help it, Kellan reached out, his fingers tracing the curve of her cheekbone. "This isn't your fault, Isabella. You had no way of knowing DuPree would find out you're a cop. You were doing your best to keep Angel safe."

A laugh crossed her lips, although the sound held no humor. "I don't...I really don't want to talk about what happened to Angel, if that's okay with you."

"Okay. Then what do you want?"

Isabella leaned her cheek against his hand for only a second before stepping in to obliterate the space between them. "I want you to let me come inside."

Her mouth met his in a rush, and holy hell, he could taste her for a month and still not want to come up for air. Capturing her face between both palms, Kellan slid his fingers through the sweet, coconut-scented fall of her hair, holding her in place so he could lay claim to every last bit of her mouth. But for as much as he took, Isabella took it right back, kissing him harder and faster until they were pressed together from mouth to chest to hips with no sign of stopping.

"This," she murmured, sliding her hand between Kellan's legs. "I want this, right now."

His cock jerked at both her touch and her demand, and yeah. Yeah, not stopping sounded like a Nobel Prize-winning idea.

The elevator rumbled softly from a few doors down, momentarily breaking the spell. "Inside," he said against her mouth, groaning at the friction of Isabella's lips on his as she nodded a fervent yes. He managed to get his key in the lock on the third try—thank you, raging hard-on—and they spilled into his foyer in a flurry of hot kisses and near-desperate grabs at body parts and clothing. But damn it, he and Moreno had been put on high alert for a reason, and the ingrained defenses of his training weren't going to let go of him, no matter how badly he wanted to pull off her jeans and fuck her right on the spot.

"Wait," Kellan grated. "Need to check the apartment, just in case."

Isabella nodded in agreement, and hell, this woman was perfect. "Your bedroom's this way?" she asked, pointing down the hallway to the right.

"Yeah. I've got the main room and the kitchen."

"Okay. I'll take the rest," she said, turning back to give him one last kiss. "Just do me a favor and don't dawdle."

Kellan kissed her back just as hard. "Believe me, sweetheart. That is the *last* thing on my mind."

He moved through his apartment, checking both the kitchen and main living space with fast, methodical precision. While the interruption and distance might have killed the mood under different circumstances, he found himself shocked to discover that the wait to have Isabella only heightened his want and turned him on more.

At least, until she didn't come out of his bedroom.

"Moreno?" Dread pushed his pulse faster against this throat. Coiling his muscles and preparing to strike, Kellan inhaled soundlessly, slipping past the door with his senses on high alert.

And then he caught sight of her, and his heartbeat sped up for a whole different reason.

"Hey." Isabella looked at him from the center of his bed, where she lay across the comforter in nothing but a lacy black bra and a matching pair of panties. "Your bedroom's clear. Took you long enough."

A chuckle rumbled up from his chest. "You're going to pay for that."

Her reply rode out over a sassy smile that made him think a thousand dirty things about her mouth. "I certainly hope so. Now come here and take off my panties."

Kellan whipped his shirt over his head and kicked off his

boots, discarding both on the floorboards at the foot of his bed. But as much as part of him was tempted to finish losing his clothes so he could lose his mind in the tight, hot space between Isabella's legs, a deeper, more instinctive part of him paused.

"No."

"What?" Her brows shot up, her spine straightening against his bed pillows.

But he didn't recant. "No."

Moving to the side of the bed, he took her in with a lingering gaze. Her lush curves surrendered to the black lace that cradled them, dusky brown nipples just visible beneath the fabric, and Kellan barely fought the urge to taste them as he slid in next to her on the mattress.

He kissed her neck, cupping one breast lightly in his palm. "I didn't spend a lot of time here the other night because I was in such a hurry to fuck you."

Letting go of a moan that nearly wrecked him, Isabella canted her hips in a touch-seeking thrust. "You say that like it's a bad thing."

"It's not a bad thing that I wanted to be inside you," Kellan agreed, skimming a thumb over her nipple, a bolt of wicked satisfaction laddering up his spine as it tightened to a stiff point behind the lace. She was so responsive, so brash in taking exactly what she wanted, and hell if that didn't make him want to slow down and touch her all the more. "But now I want to make up for my oversight."

Another moan, and she trailed a hand over the flat of her belly. "Don't make me start without you."

The thought of Isabella slipping her fingers beneath that tiny triangle of lace to make herself come sent a hard ache from the base of his spine to his balls. "Go right ahead."

Her mouth parted in a soft O, prompting Kellan to lean in and taste her surprise. "What?" she asked.

He bit down on her bottom lip with just enough pressure to skirt the boundary between pleasure and pain. "I'm about to turn you on in ways you've only imagined before now.

You don't really think I'm going to tell you no if you want to return the favor."

"You want to watch me touch myself?" Her fingers inched lower, down past the indent of her belly button, and clearly, she was warm to the idea.

Kellan grasped her hand and placed it directly between her legs, because he was fucking *incendiary* for the idea. "Yes. I want to see exactly how you need to be touched."

"What else do you want?" Isabella pushed her hips up in a slow glide, her fingers pressing against her lace-covered sex.

He bit back a groan. Jesus, she had no idea how hot her tenacity was. "I want to take this off"—he dipped his head to the slim line of her shoulder, running his tongue along the ink-colored ribbon of her bra—"so I can learn your gorgeous tits with my hands and my mouth, just like I did with your pussy the other night."

Her back arched, and Kellan didn't wait for another invitation. Moving his hand to the back of her rib cage, he found the delicate clasp nestled between her shoulder blades, freeing it with a quick turn of his wrist. Isabella looked at him, just a second's worth of sweetness in her milk chocolate eyes as she slipped the lace from her body.

Gorgeous didn't even touch this woman.

He looked back at her, wanting to memorize every nuance and curve. The way her hair framed her face and shoulders, how her nipples pointed up, tight with the need to be touched. The sight of her long fingers still pressed to the lace between her tawny thighs.

"Kellan," she whispered. "I need—"

The rest of her words became a keening cry as he closed his lips around one nipple, because as much as Isabella needed to be touched, he needed *her*, just like this. Sliding his tongue in a slow circle, Kellan tasted and sucked, angling his body over hers as she lay back on the bed.

"Ohhhh." The sound spilled from her mouth, her exhale heating the back of his neck. Her soft, sensual cries made his cock throb behind the fly of his jeans, but when her fingers delved beneath the edge of her panties, he damn near lost his mind.

Kellan let go of her breast, his eyes fixed on her fingers as they disappeared provocatively between her legs. "That's it," he grated, his breath shaky with want. "Show me what you want."

"I want…" Isabella's knees widened, her back bowing. "Don't stop doing that with your mouth. And don't stop watching."

"My pleasure."

Continuing to keep his body weight braced on one side, Kellan dropped his mouth back to her nipple, curling his fingers beneath the swell of her breast to hold her close. The angle gave him a perfect vantage point to watch her busy fingers, his breath moving faster and his sucking growing harder as she circled her fingers over her clit.

Isabella moaned, her nipple pebbling harder beneath his lips. She buried her thumb at the top of her sex, tilting her hips up and letting her fingers drift lower, then lower still.

Kellan froze, his cock turning to absolute steel as he realized exactly where she was touching herself. Keeping his mouth on her nipple, he let go of her breast, gliding his fingers over her body until they twined with hers. She stilled at the contact, but he didn't hesitate.

"Show me."

He didn't know whether to be more stunned or turned on when Isabella complied. But then she was pulling the lace from her hips, returning her hand to his and guiding it to the heat between her legs, and yeah. He'd never been so turned on in his fucking life.

Kellan slid his index finger into her pussy in one seamless stroke. She bucked against the heel of his hand, and he withdrew only long enough to grab her hand and return it to the sweet spot of her clit.

Isabella sighed her approval, stroking herself and pushing her hips up as he slipped two fingers inside. Her inner muscles squeezed, and he watched with pleasure while she touched her clit harder, faster. Kellan pumped his fingers with ease, working her sex in slow, deep thrusts, using the slickness from her pussy to draw a path toward the sweet, tight cleft of her ass.

"*Ah.*" She dug her heels into the comforter, tilting her hips to chase his touch.

Kellan looked up at her. "Show me," he demanded again.

And again, Isabella did.

Lowering her hand from the top of her sex, she delved lower between her legs. She skimmed her index finger over the tightly drawn muscle at the entrance to her ass, pressing just hard enough for him to feel the rest of her vibrate in response.

"There. *There,*" she grunted, and he replaced her finger with his in a flash.

"Like this?" Kellan confirmed. He circled her opening with the tip of his ring finger, a dark smile tugging at the corners of his mouth as Isabella moaned in reply. Her hand returned to the apex of her thighs, and between her fast ministrations above and his slow, purposeful movements below, her breaths quickly became shallow. Turning his hand, he increased the pressure just slightly, breaching her hole with the pad of his finger while reclaiming her nipple with a punishing kiss. A cry broke from the back of her throat, gravel and silk at the same time, but if anything, it only urged him not to stop. He sucked and pressed in time with the rhythm of Isabella's fingers on her clit, until finally, she began to pulse from the inside out.

"Kellan. Oh, God, I'm…"

"Show me," he demanded, thrusting the tip of his finger deeper into her ass. "I'm right here, sweetheart. Show me what you need."

Her hips jerked, her body clamping all the way down before unraveling in waves. Kellan coaxed her through all of them, lightening his touches bit by bit as her body went lax, and Christ in heaven, how could anyone be so sweet and so sinful all at once?

"Kellan."

The throaty tone of Isabella's voice made his blood race. He lifted his head from her kiss-swollen nipple, pushing himself up from beside her to return her stare through the morning sunlight. "Yeah?"

She spread her legs, pinning him with a stare he felt from breath to bones. "I need you. Right here." Her gaze flicked down at the same time her hips tilted up to give him an unimpeded view of her bare, glistening sex. "Right. Now."

Kellan's heart slammed in his chest. He knew he should take Isabella in, to go slow and discover every inch of her, but damn it, he couldn't wait.

He *wanted* her. He didn't want to be cautious or controlled or calm. He wanted to break all the boxes keeping his impulses in check, smashing every last one of them so he could fuck her until she screamed and feel it in his blood and breath and balls when she did.

The same deep-seated instinct that had driven him to take his time before now forced him into action. In the fastest movements possible, Kellan threw off his jeans and boxer briefs, pausing only briefly to grab a condom from his bedside table drawer. Seconds later, he knelt between Isabella's legs, sliding the head of his cock along her folds just once before giving in to fill her with one smooth thrust.

His breath escaped on a groan. Oh hell, her pussy was so tight and hot and absolutely perfect, he was tempted to come just from the feel of her. Kellan bit his lip to fight the throb at the base of his spine, tempering his raw, dirty pleasure with the pain. Isabella arched up, flattening her palms over his ass to keep him anchored inside her pussy, the deep squeeze of her inner muscles gripping his cock and obliterating his composure.

Fuuuuck. He didn't have a chance in hell of lasting even thirty seconds like this. He pulled back, only an inch, searching for control. Pushing back home, Kellan repeated the movement once, then again, until he and Isabella found a slow, deep rhythm. He leaned forward to place his palms on either side of her shoulders, and Isabella gasped at the change in angle, as if he'd discovered some hidden spot inside her.

Oh, hell yeah. Now *this* he could do for fucking ever. Especially if it meant she'd keep making those hot little sounds.

Kellan gripped the comforter for balance, repeating the motion and rotating his hips. "You like that," he said, and even though his words had been all statement, Isabella nodded in reply.

"Yes." Her eyes glittered through the dark sweep of her lashes as she looked up at him. Opening her knees wider, she hooked her inner thighs around his waist. "Please. Oh God, Kellan. Don't stop. *Please.*"

Something about the way her tone shaped the last word hit him square in the chest. He wasn't shy in the bedroom, and clearly, Isabella wasn't either. Talking dirty was a hell of a turn-on. But all at once, Kellan realized she wasn't asking because she liked the feel of him fucking her, or even because she wanted to come for the sake of the pleasure. In this moment, she *needed* the release, like food or water or breath.

And he was going to give it to her. Even if he had to lose control to get her there.

Kellan brushed his mouth over hers, just a fast stroke of lips on lips before beginning to thrust again. Isabella met his motions, rocking with him, daring him to move faster and harder until the space between them didn't exist. Her nails curved into the bare skin of his ass, but not even the sweet sting could distract him from his purpose. He pushed inside her, over and over, watching his cock disappear between her pretty pink folds until finally, her eyes flew wide.

"I won't stop." Kellan pistoned his hips, filling her pussy as proof. "I know what you need, sweetheart. Go on and take it. Come for me."

Her voice broke on a cry as her body began to tremble, and the combination blindsided him. His release razored up from deep between his thighs, gripping him and forcing him to let go all at once. Isabella knotted her legs around his waist, her muscles clasped against him both inside and out, and the sensation was too much. With a moan that turned into a shout, Kellan climaxed, burying his cock deep as he came in wave after wave of uncut pleasure.

They lay together, forehead to forehead, chest to chest, bodies joined, until inevitably, he had to slip across the hall for a quick clean-up. He returned to find Isabella still in the middle of his bed, holding her T-shirt over her otherwise still-bare chest.

Although Kellan's gut knotted in concern, he kept the emotion far from his face. "Hey. You okay?"

"Yeah. Absolutely," she said, although he could've spotted the lie from forty paces out. "I should probably go."

But she didn't make a move to do it.

"You don't have to," Kellan told her. Yeah, saying so was a risk. But for fuck's sake, the look on her face matched her lack of definitive movement toward the door. Something had happened yesterday, something that had prompted Isabella to come over to his apartment and wait for him to come home.

"I know," she said, dropping her gaze to the black cotton still clutched across her front. But again, she didn't move, and screw propriety and impulse and risk.

He wanted Isabella to stay.

Kellan grabbed his boxer briefs, slipping them over his hips before sitting down on the bed next to her. "Is that what you really want? To go?"

For a second, he thought she'd say yes—Christ, her knuckles were damn near white from her death grip on that T-shirt.

But then she looked up at him, her gorgeous brown eyes brimming with too many emotions to name, and shocked him by whispering, "No. I don't want to go."

CHAPTER TWENTY

Girl, it's official. You have lost your goddamn mind.

Isabella closed her eyes, digging deep for a breath that would calm her racing heartbeat and slap some sense back into her clearly malfunctioning brain. After dividing her night between pacing the floor in her living room and staring at the ceiling in her bedroom, she'd finally given up at dawn and left her apartment. She'd thought about going to the gym or taking a nice, long trip to the gun range—or hell, even making an about face back home to crack open the bottle of Patrón Silver she kept in the cabinet over her fridge in case of emergencies. But what she'd really wanted was to lose herself, to forget for just a little while that Angel had been killed and that Sinclair had tossed her off this case, and she'd come to Kellan's apartment to do just that.

But now she didn't want to forget at all. As impulsive and uncharacteristic and insane as it was, Isabella wanted to tell him everything.

"Okay." Kellan's voice brought her back to the reality of his bedroom, smoothing over her frayed nerves. He shifted from the mattress to the floorboards, pulling down one edge of the dark blue comforter to reveal a set of crisp white sheets. "Come on," he said, getting under the covers.

For a second, she nearly panicked. She'd never post-sex-snuggled anyone in her life. Was there some kind of protocol for this? Something she was supposed to do or say?

As if he'd lasered in on her thoughts, Kellan said, "Hey. None of the questions have to be hard, remember?"

His expression was so easy, so laid back and no-great-shakes, that before her defenses could protest, Isabella pulled her T-shirt over her head and slid in next to him.

Letting Kellan in might be insane, but it also didn't feel wrong.

"Okay," she whispered. She turned to her side, and Kellan pulled her close just like he had the other morning on his couch, his body warm and solid behind hers. Although they were way less than fully dressed, the contact felt more comforting than sexual, and her muscles relaxed, breath by breath.

"Moreno?" His voice rumbled at her ear, and whether it was the post-sex endorphins or the pure, shocking goodness she felt at lying wrapped up in Kellan's arms, she couldn't be sure.

But something prompted her to say, "Isabella."

"What?" Confusion crept into his tone, sweet enough to knock her unease down another peg.

"We've seen each other naked more than once." She pressed a smile between her lips at the memory. "I'm pretty sure that means we should be on a strictly first-name basis from now on."

Kellan's chuckle was warm in her hair. "Okay, Isabella. Tell me something about you."

Unable to help it, she matched his laughter with her own. "More pizza toppings? Or did you want to go for favorite flavor of ice cream this time?"

"Not quite," he said, his voice strong and steady in her ear. "Actually, I was hoping you'd tell me what happened to make you show up on my doorstep. Not that I mind, but—"

"Sinclair benched me."

Her heart stuttered. She hadn't meant to blurt the words so gracelessly—God, she wasn't even sure she'd meant to say them at all. And she *really* hadn't expected to feel so relieved now that she'd let them loose.

Kellan's arm tightened around her waist. "He took you off the case?" At her wordless nod, he continued, indignant. "He can't do that. You busted your ass to make this case happen."

"After he told me not to," Isabella said, trying like hell not to let the bitter taste of the words filter into her tone. She took a deep breath to meter the ache blooming behind her breastbone. "I broke the rules by pursuing DuPree on my own. I had my reasons, but Sinclair thinks I don't trust him or my team, so…"

"Do you?"

Now it was Isabella's turn to stiffen against Kellan's chest. "Are you out of your mind?"

"No. I'm just asking a question," he said, so matter-of-fact that she answered without thinking.

"We work together in literal life or death situations. Of course I trust my team."

For a minute, Kellan said nothing. Then, "But you didn't for this. Your partner."

He paused, and she filled in the blank. "Hollister. Liam."

"Right. Hollister. He seems like a decent guy. He wouldn't have backed you up? At least on the walk and talk with Carmen?"

Isabella bit her lip, the ache of her sadness growing more insistent between her ribs. Confiding what had happened with Sinclair was one thing. But she couldn't tell Kellan this part. She couldn't tell him why she kept her distance from her team, hell, from everyone.

She couldn't tell him that her cousin—the very best friend she'd ever known—had been murdered eleven years ago, and it was her fault. That when people trusted her, they died.

She couldn't let Kellan get *that* close. So she said, "He might have backed me up. I don't know. But it doesn't matter. I still screwed up in the end."

"Sorry, I don't follow. You got Sinclair to open a case, right?"

Isabella laughed, hating the harshness in the sound, and every emotion she'd been trying to keep at bay pushed forward all at once. "What good does that do Angel now? I promised…I promised her she'd be safe. I *promised*, but still she's…he still…"

Kellan wrapped his arm around her tighter, saving her from having to speak the one word that would wreck her right now.

Dead. Angel was dead. Just like Marisol.

And just like Marisol, it was her fault.

"Okay. Okay," Kellan said softly, but her anger welled up, driving her to fight his embrace.

"It's not okay!" she snapped, unable to stop her emotions from clawing their way out. "Angel is *dead*, Kellan. DuPree killed her because she was coming to talk to me. Not the FBI or Sinclair or anyone on my team. I'm the one who promised to keep her safe. Sinclair was right to take me off this case! I did this. It's my fault."

"No." Kellan pulled back, closing both palms over her shoulders. Turning her so they were face to face, he pinned her with a scalpel-sharp stare. "Think about the conversation you had with this mystery guy who called when you were in the diner. He said 'now that I know you're a cop', right?"

Isabella blinked, the question stealing just enough of her fight for her to actually answer. "Yeah. So?"

"So, DuPree didn't know you were a cop until after we left."

"There's no chance he'd have let us make it to the door if he'd known all along," she agreed. "But it doesn't matter. He still found out, and Angel is still dead because of me."

"It does matter," Kellan insisted. "DuPree's got to have

one hell of a security guy to find out you're a cop as fast as he did, which means he'd have almost certainly known if the FBI had opened an investigation into his parties. If you'd gone to Sinclair from the beginning, DuPree would've seen you coming. You'd never have made it past the door of that penthouse, and you wouldn't have the intel you need to build this case."

Isabella's brain spun. Could he be right? "We did get a lot of intel from that party that we'd never have gotten otherwise. But that doesn't change the fact that Angel is dead."

Kellan's eyes darkened, stormy blue and fierce with emotion. "You're right, and her death is a horrible thing. But Angel wasn't stupid. She knew who you were. She knew the risks involved in talking to you, and she wanted her freedom badly enough to take them."

"I…" Isabella's heart squeezed, and she pressed her forehead to Kellan's. His arms felt so good, holding her close beneath the bed sheets, that she whispered the truth without thinking twice. "I know, but I promised. She died on my watch. Not Sinclair's or Peterson's. Mine."

"But you didn't kill her, and I'm not going to let you say you did." Kellan's jaw tightened, his muscles pulling taut beneath the dark stubble covering them. "DuPree killed Angel, and now that Sinclair is opening an investigation, he's going to go down for that."

Despite the sadness still crowding her chest, Isabella nodded. Sinclair might not agree with her methods, but he'd believed her when she'd insisted DuPree was behind these murders. He wouldn't stop until the case was closed.

A thought that had been lodged in her brain for the past twenty-four hours reared up, and she swallowed past the knot in her throat to ask, "You pulled her from the house, right? That's what you told Sinclair yesterday, when we were going over the fire scene."

Kellan exhaled, his callused fingers brushing her cheek in a shockingly soft touch. "Isabella, don't. Don't do this to yourself."

"I need to know, Kellan. I just…please. I need to know."

After a second, he nodded. "Yes. I found Angel in the bathroom, and I brought her down to our paramedic, Quinn. The two of us did every single thing in our power to try and save her."

"I know you did," Isabella whispered. "Thank you."

"This isn't your fault."

Although she didn't agree—how the hell could she?—she was also beginning to learn Kellan's expressions. The V between his dark brows and the ice-blue intensity of his stare said with certainty that he wouldn't let this go, so she eked out a nod.

"I guess I'm just fried," she said, because *that* was true enough. God, the last few days felt like they'd lasted for a month.

Kellan pulled her close, turning to his back and fitting her tightly against his side. "You've had a hell of a long twenty-four hours. Why don't you try to get some sleep, and we can talk about this more in a little while."

Isabella knew she should dodge the topic, just like she knew she should get out of Kellan's bed and regain the space that would keep her safe. Letting him get too close was dangerous. She needed distance.

But instead, she fell asleep in his arms.

* * *

Julian waited until the last possible second before taking off his bathrobe to enter the shower. Although his en suite was as private as the rest of his quarters—perhaps even more so, considering the extra set of biometrically locked doors keeping it separate from his bedroom—he still couldn't be too careful.

No one had ever seen his scars. At least, no one who still breathed, and he was already light on dependable staff.

Speaking of which…

Julian stepped beneath the spray, welcoming the pain of the scalding water on his hyper-sensitive skin for a moment before turning his thoughts toward business. Although the house fire had gone exactly as planned, there were still a few necessary moves to be made in order to have Detective Moreno exactly where he wanted her.

Detective Moreno.

Julian's breath quickened, his member stirring between his scarred thighs. Shame filled him at his impure reaction to such a filthy, brazen woman, and he turned the water even hotter until it blistered his skin.

Dirty boy! The voice screamed up from his past. *You're a dirty, disgusting boy, and you must be punished for your sins!*

No. Detective Moreno needed to be punished. She made him feel this way, with her whore smiles and her hidden agenda. She thought she could outsmart him, but she was wrong. He knew all about her past. The cousin who'd died after three long days of being locked in a basement and repeatedly raped. The ridiculous dedication she'd thrown into becoming a police detective, almost certainly to avenge the crime. The way she'd shamelessly thrown herself at that firefighter, rutting against him for the sole purpose of getting what she wanted. Of trying to get to him and shut him down.

Isabella Moreno was dirty and disgusting and the worst sort of whore. And he was going to break her.

Scrubbing his body until the pain made him numb, Julian finished his shower. He dressed quickly, rebuilding his composure with each movement. He couldn't allow savage anger to lead him toward mistakes.

He would kill Isabella Moreno. But first, he would make her pay.

Julian made his way to the surveillance room, where Vaughn and Charles and Franco had gathered at his demand. "Gentlemen," he said, though the address was far enough from the mark to leave a foul taste in his mouth. "An update, if you please."

All three men exchanged uncomfortable glances from across the bank of computer monitors, and finally, Vaughn spoke. "The news isn't great, boss. The fire department is ruling the, uh, incident on Oakmont as 'undetermined', which wouldn't be so bad, except the RPD just reached out to their friendly neighborhood field office to request an official investigation into the deaths. All they need is one connection between you and Angel or Marcus, and they'll be on us like a bad rash."

Julian arched a brow at Vaughn. From the other two, he'd expect this lack of insight. Perhaps his hacker was slipping. "Fine," he said, waving a dismissive hand. "Then things are proceeding exactly as expected."

"You want the Feds crawling up your ass?" Franco asked, shock covering his scarred face. Christ, the man was as big an idiot as he was a brute.

"Of course not," Julian replied, speaking as he might to a child. "But their investigation will serve as a means to an end. The FBI, like the fire department, won't find anything they can use to indict me, for the deaths or for my gatherings. While they struggle in vain to try, however, I'll gain access to something I want very much."

"I don't get it," Charles said, blinking his beady eyes. "What do the cops have that you want?"

Vaughn straightened, staring at Julian from beneath the hood of that infernal sweatshirt. "The woman. You want the woman."

At last, a light among the dimwits. "Bravo, Mr. Vaughn. I want the lovely Detective Moreno to pay for her audacity, and what better way than to have her come to me."

"You think she'll come to you as part of the investigation?" Charles asked, and truly, Julian had to question how the man functioned with such slow uptake.

"I think she came to me when there was no investigation. She's too impulsive for her own well-being. Certainly we can motivate her to act without too much effort. And when she does, I'll be ready." He turned toward

Vaughn and lifted his eyebrows expectantly. "So tell me, do we have eyes on the detective's apartment?"

Vaughn clacked a series of commands over the nearest keyboard, one-handed. "Yup, sure do. I tapped into the security feed for her building—piece of fucking cake, by the way—but she's not there now. The camera in the lobby has her leaving at about oh-five-hundred this morning. Interestingly enough, she landed on the firefighter's doorstep." Another clack, and the grainy image on the computer monitor changed. "They got hot and heavy on their way into his place a couple hours ago, and haven't come out since."

Julian smiled. This was going to be even easier than he'd anticipated. "Excellent. Don't take your eyes off that feed. If either one of them so much as sets a toe over the threshold, I want to be informed on my cell phone."

"You're headed out?" Vaughn's fleece-covered head pulled back in surprise.

Julian's heart beat faster, his blood beginning to rush at the dark pleasure of the task in front of him.

"Yes. Charles and Franco and I have some work to do. It's time to bait the hook."

CHAPTER TWENTY-ONE

Kellan sank his shoulders beneath his RFD hoodie, blocking out the early October chill as he surveyed the front of Isabella's tidy, three-story apartment building along with the two on either side of it. Evening sunlight still illuminated the city block, although the collection of evenly placed streetlights would take over the job in less than an hour. The handful of people crossing the leaf-covered sidewalk looked friendly and perfectly in-place as they walked their dogs or strolled by, and after his second three-sixty, Isabella cleared her throat from beside him.

"You do realize this is completely unnecessary," she argued—albeit lightly—for the thousandth time.

And for the thousandth time, Kellan argued right back. "Look, you can blame my lieutenant for this. But if I have to check in with him every twelve hours as a just-in-case, then you can put up with me doing a little look-see while I walk you to your door."

"A little look-see?" Isabella's caramel-colored brows lifted in challenge, and okay, she might have him there.

Too bad for her, the last ten years had honed his ability to field a raft of shit like a consummate pro. "Suck it up, buttercup. I like you. I'm not going to apologize for wanting to make sure you get into your apartment safe and sound."

Although he'd intended the words as a tease, Kellan couldn't help but realize how much truth hid behind them, too. Yes, the sex had once again been mind-blowing, and he and Isabella were clearly compatible between the sheets. But then she'd opened up about Angel and getting taken off this case, trusting him enough to let him in, then spend an entire day with him besides, and damn it, Kellan couldn't deny what was right in front of him.

He *did* like her.

Which would be dangerous, except for the fact that right now, in this moment, it felt too fucking good to scare him.

"Fine." Isabella's throaty voice brought him back to reality with a sexy snap. She tucked a wayward strand of hair behind her ear, a tiny smile shaping her mouth as she turned and started to move over the sidewalk. "But don't say I didn't warn you. If you insist on checking under my bed, you're going to find a legion of dust bunnies. They may or may not be friendly."

"You're a badass," he said, falling into step beside her and nudging her shoulder with his. "I'm willing to bet you can take the dust bunnies."

"You're lucky I like you, too. Otherwise I'd make you fend for yourself," Isabella quipped back. She pulled her key ring from her jacket pocket, unlocking the main door to the building and holding it wide to usher him over the threshold. "Here we are. Home sweet home."

Kellan scanned the tiled, hallway-style lobby, and nice, there were two—make that three surveillance cameras in place. "Not bad security," he said, jutting his chin at the acrylic dome anchored to the ceiling by the bank of metal mailboxes lining the main corridor.

She nodded. "The feeds aren't monitored live, but the cameras are a nice deterrent. We haven't had so much as a purse-snatching since they were installed a couple of years ago." She pressed the up button, stepping onto the elevator when the doors opened a few seconds later.

Kellan followed, and as much as he knew his segue to the next topic might tempt her to clam up, he also knew he couldn't dodge it. "Are you going to be okay, not working on this case?"

Isabella's shoulders tensed around her neck. Still, she answered. "I don't know. The most important thing is that DuPree gets caught. But this is personal. My c—"

Her lashes fanned wide for just a breath before her eyes dropped to the thin carpet covering the elevator floor, and Christ, the sadness on her face was enough to gut him.

"Hey." Kellan stepped in, hooking a finger beneath her chin. "I know you feel responsible for Angel. Your team will get DuPree, Moreno."

By the time Isabella lifted her gaze back to his, she'd nailed her guard back into place. "I know," she said, her smile as small as it was brief. Before he could answer—or call her out on her answer—the elevator bumped to a stop, the doors sliding open at the third floor. He and Isabella moved down the hall, the jingle of her keys breaking the silence as she flipped them against her palm.

"This is me," she said, stopping in front of a glossy black door labeled with a brass plaque reading 311. The hallway looked as bright and well-kept as the rest of the building, the door solid and undisturbed, and Kellan's muscles loosened with ease.

Right up until Isabella turned her key in the lock, and the deadbolt didn't click.

She whipped her hand from the door just as a shot of adrenaline punched through Kellan's chest. "I always lock it," she whispered, bending down noiselessly to liberate the Glock 43 from the ankle holster beneath the cuff of her jeans.

Fuck. He reached beneath his hoodie for the holster at his side, pulling out the SIG Sauer P229 he'd been licensed to carry ever since he'd been discharged from the Army. Sending one last split-second gaze over the hallway, Kellan double-checked to be sure the space was empty of either potential threats or friendlies who could get hurt.

"You're clear," he whispered.

She nodded, one hard dip of her chin. "My kitchen is at three o'clock, and there's a breakfast nook next to it. Clear that space while I check the bedroom on the other side. You copy?"

"*Affirmative.*" *Focus. See what's in front of you. Breathe.* "I've got your six. Go."

Reaching down with her left hand while she held the Glock steady in her right, Isabella turned the knob, pushing her way inside the apartment. Her body tensed three steps over the threshold, and holy hell.

The place was ruined.

A hard prickle of warning set in over the back of Kellan's neck, growing sharper with each passing second. Daylight slanted in past the mostly closed blinds, outlining the wreckage of what looked to have once been her living room. An upholstered love seat sat in the middle of the room, sideways and slashed to ribbons. The coffee table in front of it had been upended, the TV beyond smashed and scattered to the four corners of the hardwood floors. Although the room wasn't particularly large or overly cluttered, everything Kellan could see—picture frames, a handful of throw pillows, books that had presumably been yanked from the shelf on the wall—was all shattered or shredded beyond repair.

Although her eyes were saucer-wide, Isabella still remained on point, her movements quiet and her muscles spring-loaded and ready to strike. With her left hand, she indicated for him to head to the right side of the apartment, leading with her Glock as she headed down the hallway to the left.

Air so hot it hurt to breathe...sunlight scorching in through the windows...

"If you move, I will kill your friend. You'll watch him die screaming, and then I'll kill you just as slowly."

Old emotions threatened to burn bright and bubble up, but Kellan set his mind on the here and now of Isabella's apartment. *Focus.*

He inhaled, marshaling his heartbeat to a steady rhythm and squeezing his shoulders in readiness. The kitchen was as trashed as the living room, pine cabinets gaping wide, dishes scattered in pieces over the terra cotta floor tiles. But both it and the breakfast nook were thankfully free from threats.

Or at least the people who had caused them. For now.

"Clear," Kellan called out, his voice sounding canon fire-loud in his ears. Relief spun through him as Isabella echoed the sentiment a few seconds later, and he retraced his steps back to the living room.

"The place has been completely tossed," he said, holstering his weapon and waiting for her to do the same before reaching out to put a hand on her shoulder. "This had to be DuPree."

Isabella let out a slow exhale, her expression unreadable. "It was."

Concern mixed with confusion in Kellan's veins. Both must have shown on his face, because she turned on her heel to lead the way to her bedroom. The quilt had been pulled from her bed along with the powder blue top sheet, and Kellan's blood turned to ice at the sight of the deep gouges cut into the mattress, all the way down to the fabric-wrapped springs. Every dresser drawer had been yanked open and emptied, her underwear strewn all around the room as if on display. But it was what hung over the full-length mirror in the corner of the once-cozy space that made Kellan's heart go ballistic.

"Is that…?"

"The dress I wore to the party," Isabella finished, her eyes moving from the photograph pinned to the thin strap of the dress to the message scribbled on the glass beneath the cherry-red hemline.

See you soon.

"I need to call Sinclair," she said, and Kellan turned, his legs not quite steady but the rest of him one hundred percent goddamn sure as he replied.

"Yes, you do. And when you get him on the phone, make sure you tell him that either he finds this guy, or I will."

* * *

Isabella looked around her ruined bedroom and tried with all her might not to kick the crap out of something. Even though nearly an hour had passed since she and Kellan had found her apartment ripped open and ransacked, the damage still sent shockwaves down her spine. The knowledge that DuPree had been in her space, riffling through her panty drawer and carving up the spot where she slept like a Thanksgiving turkey, was enough to tempt her to vomit.

The way the slimy bastard had ripped the photograph of her and Marisol out of the frame by her bedside and pinned it to the top of the dress in a clear-cut effort to rattle her? Now that made Isabella want to head straight for his penthouse to drag him down all forty flights of stairs and into the precinct with her bare freaking hands.

This case had just gotten personal on a whole new level, and there wasn't a damned thing she could do about it from behind her desk. Just like there hadn't been a damned thing she could do for her cousin eleven years ago once she'd made the fateful phone call that had led to Marisol's death.

No. *No.* Isabella would not—*could not*—be bullied by Julian DuPree. Now more than ever, she had to stop him from hurting any more women. Which meant she had to prove to Sinclair that she trusted her team so he'd put her back on this case.

No matter what.

"All right," Sinclair said, rocking back on the heels of his heavy-soled boots to give her bedroom one last look before fixing her with a gray stare that meant business. "The crime scene techs are on their way. Maxwell is canvassing the building to see if any of your neighbors saw or heard anything unusual. Hollister and Hale are talking to your landlord, but our initial check with dispatch doesn't have any other reported break-ins on this block today."

Isabella had to give Sam credit. For as pissed as he surely still was that she'd pursued DuPree on her own in the beginning, he had to have walked out his door less than a minute after she'd called to tell him she and Kellan had discovered this mess.

God, this mess was her *apartment*. Her personal, private space.

"Okay," she said, taking a deep inhale and trying to organize her spinning thoughts. There had to be some way of proving DuPree was responsible for this. He might be cagey, but he wasn't the goddamned Invisible Man.

"Did you have the building's security company pull the footage from the cameras in the lobby?" Kellan asked from beside her, putting her thoughts into words.

Sinclair lifted a brow at him before sending his answer in her direction. "Capelli's on the footage, but it's going to take him a little time. Is there anything obvious that's missing?"

Isabella knew he had to ask, but still... "Other than my sanity, you mean? Come on, Sam. You know this wasn't some random break-in." Between the threat and the dress and the picture of Marisol, the mess had DuPree tattooed all over it.

To her surprise, he kept his cool. "Just like *you* know I can't exactly ask Peterson for an arrest warrant labeled 'because I said so.' Now you want to try again? In order to rule DuPree in, we have to rule everything else out."

"Fine," she said, because as much as she hated it, he wasn't wrong. "I don't really have anything all that valuable. My SIG is in the safe in the closet." She'd checked about two seconds after she'd called him, leaving everything else untouched. A stolen weapon was bad enough. A stolen weapon that belonged to a cop? Now that was a bad fucking day. "Everything else looks like it's here. In pieces, but still here."

"And you were gone all day?" Sinclair asked, and Isabella nodded, going through the drill.

"I left at five this morning. When Kellan and I came back from his place about an hour ago, my apartment looked like this."

"You two have been together the whole time." Sinclair shifted his gaze from her to Kellan and then back again, his brows rising just enough to let her know he'd read between the lines, and although her gut tightened, she didn't hold back the truth.

"Yes. We've been together all day."

Kellan stiffened from his spot next to her on the floorboards. "Sorry," he said, his arms forming a knot over the front of his dark blue hoodie. "What does that have to do with the fact that DuPree trashed Isabella's apartment, exactly?"

Her pulse jumped. Time to step in so Sinclair wouldn't. "He just needs to confirm there was no threat made to you, too, since we were both at the party together. Don't worry, it's standard procedure to ask."

Kellan's shoulders lowered, if only a fraction. "Oh. No, nothing out of the ordinary on my end. My buddy Devon has my sister covered. He'd have called if something went pear-shaped there."

"Okay, good." Sinclair paused to look around Isabella's wrecked bedroom, the frown lines bracketing his mouth turning softer. "Well, you know the drill, Moreno. We're going to need to get you into protective custody."

Her pulse clattered in yet another round of you can't be serious. "What? No."

"A clear and present threat was made against you," Sinclair said, gesturing to the mirror where her dress and the ominous message still stood like a taunt. "What else would you suggest we do?"

"Let me back on the case?" she asked with a little bit of sarcasm and a whole lot of honest suggestion. "This is beyond personal now, Sam. You can't really expect me to sit in protective custody while you guys track this bastard down."

Aha. The look on Sinclair's face said her words had found their mark. Still, he asked, "Are you refusing protective custody?"

Isabella answered with care. "I'm not an idiot. I know how to watch my back and I'll check in at regular intervals. But as far as staying in some safe house in the hinterlands of the city, yeah. I'm refusing protective custody."

Sinclair frowned, but he also didn't argue. Thank God. "You're going to have to stay somewhere else, at least for tonight while CSU goes over this place and we look into leads. If one of them points at DuPree, we'll let you know."

A protest formed, hot and quick on her tongue, but Kellan jumped in before she could say a word, his arms knotting across his chest. "Wait. You're really not putting her back on the case?"

Now it was Sinclair's turn to cross his arms and go for the stare-down. "Walker, you're here right now as a courtesy to Isabella. Don't make me regret being nice."

"No, I'm here because I was with her when she came home and found her apartment trashed. I'm part of this, just like she is. And if booting her from this case after this sonofabitch DuPree just threatened her is your definition of nice, I'd hate to see you act like a dick."

In an instant, the air seemed to vanish from the room, and Sinclair's stare turned razor-wire sharp as he pinned Kellan with a glare strong enough to be weaponized. "That's unfortunate, because you're about to make me cross that line."

"Be my guest," Kellan shot back. "You could use a little riling up as far as this case is concerned."

Even in the face of Sinclair's badge and Beretta, he didn't

take one toe off the proverbial line, and sweet Jesus, things were really mission critical if she had to be the voice of reason.

"Okay, you two," Isabella said, wrestling her voice into calmness despite the game of high-velocity tag her heart was playing with every last one of her ribs. "I get that things are a little tense, but we're all on the same side here."

Sinclair broke the standoff first. "You're right, we are. But I can't put you back on this case until you start following the chain of command and learn how to trust your team. Especially now that you're a potential target."

Kellan snorted. "What do you think she just did?"

Stunned, Isabella turned to stare at him, Sinclair mirroring her surprise as his chin snapped around to do the same.

But Kellan either didn't notice their shock or didn't care that they were both gaping like fish on dry land. "As soon as I told Isabella we'd found Angel in that fire, she called you," he said. "She knew her ass was on the line, but that didn't stop her, even for a second. She knew she needed help, and she trusted you to give it. And just now, when she and I came in here and found this place trashed, with her dress on display and that message obviously left to taunt her, what's the first thing she did? She called you. She knows exactly where DuPree lives. She could've gone over there all commando to take care of the threat herself, but she didn't. She called you. Do you really think she'd do that if she didn't honor your chain of command? Or if she didn't trust you? Because I sure as shit don't. She's a good cop, Sinclair. She cares about finding justice for these women, and she deserves to be back on this goddamn case."

Holy…hell.

For a second, Isabella couldn't breathe. Kellan wasn't wrong about her trusting Sinclair—in fact, he'd made the same argument she'd been ready to launch, albeit maybe a bit more bluntly. Not only had he beaten her to the punch, but the absolute certainty of what he'd said rang hard in her ears.

He didn't just believe her, and he didn't just think she was good at her job.

He had her back.

"Walker." Sinclair's voice broke the silence, gravelly and low. "Can you give me a minute with my detective? And before you think about arguing with me, you should know that I'm not really asking."

Kellan paused, and Isabella's heart gave up an involuntary squeeze. She stepped in next to him, her boots quiet on the floorboards even though her pulse pounded like a runaway freight train in her ears.

"It's okay. Why don't you check in with the rest of the unit and let them know I'm good. I don't want them to worry."

"I'll be right in the next room," he said, sliding one last frost-blue glance at Sinclair before stepping carefully through the mess and out her bedroom door.

Isabella braced herself for Sinclair's reaction, and true to form, he didn't disappoint. "Your boyfriend's a little territorial."

She bit back the urge to tell him she hadn't had a boyfriend since she'd been seventeen. Not that it wasn't the God's honest, but all things considered, they had bigger fish to fry.

Speaking of which… "Yeah, I think DuPree has us all a little on edge right now," Isabella said, and fuck it. Scaling back on the truth in the face of a little intensity had never been her thing anyway. "He's dangerous as hell, Sam, and he absolutely did this."

Sinclair followed her gesture around the room, a muscle ticking beneath the gold-gray stubble on his jawline as his stare lingered on her deeply gouged mattress. "I know."

She kept her surprise in check, but barely. "Well I'm glad, because Walker's right. I might keep some things close to the vest, but I do trust you, and I should be back on this case. DuPree trashed my apartment, or at the very least, he was behind it. Plus, the threat on the mirror is pretty cut and dried, and the photograph…" Isabella swallowed past the tightness pinching at her words. "I want to help get this guy."

"The threat on the mirror is real," Sinclair said. "Putting you back on this case also puts you at risk."

"But I'm already at risk." Despite her urge to argue, Isabella took a deep breath. Losing her cool wouldn't get her anywhere, no matter how tempted she might be to do it. "DuPree clearly knows we're onto him, and he's trying to get a rise out of me—out of all of us—with this stunt. But if he wants me as bait, then use me as bait. The more personal this gets, the more likely he is to make a mistake."

Sinclair huffed out a humorless laugh. "Just as long as you don't make one first. This *is* personal, on both sides. DuPree knows who you are. He obviously knows what happened to Marisol. He's not going to hesitate to use your past to get inside your head."

Isabella's stomach pitched behind the black cotton of her T-shirt, guilt and dread and anger threatening to fill her completely, but she had to hold steady. "Let him give it his best shot. He's not going to get to me. Look"—she took a step forward, and there was no sense holding back now. "You want me to trust you? Let me back on this case. Let me trust the intelligence unit to catch this guy if he's after me, and trust me to help you do it. DuPree killed this woman, and he's hurt who knows how many more. He needs to pay for that, and I know we can make that happen. Please. I promise you, Sam. I'm good for this."

A minute ticked by, then another, her palms growing slicker with each second of deafening silence, until finally, Sinclair said, "There are no half measures on a case like this, Isabella. I need to be one hundred percent sure I can trust you."

"You can. I swear it, Sam. No freelancing. No flying solo," she said with zero hesitation.

Not even when Sinclair jutted his chin toward the door

that Kellan had passed through after having promised to stay close.

Close.

"And can you trust him?" Sinclair asked.

Isabella's defenses prickled beneath her skin, warning her to say no. Casual sex and a few good conversations were one thing, and easy things at that. But trusting Kellan meant letting him in. Letting him get close.

Letting herself care about him.

But again, she didn't hesitate. "Yes. I trust him."

"Good." Sinclair smiled, the first one she could remember since they'd started this case weeks ago, and it sent a hard shot of relief all the way through her gut. "Assuming you'll be staying at his place while CSU works here, I'll put a squad car in front of Walker's building tonight, and you'll need to check in every eight hours. Now let's finish up so you can get out of here and get some rest."

"I'm really fine," Isabella said, and to her surprise, Sinclair answered with a nod.

"I know. But you're going to need all the energy you can get. Peterson gave intelligence full jurisdiction to investigate this case. Which means first thing tomorrow morning, we have a killer to catch."

CHAPTER TWENTY-TWO

Kellan got out of his Camaro, taking the last sip of coffee from his to-go cup before blinking past the morning sunlight and scanning the street for serious threats. Although the habit was as ingrained as breathing, he took extra care with his awareness as he crossed the sidewalk in front of the two-story apartment building, pressing the buzzer for 2B and adjusting his RFD baseball hat as he waited for an answer.

"Who is it?" came the familiar female voice from the intercom speaker.

"It's me." Kellan waited just a beat before hitting the button again to add, "I'm here to deliver the jelly donuts."

Okay, so maybe Gamble's code word wasn't the weirdest thing going. That's what he got for letting Kylie, who had been thirteen at the time, choose the phrase for their all-clear.

A few seconds later, the building's main door sounded off with a heavy click, allowing Kellan to cross into the lobby and head up the single flight of stairs. Relief spread beneath the game face he'd had locked into place for the last twelve hours, and he placed a crisp knock on the door in front of him. "Still me," he said.

"Gah, it's about time!" The rattle of the chain sounded off from the other side of the door, followed by the click of not one but two deadbolts. A second later, he was being hauled over the threshold by his deceptively slender sister.

"Jesus, Ky. What's with the—oof!" Kellan's breath shot from his lungs as she threw her arms around him and held on for dear life.

"Thank God you're okay." She pulled back to hold him at arm's length, examining him from baseball hat to boots. "You are okay, right? No blood? No bruises?"

Unable to help it, he looked over Kylie's shoulder, where Devon stood in their living room wearing an Army T-shirt, a pair of jeans, and an I-tried expression. "Has she been like this the whole time?" Kellan asked.

"Ever since you called last night," Devon confirmed, leaning in to shake his hand and clap him on the shoulder. "I told her you were fine, but—"

"Please." Kylie released an unladylike snort that reminded Kellan all too well how tough—and smart—she was. "Your arm could be hanging on by a tendon and a Hail Mary and you'd both try to convince me it was a flesh wound. Anyway, Devon has barely let me out of his sight ever since you gave us the update on what happened at Detective Moreno's place, and he told me the intelligence unit had a patrol car camped out in front of your apartment all night, so yeah. I was worried."

He should've known she'd be too perceptive not to pick up on the subtle changes that went with a heightened threat. And damn, did Julian DuPree ever fit the bill. "The cloak and dagger stuff is mostly just precautionary. Better safe than sorry."

"Believe me, I remember." Kylie linked her arm through his and guided him through her apartment while he tried like hell to forget that less than four short months ago, Xavier Fagan had held her at gunpoint and threatened to kill her half a dozen ways. "Anyway, I'm glad you came over," she said. "I wouldn't have been able to rest easy without seeing you in person."

Kellan tried on a smile, forcing the expression to look nice and easy even though it was two sizes too small. "Of course I came over. I'm not on-shift until tomorrow, and you promised to feed me. And honestly, I'm fine."

Okay, so fine was kind of relative in light of recent events. But the last thing he wanted was for his sister to worry. She'd been through enough with Fagan, and for all intent and purpose, he really *was* fine.

Just as long as he didn't think about DuPree threatening Isabella. Or how she'd seemed to land directly in the bastard's crosshairs. Or how she'd looked all sexy and sleepy and perfect the minute she'd woken up this morning, and Christ, Kellan needed to stick to facts, not feelings.

Kylie reclaimed his attention with a cluck of her tongue. "Fine enough to have cops on your threshold all night?"

"Those two patrolmen had the most boring night ever. No sign of trouble," he said. "Not even a jaywalker."

From the look on her face, she remained unconvinced. "Hmm." She steered him into the kitchen, where something smelled damn close to heaven. "Well that's a relief, considering Isabella's apartment was pretty wrecked, right?"

Annnnd time to get selective with the truth. Kylie was already worried enough. Plus, thinking about Isabella's apartment—and the chilling threat that had been left in it— wasn't going to do a damn thing for his already iffy composure.

"Someone definitely ransacked the place." Kellan sent a covert glance in Devon's direction, meeting his eyes as his buddy pulled a pair of mugs from the cupboard and filled them both from the coffeepot on the counter. Thankfully, they were still fluent in the nonverbal shorthand they'd cultivated together in Afghanistan. The nearly imperceptible nod Devon gave Kellan along with one of the cups of coffee said he'd be on full watchdog status around Kylie until DuPree had been caught.

Kellan pulled a chair from beneath the kitchen table in the sun-filled breakfast nook, taking a long draw from his mug before saying, "Isabella's headed to the precinct right now, and the intelligence unit is investigating the case with the FBI's authorization. They'll catch this guy."

"Good." Devon moved over the kitchen tiles, and even though the kiss he pressed to Kylie's temple was chaste, the fierceness of his feelings for her practically radiated out of the guy.

And don't you just know that feeling firsthand.

Kellan's heart kicked faster behind his T-shirt and the plaid button-down shirt he'd slung over it. So he liked Isabella and didn't want her to get mauled by a homicidal maniac, and yeah, she smelled really good and they had out-fucking-standing sex and he slept better than he had in ages when she was wrapped up in his arms. It didn't mean anything. Definitely not anything major.

Shit. The whole thing was *completely* major. He liked her. A lot.

And as dangerous as that was, he didn't want to stop.

The rumble of Devon clearing his throat brought Kellan back to planet earth. "I'm going to let you two talk," he said. "You'll let me know if there are any updates?"

As if that was even a question. "Of course," Kellan said, tacking a silent *thank you* to the end of the sentence. Knowing Devon had Kylie's back let him breathe a little easier, and he needed all the calm he could get.

Kylie scooped up the plates she'd been loading with French toast, watching Devon walk back to the living room with a giant, goofy smile on her face before turning back to Kellan. "Okay. Breakfast is served."

He grabbed one of the forks that had been lying in wait on the table, his stomach going for a high-powered growl as he inhaled the spicy-sweet scents of cinnamon and maple syrup goodness. "Thanks. I'm starving."

She laughed, handing over his plate and sitting next to him with her own. "It's not cold pizza, but it'll do."

"Ha-ha," Kellan said, digging into the edge of one golden-brown piece of French toast. A few seconds later, his taste buds damn near exploded. "Jeez, Ky." In went another bite, then another, and screw manners. He'd lick the plate to get every last crumb into his cakehole. "Did you put crack in these? Because seriously. They're off the chain."

"Nope." She popped a bite into her mouth, but it still didn't hide her smile. "Just regular pantry ingredients. I can write down the recipe if you want to make them for Isabella."

Kellan's fork dropped to his plate with an inelegant clatter. "Uh," he managed. "What makes you think I'd be cooking breakfast for her?"

Kylie arched a dark brown brow at him over the table. "Come on. You told Devon she's staying with you while her apartment gets cleaned up, and any idiot can see that you two are into each other."

"There's a little more to it than that," Kellan argued.

But Kylie just rolled her eyes. "Actually, there isn't. You like her, she likes you. I hate to break it to you, but this is how relationships are supposed to work."

"Okay, Isabella and I aren't…" He broke off at his sister's don't-even-try-it stare, and jeez, she really was a barracuda. "We've only been, ah, spending time together for a couple of weeks."

Mercifully, Kylie let his awkward semantics slide. "Yeah, but you've known her for months. Plus, you two have been through a lot together lately. This DuPree guy sounds awful."

"He's not a Boy Scout," Kellan said, and left it at that. "But just because I helped Isabella work this case and she's staying with me until her place is right side up doesn't mean things are serious."

Serious meant emotions, and emotions were dangerous. He needed to stay steady. He couldn't lose control. Which meant everything he felt for Isabella needed to stay way down deep.

Didn't it?

"Okay," Kylie said. Rather than pin the word with a bunch of sass or sarcasm, though, she simply smiled and hopped up from the table. "At any rate, Devon mentioned that Isabella probably wouldn't be able to take anything out of her apartment for at least a day, and knowing her, she's not going to want to stop working on this case even to pee, let alone shop for toiletries and a change of clothes. So I ran out this morning to grab a few things for her."

Surprise worked its way up Kellan's spine as he looked inside one of the three plastic shopping bags Kylie had grabbed from the side table by the pantry. "That was really cool of you."

"Well, you like her, so..." Kylie shrugged, but her smile was impossible to miss. "Plus, she did kind of go above and beyond to catch the crooked cop who nearly got me and Devon killed, so y'know. There's that, too."

Kellan's gaze caught on something inside the bag, and wait. Was that...?

"Really, Ky?" he asked, the back of his neck heating as he lifted a silky, dark green thong from between a T-shirt and a toothbrush.

His sister, who seemed utterly unaffected, waggled her brows and popped a bite of French toast into her mouth. "Mmmkay," she murmured between chews. "So you like her a lot. It's fine to say so out loud, even if things aren't serious."

Whether it was Kylie's unexpected generosity or the ease with which she spoke about such a potentially serious topic, Kellan couldn't be sure. But something prompted him to ask, "How come you didn't say anything? A couple of months ago, when Isabella told you she'd gone back to Chicago to nail Burton and seal up your case. How come you didn't tell me?"

Kylie lowered her fork, but she didn't shy away from the question. "Because. As scary as those memories are, I lived through that part of my life, and it got me where I am now.

Don't get me wrong"—she paused, her wide-open expression growing slightly sharp around the edges—"I'm glad Burton got caught and that he'll be punished for telling Fagan where I was. But I didn't say anything to you when Isabella told me because I want all that behind me. I don't want to be scared to live my life, or have a great new career, or be in love with Devon. I can't let the emotions of what happened in the past keep me from acting now. I want to look forward, not back."

Kellan's breath abandoned his lungs. Holy hell. He'd spent so much time stuffing back every emotion, good, bad, or indifferent, that it had never occurred to him that he could feel some while keeping the others in check. The boxes had always been all or nothing, like a dam holding water at bay. Letting go of one meant all the others would rush out, and if that happened, surely Kellan would break.

Except...

Kylie hadn't. Fagan had put her through hell. She'd witnessed a murder and nearly been murdered herself. She'd been chased and shot at and genuinely feared for her life. Yet she'd also moved across the country, embarked on a brand-new career path, and fallen in love with her bodyguard, all things Kellan would have counted as impulsive. Dangerous.

Only maybe they weren't. Maybe they were just part of living.

And maybe he hadn't been living for far too long.

"I don't know," Kylie said, filling the silence Kellan just now recognized as having gone on for half a minute with a nervous laugh. "I guess that sounds a little new-agey and weird. You probably think I'm crazy."

"No." He shook his head and let out the unvarnished truth. "I don't think you're crazy at all. In fact, I know exactly how you feel."

Because dangerous or not, he wanted to move forward with Isabella Moreno.

CHAPTER TWENTY-THREE

Isabella took the steps to the Thirty-Third precinct two at a time, her arms overloaded with case files and her chest chock-full of determination. Okay, so it was a little early by intelligence standards. After all, big and bad tended to favor the middle of the night over eight o'clock on a Monday morning. But she still had a metric ton of case details to catch up on from the day and a half she'd missed, an update to grab from the crime scene techs who were processing her apartment, security footage to review, reports from the fire marshal to check on, and damn, she needed to find a cup of—

"Chamomile?" Hollister asked, lifting a to-go cup with a tea tag dangling over the edge from the blotter on his desk.

Isabella blinked past all the *whoa* bouncing around in her chest. "What are you doing here?" she asked, hearing the sheer gracelessness of the question only after it had crossed her lips.

But her partner just broke into a knowing grin. "Good morning to you, too." He crossed the otherwise empty office space, trading the cup of tea for half the files in her grasp.

"Sorry. And thanks." Her cheeks prickled with the full force of her chagrin, and yeah, time for take two. "I guess what I meant was, you're here awfully early all things considered." He'd been at her apartment until ten last night, talking to her landlord and helping Maxwell and Hale canvas the building.

A fact which didn't seem to faze him in the least. "Eh." He lifted a shoulder and let it fall beneath his holster and gray Henley shirt. "Sleep is overrated. You okay?"

The stare that accompanied the question said Hollister wasn't asking as a pleasantry. "Yeah," Isabella said, making sure her return expression backed up the sentiment. "Eager to nail this guy, but otherwise I'm fine."

One corner of Hollister's mouth lifted. "Good to see your short time off hasn't affected that bulletproof work ethic of yours."

Ah, busted. Still, a girl had to save face. "I'm behind the rest of you guys by a day and a half, so I wanted to catch up. Especially since the Feds are letting us take lead."

"Letting us? Please." Hollister huffed out a sound that was half laughter, all sarcasm. "Sinclair all but told Peterson that if he didn't let intelligence break this case, he'd never get a willing assist from anyone in this precinct again."

Isabella's lips fell open in shock. "He did?"

"Yeah," Hollister said, as if she'd just asked for clarification that two plus two did indeed equal four. "You said you were sure, so Sinclair went to bat for you. Plus, this guy broke into your apartment, Moreno. We take care of our own."

She lowered the stack of file folders from her hip to her desktop, letting his words sink in. Hollister had always been a solid partner, one she'd been proud to work with. Just because she'd always thought so didn't mean he knew so, and Sinclair was right. Her unit had to know she trusted them.

"Listen," she said, waiting for him to look up from the desk across from hers before she continued. "I know I'm not really a share-all kind of person, but this job is important to me. This *team* is important to me."

Hollister's brows lifted in what had to be surprise, although he had a better poker face than most people when he decided to trot it out. "The team is important to me too."

"I'm probably not the easiest partner to work with," Isabella continued, and at that, he let go of a soft laugh.

"You're a little bit of a puzzle," he agreed. "But you're not a bad person. And you're definitely a good cop. I figure you've got your reasons for liking the outskirts."

The thought of Marisol, of the one damned phone call that had kicked so many horrible, irreversible things into motion, punched through her gut. "Yeah."

Hollister sat back in his desk chair, and even though she was certain he hadn't missed a thing—her poker face wasn't nearly as high-quality as his, and the guy was a fucking detective, for God's sake—he also didn't push. "If it makes you feel any better, we all have things we don't advertise. You ever feel like talking about yours, I'm not a bad listener. I don't just have your back on the job, you know?"

"Thanks. I…" Isabella paused for a breath. "Thanks."

"Sure." Hollister cleared his throat, tapping the stack of case files on the desk in front of him. "So I take it the rest of your night was quiet after you left your apartment?"

Isabella nodded, taking a long sip of tea as she kicked back into work mode. "Yup."

For as trashed as her apartment had been, Kellan's had remained untouched. At this point, she'd take whatever silver linings she could get.

"Good," Hollister said. "I took a trip out to North Point to check on Carmen after I left your place last night. I know she never worked for DuPree, but since she's the one who gave up the intel on Danny Marcus, I figured a knock and talk couldn't hurt."

Oh. God. Isabella's mouth went as dry as sand despite the tea she'd just thrown back. "She's okay, right? She's safe?"

Hollister made a rude noise and a face to match. "She's

a righteous pain in the ass, is what she is. But yeah. Carmen's fine."

Relief skated through her, followed by a hard shot of curiosity. One day, she'd have to ask what the deal was between the two of them, but since Carmen was safe and the girls at DuPree's parties weren't, today wasn't going to be that day.

"Okay, good." Isabella dropped her eyes to the pile of gray folders on her desk, each one stamped with the RPD crest, then shot a glance at the matching stack of paperwork in front of her partner. "So you want to catch me up, here? I'd like to be useful by the time Sinclair gets in."

Hollister grinned. "Sure. Let's get to work."

They spent the next forty minutes going over what the intelligence unit had turned up in her absence. It was still too soon to have much of anything from last night yet, and the rest of what they did have was disappointingly thin. But the fact that the FBI had given them jurisdiction to investigate meant Isabella could dive into this case even harder than she'd hoped. There might be a lot of maybes, and even more what-ifs. But even if she couldn't prove it yet, she knew the truth.

Julian DuPree was hurting women in the worst ways imaginable, and she wasn't going to stop until he'd been stopped. All she had to do now was get him to make one wrong move.

"Well look who's back in action." Maxwell's voice sounded off from the front of the office, snagging Isabella's attention. "You okay, Hardball?"

She laughed at the unexpected nickname. "Yeah. I wish I could say the same for my furniture, but I'm good."

"Glad to hear it. And good to see you back." Although Maxwell was about as far from clean-cut as possible, with his shaved head and multiple piercings and dark eyes that seemed to have seen far too much for a guy who had way more of his life ahead of him than behind, his smile still curved around the welcome enough to tell her she'd been missed.

"Yeah, looks like you guys are stuck with me after all," Isabella said, sending her grin from Maxwell to Hale and Capelli, who had walked into the intelligence office alongside him.

"Oh thank *God*," Hale said in her usual all-in manner. "I know it was only a couple of days, but I missed the crap out of you." She twirled her finger in an imaginary circle to encompass the rest of their unit. "These three chuckleheads tried to gang up on me in a guys versus girls pool tournament down at the Crooked Angel on Saturday night. Thankfully Shae McCullough from Seventeen was cool enough to help me out."

Capelli frowned, moving past Hale to park himself at an L-shaped desk with three state-of-the-art computer monitors on each branch. "McCullough's scores shouldn't count. That woman is an anomaly."

"You're just mad because she managed to defy all those probability statistics you used to try and calculate whether or not she'd be any good at shooting pool," Hale said, and Hollister added a laugh.

"Welcome to my world, Capelli. I've never been able to figure out women, either."

"I didn't say I couldn't figure out women," Capelli grumbled. "Only that *this* particular woman is an anomaly."

Hale snorted. "Whatever. You still can't figure her out. And even though you didn't put any money on the game, as usual, that's got to be driving your boy-genius brain bat-shit crazy."

Isabella opened her mouth to agree with Hale—Capelli was very rarely wrong, even less so when fact-based predictions were concerned, and it probably was making him nuts on toast. But instead she was interrupted by the very familiar, very serious sound of a throat being cleared.

"Ladies and gentlemen." Sinclair walked across the linoleum, pausing to hit each one of them with a stare that meant business, and *damn*, she loved this job. "Now that

Moreno's clearly gotten the welcome back she deserves, where are we on this DuPree case? Peterson might've kicked this investigation over to us, but he's going to want leads to go with the bright, shiny indictment we promised, and I'm not inclined to tell him we don't have any."

It took less than thirty seconds for all five of them to find both their desks and their work ethics, although not necessarily in that order, and Maxwell was the first to chime in with a reply.

"Right. Well, starting with last night's break-in, we got a whole lot of nothing from canvassing Moreno's building. No one heard or saw a damned thing, which means this guy knew exactly what he was doing. Low profile all the way."

Ugh. Isabella had figured as much. DuPree hadn't gotten this far by throwing down bad-guy calling cards everywhere he went. But if they could put him in the building some other way, that would be a huge step forward in the concrete evidence department. "What about the surveillance video?"

"Yeah, that's me," Capelli said, leaning in to examine one of his six monitors. "Looks like our guy was actually three guys. The only people on yesterday's feed who didn't check out as residents, guests, or delivery people are three males who entered the building at ten forty-six yesterday morning. A closer look at the entry log shows their key card as a fake."

Isabella's pulse perked to life. "That's a good sign."

But Capelli adjusted his glasses, pausing to grimace at the image he'd pulled up. "Not as good as it sounds. The video shows these men entering the building and going up to the third floor on the elevator, but that's *all* it shows. There are no security cams on the third floor, and all three men kept their heads down. No facials to ID. No distinguishing features. Just dark clothes and baseball hats with no logos, and no definitive proof that they did anything other than sneak in and ride the elevator."

"Strike two," Sinclair said, his frown growing deeper. "What about forensics in the apartment?"

"Still being processed." Maxwell looked up from his

desk across the open office space. "First glance though? No prints, nothing unusual left behind. Although it's going to take them a while to go through everything because the place was so trashed."

Great. Isabella didn't know if that should make her feel hopeful or even more hacked off. "Okay, so let's work backward. How about the fire? Anything new since yesterday?"

"Ah." Hale leaned in, phone in hand. "Yes, actually. Autopsies just came back on both Angel and Danny Marcus." She scrolled down, her eyes widening with interest and surprise as she continued. "Check this out. They both died of asphyxiation, and time of death is consistent with the approximate time of the fire. But neither one of them had any trace of smoke or soot in their lungs. Which means…"

Isabella's heart slammed against her sternum as Hale's words connected. "They were dead before the fire even started."

"Exactly," Hale said. "Tox screen shows high levels of heroin in both victims. Not enough to kill either of them, but—"

"Enough to make them drowsy and non-combative," Isabella finished. Oh, Angel.

Hale nodded, sliding a sympathetic look in her direction before continuing. "Yes. No ligature marks on the bodies to suggest strangulation, but the ME did find small cuts and some bruising on the inside of both victims' mouths that are telltale signs of suffocation. She's officially ruling both as homicides."

"That's a step in the right direction, isn't it?" Hollister asked, but Sinclair shook his head, punctuating the sadness twisting deep between Isabella's ribs.

"Not a very big one if we can't link DuPree to the crime," he said. "Talk to me about the scene."

"The house is"—Isabella paused. Scraped in a shaky breath. Reset her determination—"*was* vacant and empty, just like that first fire scene where Kellan found the photos. This one was a foreclosure, supposed to go up for auction in about two weeks."

Sinclair crossed his arms, shooting her a glance from the spot where he stood in front of the floor-to-ceiling window in front of his office. "I'm sure it's too much to ask that there's a paper trail connecting DuPree to either property?"

Oh, if only. "Sadly, it is," Isabella confirmed. "There's no connection between DuPree and any of the previous owners or tenants, and he never owned or rented either house. He makes most of his on-the-books money in real estate, though, so it follows that he'd have a line on vacant properties." She'd looked into his business dealings at length last week. They were clean enough to squeak from every angle. Unfortunately. "It's possible he scouted empty houses and had Franco and the big guy, Rampage, keep the girls in these places."

"It would explain the extra locks on the doors in both locations," Maxwell said, and the idea gained momentum in Isabella's brain.

"It would also keep DuPree's name off any leases. If he paid other people to squat in these houses and do his dirty work for him, there wouldn't be any way to put him or any of his associates there without witnesses."

"In North Point?" Hollister let out an exhale tinged heavily with doubt. "Good luck. Nobody talks to the cops down there."

Which DuPree had almost certainly counted on. Christ, he was as slippery as he was smart.

"Okay." Isabella dipped her chin in thought, ordering and re-ordering the facts like the pieces to a puzzle as she tried to line up the edges and curves. "So we've got Franco and Rampage who are clearly on DuPree's payroll. Any ID on the guy who called my cell phone? His voice wasn't familiar."

Capelli shook his head, his brows bent in concentration. "I pulled the records from the phone company, but the call was made from a payphone in the middle of downtown Remington."

"They still have those?" Hale asked, and Isabella got the impression she was only half-joking.

Unfortunately, Capelli was all serious. "Only in the busiest parts of the city, and this one is about a block from Remington Hospital but just outside the reach of any city cams, so yeah, we don't even have a snowball's chance of figuring out who placed the call."

"Great." Isabella tugged a hand through her hair in frustration. DuPree was clearly meticulous. But there was no such thing as the perfect crime. There had to be something they could go by, some small slip-up that would turn into a big lead.

"There is something a little weird about this call, though." Capelli sifted through the paperwork on his desk, coming up with the paper placemat where she'd recorded the grim details of her conversation in the diner. "Moreno, you're sure you wrote down everything the guy said, word for word?"

"As much as I could remember, yeah." Details grew hazy over time, even for the best of cops, and she'd broken too many cases wide open over verbal missteps criminals thought would be overlooked.

Capelli shook his head, his eyes narrowing behind the dark frames of his glasses while he read once, twice, then again for good measure. "This one line, right here where he said, 'beyond the shadow of a doubt'. It's so familiar. Almost like…" In one swift motion, he jerked back against his desk chair hard enough to make the thing squeal in protest. "Oh, shit. I know who DuPree's security guy is."

"Are you sure?" she asked, then backtracked with a shake of her head, because, hello. Capelli. "Who is it?"

"He's a hacker, goes by the alias of the Shadow. His real name is Conrad Vaughn, although not a lot of people know that. Last I heard, he was in Tokyo, but honestly, the guy could be in this room and we probably wouldn't know it.

He's crazy-smart and even more dangerous. Although no one's proved it, he's credited with crashing Twitter last month."

"Are you kidding me?" Hollister asked, sitting up straight in shock. "The site was down for like eight hours."

"Nine hours and twenty-two minutes, to be exact," Capelli said. "He loves to talk in riddles, always about shadows and light. And if he's behind DuPree's security, you can bet the guy's tracks aren't just covered. They're *gone*. The Shadow never leaves a trace."

"There's always a trace," Sinclair said, cutting into Isabella's dread with absolute certainty. "We just need to find it. Maxwell, I want you and Hale to dig deeper on Danny Marcus's end—connections between him and DuPree, these parties, the wrestler, anything. Moreno and Hollister, go to North Point and see if someone on Oakmont can't ID any of these guys at that house, Saturday morning or otherwise. Make it worth their while to have accurate memories. Capelli, figure out how this Shadow guy is getting his intel. I want to know what he knows, how he knows it—and let's jam him up so he can't get anything else while we're at it. I want concrete evidence that DuPree's behind these murders and I want it past tense. Let's connect the dots, people."

"Okay boss," Isabella said, double-checking the Glock in her holster before asking, "What are you going to do?"

"I'm going to take a field trip to the Metropolitan. Let's see what our boy DuPree has to say for himself."

CHAPTER TWENTY-FOUR

Kellan pushed up from his couch, processing the intercom buzz that signaled a visitor with equal parts trepidation and relief. Isabella had called him twenty minutes ago to say she was finally on her way over from the precinct, and he hardly thought anyone wishing him harm would tip him off with a call in advance from downstairs, but still. A guy couldn't be too careful.

As was evidenced by the hulking Marine who had beat Kellan to the intercom box in the foyer.

"Who is it?" Gamble grated into the speaker by the front door, and whoa, Kellan thought the guy was serious at the firehouse.

"Dude, I'm sure it's just…"

The intercom crackled to life from four floors down. "It's Moreno. Jackass," she added, making Kellan laugh despite the seriousness of the situation.

Gamble raised one black brow, wordlessly pressing the button to release the security lock on the building's main door. After a handful of minutes and a brisk knock at the door, Isabella was safely in his apartment, and Jesus, she was the only woman alive who looked even hotter after a day's worth of work than she had when she'd left.

"Hey." She shrugged out of her jacket, then the shoulder holster holding her SIG before lifting her hands as she smiled at Gamble. "Did you want to frisk me, too, or are we good?"

Kellan couldn't help it. His laugh escaped for round two. Not that he wouldn't be just as cautious if their roles were reversed and Gamble needed the backup, but the look on his lieutenant's serious, stubbled face? Fucking priceless.

"We're good," Gamble said, shocking the crap out of Kellan when one corner of his mouth kicked up into the closest thing the guy had to a smile. "Just stay on your toes and keep it that way, Detective."

Isabella nodded, her expression going from sassy to soft. "Copy that, Lieutenant. And thanks."

Gamble skinned into his black leather jacket and palmed his motorcycle helmet from its resting spot in Kellan's foyer. "We take care of our own." He turned toward Kellan, lifting his chin as he made his exit. "I'll see you at roll call tomorrow."

"Fifty bucks says I'll see you first," Kellan said, clapping the guy on the shoulder as he ushered him out. Flipping the deadbolt firmly back into place, he retraced his steps back into the foyer, and Isabella met him halfway across the hardwoods.

"Now there's a proper greeting," she said, her fingers sliding with delicious friction against the back of his neck as he pulled her in close to press his mouth over hers.

He knew he shouldn't mess with her, but, hell, it was too good to pass up. "I don't know. Maybe I should frisk you, just in case."

Isabella deepened the kiss, slanting her tongue over his in a dirty suggestion of what she could do with it before she broke their contact with a grin. "Go right ahead. But turnabout is fair play, and I've got handcuffs."

Good Christ, this woman was going to ruin him before they made it to the living room.

Despite the protest from his dick, Kellan pulled back to lead her into the kitchen. As badly as he wanted to get naked with her (damn, he really, *really* wanted to get naked with her), he also knew Isabella had likely had a hell of a day. Even though she didn't say so out loud, the vulnerability hiding behind that layer of toughness in her eyes told him in no uncertain terms that she still felt responsible for Angel's death. Making sure Isabella was okay was his number one priority right now.

"You hungry? I've got a lasagna in the oven," Kellan said, biting back a laugh as her eyes went wide over a hell-yes smile.

"Damn. You made a freaking lasagna? You've been holding out on me in the skills department." She inhaled, the rise of her breasts beneath the V-neck of her dark red top making Kellan second-guess his decision not to strip it off of her.

Focus. "Actually, I can't take any credit. Kylie made the lasagna. All I did was put it in the oven. Oh, and before I forget"—he broke off just long enough to grab the bags his sister had given him, passing them to Isabella—"she picked up a few things to tide you over until you can get back into your place. She had to guess at the sizes, but she's pretty good at that sort of thing."

Isabella blinked twice before staring down at the bags in surprise. "That was really nice of her. CSU is still processing my apartment because there was so much damage to sift through, and to be honest, I had one hell of a long day with this case. I kind of forgot I'd need a few things."

"She thought you might say that."

"I'll have to pay her back next time I see her."

Kellan laughed. Isabella was nothing if not true to form. "Kylie thought you might say that too. She told me to tell you, and I quote, 'After all you did to find that asshole Burton, don't even think about paying me back for these.'"

Pressing a smile between her lips, Isabella set the bags in an out-of-the-way spot and moved back through the kitchen. "Your sister's kind of a badass," she said, pointing toward the cabinets with her brows up in wordless question. At his nod, she unearthed two plates, repeating the process with the drawer below to add silverware. "Kylie's safe, right?"

"Are you kidding?" They might have a truckload of shit to worry about with DuPree still on the loose, but thankfully, his sister's safety was a no-brainer. "Like you said, she's kind of a badass. Anyway, Devon's even more protective of her than I am, and that's saying something."

"Good." Her brown eyes turned serious in the soft overhead light of his kitchen as she kicked into work mode. "DuPree's been quiet since he shook things up at my apartment, but after today, I'm sure he won't stay that way."

Isabella proceeded to fill him in on the case details as he dished up two double-portions of lasagna and led her to the tiny table in his breakfast nook. His shock that Angel's death had been ruled a homicide turned into anger at the lack of evidence to connect it to DuPree, and damn, between the confirmation that they were up against some top-notch security with this Shadow hacker and the fact that DuPree clearly knew how to outsmart everyone in his path, the intelligence unit definitely had their work cut out for them.

"So Sinclair didn't get anywhere with this bastard at all?" Kellan asked, stacking his empty plate on top of Isabella's and bringing both to the kitchen sink a few steps away.

Isabella shook her head, following him to the counter. "Sinclair didn't even get in the door," she corrected. "He got dead silence at the Metropolitan, and when he tried DuPree's office, the receptionist kept telling him the bastard was 'unavailable.' We can't even be sure he was in either place."

"Damn. How about a search warrant for the penthouse?" Not even DuPree would be able to snake around that.

"Unfortunately, the State's Attorney can't use anything we turned up at that party to get search warrants for

DuPree's penthouse or surveillance equipment," Isabella said with a frown. "The conversations you and I had with both Danny and Angel can't be corroborated, plus we didn't have a warrant to be in the penthouse to begin with. If a judge finds out we went to that party before an active investigation was opened on top of that…"

Fuck. "You'll get laughed right out of the courthouse."

"Exactly."

Kellan blew out a slow breath. "And you didn't get anywhere with the canvas out in North Point?"

Isabella shook her head, dark hair spilling over her shoulders. "Hollister and I knocked on every door in that damned neighborhood today. Not one person can put DuPree or anyone on his payroll at the scene of Angel's murder, and Hale and Maxwell came up empty on Danny Marcus's end too. There's no trace of this guy anywhere near these crimes. DuPree might as well be a ghost."

Finishing with the dishes, Kellan led her to the living room, parking himself next to her on the couch and saying the only thing he could think of. "I'm sorry."

To his surprise, she simply nodded. "Thanks. It's not all a loss, though. Just because we can't use what you and I saw at the party to indict doesn't mean the intel doesn't help the investigation. We know DuPree is forcing these women into prostitution, and we know how he operates. We just have to keep digging to find a way to prove what we know. And once we do that…"

"You'll have enough to tie him to the parties and the murders," Kellan finished. He sat back against the couch cushions, looking at Isabella in the last of the evening light filtering in through the picture windows. She met his stare, holding on to it for just a minute before smiling and shocking the hell out of him.

"So tell me something about you."

His brows shot upward, and God, would she ever stop being both the opposite of what he expected and exactly what he wanted all at once? "You want to know something about me?"

She stilled. "Yes. No. I mean"—she paused, but the glimmer turning her eyes the color of whiskey over ice told him she wasn't backing down, regardless of the flush climbing over her cheeks—"Believe me, I want to break this case. But I've been thinking about it nonstop for nearly two weeks straight, and I'll be thinking about it first thing tomorrow morning, too. I just need…something else right now. So yeah. Tell me something about you."

For a second, Kellan paused. He knew he should pop off with something like his favorite baseball team or where he'd spend his next vacation if money were no object. Those were the easy things, the things they'd stuck to before now, and she'd had a hell of a long day. But something about the way she was looking at him, the warmth of her closeness and the at-odds combination of strength and need buried deep in her stare, made the truth launch past his lips.

"When I was deployed, I saw a lot of things that make it hard to sleep at night."

Isabella's brows lifted. "I'm sure you did," she said slowly. "Two tours in the Middle East couldn't have been easy."

"No," Kellan agreed. "I learned pretty quickly how to stuff everything down." It had been as basic a survival skill as keeping your head on a swivel and having your M9 ready on the fly.

"So why did you choose such a high-pressure job when you got out of the Army?" Isabella asked. "That can't be easy, either."

"Because it's not like I could've become an accountant," Kellan said. "No disrespect to number-crunchers—they're smart as hell in ways I'm not. But that's just it. I'm not like that."

"I'm not sure I follow," she said, a frown shaping her pretty mouth. But God, even though he knew he shouldn't, Kellan wanted to explain it to her.

As dangerous as it was to show her the boxes where he

kept every last thing that could make him vulnerable or weak, he couldn't deny the simple fact that he wanted to let her in.

"My dad died when I was twenty-one, after being sick for over a year."

Isabella stilled, but only for a breath before shifting on the couch cushions to brush her hand over his forearm. "I'm so sorry."

"Thanks." Kellan waited for the loss to sink hooks into his chest and paralyze him like it had in those early months before he'd learned to pack it away, but funny, it didn't.

So he kept talking. "It was just him and me and Kylie, so we were close. He worked a lot, trying to support us on his own. When he was diagnosed with lung cancer, I did my best to take care of him and Kylie, but he got really sick, really fast, and…"

"You were twenty-one," she whispered. Her fingers tightened on his forearm, and fuck, the warmth felt so much better than it should.

He swallowed past the dryness in his throat. "After he died, I didn't really know how to handle all the emotions that went with losing him, you know? I was pissed and hurt and about a thousand other things that messed with my head. Kylie and I were close, but she needed stability I couldn't give her. She had a friend whose parents agreed to let her live with them for two years until she turned eighteen. I needed something to get me right side up."

Isabella paused, her expression letting him know she'd connected the dots a second later. "So you enlisted."

"Yeah. At first I hated the Army." Okay, so it was an understatement. He'd survived basic training by equal amounts pure luck and sheer, screw-you grit. "I haven't always been so great at being told what to do."

"I can empathize," she said on a soft puff of laughter. "Let's just say my first few weeks at the police academy were a bit of a challenge."

At that, Kellan had to laugh too. "Eventually, though, I

learned how to push back on everything inside my head. I packed down my feelings and focused on what was in front of me. My training showed me what I was good at, and it wasn't long before I knew I wanted to be a Ranger." Now his laughter disappeared. "But there were parts of being a Ranger that came with a price."

"You had an aptitude for sniper skills."

Ah. Of course Isabella would know you don't choose becoming a sniper; it chooses you. Or more specifically, the Army chooses you for the job based on a whole battery of skills and training, and hell if Kellan hadn't had the perfect cocktail on his resume.

"I did," he said. "Which means I saw a lot of things no one should have to see." Those were the things he'd kept locked up the tightest. The boxes he feared the most. "Have you ever killed anyone in the line of duty, Isabella?"

A pop of surprise flashed in her eyes, there then gone before she shook her head. "I've fired my weapon a bunch of times on the job. Three hits, all clean. But none of those people died, no."

"You'd think it'd be cut and dried, you know. And in a way, it is. You're trained to assess threats. To protect and defend. To act." Even now, he couldn't so much as hit the head in the Crooked Angel without scanning the bar three times for potential danger. "So that's what you do. You calculate. You eliminate threats. You pull the trigger to keep yourself alive."

"If someone's posing a clear and present danger, defending yourself in order to survive is necessary, Kellan."

But the smile that pulled at his lips in response held no joy. "It's not the actions that fuck with you. It's what comes after."

Kellan thought the words would feel sharper or more rusty upon exit—he'd never spoken them to a soul.But they flowed into the warm, softly lit space between him and Isabella with ease, so he opened his mouth and came out with the rest.

"Devon and I were in Afghanistan toward the end of our second tour, way the hell out in a remote part of the country. Our unit was tasked with doing routine sweeps on a couple of different villages. Part of our job was to look out for insurgents who wanted to hurt us, but we were also there to make sure the locals remained safe."

Isabella didn't move or interrupt, just kept her hand steady on his arm as she listened, and the story rushed from the box in Kellan's memory right past his lips.

"Devon and I paired off to check this one dwelling, just like we'd done on probably twenty other days just like that one. Only this time, an insurgent who had been hiding in the back took Devon hostage with a gun to his head, point-blank."

"Jesus," Isabella gasped, her fingers tightening. "What did you do?"

Kellan paused, allowing himself just a split second to remember the heat that had punched through his lungs instead of air, and the cold, hateful cadence of the man's voice as he'd spoken.

If you move, I will kill your friend. You'll watch him die screaming, and then I'll kill you just as slowly. Your men will come running, and they too will die. All of you will die today.

"I shot the guy between the eyes within the span of a heartbeat."

Isabella's lashes fanned upward. "He had a gun to Devon's head. You did what you had to in order to save your best friend's life."

"And I don't regret it," Kellan said, the truth tumbling out unchecked. "The guy would've killed me and Devon and every last man in our unit if he'd had the chance. But I didn't think. I didn't feel. Christ, I wasn't even scared. I pulled that trigger and killed that man, and then I took all the emotions that came afterward and I locked them the fuck away, just like I do when I run into burning buildings. That's what I'm good at, and it's why I chose to become a firefighter. I don't think about the danger. I scan, I assess, I focus, but I never, ever feel."

He broke off, his defenses giving up a last-ditch warning to shut his trap and keep his emotions where they belonged, buried deep below the surface of his control. But Isabella was right there in front of him, with her fiery convictions and her bold words and that honest stare that saw right fucking through him, and he didn't stop talking at all.

He trusted her.

"I've spent the last ten years compartmentalizing every emotion I have, because if I don't, I can't act. So instead I keep everything packed away. But I'm really just going through the motions. I can't let go and really feel something with all I've got, even if that thing is good, because I don't know how to do that without breaking."

Isabella leaned in, her eyes never moving from his. "Is that what you want? To really feel something good with all you've got?"

Yes. God, yes.

Kellan realized he'd said the words out loud only when she reached up to curve her palm over his face and answered, "Then let me give it to you."

"Isabella," he started, but her fingers pressed against the center of his mouth, halting the rest.

"You've been here for me this whole time. You've had my back, even in the beginning when I fought you every step of the way. You deserve for someone to show you the good man that you are. You deserve to feel good, without holding back."

She moved close enough that he could feel the heat of her body and breath, and Christ, he'd never wanted to let go and just feel so badly in his life.

"Let me give this to you, Kellan. Let me have you for a change. Let me make you feel everything, no holding back."

CHAPTER TWENTY-FIVE

Isabella's heart pounded against her breastbone as she angled her mouth over Kellan's in one fluid movement. Her offer had been brash, she knew. But the ragged need in his eyes when he'd said he wanted to feel without holding back had shot all the way through her, filling her with certainty.

He was a good man. A brave, fierce, incredible man. He didn't just deserve to hear that. He deserved to really *feel* it, all the way in his blood and bones.

And Isabella was going to show it to him the best way she knew how.

"Come with me," she said, shifting her feet to the floorboards and straightening to a stand in front of him.

Although Kellan didn't say anything, he complied, letting her thread her fingers through his as she led him to his bedroom, not stopping until they were a few feet shy of the mattress.

"Come here."

He stepped in until only a few inches separated their bodies. Reaching up to cradle his face between both hands, Isabella slanted her lips over his. But where all their other kisses until now had been preludes, hot and hungry with the suggestion of what would come after them, this one was the polar opposite. This kiss wasn't meant to be anything other than exactly what it was—mouths touching, breath mingling, pure closeness—and the simplicity was a bigger turn-on than anything Isabella could've imagined. Slowly, she pressed her lips against Kellan's a little harder, taking her time as she explored his mouth.

Oh, his mouth. His lips were surprisingly soft, but firm too, and a small, dark thrill shot up her spine at the juxtaposition she'd never quite noticed. Focusing her attention on just his mouth, she nibbled and tasted and kissed with feather-light movements. She worked her way from one corner to the other with mostly chaste movements, darting her tongue out only long enough to trace the very edge of his bottom lip where his bare, smooth skin met the coarse stubble of his goatee.

"Jesus." Kellan groaned, his breath hot on her mouth. "Isabella, you're killing me."

She placed her lips back over his before parting them in a smile that tasted as wicked as it felt. "Do you feel good?"

"*You* feel good." His mouth parted, his tongue sliding hotly over the seam of her lips. "The way you're kissing me, how you're giving and teasing at the same time…you're driving me crazy."

"Like this?" Isabella arched forward to kiss him again, capturing his top lip between her teeth. Moving them back and forth, she worked his skin just hard enough to let him know where she'd been, and her nipples hardened at the growl climbing the back of his throat.

"Yeah," he said, pulling back to fasten her with a smoldering stare through the shadows in his room. His eyes glittered, dark blue and primal, and God, he was beautiful. "Like that."

"What else do you want, Kellan?" Isabella hovered her mouth in front of his, just shy of contact, and he didn't wait to answer her question.

"I want you pressed up against me." His heated gaze

traveled lower, lingering on the deep V of her top before he hooked his hands beneath her arms to bring their bodies flush. "Your mouth isn't the only thing I want to feel."

Oh God, yes. In a flash, she swung his back to the bed and pushed all the way forward, shifting their bodies lengthwise over the mattress. Kellan's shoulder blades met the sleep-rumpled sheets with a thump, and she bracketed his shoulders with both hands, straddling his lap and fitting her body against his from mouth to chest to hips.

"Oh, *fuck.*"

His moan made Isabella's sex grow slick behind the seam of her jeans. Her nipples pearled at the contact with the hard plane of his chest, and his fully erect cock sent tremors of heat to her clit, even through the layers of their clothes. Their bodies were cloaked in more shadow than light in the wake of the sunset, but the ambient glow filtering in from the hallway outlined the needful glint in his stare, and Isabella moved without thinking.

She returned her mouth to his, only this time, she didn't go slow. With a single, bold sweep of her tongue, she parted his lips, knotting her fingers in his hair to hold him close as she deepened the kiss. Kellan surrendered to her advance, letting her give and take and give again until finally, he pulled back with a sharp exhale.

"Isabella." His muscles thrummed beneath her body, and she leaned in to place her mouth beside his ear.

"You don't have to hide this away, Kellan. Tell me what you want to feel."

"I want more of you," he said, honesty and need wrapped tight around the words. "I want to feel your skin on mine."

Isabella slid off his lap and let her feet find the floor in front of him. Her body protested the loss of contact, sending a shiver all the way through her, but she didn't stop moving. She undressed quickly but with purpose, keeping her eyes locked on Kellan's as she lifted her T-shirt over her head, then slipped out of her boots so her jeans could follow. Leaving her bra and lacy white thong in place, she crooked one finger in a c'mere motion.

"Now you," she said. Kellan answered without a word, pushing up to a seated position on the bed, and she reached down low to grab the hem of his T-shirt. Heat pooled between her thighs at the sight of him, the indent of his chiseled shoulders, the flex and release of his biceps that made the scrolling ink on his arm seem to ripple with strength.

But despite the obvious appeal of his body, what Isabella really wanted was to give Kellan what he wanted, so she flattened her palms over his chest, guiding him back over the bed so she could reclaim her spot in his lap.

Oh. Sweet. Jesus.

A moan crossed her lips, completely without her consent. Her thong provided only a thin barrier between their bodies, and the friction of Kellan's denim-covered cock on her already-sensitive clit sent tiny bursts of pleasure deep between her hips. A wicked smile tore over his lips as he thrust against her sex in another suggestive glide.

"Looks like I'm not the only one who wants more," he said, and Isabella hinged her hips, leaning in to slide her mouth over his.

"I want *you*," she said, trailing her lips down the column of his neck. Kellan's breath hitched, releasing on a soft groan, and realization unfolded in her mind.

She slid an open-mouthed kiss over his collarbone, then another, and yes. There was the shudder. "Kellan?"

"Ah." The sound was more exhale than word. "Yeah?"

"What do you want?" Isabella slid lower. Found the dip right between his pectoral muscles. Licked.

He moaned again, lighting a fire way down deep in her belly. "I want…" Kellan's cock pressed harder against her pussy, and she canted her hips over his for one more delicious thrust before unhooking her leg and moving to his side.

"Mmm hmm?" she asked, returning her mouth to his

chest. His muscles flexed and jumped beneath her touch, making the heat in her belly double. She might have promised to make Kellan feel everything, but oh God, the promise of delivering that pleasure had *her* wanting to come.

His hips lifted off the mattress. Letting her fingers join her mouth, Isabella skimmed a hand over his chest, taking in the smooth, warm expanse of bare skin, then the flat of his belly before moving over the crisp scattering of hair leading into the top of his jeans.

"Isabella." His voice was pure gravel, her name so intense that her heart stuttered as he said it. She lifted her chin to meet his eyes, her heart slamming even harder at the fierce desire she found in his stare.

"I want your mouth on my cock."

Isabella's fingers shook with anticipation, but she managed to loosen the button and zipper on his jeans, and Kellan helped her lose the rest of his clothes with only a few twists and tugs. Sliding lower over the sheets, she splayed one hand wide next to his hip, balancing the rest of her weight on her knees beside him as she wrapped the fingers on her other hand around his cock.

Kellan bit out a curse when she started to stroke, then another when she lowered her mouth to his abdomen. Isabella explored his body with soft, slow touches just as she had with his mouth, teasing here, taking there. She kissed a path from his navel downward, wetness blooming between her thighs when she reached the head of his cock. Pressing her lips over the crown, she spread her lips just wide enough to flick her tongue out for a salty-sweet taste.

"God damn," Kellan said over a moan. "That feels…"

She opened her lips wider, letting her tongue linger over his smooth, hot skin. "Good?"

"Everything. Christ, sweetheart, you feel like everything."

The words unraveled Isabella's control. She parted her mouth over his cock, taking as much of him as she could before returning to the top and starting to suck. The motions of her hand chased the slide of her lips until she found a rhythm both slow and steady. Gliding her tongue all the way down the seam of his cock, she paused to take him deep inside her mouth for a heartbeat, then another, before pursing her lips on an upward slide.

Kellan exhaled his approval, his breath coasting hot and low over her shoulder. He thrust in time with her hand and mouth, guiding her faster, then faster again. Isabella worked his cock in long strokes, wanting him to feel everything and wanting to take everything he had to give. With every pass, need built in her sex like a bright demand, spreading up to make her clit throb and her nipples ache, but still, she didn't stop.

"Isabella…" His hands hooked in the wild spill of her hair, his muscles coiled so tightly she could feel the need for release pulsing desperately beneath his skin. "I want…*fuck*, I want…"

"It's okay," she murmured, pumping her hand over his slick length. "Go ahead and feel everything. I have you."

"But I want to have you."

So fast Isabella could barely process his motions, Kellan levered up from the mattress, separating their bodies for just a breath before grabbing her shoulders to roll her beneath the hard frame of his arms and hips.

He thrust against her, hard enough to knock the air from her lungs on a gasp. "I want you under me, screaming my name," he said, pulling off her panties with one rough yank. A primal sound left his throat as he looked at her bare sex, and it sent another shockwave through her.

"I want to feel your sweet, hot pussy grip me tight when I fuck you," he continued, taking a condom from his bedside table drawer, sheathing himself in seconds. Isabella's sex clenched at the promise, and oh God, she wanted him inside her, fucking her any way he wanted until they both shattered together.

She spread her legs wider, and Kellan licked his bottom lip before leaning in to hover over her. *Close. So close.*

"And as hot as your smart mouth is, I want my cock deep inside you when I come. I want to feel everything, Isabella. I want to feel *you*."

He filled her in one hard thrust, and for a second, the riot of sensation stole her breath. The blunt pressure of his cock buried deep between her legs made her inner muscles squeeze, her clit pulsing at the friction of the contact. Isabella arched up from the mattress, desperate not to lose even a fraction of their touch.

But then Kellan started to move.

"Oh...holy...Kellan, you feel..."

There was nothing she could say that would complete the sentence. Her sex grew slicker as he began to thrust. What started as slow, shallow movements quickly became more. He reached into the slight space where they were joined, teasing her needy clit with his thumb.

"You feel like that, too," he said. Gripping her hips, he pushed deep, filling her pussy in long, hard strokes, and the sensation was too much. Isabella's climax ripped through her in wave after wave. Kellan worked her through each one, slowing his movements as the intensity of her orgasm ebbed. But her want only doubled, and she bent her knees, clasping her thighs tight over the corded line of his waist.

"Do you feel me now?" she asked, lifting her hips to draw his cock deeper inside.

Kellan thrust back. "Yes."

"Then don't stop." Her heart pounded, but she didn't hold back. "Please, Kellan. Don't stop until you feel everything."

His hands dug into the bed sheets beside her shoulders as he pressed forward to fill Isabella to the hilt. He pumped faster, harder, swiveling his hips in a motion that tempted her to scream. Grabbing the backs of her knees, she lifted up, until his cock was so deep inside of her, she was certain she'd fly apart. Kellan pistoned his hips, thrusting over and over until his body went bowstring tight against hers. He pressed inside her pussy, closing all the space between them as the tension in his muscles came undone on a guttural moan.

Isabella's breath returned slowly, and Kellan lowered his forehead to hers.

"You feel like everything," he whispered, and she wrapped her arms around him even tighter.

* * *

Isabella lay in the shadows of Kellan's bedroom, her body exhausted but her brain refusing to go slower than warp speed. Logically, she knew she could blame her insomnia on the combination of a high-stress, high-risk case and the wheelbarrowful of great-sex endorphins running amok in her system. But logic had very little to do with what she felt deep beneath her breastbone right now.

Everything. You feel like everything.

Kellan trusted her. He had her back. He was close.

And even though it scared her shitless, close was exactly where she wanted him, because she trusted him too. Maybe even enough to fall for him.

"Hey." He stirred from behind her, turning to his side to press a kiss between her shoulder blades. "It's almost one. Awfully late for you to be awake."

Shit. Isabella's belly tightened with guilt. He had enough trouble sleeping as it was. "I'm sorry," she said, sending the whisper over her shoulder without turning around. "Am I keeping you up?"

"Nope." He slid his hand over her hip, his fingers tracing light circles beneath the covers, and how could such a simple touch feel so purely, deeply good? "You thinking about the case?"

"Not exactly," she hedged.

Kellan's pause held no small measure of concern. "You okay?"

Isabella exhaled, her pulse pressing hard against her eardrums in the quiet, moonlit room. "Not exactly."

"I see." He moved his hand from her hip to her back, his touch never faltering. "Tell me something about you, Isabella. Tell me what's making you not okay so I can help you."

She hitched, her heart in her throat. But he'd trusted her enough to let her in tonight, to let her see things he'd kept locked away for a decade.

She trusted him, too.

"Do you remember the story I told you? About my cousin Marisol?"

"Yeah." Confusion clung to his tone, but God, now that she'd started, Isabella couldn't stop the words.

"She was abducted eleven years ago, a couple of weeks before her fifteenth birthday. The man who kidnapped her kept her for three days, sexually assaulting her multiple times before strangling her and leaving her body in the basement of an old apartment building."

Kellan went utterly still behind her. "Jesus," he whispered after a minute. "Isabella, I'm so sorry."

Despite the shock in his voice, his breath was warm on her neck, his chest so strong and solid and there behind her that everything she'd tried so hard to forget just kept coming out.

"I remember thinking it had to be some kind of mistake. That she'd walk through the front door at any minute with a big smile on her face and ask why we all looked so worried. But instead, the police came to her parents' house on that third day. They're the ones who knocked on the door, and they weren't smiling."

"That's why you became a cop, isn't it?" Kellan asked, understanding dawning in his voice. "Why you throw yourself into the job so hard? You want to protect people like Marisol."

Protect. The irony rang in Isabella's ears hard enough to hurt, and she followed them with a bitter laugh. "I became a cop because I didn't protect my cousin at all. Her death was my fault."

A pause opened between them, lasting for a full breath before he said, "What are you talking about?"

Guilt rushed up with the memory, heavy enough to crush her chest, but the rest of the story—the part that no one knew except for her family and the detectives who had investigated Marisol's murder—poured out of her on a tide of sadness.

"We were supposed to go to a party that night, some high school thing to celebrate homecoming." God, how stupid it had all seemed in hindsight. How easily she could have made a thousand different choices that would have led to a different outcome. An outcome that wouldn't have ripped out her family's heart. An outcome where Mari would have lived.

Closing her eyes, Isabella continued. "I'd been invited by this guy I really liked, but my parents made me promise to take Marisol, too. She was so excited. She'd just started her freshman year, and a party like that was a big deal. I was supposed to pick her up."

She could still remember the night as if it had been a minute ago, the feel in the air that wasn't warm enough to be summer anymore, but not quite chilly enough to be fall. At the time Isabella had thought that night would be perfect. How stupid she'd been. How careless.

"But I didn't," she said, the words wobbling traitorously through the dark of Kellan's room. "I told her to walk to our house instead so I could have extra time to get ready. I promised her it would be no big deal, that she'd be safe. I promised, and she believed me, and because of that, she died."

"*No.*" Although the protest was little more than a whisper, it cracked through the room as if Kellan had shouted it.

A sob worked upward from Isabella's chest, and God, she hated herself even more. "Yes. I—"

"No." Grabbing her shoulders, he swung her to face him. "It's not your fault. Just like you weren't responsible for Angel's death, you aren't responsible for Marisol's either."

"But I promised." Tears burned behind her eyelids, and she slammed her eyes shut to ward them off, to no avail. "She was my best friend, my closest friend. If only I'd gone to get her...I should have protected her."

"Isabella, you didn't know." Kellan cupped her face. "You couldn't have known. You were only seventeen. Marisol's death is a terrible thing, a thing that shouldn't happen to anyone. But you didn't kill her, Isabella. This isn't your fault."

He thumbed away the tears spilling freely over her face now, and oh, she wanted to believe him so badly. "I miss her," Isabella said. "I miss her so much."

"Okay. It's okay." Kellan wrapped his arms around her, and just like that, she broke apart. Lying in the safety of his embrace, Isabella let out the guilt that had wracked her for so long. He never budged, just held her and took the brunt of her grief as it tumbled out of her in wave after wave. Finally, her bone-deep cries subsided into softness, and he pulled back to look at her with so much certainty, she ached.

"I've got you too, sweetheart. It's okay."

This time when he said it, Isabella believed him.

CHAPTER TWENTY-SIX

Kellan sat in the lobby of the Thirty-Third precinct, watching the controlled chaos around him with no small amount of awe. The place hummed with way more activity than a Wednesday afternoon should allow, from the steady stream of uniformed officers moving past the front doors to the near-constant ringing of the phone in the main office space to the desk sergeant barking orders at damn near everyone walking by. Kellan supposed the firehouse wasn't too much different from a visitor's perspective; in fact, Sinclair's daughter, January, ran the office at Seventeen much like her father ran his intelligence unit—no bullshit, all the time. Still, the Thirty-Third was kind of a daunting place if you didn't have backup.

"Hey!" came a familiar voice Kellan was growing all too accustomed to, and okay, maybe this place wasn't so bad after all.

"Hey," he said, standing to greet Isabella as she descended the last of the steps to the lobby. She looked just like she always did, a few wisps of hair defying her ponytail to frame her face, jeans hugging her curves, and her SIG and badge at her side. But damn, she was the most beautiful woman Kellan had ever clapped eyes on, and the pang in his gut grew twice as strong when she pressed to her toes to brush a kiss over his cheek.

He cleared his throat, although it probably didn't do much to kill his idiot grin. "Sorry to barge in on you like this, but I was at loose ends after catching up on my sleep from yesterday's shift. Thought I'd bring you lunch."

Isabella's eyes brightened at the sight of the carry out bag from the Fork in the Road. "Is that what I think it is?"

"Club sandwich and fries, extra pickles. Oh, and a giant vat of tea." He held up the oversized cardboard cup—the biggest one the guy at the diner could find, as a matter of fact—unable to cage his laughter as her expression went from happiness to full-on bliss.

"You're a peach, you know that?" She took the bag and the cup, tilting her head toward the staircase leading up to the second floor. "Why don't you come on up? We just got the reports back from CSU on my apartment. Hollister and I were about to dig in."

Surprise made Kellan blink. "Okay, if you're sure."

Truth was, he'd been climbing the walls at his apartment. If he could help them get closer to nailing DuPree? Even better.

"Of course I'm sure," Isabella said, matter-of-fact. With a flash of her badge and a quick jaunt through the metal detectors, they climbed the steps to the intelligence office. The place was mostly empty, with three of the five desks vacant. Kellan followed Isabella over to one covered with case files and photographs and abandoned tea cups, where her partner sat a few feet away in a similar pile of paperwork.

"Hey, Walker." If Hollister was shocked to see him, the guy didn't show it, although the guy probably wore a poker face as an occupational hazard.

"Hollister. Good to see you," Kellan said, leaning in to shake the guy's hand.

"Kellan's not on-shift today, so I figured it wouldn't hurt if he kept us company while we shuffled through these on our lunch break." Isabella pointed to the file folders, and Hollister sent a frown in the same direction.

"Only if you want indigestion, my man. These are about as useless as a screen door on a submarine."

Isabella's brows shot up before sinking in disappointment. "They didn't come up with anything?"

"'Fraid not," Hollister said. "No fingerprints, no hair, no fibers, and no boot prints on the hardwoods. The slashes to the couch and mattress were made with an undetermined serrated weapon, of which I can think of about two dozen varieties off the top of my head, and the marker used to write the message on the mirror is the most widely manufactured in the country. Truth? We've seen serial killers less methodical than this fucking guy."

"Dammit." Isabella slumped in her chair. "So we have nothing on the break-in and nothing on the fire."

"Nope. Maxwell and Hale are still finishing up that assault case from this morning, but they checked in to say they've heard exactly zip on the final report from the fire marshal."

Kellan's gut dropped. "Yeah, I pulled the reports that both Gamble and Hawkins made from the call. Looks like the water probably trashed any evidence you might find that DuPree or any of his guys were in the house when the fire started."

"Great," she said, pinching the bridge of her nose between her thumb and forefinger. "So we're back at square one."

"Not necessarily!"

The words snagged Kellan's full attention, and he turned toward the top of the stairs, where the intelligence unit's tech guy was hightailing it into the office.

Isabella lasered her sights in on him, her eyes sparking with hope. "Capelli, tell me you have something."

"That I do. Grab the boss. He's gonna want to hear this," Capelli said. A few seconds later, when Sinclair had come out of his office, the guy continued. "I just got some background on our guy, and it's a doozy. Ah—"

He paused to look up at Kellan, his eyes darting to Sinclair in obvious hesitation, and Kellan got the message loud and clear.

"I can go." He shifted to find his feet, but a pair of protests stopped him mid-move.

"No."

Kellan processed the *holy shit* pumping through his veins at the fact that Sinclair's voice had been the one to join Isabella's.

"We don't normally disclose case details with members outside of the unit, and that rule still stands," Sinclair said. "But given the extenuating circumstances of Walker's involvement and the fact that he could still be a potential target, he might as well stick around for the update."

He turned to level Kellan with a frosty stare, and ooookay, guess the guy hadn't quite gone the forgive-and-forget route on the mouthing off Kellan had given him a few days ago.

"Provided that you keep everything discussed here strictly confidential," Sinclair added.

Kellan dipped his chin in a deferent nod. "Copy that."

Capelli blinked, but quickly got back to business. "Right. So I had a friend over at the FBI field office run some background checks for me, to see if there was anything higher up the food chain than I had access to. Turns out, he got a hit on one of the government databases in New York."

"New York?" Isabella asked, stepping back on the linoleum in obvious confusion, and yeah, sign Kellan up for the sentiment, too. "I never found any record of DuPree living or working in New York."

"*That* is because he was a minor at the time. The hit is from the Department of Child and Family Services in Syracuse, and the case file was sealed, which is why it took a couple of days' worth of digging to find."

"Sealed why?" Hollister asked. "Even if DuPree was a minor at the time, the record should still at least show that files were charged against him."

Capelli's brows went up. "Not if he was the victim."

Kellan's jaw unhinged. No way had he just heard that right. "DuPree was the *victim*?"

"Yep. Looks like there was an investigation into abuse by his mother. A school guidance counselor noticed what she listed as 'abnormal behavior', so she requested a follow-up from DCFS. DuPree initially accused the mother of abuse, but it looks like he later rescinded."

"So no charges were ever filed?" Sinclair asked.

"No," Capelli said, shaking his head. "And mom fell off the radar not long after that. The notes from DCFS are sparse, but the school counselor was pretty adamant that DuPree was potentially dangerous."

Isabella froze beside him. "Dangerous how?"

Capelli's pause definitely wasn't lost on Kellan, or probably anyone else standing in the intelligence office. "According to this, he was 'substantially anti-social, distant, displayed a lack of empathy for those around him as well as a lack of remorse for wrongdoings.'"

"Wrongdoings," Hollister repeated, and this time Capelli's pause lasted longer.

"The list is pretty long, but the *Reader's Digest* version is that he threatened two teachers with bodily harm, followed through on similar threats made to at least a half a dozen students, and although it was never proven, he was looked at pretty hard for vandalism to the school principal's car and for killing a neighbor's cat."

Kellan couldn't think of a single curse word that adequately covered this. "The guy is a freaking sociopath."

"At first glance?" Capelli asked. "Yeah."

"Okay," Sinclair said. "I want our profiler on this, right now. Moreno"—he turned to look at her, and oh hell, Kellan knew the look in the sergeant's eyes couldn't mean anything Isabella would like—"I want you in protective custody."

"Sam," she said, her brows winging sky-high. "Come on.

DuPree has been church-mouse quiet for three days."

"Yeah, and seventy-two hours ago he was turning your furniture into kindling. I mean it. This guy is unhinged."

Before Kellan could open his mouth to suggest that Sinclair wasn't wrong, Hollister beat him to the one-two. "Moreno, he's kind of got a point. It sounds like DuPree is off the deep end, and he clearly has a hard-on for trying to get to you."

"Then let him try," Isabella said, jamming her hands over her hips and planting her boots into the linoleum. "Look, I understand he's dangerous, and I'm not saying I won't be careful. I'll still check in and take extra safety precautions. But if DuPree is antsy enough to make a move, we'll have him right where we want him. We might not get him any other way."

Annnnnnd fuck. Now Isabella had a point, too. Kellan didn't want her in harm's way—the thought alone made him want to throat-punch someone. But she was a cop, which meant her job came with a certain amount of risk. While he wasn't on board with her taking unnecessary ones, at some point he had to trust that she'd be both smart and okay.

"If it makes you feel any better, I've got Isabella's back," Kellan said. "I know you guys are her team and everything, but when she's not with you...I promise to keep her safe."

For a minute, nobody said anything, the silence stretching thinner and thinner. Finally, Sinclair ran a hand over his crew cut and turned back toward Capelli.

"I want something from the profiler by morning, and keep on the hacker. We still might get a nugget on these parties or these murders. Moreno, I've never minced words and I'm sure as hell not going to start now. I don't like this. That said, I have to trust that you're making the right call. But you will be taking every extra security measure under the sun."

"Yes, sir," she said.

"Good. Now let's get back to work. And Walker?" Sinclair waited for him to make eye contact before adding,

"You'd better."

"I do," he said, and they were the easiest two words he'd ever spoken.

* * *

Julian DuPree was not a patient man. He stood in the middle of his penthouse, looking down at the city lights signaling a Friday night in full swing, while everything around him was quiet and still.

All because Isabella Moreno had miraculously and unexpectedly grown some fucking restraint.

The silence around Julian grated on his nerves, his anger writhing under his skin. One week ago, everything was normal. He'd stood here in this exact spot, watching every depraved whore he owned getting used and abused just as she should.

No room for filth! screamed the voice in his head, and he slipped his fingers to his temple in order to shut it up.

But still, it came. *Filth needs to be punished! I'll beat it out of you, you vulgar boy!*

And the voice had tried. She'd taken the switch from the cupboard in the kitchen, just as she'd done all the times before. The house was far from any neighbors, and no one had visited since the woman from DCFS, who Julian had told about the voice. He'd paid for that, having to take it back and say it was a lie after the voice had given him the scars. But a year had passed by then, on the night the voice got the switch. Julian had been bigger then than when she'd first started raging about the filth. Biding his time since she'd given him the scars. Planning. Waiting for the right time to kill her.

And then he'd beaten her to death in that kitchen, snapping every last one of her bones before dismembering her and burying her bit by bit in their backyard.

Julian exhaled, adjusting the cuffs of his dress shirt as he examined the city through the wall of windows. Detective

Moreno had led the RPD to his doorstep, a doorstep which he prided himself on keeping covered. He was meticulous, he was smarter than all of them, and therefore he didn't get caught. But now he was being watched, his parties on hold, and his pent-up need to inflict pain was growing urgent.

He wanted to hurt her. In the worst way possible. He wanted to take everything from her, as she was doing to him.

But the detective wasn't just staying away from Julian, sending her pig of a boss to try and question him instead. She was well-protected. Walker never left her side, and while the man was the worst sort of brute, he was also highly trained. If Julian tried to take them both, he'd sustain casualties at the very least. Casualties meant mess, and mess meant loose ends that could get him caught. He needed another way.

He needed to separate them. To get Detective Moreno to act brashly, and alone.

It was time to up the stakes and end this game, once and for all.

CHAPTER TWENTY-SEVEN

Isabella stood in her freshly cleaned bedroom, tucking the last edge of a light blue sheet beneath the corner of her brand-new mattress.

"You do know that's probably a waste of time, right?" Kellan's voice snared her attention from the spot where he'd appeared in the doorway.

"How's that?" she asked, a flush heating a path over her cheeks at the dark and sexy half-smile riding his mouth in reply.

"Because I'm just going to strip you naked and make you want to tear those sheets right back off."

The "oh" tumbling from Isabella's lips was more moan than actual word. "Well, it does make sense to test out the new bed. Quality control, and all that."

Kellan crossed the floorboards, leaning in to slide a sweet and sinful kiss over her mouth, and oh God, she was totally stupid for this man. "I like how you think. But we should probably eat dinner first."

"You want to wait?"

"No. I want to lay you down and fuck you senseless. But it's late and I know you better than to think you actually took a break for lunch today. Plus, that chicken casserole Kylie brought over has been in your oven for twenty minutes, and I can't lie. It's starting to smell insane."

Isabella laughed, although her happiness was short-lived. "Okay, okay. So you're not wrong about work." She followed him down the hall to the living room, her brain still trying to get on board with the sight of the new furniture that had been delivered just a few hours ago. "But we're behind the eight ball now more than ever. DuPree has been underground for a whole week. Not only do we have no new leads, but we can't even confirm for certain that the scumbag is in Remington."

"Is there anything the Feds can do?" Kellan asked, and a fresh shot of frustration spread out beneath her skin.

"No. Sinclair has tried to interview DuPree every day this week. He gets the same stonewall every time. No answer at the Metropolitan, no joy at DuPree's office. Without sufficient evidence to suspect him, we can't get a warrant to get any farther than the lobby of either place. Not even the FBI can get around that."

Isabella flopped down on the couch, jamming a hand through her hair. Her tension had been steadily building all week, and as hard as intelligence was working, nothing was working.

She said, "We can't get anywhere because DuPree has covered his tracks so well, and meanwhile, he's got a bunch of women holed up in some shitty flophouse somewhere in North Point, having God-only-knows-what done to them by Franco and Rampage. We need a break, and we're not getting anywhere by waiting."

Realization flickered, chilling Kellan's stare to an icy blue. "You're not thinking of going down there instead of Sinclair."

"Why not?" Okay, so she hadn't meant to just pop off with the words, but come on. Nothing else was working.

Of course, she should've known the suggestion would bring Kellan's defensive side out to play. "Ah, let's see.

Because DuPree is crazy." He lifted a finger, keeping count. "He trashed your apartment and threatened you." Another finger. Check. "And because Sinclair would never okay it, and you promised to work with the rest of your unit as a team."

Isabella's brain knew he had a point. But her gut? Not such an easy sell. "You're exactly right. DuPree is crazy, which is why he needs to be stopped. Kellan, he killed Angel and Danny Marcus, and he's doing despicable things to these other girls. So what if there's a little risk involved in taking him down?"

Kellan didn't budge. If anything, his expression only grew more fierce. "You confronting him isn't a little risk."

"I know," she said, because in truth, she did. The full report from their profiler had sent chills down her spine, and that was just based on the abstract. Knowing DuPree, the reality was likely worse. "I'm just frustrated. I want to catch this guy."

"I know you do, and you will." Kellan slid over the couch cushions to press a kiss to her forehead.

"Easier said than done," Isabella grumbled.

"Tell you what. Let's have some dinner and I'll help you go over the case files. Maybe you'll catch something new by talking out the details."

She exhaled, but gave up a nod. "Okay, yeah. It can't hurt."

"Great. Just let me call Devon and Kylie to check in, and by then dinner should be done."

Kellan kissed her one more time before standing up to unearth his cell phone from the back pocket of his jeans and head toward the kitchen. The strains of his conversation with Kylie floated into the living room, so easygoing and relaxed that Isabella had to smile. Maybe Kellan was right. Maybe they'd get their break by looking at all the facts again.

But God, she'd already done that a thousand times. Today.

Her cell phone vibrated from her back pocket, sending

a ribbon of hope uncurling through her belly. Capelli had been sifting through DuPree's business transactions when she'd left the precinct. Maybe he'd gotten a hit on something.

Unknown caller.

The hairs on the back of Isabella's neck stood on end as she stared at her cell phone. Trying—and failing—to steady her hands, she tapped the icon to take the call and lifted the phone to her ear.

"Moreno."

"Hello, Detective. I hope you're having a lovely evening so far." DuPree's melodic voice hit her with all the force of an anvil, and for a second, her answer wedged in her throat.

"Mr. DuPree," she said, her thoughts going from zero to a million and sixty as she fast-tracked her way into her bedroom to grab a pen and a piece of paper. The phone company might be able to pull the call details later, but DuPree was slicker than snot. Who knew how long he'd stay on the line?

As if he could read her mind, he said, "I've been assured this line is secure. Try as you might, you won't be able to trace this call."

God *damn* that hacker! "What do you want?"

"To put it bluntly, I want you, Detective."

Isabella's palms went slick, but she channeled all her effort into calming her words despite the physiological response. "I'm at the Thirty-Third nearly every day, Mr. DuPree. You're welcome to come in any time you'd like to chat."

"You are tenacious, aren't you?" His voice tightened, just slightly but it was enough. "I'll admit to being rather disappointed to find out you're a detective, Isabella."

"Telling you last week would've spoiled the fun." She trapped her tongue between her teeth, too late to pull back her emotions. *Come on, girl. Breathe deep.* "But we don't have to let that stand in the way of us having a sit-down."

"Full marks for effort, Detective. But I won't be giving

you the advantage of meeting you on your own ground. Come to my penthouse at the Metropolitan—alone, of course. Midnight tonight. I believe you remember the way."

Isabella's stomach clenched. "And what makes you think I'll come to you?"

His answer was as immediate as it was matter-of-fact. "Because if you don't, I'll start purging my inventory. One girl every four hours. And trust me when I tell you, it will take that long for them to die."

For a second, she couldn't breathe. "You wouldn't."

DuPree's laugh was sharp enough to cut glass. "I think we both know that I would.

I do hate to waste commodities, but there will always be more where they came from. And alas, there's only one you, Detective Moreno. There will be a keycard for you in the lobby. If you tell anyone else about this meeting—and I will know if you do—I'll start killing girls immediately. So do take care to be discreet."

Her mind scrambled for a last-ditch ploy, anything to give her leverage. "You don't really think I'm going to walk in there without backup, do you?"

"Seeing as how this is your only chance at getting anywhere near me, yes, I actually do. Oh, I nearly forgot. Do us both a favor and don't arrive armed. That would be poor form. Am I clear?"

She had no choice but to say, "Perfectly."

"Then we have a date."

The line went dead, and dread filled Isabella's chest like ice water.

But the sensation was nothing compared to what she felt when she turned around and saw Kellan standing in the doorway.

* * *

Kellan scraped in a breath, doing his best to hold on to the last ounce of his composure as the conversation he'd just overheard trickled all the way into his brain.

You don't really think I'm going to walk in there without backup, do you?

Nope. Screw composure. He was about to lose his fucking mind.

"What the hell are you thinking?" he asked, closing the space between them in only a few strides. "You're going to meet with DuPree? Alone?"

A look of panic stole across Isabella's face. "I'm...that's what he wants."

"No." Kellan fired off the word like a mortar. "Isabella, you have to call Sinclair."

"No!" The force of her emotions brought her chin snapping upward. "I can't."

She had to be kidding. "He's your boss. Why the hell not?"

"*Because* he's my boss," she said, and damn, she so wasn't kidding.

"Start talking. Right now."

Although the whiskey-warm flash in her eyes said Kellan was pushing the boundaries of her tolerance by getting chippy, she started to explain. "DuPree wants a meeting with just me, at his penthouse. No backup, no weapons. Just me and him."

Jesus. This guy had stones the size of an aircraft carrier. "He really is insane if he thinks you'll agree to that."

Although Kellan didn't think it was possible, Isabella's expression grew even more grim. "He's going to start torturing and killing the girls from the party if I don't."

His blood whooshed hard enough in his veins that his knees loosened. "What?"

"One every four hours, starting at midnight, if I don't show or if I tell anyone. And believe me, he means it."

"He's fucking deranged." Kellan bit each syllable to the quick. "He wants to hurt you, and he won't stop at anything until he does. You need to call Sinclair. Or at the very least let me go with you."

Isabella's breath flew out in a frustrated huff. "I can't. I have to protect these women. Don't you see? I don't have a choice here. If I don't go completely alone, he's going to start killing people. I *have* to do this his way."

Fear exploded in Kellan's chest, hell-hot and frigid at the same time. She couldn't do this. She could not.

"But you don't," he said, all the emotion he knew he should hold back rushing to the forefront and directly out of his mouth. "You don't have to catch DuPree all by yourself, and you don't have to keep chasing ghosts. Putting yourself on the line like this isn't going to bring Marisol back."

She froze, just for an instant before her spine straightened into a rigid line, and fuck. *Fuck.* "What did you say?"

"Isabella, I didn't mean—"

"Oh yes you did." She stepped back on the floorboards to nail him with a glare. "Let me assure you, I know all too well that *nothing* will bring Marisol back. She's dead. She was raped and murdered by a man just like DuPree. I know that. I live with that every single day, and I'm not going to sit around and let it happen to any more women just because I'm afraid of taking a risk!"

Realization sank into Kellan with razor-wire teeth. "You're going to do this no matter what I say, aren't you?"

Isabella hesitated, and for one thin second, hope ignited in his belly.

But then she shook her head, snuffing it out. "This is the only shot we will ever have at getting DuPree. This is his misstep, Kellan. *This* is what we've been waiting for, and I can't let him kill any more women. I need to go and take him down, and I need to do it alone. If you can't stand by that"—she sent her gaze over his shoulder—"then you should go."

Kellan stood in front of her, completely shell-shocked, for only a second before his defenses locked his shoulders into place and the rest of his body shut. "Fine," he said, slamming down on his emotions until he felt nothing but numb. "Have it your way. You're on your own."

He turned on his heel and left.

CHAPTER TWENTY-EIGHT

Kellan got all of ninety feet from the back exit of Isabella's apartment building before he realized he'd left both his cell phone and the keys to his Camaro on her kitchen counter.

Fuck.

He flipped his wrist, checking his watch with a frown. Okay, so it was barely twenty-hundred, which meant there were a solid four hours before Isabella was set to show up at DuPree's penthouse. That would give Kellan plenty of time to get to a phone to call Sinclair.

Isabella would be furious, but at least she wouldn't be dead.

Check that. She was already furious. If he told Sinclair about the phone call she'd gotten from DuPree and the plans she had to go with it, Isabella would never speak to him again.

You're kind of already there, aren't you buddy?

Kellan mashed back on the emotions brewing between his ribs. Kicking his feet into motion, he aimed himself toward the sidewalk and started to hoof it, eyes peeled for a payphone. One block turned into the next, which turned into a dozen more, and despite his effort, he couldn't wipe the thought of Isabella from his head as he walked. The way she made at least five cups of tea in the morning, but only drank half of each one. The pure excitement that lit her face when she talked about things like the gun range and tactical weapons training. The way her body tightened and hummed just before she broke apart in climax.

The images rolled by on a continuous loop in Kellan's head over and over, and damn it, screw it and fuck it all to hell, he couldn't lock her away. He didn't want to lock her away. So he didn't.

He also didn't hear the men behind him until one of them jabbed a needle into his neck, and the other threw a canvas bag over his head, turning his world pitch black.

* * *

Isabella paced over her living room floor so hard, she was shocked she didn't carve a visible path in the hardwoods. Kellan had only been gone for an hour, but God, it felt like a thousand, and their argument welled up in her memory like a nasty cut. While she wasn't shocked at his anger over her desire to confront DuPree, his mention of Marisol had smarted like a slap. Of *course* Isabella knew she couldn't bring her cousin back—she'd tried just about everything to dull that pain. But now she could keep other women from being hurt, too. How could she refuse?

She owed it to them to do her job. And her job was to take down Julian DuPree. With or without Kellan's blessing.

And despite the bone-deep ache in the center of her chest.

An electronic ringtone cut into Isabella's awareness, sending her pulse through the roof. But her cell phone was right here, silent in her palm. So what the hell was ringing?

She walked into her kitchen, quickly realizing that Kellan's cell phone lay sunny-side-up on her counter next to the now-cool casserole. The incoming call was labeled

Gamble, and even though she hesitated for just a second, she scooped up the phone and put it to her ear.

"Hey, Gamble. It's Isabella. I—"

"Is he with you?"

Fear laddered down her spine at the gruff urgency of the demand. "No. He left about an hour ago. Why?"

Gamble didn't mince so much as a syllable. "Because he never checked in."

Isabella's chest constricted. "What? That's impossible. Wait—" Her cell phone buzzed from the spot where she'd placed it on the counter when she'd traded it for Kellan's. "Hang on, I'm getting a text. It might be…"

The rest of her words withered in her throat, her fear turning to sheer terror as she saw the image of Kellan, bleeding and blacked out and wearing the same shirt he'd left her apartment in an hour ago.

I have something you want. Midnight.

"Gamble," Isabella said, her voice wooden in her ears. "I'm sorry, I have to go."

She dropped the phone with a clatter and ran to the safe in her bedroom.

* * *

Kellan felt like he'd been smashed into a thousand pieces and glued back together by a toddler. The antique grandfather clock in the penthouse foyer told him he'd only been lights out for about an hour before the fun had started thirty minutes ago. His neck was sore from the injection site of whatever that asshole—who'd turned out to be Rampage, he'd found out when he'd come to—had stuck him with to knock him out, and his temple throbbed like a motherfucker from where that other asshole—everyone's least favorite pimp Franco—had pistol-whipped him with the Glock he'd shoved in his waistband. Kellan had left his SIG in Isabella's apartment along with his keys and cell phone to complete the trifecta of stupid, so his only hope now was that Franco might get a touch more careless with that weapon and either shoot his own ass off or give Kellan a chance to take it.

That second one didn't seem likely, seeing as his hands were zip tied in front of him and he'd taken enough of a beating after he'd regained consciousness to be seeing double and spitting blood.

Oh hell. Isabella was going to walk right into this. DuPree was going to do the same to her, and it would only get worse.

Kellan had to get out of these restraints and take that gun.

"Get up, pretty boy. The boss wants you." Rampage grabbed him by the back of the neck and hauled him to his feet. Kellan forced his body to remain lax, allowing his head to loll deeply even though the move sent stars sparking across his field of vision. Better to let them think he was still off-kilter to keep their guards lower.

Rampage kicked at Kellan's heels, shoving him from behind. He stumbled his way out of the penthouse's main room—nineteen steps—down a back hallway—twelve steps—and into a wood-paneled room that looked as if it had been horked out by *Masterpiece Theater*. DuPree sat behind a huge mahogany desk, looking as smarmy as ever in a navy blue suit and a repulsive smile.

"Ah, Mr. Walker. So nice of you to join us." He gestured to the spot in front of his desk, and Rampage gave Kellan an extra shove for his trouble.

"Sorry." Kellan slurred on purpose, slipping one thumb around the zip tie at his wrists to test their thickness. Damn, this was going to take some doing. "I didn't realize I had a choice."

DuPree's expression read *good point*. "Yes. Well, I have to say it was quite the happy coincidence that you left Detective Moreno's apartment after she and I set up our engagement. The truth is, I've been waiting for the two of you to separate all week. Divide and conquer, you know. I thought the plan to use those cock-sucking whores to goad her here was rather clever, but you…" He wagged a finger, and Christ, Kellan was tempted to bite the digit clean off. "When I saw you walk out of her apartment building a few hours ago, you made things all too perfect."

"You saw me?" Kellan blanked his expression to keep his emotions hidden, but DuPree's were on full display, the pride practically pouring out of him.

"Don't you know by now, I see everything? Accessing the security feeds for her building was all too easy, and now I have her where it hurts the most. She's a dirty little slut, letting her brazen impulses lead her into my party, trying to outsmart me, to make me look weak. She needs to be punished."

Kellan's stomach pitched, his heart beating faster in his chest. This guy had gone around the bend. "So you're going to punish her?"

DuPree smiled, pure evil in his soulless eyes. "And you're going to watch."

Kellan felt his lunge forward only after his body had decided to go. Pain detonated across his already-injured temple, stunning him into place, and the sticky warmth of fresh blood trickled over his jaw and into the neck of his T-shirt. Anger sizzled like a living, breathing thing under his skin, stealing his focus and snatching at his composure.

Breathe. In, two, three, four, five. Out, two, three. Breathe.

Kellan buckled down, bracing to take the next blow. Only what came instead was a tense voice through the intercom speaker on the cherry-paneled wall by the door.

"Uh, boss. I hate to interrupt, but it looks like your girl is early."

Kellan's heart tripped against his sternum. *Isabella.*

Rampage paused, his hand still raised in an upswing, and DuPree's expression turned to granite. "I'm sorry," DuPree hissed. "How is that possible?"

"None of the feeds at her apartment show her leaving the place at all, but she just popped up in the lobby downstairs. She's solo, and no phone calls went in or out on her cell, the firefighter's cell, or her landline. I have no idea how she slipped the surveillance, but if she contacted anybody, it was either by smoke signals or fucking semaphore," said Intercom Boy.

"Of course." The muscles along DuPree's clean-shaven jawline jumped, and yeah, Kellan thought as he covertly angled the locking mechanism of the zip tie between both wrists. He was running out of time.

"She's trying to throw me off by changing the rules. Insolent bitch. Charles, watch him," DuPree said, jerking his head toward Kellan. "Franco, go escort the detective in. It looks as if we're starting this party early."

* * *

Isabella slid her finger beneath the thin silver chain around her neck, focusing on her breathing even though her lungs were filled with far more adrenaline than air. But her plan was in place—was already in motion—and she was one hundred percent certain it would work.

She'd done the right thing. She had Kellan's back.

Now she was going to *get* him back.

The thought steadied her hands along with her nerves as the elevator whispered up on a nonstop route to the penthouse, and she tacked on her poker face when the doors opened to reveal Franco, aka Scarface from the party.

Here we go. "I'm here to see your boss."

"You're early," Franco said with a sneer.

"He'll see me anyway," Isabella flipped back, and Franco's face split into a crooked-toothed grin.

"He's gonna love making you pay for that." Franco proceeded to frisk her, his grabby hands lingering in all the places she'd expected them to before he led her past the front door.

"What, he's not going to entertain me in the main living space?" she asked, the hard soles of her boots calling out each of her footsteps over the marble.

"No. All the good private shows go down in his study."
A minute later, Franco nudged her over the threshold of a
darkly-paneled office space, and she got barely two steps in
before fear funneled all the way through her.

"Kellan."

The whisper slipped out, and she dug her nails into her
palms in order to keep from running to him. He was
upright, although barely, one eye swollen shut and the other
on its way. A brutal gash, small but deep, sliced over his
temple, and there was enough blood leading down his neck
and into his gray T-shirt to tell her the wound wasn't child's
play. She met his gaze for just a brief second, trying with all
her power to stay calm.

And then she looked at DuPree, and so much for that.

"Detective Moreno. You are full of surprises," he said,
regarding her from behind his desk. "It's eleven-oh-five.
Did we not agree on midnight?"

"You said midnight," Isabella corrected, working up a
smile that would thoroughly piss him off. "I never agreed."

"I make the rules," DuPree spat, and yeah. Keep
coming.

"If you say so."

"You want me to zip-tie her, boss?" Franco asked,
stepping forward, but much to the relief she refused to let
show, DuPree shook his head.

"No." At the thug's obvious shock, he said, "I want
Detective Moreno unrestrained. We're going to play one of
my favorite games."

Isabella tensed, but said nothing as DuPree opened one
of his desk drawers. "Since you're so fond of boundary-
testing, Detective, I thought a bit of chicken was in order."

A fine sheen of sweat beaded on her forehead, turning
instantly cold as he began laying knife after knife on the
smooth mahogany desktop. "Blades, huh?" she asked,
carefully edging her fingers from her sides to her hips. She
needed to keep him angry. "I didn't figure you for the messy

322

type."

"No?" he asked, the eight-inch fillet knife in his grasp glinting in the overhead light as he examined it.

She swallowed, moving her hands to the small of her back. "Nope. Frankly, I didn't think you had the balls."

Bingo. DuPree slammed the knife to the desktop with a hard crack. "It's time to shut that filthy mouth." He rounded the desk, stepping in front of Kellan. "We're going to find out how high your fuckmate's pain tolerance is. You won't scream," he said, looking from Kellan to Isabella. "You won't move a muscle. Because if you do, the cuts get deeper until he loses a limb."

Adrenaline free-flowed in her veins, the tide changing the instant her fingers found purchase. "You're not going to hurt him, jackass."

Both Kellan and DuPree's heads snapped up at the word. "And why is that?" DuPree sneered.

The answer came by way of a loud crash coming from the front of the penthouse, followed by the thunder of footsteps and shouts of "RPD!", and Isabella's muscles sang with relief.

"Because we're not playing by your rules. We're playing by mine, and I don't work without backup."

Everyone moved at once. Both Franco and Rampage scrambled for the exit, leaving their boss to fend for himself. Kellan's arms shot upward, both elbows slamming down and out with enough force to snap the locking mechanism on his bindings. DuPree reached back for the knife on his desk, his face bent in a furious rage as he turned toward Isabella.

"Filthy whore!" he screamed, spittle flying from his mouth as he lunged not at her, but toward Kellan. "You'll pay!"

She jammed the two-inch blade she'd had hidden behind her belt all the way into his neck.

Time elongated, each one of her heartbeats stretching out and showing her the scene as if she were watching a movie. She saw the startled look on DuPree's face, quickly replaced by pain as his hands flew to his neck to try and stanch his free-flowing blood. She saw the door burst open, Sinclair and Hollister leading the way in with tactical gear on and guns drawn. She saw Kellan, eyes open, chest rising and falling, and oh God. Oh God, he was alive.

And then she saw the blood starting to pool at his feet.

"*No!*" Isabella's scream ricocheted off the walls, filling her ears and her chest and her everything. "No, no, no, no."

She surged forward at the same time Kellan swayed, catching him awkwardly and lowering him to the carpet, dimly aware of Hollister securing the scene and moving toward the spot where DuPree had collapsed, then Sinclair appearing in the doorway behind him.

"Kellan!" Her heart leaped as his eyes fluttered open, then catapulted against her ribs at the sight of the gaping stab wound on his shoulder. She slapped her hands over his T-shirt. "Okay, it's okay. *Sam!*" she screamed over her shoulder. "Roll an ambo out here, right fucking now!"

"Copeland and Drake are on their way up," Sinclair said, placing his hands on top of hers and pressing down with infinite calm. "We had them on standby. You both did great."

"Isabella?" Kellan groaned, his eyes darting wildly, and she leaned in with a broken nod.

"I'm right here." *I have your back. I love you.* God damn it, where were those paramedics and why weren't they moving faster?

"We got him, right?"

Tears spilled over Isabella's face even though she'd never felt them coming. "Yeah, we got him."

"Good," Kellan said.

And then his eyes closed.

CHAPTER TWENTY-NINE

Kellan came to slowly, although damn, it was a hard trip. He tested his memory before his muscles, keeping his eyes shut as he pushed on the thick fog in his brain and spun back in thought.

Walking over the cracked sidewalk...stinging pain in his neck...Franco throwing him the mother of all beatings...DuPree and those knives, reaching, turning...

Isabella.

His eyes flew open on a gasp. He regretted it in an instant, when every cell in his body shrieked in pain, the ones in his left shoulder loudest of all, but fuck, DuPree had been right there. He'd been ready to kill them both.

He'd been ready to kill Isabella.

Blood. Blood. There had been so much blood. Oh God, where was she?

"Whoa, whoa, whoa." Cool, firm hands framed his face, and Kellan blinked through the shadows to try and focus. "Take it easy. Try not to move."

He inhaled the sweet smell of coconuts, and thank Christ, she was alive.

"Isabella?" he croaked, his throat turning the word into

a tangled rasp.

"Shhh. I'm right here," she said, her fingers still resting on his cheeks. The struggle, as small as it had been, had drained what little energy he'd had, pain knifing through the left side of his body with merciless intensity. Kellan breathed in, taking a few seconds to register the hospital room, the tubes and machines to his left, and the portable cot Isabella had been lying on to his right.

"What…" His thickly wrapped shoulder ached and throbbed, his bandaged temple along with it. "Are you…" Damn it, why were his thoughts so disjointed?

"I'm fine," Isabella whispered. "But you've got to stay still, okay? You had to have surgery to repair your shoulder. It went great," she added, probably in response to his attempt to ask her what the hell. "You're going to be good as new, but it's going to take a little while for you to heal."

His brain raced as he tried to piece everything back together. Nope. No go. "DuPree?"

She paused, but only for a fraction of a second. "Died from his injuries on the way to the hospital. He's never going to hurt anyone again."

Emotions filled Kellan's chest, pushing out more questions. "How…how did you get past DuPree's security in the first place? He had eyes on your building."

She nodded. "I figured he had to be watching me somehow once he called with the threat, so I used the fire escape to get out of my building, then I called Sinclair from the burner phone I used on the night of the party."

Shock lifted Kellan's brows. "You saved that burner phone?"

"DuPree never knew I had it. I locked it in my bedroom safe after the party."

Well that explained how it survived the break-in. "Hell of a rescue plan," Kellan said, and Isabella released a soft laugh.

"It was teamwork. The profiler told me how to work DuPree in order to get him riled up and make a mistake.

Intelligence had me mic'd up with a necklace pendant, and I fed them intel on our exact location through conversation with Franco. Capelli was the real mastermind, though. He's the one who figured out how to deal with the Shadow."

Kellan shifted against the pillow at his back. "I was wondering how you got in the door with no warning from the Intercom Guy."

"Turns out, we didn't have to out-hack him to out-smart him," Isabella said. "The guy is a rogue, which means no loyalty. Capelli knew the odds of the Shadow sticking around once he saw all of us swarming the Metropolitan were extremely low, especially if we took him by surprise. We had to get creative with coms, but once he saw us in the lobby, he bailed to save his own skin. Just like Capelli predicted."

"Did you catch him?" Kellan asked, but she frowned and shook her head.

"Unfortunately, no. But we got both Franco and Rampage as they tried to escape." A smile lifted the corners of her mouth. "The big guy sang like a canary. He led us right to the flophouse where they'd been keeping the girls. None of them were hurt last night, and we're working on getting them counseling and rehab services."

Relief flooded through him, despite the news about the Shadow. "Good. I'm glad."

"Me too." Isabella dropped her chin, her eyes flashing with emotion as she stared at the thick layer of bandages sticking out of his hospital gown. "Kellan, I'm so sorry."

He blinked at the unexpected words. "Sorry for what?"

"I shouldn't have considered going to DuPree's without backup," she said, her voice shaky and soft. "I shouldn't have even thought about it for a second. I was just so scared he'd hurt those girls that I didn't stop to think there could be another way. The *right* way. You knew, and you tried to tell me, but...I didn't listen. I'm so sorry."

"But you did," he said, his own emotions rising as he reached out to grab her fingers with his good hand. "You did listen. You went to Sinclair. You relied on your team," he said, pulling her close. "I shouldn't have left you in the first place."

Isabella shook her head, adamant. "I told you to."

"Okay, you are kind of feisty." Kellan reached up to cup her face, loving the feel of her smile beneath his palm as she gave up a tiny laugh. "But I'll learn to live with it. Come here."

Maneuvering around all the tubes—damn, there were a bunch of them—they carefully shifted things around to fit her in at his good side.

"So tell me something about you," she whispered.

Kellan's emotions answered for him, and he didn't hesitate. "I'm in love with you."

"You...what?"

Isabella pulled back to stare at him, but he'd never been so sure of anything in his life.

"I've been on countless ops, and I've run into nearly as many burning buildings, and none of that ever scared me. But the thought of DuPree getting his hands on you"—Kellan paused for a steadying breath before opening up to let his feelings all the way out—"the thought of losing you? That terrified me. I love you, Isabella, and I don't want to put that emotion in a box. I want to live it, every day. I don't want be without you."

"Well good," she said, her body feeling warm and right and perfect as she held him even tighter. "Because I love you too. I've got your back, Kellan. And I'm never going to let you go."

ABOUT THE AUTHOR

Kimberly Kincaid writes contemporary romance that splits the difference between sexy and sweet and hot and edgy romantic suspense. When she's not sitting cross-legged in an ancient desk chair known as "The Pleather Bomber", she can be found practicing obscene amounts of yoga, whipping up anything from enchiladas to éclairs in her kitchen, or curled up with her nose in a book. Kimberly is a USA Today best-selling author and a 2016 and 2015 RWA RITA® finalist and 2014 Bookseller's Best nominee who lives (and writes!) by the mantra that food is love. Kimberly resides in Virginia with her wildly patient husband and their three daughters. Visit her any time at www.kimberlykincaid.com

ALSO BY KIMBERLY KINCAID

Want hot heroes, exclusive freebies, and all the latest updates on new releases? Sign up for Kimberly Kincaid's newsletter, and check out these other sexy titles, available at your favorite retailers!

The Station Seventeen series:
Deep Trouble (prequel)

The Line series:
Love On the Line
Drawing the Line
Outside the Lines
Pushing the Line

The Pine Mountain Series:
The Sugar Cookie Sweetheart Swap, with Donna Kauffman and Kate Angell
Turn Up the Heat
Gimme Some Sugar
Stirring Up Trouble
Fire Me Up
Just One Taste
All Wrapped Up

The Rescue Squad series:
Reckless
Fearless

Stand-alones:
Something Borrowed